ONE KNIGHT'S DESIRE

A MEDIEVAL ROMANCE

CLAIRE DELACROIX

DEBORAH A. COOKE

One Knight's Desire
by Claire Delacroix

Copyright ©2023 Deborah A. Cooke.

All Rights Reserved.
Cover by Kim Killion.

❀ Created with Vellum

DEAR READER

One Knight's Desire is the third book in my Rogues & Angels series of medieval romances. I had originally planned for this to be the story of Heloise (the Lord de Tulley's niece) and Niall MacGillivray, a charming rogue who never intends to be bound to a single woman. My characters had a surprise for me. The woman believed to be Heloise is actually that lady's former maid. She has won the Lord de Tulley's affection for her kindness, a trait he knows his niece does not possess, and the old lord is determined to ensure the happy future of this mysterious maiden—which will not include Niall.

When Lothair, a knight and healer, is summoned to Tulley, he is astonished to be offered the post of Captain of the Guard, but intrigued by the old lord's challenge to him to unfurl the lovely maiden's secrets. Will Magdala's decision to confide in the taciturn knight set all to rights? Will the Lord de Tulley's meddling result in a happy marriage? Or will Magdala's hidden past conspire against the dawning love between herself and Lothair? I really enjoyed how these two had to learn to trust and to put their respective pasts behind them to build a new future. You'll see why I trust my characters when they tell me I have the story wrong—this story is much more interesting than the one I had planned!

This story, like the others in the series is available in ebook and trade paperback.

I hope you enjoy Lothair and Magdala's story, and also the companion knights of the **Rogues & Angels** series.

All my best–

Claire

http://delacroix.net

ONE KNIGHT'S DESIRE

PROLOGUE

February 1103

It all went awry.

Magdala should have expected as much. It was the curse of her blood that nothing ever turned out as it should, and she knew it was folly to hope otherwise.

That did not stop her from trying to evade the inevitable.

She had liked the abbey and had been glad that her parents had surrendered her there. There had been enough to eat, though the food was simple; she had been clean and safe from harm. She had been useful, too, for the abbess had given her responsibilities and praised her when she did them well. When Lady Verena had chosen her to be a maid to her daughter, Magdala had not wanted to go, but the abbess had insisted.

That daughter, Heloise von Idelstein, proved to be a maiden who shared a passing resemblance with Magdala. Perhaps that had been why Magdala had been chosen. All had seemed to be well, but Magdala's ill fortune had followed her to Idelstein. She blamed herself for the illness and sudden death of the lord and lady. Then Lady Heloise had chosen to journey to visit her elderly uncle at Château

Tulley. That lady had insisted upon trading places with her maid for the journey, following her own mother's precaution, each assuming the name and clothing of the other.

But their party had been attacked and Heloise had been killed.

Magdala had continued to Tulley, veiled in sorrow to hide her face. She had intended to bring the sorry tidings to Heloise's uncle, but the Lord de Tulley had mistaken her for his niece, accepting the disguise. A decade had passed since Heloise's last visit and perhaps his eyesight faded. He had greeted Magdala with such joy that she had lost the opportunity to tell him the truth.

Each day, she planned to confess and each day, the Lord de Tulley expressed such delight in her presence that she could not do it. He confided in her that he had no other living family. No one else guessed at her deception.

Days passed to months and thence to a year, and then another. It became impossible to disappoint the grumpy but affectionate old lord with the truth. Magdala liked him too well.

But now the Lord de Tulley struggled with a ferocious illness, and Magdala knew her curse made itself known once again. There could be no contentment and stability in her days: all those she held in affection would die. Magdala tended him vigilantly, never leaving his side, not caring what the other servants said. He *had* to survive. She could not bear if she was responsible for the demise of this man who had shown her kindness. His every cough tore at her heart. When he shivered, she tucked the furs around him. She fed him broth and wiped his brow, trying to encourage his recovery by force of will.

Niall MacGillivray, a handsome warrior in the service of Quinn de Sayerne, came from Annossy late on the third day of the Lord de Tulley's illness, insisting he had to speak with her. He was a frivolous man in her view, though she knew Heloise would have appreciated his attentions. They were alike, the pair of them, attractive and confident, assured that all would turn to their advantage. As Heloise, she jested with him, knowing the old lord would expect nothing else.

On this day, Magdala could not pretend. She left the solar with reluctance, closing the door behind herself to greet the knight. It was not fitting that anyone saw the Lord de Tulley in his current state.

"Aye?" She saw immediately that Niall was puzzled by her brisk manner.

"I bring a potion from the wife of the miller at Annossy," he said, offering a crockery vessel to her along with a smile. "She insists it will aid him, as it aided her youngest son last spring. He had a similar malady."

Magdala removed the stopper, grimacing at the pungent smell. "Is she a healer?"

"She said she learned its formulation from Lothair."

Magdala remembered the tall grim knight who had been amongst Quinn's comrades. She had been relieved when he left, for he was quiet and watchful, his pale eyes seeming to perceive every secret—and Magdala had a host of them. "I thought he was a warrior."

"And a most effective one," Niall agreed easily. He sidled closer. "But he also is a healer."

Magdala had not known as much. "If the smell is an indication of its power," she said under her breath and Niall chuckled.

"It must be heated and a measure of it given thrice daily until his fever breaks."

The Lord de Tulley cried out incoherently from the chamber behind Magdala and Niall was visibly startled.

"He dreams," Magdala confided with a shake of her head. "Terrible dreams."

"You are fond of the old cur," Niall said, sounding surprised.

"He has been good to me, with little cause to do so." She felt her eyes fill with tears. "I would see him healed, whatever the price."

"Little cause?" Niall protested. "But you are his niece!"

Magdala did not look at him, and could not find it within herself to buttress the lie. "But not his daughter," she said instead. "He did not have to welcome me and I know it well. Excuse me, as I must give him this in the hope that it is of aid."

"But you are a favored niece," the knight noted when she had turned away. "Anyone else would be encouraging the old man's demise, that his holding and wealth might fall into your grasp."

"Do not speak thus!" Magdala cried, rounding upon him in fury. Niall retreated with obvious alarm. "Even uttering that notion aloud might make it so." She spoke fiercely. "I would have him recover. I would hear him bellow in the hall over some matter or other. And I will do whatever I must to make it so, no matter the price."

Niall shook his head, apparently thinking she had lost her wits. "The choice is not yours to make, Lady Heloise."

"I will do my utmost," Magdala insisted.

"I daresay you have need of some sleep. Have you tended him without rest?"

"I do my duty, sir," she said, fixing the knight with a look that must have burned with intensity for he retreated another step. "Perhaps you might depart to do your own."

"I had thought to sit with you a while..." he began, once again turning a smile upon her.

His expression should have charmed her, but Magdala turned away. "Not before my uncle is hale," she said with resolve.

Niall blinked, then with obvious reluctance, he retreated down the stairs.

The Lord de Tulley mumbled something when Magdala entered his chamber again, his fist pounding weakly on the side of his bed in frustration at some imagined torment. Magdala heated a cup of the potion on the brazier, wishing it might simmer with more haste. She tested the heat of the potion then moved to his side, lifting him and aiding him to drink. "This will aid you, Uncle," she said softly. "Though it smells most horrible."

"Heloise," he whispered when he had sipped some of it. He coughed mightily but it did sound as if his chest cleared. His eyes opened and he studied her, as if amazed that she was beside him. "You are the blessing of my elder days."

"What else should I be, sir, when you have given me a home?" She touched her lips to his brow in a chaste kiss. "Please drink a measure more. It is a potion devised by Lothair, that healer in Quinn de Sayerne's company."

"But he left," the older man said, shaking his head as if to clear his confusion. He studied her and his gaze was clouded. "Did he not?"

"You are right. He left, Uncle, but he shared some of his knowledge with the wife of the miller at Annossy before his departure." She held the cup and he sipped again, grimacing at the taste.

"'Twill cure me or kill me," he muttered with a trace of his usual manner. But he finished it without further complaint and it seemed to Magdala that he slept more easily than had previously been the case.

She stoked up the fire in the brazier and tucked him in, wiped his brow and listened to his ragged breathing. Then she fell to her knees beside his bed and prayed, for there was little more she could do to aid this man who had given her so much.

OVER THE COURSE of that night, the old lord's fever broke. His skin cooled and his nightmares faded. His breathing cleared.

When the sun shone through the window of the solar of Tulley, that chamber at the pinnacle of both keep and mount, the Lord de Tulley awakened to find that the maiden who had tended him so diligently was sleeping. Her golden hair slipped loose of her braid to fall over her slender shoulders. There were shadows beneath her eyes, but the greater sign of her exhaustion was she slept in an awkward position, as if she had been watching over him for as long as she could keep her eyes open. She sat on a stool beside his bed, her head resting on the mattress, her body bent as if she had fallen there.

The blessing of his elder days indeed.

The Lord de Tulley was not a sentimental man but his heart swelled that this maiden's nature was so good and so kind. Another would have hastened him on his way, intent upon claiming an inheritance, but not this one. He might have said that her nature was the opposite of her parents, for the Lord von Idelstein had been greedy and his lady, the Lord de Tulley's own sister, had been selfish. The truth was, though, that he knew that this maiden shared no blood with either. She was not Heloise and Tulley knew it, but he did not know who she was.

He had a suspicion, one that he hoped was true.

But he would demand a considerable measure of truth to believe as much, never mind to act upon it.

He did not know what she desired of him or what she sought at Château Tulley. He was not even certain why she had come to his gates disguised as his niece. Where *was* Heloise? In watching this maiden who claimed to be who she was not, his suspicions had faded steadily and his curiosity had grown.

With this deed, this tending of him with such devotion, Tulley knew her heart was true.

Whatever her name might be.

Whatever cruel fate had befallen his niece. He knew that Heloise would have arrived at his gates by now, if she still drew breath. He could not believe that this maiden had contrived his niece's demise, but still he had so many questions.

He dared not ask her outright, lest she vanish. He did not wish to lose her company.

He laid a hand upon her head, knowing he had to repay this debt to her. He would find this gem of a maiden a suitable match and soon. She deserved far better than that Niall MacGillivray, the silver-tongued rogue of a mercenary who served Quinn de Sayerne. That warrior visited often and tempted her laughter, but he was too friv-olous for this lady. Truly, Tulley believed Niall's interest was in the hunt and once any lady surrendered to him, he would pursue another.

This maiden deserved a man who would love her for herself, and for all time. She deserved a man of noble heart, perhaps one of less charm than Niall but one more steadfast.

When he learned later that morning whose concoction had ensured his cure, the Lord de Tulley knew who that man had to be.

He sent for Quinn to learn Lothair's whereabouts that he might set matters in motion with all haste.

His mysterious maiden would be happy with the match he made, the Lord de Tulley knew it well.

He had only to ensure that the vows were exchanged. Would the knight be interested? The Lord de Tulley might have to offer greater inducement than the lady herself—though he would prefer that Lothair have the wits to recognize a true prize.

Aye, ensuring the happiness of this maiden would be a fitting challenge for his final days.

CHAPTER 1

June 1103

othair of Sutherland, often called the Viking, had not realized his squire's compulsive need to fill a silence until he had left his fellow knights. If Calum had talked so incessantly amongst the other squires, Lothair had not been compelled to listen to his words. When they two rode together, he had little choice.

The youth was markedly fulsome.

They had ridden together for nine years, since Lothair's departure from Moray, since his patron had insisted that his young son had to train with Lothair. Calum had seen merely eight summers then or so, a cheerful sturdy boy who had never ventured far from home. Now, he was lanky, as tall as a man but not yet as broad, with a fearsome appetite—apparently as well as a tendency to chatter.

Lothair himself was not inclined to conversation, but Calum's chatter made even him less likely to speak. By the time Château Tulley was in view, he uttered only the occasional agreement while the youth talked on and on—and on. Lothair wondered when his squire managed to catch his breath.

9

He was certain Calum had not been so inclined to talk when they left Scotland to journey south, though it had been years.

"What a marvel to return to Tulley, sir!" Calum declared as they passed through the gates across the road at the base of the mount. "This keep is remarkable, to be sure, and it is fortunate to have another opportunity to appreciate its details. My father will be delighted to learn of it."

That was true enough. Ahead of them, the road wound upward, spiraling around the rocky peak that supported the keep. Château Tulley perched at the summit, its village clustered below it and seemingly clinging to the rock face. The peak erupted from the base of a valley, as imposing as Lothair recalled, mountains rising on either side of the valley. It was a great finger in the midst of the valley, a rocky outcropping formed naturally and used to advantage in the building of the château. From the keep at the summit, one could see all activity on the road and defend the sheltered valley beyond. The holding of Tulley included all those fortifications in the valley that spread to the east, the keep frowning down on the road that led south and north.

The road to the keep twisted and turned, winding ever upward at a steep pitch. Houses and shops clustered close to the road, which was faced with stone. It was an ancient fortification and one that could be readily defended. Position alone made Tulley a rich holding, and the fertility of that sheltered valley contributed to that wealth. Lothair suspected that the Lord de Tulley had made it richer in his time—his strongest impression of the old lord was that he was shrewd and strategic. It seemed they arrived late enough in the season to have missed the spring rains, which Lothair also recalled as impressive. On this day, the sun was bright overhead and the valley was lush with new growth.

Lothair dismounted once inside the gates and led his destrier, Sleipnir, up the road, wanting to see more of the holding as they climbed to the keep.

Calum, of course, followed suit, leading both palfreys without falling silent for a moment. "But then, since the Lord de Tulley summoned you for a reward, you could scarce refuse. What manner of reward do you think he intends to grant to you, sir?"

Lothair shrugged. He would know soon enough and had little interest in fruitless speculation. He did, however, regret that he had been compelled to leave Provins so soon. The apothecary there had been most experienced in the medicinal powers of roses and Lothair had been hoping to learn more. The summons from Tulley—for it had not been a mere invitation—had not reached him at the best moment.

Perhaps he could resolve matters here and return to Provins before that learned apothecary moved on.

"It could be a gem, sir, or a sack of gold," Calum said with enthusiasm. "They say the lord's treasury is as rich as a dragon's hoard."

Lothair glanced back. "Who says?"

"I heard as much when last we were here, sir. They talked in the tavern of his wealth."

Lothair's curiosity was dismissed. Peasants knew little of their overlord's true affluence, in his experience, and often embellished their tales—especially when consuming ale. He considered the merit of chastising his squire for spending time in the taverns, but a transgression so long past was best forgotten.

"But then," Calum continued. "You already possess a gold coin from a dragon's hoard."

Lothair sniffed at that tale, to which he gave little credence. "It will spend as well as any other," he said gruffly.

"Nay, nay!" Calum protested. "It alone can buy back your soul. That was what Marcus said." He referred to the tavern keeper in Jerusalem who had granted gifts to all of the knights in their company upon their departure. "There is a matter we argued mightily in the stables, for there were those—I will not name them, sir—who insisted you had no soul at all. I know better, of course."

"Enough of the coin," Lothair said tersely.

Calum, accustomed to such corrections, changed the subject. "To think that the old lord was cured by your potion, sir." He sighed with satisfaction. "And now, he would reward you for saving his life even though you were not even here! There might be a tale composed of it, sir, one sung in the taverns of this holding and others. Why, you might gain great fame!"

Lothair shook his head at such whimsy. The potion that he had taught the wife of the miller at Annossy to prepare had done precisely what it was intended to do, to his thinking. It was a mark of her good sense that she had sent some of it to the Lord de Tulley. It was a remedy for a profound cough, learned from a healer far in the north, and it was, in his experience, infallible. That it was so once again was no tale worthy of a bard's verse.

He would confirm the lord's symptoms, though, in case the potion had shown a previously unnoticed efficacy.

Lothair certainly had not saved the lord's life himself. Should he decline the reward? To Lothair's thinking, it was the miller's wife who had earned a reward. That might grant him a gracious way of declining an unwanted gift.

They strode past house after house, each as well-tended and comfortable as Lothair recalled, Calum commenting on the fine construction and made note of any miniscule changes in their absence. There was no doubt that the Lord de Tulley's holding was an affluent one, independent of the contents of his treasury.

Halfway up the rocky outcropping, there was a spectacular vantage point with views to the north and east, a glimpse of the entire valley sworn to the Lord de Tulley. Lothair slowed to survey it in admiration.

The mountains rose tall in the distance, their peaks still adorned with snow. He doubted they were ever bare. The fields in the long valley were lush again, the crops growing with vigor, the sun seeming more benevolent in this fertile corner of Christendom than anywhere else he had visited.

He could identify Annossy in the distance, but just barely, and hoped that his former comrade Quinn was well. Quinn's wife had been with child when Lothair had left but he could not even think of the inevitable arrival of that infant. He prayed that all had gone well. He spied greenery there and recalled that Annossy was famed for its wine. There was a small party on the road between Tulley and Annossy, one that approached this very keep. For a moment, Lothair thought that he might see his former comrades again, but truly, it could have been a party of merchants or other travelers.

Sayerne lay beyond Annossy, though it was beyond view. Quinn's hereditary estate was managed by Bayard, another of their small company returned home from crusade. Of the eight knights who had fought together and left Outremer together, three were currently at Tulley and Lothair would make a fourth for the moment.

Niall MacGillivray had chosen to remain in Quinn's service, while their other comrades had ridden onward. Lothair suspected that his former companion, who had a tremendous fondness for the company of women, had truly stayed to persist in his amorous pursuit of Lady Heloise von Idelstein, the Lord de Tulley's beautiful niece. Perhaps she had already succumbed to Niall's charms. She certainly had seemed to welcome his attentions. Lothair hoped that she was more perceptive than he believed her to be. He knew Niall would never fix his affections upon a single woman for long. The lady's romantic choices were not, however, his concern.

Lothair saluted the gatekeeper who stood beneath the gate to the keep itself. That man bowed, evidently having expected him. They exchanged a polite greeting and Lothair was gestured to the stables. He continued across the bailey, Calum fast behind and momentarily awed to silence.

The situation would not last, Lothair knew.

"It is a wondrous keep, is it not, sir?" the youth whispered.

"Finely wrought, indeed," Lothair agreed, the strength of the château's defenses making him fulsome. At his gesture, Calum took the reins of Lothair's destrier to lead him to the stables. Lothair looked about himself, appreciating how the ramparts seemed to stretch to the very heavens, and liking the fierce blue of the sky overhead. The wind was crisp, and he had the sudden conviction that only a north wind could ensure a man saw clearly. He had time to decide that it was not all bad to return to this holding when a woman spoke.

"And so you are come, Lothair of Sutherland," she said and Lothair turned to find Lady Heloise herself watching him from the portal to the keep. His heart leapt as it should not have done, and that was even before she smiled. "My uncle will be pleased."

The lady was as lovely as ever and Lothair caught his breath at the sight of her. If ever there had been a woman perfect in every facet of her appearance, it would be Lady Heloise. Her hair was not as pale a blond as his own, but tended to a more golden hue. Her eyes were green and thickly lashed, her brows as dark as her lashes. This gave her a striking appearance, especially with the red of her lips and the flush of pink that routinely touched her cheeks. She was both beautiful and of robust good health, not a maiden who sat idly for hours but one who was active in her endeavors. Lothair told himself that was the source of his admiration but even he recognized that the lady's allure was due to more than her vitality.

On this day, she wore a kirtle of deepest burgundy, a hue that favored her own coloring well, which was laced to show her slender figure to advantage. The garment was adorned with gold embroidery on the hems and cuffs, and her chemise beneath was pale gold. He thought it might have been silk given the shimmer of the cloth. Around her hips was a wide girdle thick with golden embroidery, a detail that only drew his appreciative gaze to her narrow waist. She wore no cloak, for the sun was warm, and her hair was braided into a corona. A crucifix of gold set with large garnets gleamed against the front of the kirtle.

She was a truly glorious woman. It was more than her appearance that had prompted Lothair's admiration when last he had visited. Her voice was low and her words intelligent. She moved with grace, as if she danced all the time. He guessed that she was some fifteen summers younger than he and knew that her beauty would only increase with age.

The sole thing that Lothair found unattractive about the lady was her vivacious nature. She was never still. She was always laughing, always talking, always demanding a tale and insisting upon being the center of attention in any gathering. Just watching her wearied him, but her manner also made her attractive to a man like Niall, whose gaze might wander otherwise.

Perhaps they were well-suited to each other. Indeed, it was dizzying to listen to the pair of them together.

Her smile broadened and her eyes sparkled as she curtseyed. "As taciturn as ever, I see, sir."

Lothair bowed. "My lady." In truth, he could not think of another word to say.

"My uncle would greet you in the hall, at your convenience."

"I will come immediately, if that is suitable." Lothair was aware that Calum glanced at him with amazement, and felt the back of his neck heat that he had said so many words in sequence.

The lady was evidently unaware of her influence. Her eyes twinkled and her voice dropped to a mischievous whisper. "Immediately always suits the Lord de Tulley best," she confided, then laughed lightly. Even the sound of her amusement prompted Lothair's smile. Indeed, his exhaustion seemed to vanish in this lady's presence and his step felt lighter.

She might have been a restorative balm herself, but one no apothecary's wares could rival.

She led Lothair inside, her footsteps almost silent on the stone. Despite her smaller stature, she moved quickly and he did not have to slow his pace at all.

"My uncle will be gratified that you responded so quickly to his invitation."

"Was it an invitation?"

Again, he was granted that sparkling glance. "You thought it a summons?" At his nod, she laughed again and Lothair found himself enchanted. "You are probably right in that. He does like to see matters his own way."

Lothair could believe that readily.

"I do not doubt that you will notice changes at Château Tulley. We have a new squire in the hall, the grandson of the miller at Annossy. Quentin always wished to become a knight, though any such opportunity was unlikely given his lack of noble blood."

"And yet?" Lothair asked when she fell silent.

"When the miller's wife brought your potion and the Lord de Tulley recovered, he offered to grant her whatever she desired. She requested that Quentin might enter service and train for his spurs. I believe the Lord de Tulley was surprised."

"I can believe as much," Lothair said quietly. If the miller's wife had already gained her reward, then he would no longer have an excuse to decline his own.

"But the detail of import is that he agreed. You might see Quentin in the stables. He is most diligent and shows a rare enthusiasm for his lessons. Uncle may have been skeptical but he has come to believe that Quentin will make a fine knight despite his lineage."

"Lineage is not the sole detail of import in a warrior," Lothair found himself saying, reminded keenly of his own humble origins—and the indulgence of the rich man who had become his patron.

"I expect you are right," the lady said. "I know little of such matters, but have always understood the expense of years of training, and the need for both horse and weapon, to make such an apprenticeship expensive. That would seem to be the greater barrier than lineage."

Lothair contented himself with a nod of agreement.

The lady smiled. "Perhaps *more* taciturn than ever," she murmured and Lothair felt the back of his neck heat again.

He cleared his throat. "The Captain of the Guard must be pleased to have such aid."

"He was," Heloise agreed readily. "At least so long as he was here. That is another change, and one most unexpected. The Lord de Tulley dismissed that man from his post but a week ago. It is said he rode for Idelstein."

Idelstein. Was that not the lady's home estate? "To serve your father?" Lothair asked.

She flushed. "My older brother is Lord von Idelstein in these times. My parents draw breath no more." She crossed herself and pressed her lips together tightly, a sign to Lothair that she missed them. Perhaps that was why she had come to Tulley. Perhaps she and her brother had disagreed. Indeed, her manner changed so much that he felt a cur for even mentioning them to her.

"My condolences," he said gruffly and she flicked a warm glance his way.

"Thank you, sir. I wager you are accustomed to death, given both of your trades, but I would prefer to see none of it. It seems that I no sooner become fond of some person than he or she must die." She shivered. "I know that is folly, if not an impossibility, but I would like all to be hale forever."

"That is not folly," Lothair ceded but she did not seem to hear him.

She frowned a little as a servant bustled past them, falling silent until the older maid was out of earshot. That woman had a shrewd glance and had surveyed them both boldly.

"Did you hear the tale of Uncle's illness?" Lady Heloise asked softly and Lothair shrugged, wanting to hear it from her lips. He did not mind that she drew closer to him, no less that the scent of her skin assailed him. An unexpected desire unfurled within him, one that was most unwelcome and yet utterly seductive.

"He was terribly ill last winter. I feared to lose him," she whispered, then paused. She glanced up and he saw concern light her eyes.

"Because you are fond of him," he guessed and she smiled a little.

"I am. He is gruff and can be demanding, but his heart is the very best."

Lothair wondered at that.

"The influence of your potion was almost immediate, to my own relief. I thank you for that." Lothair might have asked for a list of symptoms, but the lady hastened onward. "Uncle was most grateful and declared that you had to be found. He has insisted that a reward is due and that he will not shirk his responsibility." She smiled. "Perhaps you do not know his resolve, but I assure you, it can be considerable."

Lothair already had the impression that the old lord was determined in his views.

"If my knowledge had any part in his recovery, I am gratified," he said with a slight bow. He cleared his throat, intending to ask for those symptoms, but the lady stepped even closer to him. Her sudden proximity both startled and pleased him, and any words died on his lips.

"As am I!" she whispered, touching his arm quickly. The chain mail of his hauberk covered his arm to the wrist, the leather gauntlet of his glove also covered his forearm, but he felt the slight weight of her fingertip all the same. Lothair's heart leapt, but she had already turned away.

Truly, he had been alone too long. He had no right to find a noblewoman like Lady Heloise alluring, and he knew she could possess no interest in him.

She admired Niall, after all, and there could be no man alive more different from Lothair.

His future was one of solitude, as a healer, and he reminded himself that he was glad of it. One wife had been more than sufficient for him.

Meanwhile, the lady hastened into the hall ahead of him, moving as quickly as a butterfly. "Uncle! Here is Lothair of Sutherland, the knight summoned at your request."

Lothair followed, bowed, and considered the great hall. It was large and well-constructed. The ceiling was high and the supporting beams were both painted and carved most artfully. A massive stone fireplace nigh filled one wall, so large that Calum could have stood within the space with three squires, and a fire blazed upon it, even given the season and time of day. Near the fire was a great carved chair of dark wood, and upon that chair sat the Lord de Tulley, tucked beneath furs and velvets.

That man raised a hand in greeting and Lothair saw immediately that illness had taken a toll. The older man looked both smaller and more frail than he had just a year before and when he rose to his feet to greet Lothair, he was less steady than once he had been. His gaze was still sharp, though, his blue eyes snapping, and the force of his will could not be denied.

"I hope you did not ride too far," he said, a sign to Lothair's thinking that this reward would not be excessively generous.

Lothair dropped to one knee before the older man, who sank again to his great chair. Heloise retreated, though she remained in the hall. Lothair ensured that his gaze did not follow her, for he knew that the Lord de Tulley would not miss his apparent interest. "I was in Provins, sir."

"Provins? Is that not a small burg of no import? South and east of Paris, I believe."

"Aye, sir."

"Why there?" The older man's tone sharpened. "A woman?"

"An apothecary, sir, with much experience in the medicinal use of roses."

"Roses?" the old lord scoffed.

"Roses! How wonderful to have such knowledge," Heloise said with a smile. "It is a gift, indeed. You should plant a garden of your own, one with all the healing plants."

"Perhaps one day, my lady."

"We have a garden," the Lord de Tulley said gruffly. "You will not have seen it on your previous visit. My grandmother had it planted, though it has languished of late."

Heloise, to Lothair's surprise, caught her breath. "It is all weeds, Uncle. No guest would find it as beguiling as you and I do."

"But once it was a wonder. People came to see it and the apothecary in the village used its bounty. You should look at it." The Lord de Tulley nodded at Lothair. "You of all men will see its beauty."

"But, Uncle, our guest has only just arrived," the lady protested. "He has had no refreshment."

Lothair had the sense that Heloise did not wish him to see the garden, which made no sense.

"He can partake of some later. You have the key, Heloise. Show him."

Something flashed in her eyes that surprised Lothair, but it was gone so quickly that he might have imagined it. He bowed to the old lord. "I welcome the opportunity, sir."

"Heloise will take you there immediately," the Lord de Tulley said, clearly granting a command. "You should know that I invited your former comrades from Annossy as soon as you were spied upon the road. We will feast together on this night to celebrate your assistance and my survival, and your reward will be granted to you before the entire company." The older man's gaze sharpened. "I trust this is acceptable?"

Lothair bowed again, wondering anew at this reward. He began to fear it was some item he did not desire—and his former comrades would see the truth. He was not a man who managed to hide his reactions well when he was surprised, let alone one who could successfully feign enthusiasm. "I am at your disposal, sir."

"Excellent. Heloise, escort our guest to the garden. Then you may ensure that he has a light meal to restore him after his journey. The ostler will see to his horses and squire."

"Of course, Uncle." The lady looked to be slightly irked, which prompted Lothair's curiosity.

The Lord de Tulley sighed and settled back in his chair, his eyes closing. "Go then," he said, his voice markedly weaker. "I will speak with you again this evening."

"Of course, sir."

"Of course, Uncle." Heloise tucked the covers and furs more securely around the older man, for they had been dislodged when he rose to greet Lothair. By the time she was done, the older man's eyes had closed. His lids flickered when she kissed his cheek. "Such a good girl," he whispered.

Her throat worked when she turned away and she exchanged a

glance with the châtelain who stood attentively near the portal to the kitchens. Lothair did not doubt that between the two of them, they kept vigil over the older man.

"He still recovers," she said to Lothair, forcing a smile. "But he grows stronger each day."

Lothair did not reply. He guessed the opposite was true and that the Lord de Tulley faded. He followed the lady and wondered who would inherit the holding. He had assumed that Lady Heloise was the older man's sole relation, but she had herself admitted to an older brother. Why had the Lord de Tulley's former Captain of the Guard gone to Idelstein? Did he seek a post, or had he been dispatched on an errand. Perhaps the old lord meant to avert a war over the rich prize that was Tulley by surrendering it to his nephew early.

Lothair did not ask, for it was not his concern.

He was curious about this garden—not to mention the lady's reluctance to show it to him. He waited with a measure of impatience as she discussed arrangements with the châtelain, ensuring that there would be a meal for himself and Calum shortly, then followed her from the hall.

As they walked, Lothair acknowledged that he was curious about more than the garden.

HAD she ever met a man so disinclined to speak? Tall and taciturn with all the emotion of a pebble found in the river, Lothair of Sutherland was inscrutable. He was also formidable, a warrior who moved with power and confidence. The scar on his cheek was sufficient indication that he knew of war.

His eyes were as pale a blue as Magdala recalled, almost the hue of ice, and they seemed to note every detail. She did not doubt that he knew how many logs burned on the hearth, how many planks were laid on the floor, how many rings the Lord de Tulley wore on his fingers—and what their relative value might be. She wondered whether he missed any nuance and guessed that he also knew the Lord de Tulley to be dying.

Dying. Magdala could not bear to think of it.

Beyond the question of the Lord de Tulley's demise—and the world being a little less interesting without his grumpy commentary, impatient demands, and determination to ensure that all ended well for every person beneath his command or influence—there was the question of what she should do. She had never intended to linger at Château Tulley. She had certainly never intended to deceive anyone. She had planned to tell of Heloise's demise, then depart from the holding, but once mistaken for her former mistress, she had lingered another day and then another. She had not had the heart to disappoint Tulley's elderly lord, when that man had expressed such joy at the arrival of his beloved niece.

Having no destination contributed to her indecision, but the greater factor was that she liked both the Lord de Tulley and the holding itself. She admired the heavy stone of the keep and the way its towers seemed to touch the sky. She savored the crisp wind and the view over the valley.

She liked the sense of safety, as if living in a fortress meant no one could even impose upon her, let alone do her injury. Magdala knew enough of the world and its ways to be afraid of what might befall her if she was alone and undefended. More than once she had eyed the length of road that led from Tulley to Beauvoir and thence to the convent to the south of the mountain pass, and shivered at the prospect of making such a journey on her own. She doubted a maiden without defenders would even manage half the distance alone.

She feared she was destined to find out.

As for the Lord de Tulley himself, he was by turns stern and surprisingly mischievous. He surprised her and though he strove to hide any inclination to be generous—dismissing his actions as 'only good sense' or some such—he was the kindest man she had ever known. He seemed to regard all of those living upon the holding of Tulley as the children he had never had, and was as demanding and appreciative a father as could be found in any realm. Magdala, who had never known a father, thought him wondrous.

But what of Lothair? He was as different from the men she knew as possible. While the Lord de Tulley was gruff and grumpy, he at least spoke. While the knight Niall MacGillivray was garrulous and charming, his gaze sparkled as he admired her and coaxed her laughter. Lothair of Sutherland evidently possessed no interest in gaining her approval and was disinclined to speak at all. The man might have been carved of stone and was as likely as a rock to begin a conversation.

Was that why Magdala found herself so very curious about him? It seemed that a man disinclined to speak must have a thousand secrets, none of which he wished to share.

As they walked through the corridors, she became keenly aware of his silence behind her, though he could never be overlooked or forgotten. The solid tread of his boots was a sign of his presence, but more than that, he emanated a force of will that could not be ignored.

What was he thinking?

And why had the Lord de Tulley granted her this errand? That man often had an agenda and she could not help but wonder whether he schemed for some future connection between herself and this newly arrived knight.

The prospect made her tingle in a most unexpected way, though the notion was absurd. No man would match his niece with a stranger newly arrived.

Magdala recognized good sense when she heard it but still she had an uneasy feeling that more was afoot than she realized.

Perhaps her churning emotions were solely because she resented this errand. The garden was not her place, however she might consider it as much. She had no claim to it, regardless of how she had come to think of it as a haven. The garden belonged to the Lord de Tulley and if he bade her show it to this man, Magdala should be glad to do as much.

Save that she was not. She did not want this warrior there, in the place where she could find solitude and be herself. She did not want any other soul there, but particularly not this keenly observant man. She did not want him looking at it, perhaps finding fault with her one small choice. She did not wish for his judgement or his assessment or his intrusion.

Although—she cast a slow glance over her shoulder to find him as disinterested in her as might have been expected—there was one merit about him in this matter. Heloise had been a charming woman, a delightful companion with a merry laugh and a great fondness for attention. Magdala was the utter opposite. She preferred to be quiet, even solitary, to be useful. But though Heloise had not visited Tulley in the decade prior to Magdala's arrival and no one realized that Magdala was not Heloise, all recalled Heloise's merry nature. Magdala had felt obligated to maintain the illusion of being Heloise by mimicking her manner, but the task was exhausting.

This man, to his credit, did not care. Lothair was not charmed by her, even when she pretended to be Heloise. He was not fascinated. He did not seek her favor or her commentary. He was utterly disinterested in her companionship, save that she had access to the garden. He likely cared more about the thoughts of the bees Magdala could hear in the garden than for her own notions.

Which meant she could ignore him.

The garden was a walled refuge on the southern and western face of the château, one that wrapped around the keep. It was higher than the great hall, but lower than the floor with her own chamber, and certainly below the solar at the summit of the peak. They climbed the stairs from the great hall in silence, then proceeded along the corridor. They reached the garden gate without having uttered a single sound and Magdala turned the key in the lock, aware that the knight's attention sharpened in anticipation.

Nay, it had to be the healer who was intrigued by the garden's promise, not the warrior. How interesting that he had interest in both, though she supposed that anyone who had been wounded might wish to know of the treatment of injuries.

The hinge creaked as the metal gate was opened and the sunlight in the garden beyond was dazzling. Magdala had to blink several times to let her eyes adjust before she could truly look upon this beloved space.

By that time, Lothair had stepped past her. His presence was incongruous, for he was clearly a man of war. His mail hauberk hung to his knees, the tops of his high leather boots vanishing beneath its hem. There was a mail coiff gathered at his neck, which she knew could be raised as a hood, and the sleeves of his mail hauberk fell over his hands. His sleeveless tabard was deepest green with a curious insignia on the chest, one that looked like a spiral embroidered in gold. His sword belt was heavy leather, slung around his hips, his sword tip almost reaching the ground. She did not doubt that he carried more weapons, perhaps hidden by the leather gloves shoved into his belt, perhaps guarded by his squire along with his destrier. He stood in the middle of the garden, slowly turning as he surveyed it all wordlessly.

Doubtless he would be able to recite an inventory by the time his perusal was done.

Though she knew the space well, Magdala found herself doing the same. The outer wall was as robust as ever, this garden being below the keep's highest wall yet not as low as the road some distance below. It was marvelously quiet, sealed away from the bustle of the town. The sounds of wagons and people haggling, the ring of the hammer from the smithy, were familiar yet so distant that they might have carried from another realm. Here, the hum of the bees seemed to be the loudest sound. On this glorious day, those diligent insects were at work, as were the butterflies. There was only a light breeze and Magdala felt the tension ease from her shoulders.

She was always reminded of the abbey and her days beneath the instruction of the abbess, and even now, she smiled in recollection.

The garden was divided into four quadrants, with stone paths between them all and a circular stone reservoir in the middle. The paths were slightly angled toward the reservoir and there was a trough cut in the middle of each so the rainwater would gather. There was another path around the perimeter and gardens planted between it and the walls, mostly with taller plants. Most of the beds were thick with healing plants and the many weeds mingled with them. Wattle fences should have held the larger plants back, but they had been engulfed by the enthusiastic growth. It looked chaotic and disheveled —save for the neat borders of calendula.

Magdala found the spot where she had left off her labor and crouched down. She had created borders of the low-growing flower around the perimeter of each bed. It was the one plant she knew well, and she thought the orange and yellow flowers were pretty. Though the calendula grew from seed each year, by this point of the year, they were flourishing. She weeded a section quietly, ignoring Lothair, then broke apart a seed head and pushed the seeds into the soil to fill some gaps. The quiet seemed suddenly more intense and she looked up to find him watching her with that curious pale gaze.

"The garden is untended."

"Aye," she agreed, dropping her gaze to her labor. "It is said that the gardener passed four years ago, and the Lord de Tulley remains unconvinced that any other has the skill to tend the garden."

"He is fond of it?"

"It was planted by his grandmother and he considers it a legacy."

He nodded once and fell silent again, the weight of his gaze still upon her. Magdala felt her cheeks heat as she worked, but she neither looked up nor strove to encourage a conversation.

"You know this plant," he said finally. There was no question in his tone and she felt her cheeks heat yet more.

Why should she not know it? It was sufficiently common.

"Calendula, named so by the Romans because it flowers every day of the year," she said. She did not stop working because it meant she could avoid his gaze. He remained silent, waiting, and she felt compelled to continue. "It was my task as a girl to tend the calendula borders, so I do it here."

"Your task?" His tone had sharpened and she knew he had not missed her slip.

Of course, the daughter of a nobleman had no menial tasks. Magdala found herself stammering. "I, I asked to help," she said, knowing her words came too quick. "It is so pretty. I always thought of it as my responsibility, but of course, it was not."

"Where?"

"At…home, of course."

"Were its petals used to treat the skin?" His tone had softened and she risked an upward glance. He was watching her keenly, as if he had never seen a maiden at work in a garden before.

"Aye," Magdala agreed simply. The abbess had made a salve which required the dried petals and she had seen it applied to angry rashes to good effect. She had spent many an evening crushing the petals in the kitchens as the nuns prepared the other ingredients. Her thoughts were filled then with memories, tears rising that she had ever been compelled to leave that place.

Could she return there?

Did she wish to? How curious to be uncertain when she had been so happy there.

Perhaps the safety and the security of the abbey held less appeal when one had seen even an increment of the world beyond its walls.

Perhaps.

CHAPTER 2

hile Magdala was lost in her thoughts, Lothair had turned away, his attention snared by the garden again. He walked to one of the border beds and tugged on some dead growth from the previous year, clearing it away with efficient gestures. It was a great stalk with clusters of seeds at the top of it, and she watched as he shook the seeds hard over the bed before discarding the dried stalk in the pile of compost in one corner. Of course, he would be purposeful and make every moment be of merit.

Magdala found herself drawn closer by her curiosity. New green growth was revealed by his removal of the old and she bent to touch the soft fronds. There were buds emerging on taller green plants that were almost as high as her knees. The tall deadened stalks had hidden them almost completely from view.

"What is it?"

"Angelica. The soil must be more wet here."

"Because it is in the shade of the wall most of the day, and when the reservoir overflows, the water gathers here."

His gaze flicked over the bed as if to confirm her words, then he nodded again. "There is some of the dried powder of its root in that potion. It can help to clear congestion in the chest." Even as she marveled that she had never heard him utter so many words in sequence, he took a handful of seeds and crushed them in his hand with the side of his dagger. He held his palm before her, the broken seeds dark against his skin.

Magdala hesitated to draw nearer, called herself a fool, then bent to inhale of the scent.

"I recognize it." Magdala eyed the bed of angelica, thinking of the Lord de Tulley's health. Would this warrior teach her how to prepare the potion or was it a guarded secret? The miller's wife knew, but that did not mean he would confide in anyone else. "We should have more of that mixture before winter."

"More will not change the outcome next time."

She eyed him with alarm, but he had already moved to study another plant. He crouched down to pull out some small plants.

Magdala had not been certain what they were. "Are they weeds?" she asked.

He shook his head. "Dill in the clary," he said. "It must be taught to keep its own place."

Magdala smiled and bent to pull the dill, crouching alongside him. Once she pulled a plant, she smelled its distinctive scent. "Dill for the kitchen," she said, remembering.

"An infusion for colic or indigestion," he provided.

"A cure for hiccups," she said and he snorted, casting her a wry glance. "And protection from witchcraft."

He shook his head, his skepticism clear.

Magdala found herself smiling. He was clearly reluctant to speak but he would reply to her questions, and she had many of them about the plants. The air became pungent with dill and the sun was warm upon her back.

"And clary?" she dared to ask, not wanting to provoke him but curious. "It is a sage, is it not?"

He nodded. "An infusion from the seed will clear the eye of foreign matter."

She remembered that now. The abbess had made that infusion

once. That lady had always worked in silence, concocting from memory, offering no explanation. Magdala recalled the scent and smell of many of the herbs, but did not even know all their names, much less the measure required for any potion.

Would he teach her?

How long would he linger?

She might already have asked him too much. She watched his hands, strong tanned hands that dealt deftly with the invading plants. She was intrigued that he could be so gentle with the seedlings intended to survive, by the way he brushed the fronds of new growth.

The silence between them was oddly companionable—and it allowed Magdala to utter the truth. She guessed this healer with his keen gaze had seen the change in Tulley and knew its import. When she spoke as merry Heloise, she had to pretend she did not recognize the signs, that she believed all would come right in the end. Here, in the quiet, with him, she could give voice to her own fear.

"Will you stay until he passes?" Even saying the words aloud made Magdala's throat tighten.

She earned a sharp sidelong glance for that. His eyes were so very blue in this moment, his lashes long and golden. His gaze was so intent that he might have been reading her deepest secrets.

"You know." Lothair said this as if the truth was unassailable. It was a relief that he neither consoled her nor insisted she was wrong.

"I fear that he fades," she admitted. "I do not know. I am no healer."

"But you see all the same." He said no more, leaving her wonder whether he had forgotten her query. They finished clearing the bed of clary sage of tiny dill seedlings and straightened as one beside each other, looking down at the young plants.

The man was utterly inscrutable.

"Will you?" she asked finally, her words hanging in the quiet of the sunny afternoon.

Lothair frowned. "It depends."

"Upon what?"

"Upon the expectation attached to his reward."

"Why would there be an expectation?"

"There often is." He eyed her for a long moment, considering.

Magdala's heart skipped but she dropped her gaze instinctively. "But you are a healer. He will have need of aid…"

Lothair interrupted her, speaking with conviction. "It is unlikely that any healer will be able to aid him."

Her throat tightened at this confirmation of her fears, which was both welcome and troubling. She crossed the garden, returning to her calendula border, her vision blurred with tears as she began to tug weeds free again. "What was it like in Provins?" she asked, knowing she sounded like Heloise once more.

Lothair considered this question for so long that she thought he might not reply. "Interesting," he said finally.

"Will you return there?"

"Perhaps."

Magdala had a thousand questions for Lothair but he, it appeared, had few answers to share. She did not know his homeland or his history, what had driven him to join the crusade, what he had experienced in Outremer, what he would do now that he had returned from the East. She found herself curious about his choices. Some knights must have remained in the East while others had returned home. Both Quinn and Bayard had taken brides, as had Rolfe de Viandin from their company. Others must have assumed responsibility for holdings, defended their borders, even fathered children.

She could not even fathom what this man would do.

She was surprised when he crouched down beside her and helped with her task. He moved into the bed itself, leaving the border to her busy fingers, having identified the one plant that should dominate the bed.

"Lady's mantle," he said tersely, anticipating her question.

"It gathers a drop in the folds of each leaf after a rain," she said with a smile.

He flicked a glance at her, then away. "The infusion is of aid to women."

Magdala frowned, not understanding, then the back of his neck turned ruddy. "Each month?" she asked.

"It is said to diminish any pain. I do not know for certain."

He did not look at her again, as if he regretted that confidence.

He was decisive, never lingering over the identity of a plant as she did. Even when it was an intruder, she hesitated to kill what might be useful. It was companionable, to work alongside him like this, yet she felt a simmer of awareness that was new to her. She wanted to know all about this man who stirred her as no other had done.

Perhaps it was the apparent contradictions in his choices that made him intriguing. Perhaps understanding them would diminish the influence of his presence upon her heart.

"How can you be both warrior and healer?" she asked, breaking the silence again.

Lothair pursed his lips, considering the question—or perhaps how much he would confide in her. "Because I so choose."

It was half an answer and Magdala knew it, but she doubted he would elaborate. "Will you join a monastery? Many healers do."

Lothair shook his head. "I have not the faith for it."

"But you rode to crusade."

"And saw there that good does not always triumph, nor does justice." He frowned, resolute, then stood with purpose.

Magdala knew he would leave her then, perhaps because she demanded too many answers of him. He took one last long survey of the garden, then turned that bright gaze upon her. His eyes fairly glowed and she caught her breath at the sight. God in heaven, but he was a handsome man—even the scar upon his cheek did not diminish his appeal. Her heart fluttered like a bird even as her mouth went dry.

"Thank you," he said, his words deep and unexpectedly heartfelt. He was sincere and she appreciated as much. Perhaps that was the root of his allure.

"The garden is not mine," she felt obliged to note.

"But it is a place you treasure, perhaps a sanctuary," he said with conviction. "I thank you for sharing it with me, my lady." He bowed over her hand and she tingled at his salute.

That was before he touched his lips to the back of her hand, before the warmth of his breath sent a thrill to her very toes.

Magdala opened her mouth to protest, then closed it, knowing her words would sound unkind.

"I know you only did as much because it was decreed that you would." His words were unexpected, if true, and she was astonished that when he glanced up at her, his eyes were glinting with humor.

Magdala found herself staring at him in wonder.

"Aye," she confessed and the barest curve of a smile touched his lips.

"I will not share your secret, my lady," he said in a conspiratorial whisper and Magdala laughed a little. His gaze remained fixed upon her, as if he found her intriguing beyond all, and he did not relinquish his grasp upon her hand.

Here was a man of merit and honor. Here was a man who would not seek to overcome her or take his desire, regardless of her view. Here was a man who could be trusted.

On impulse, Magdala took a step closer, reached up and touched her lips to Lothair's cheek. She felt his surprise and heard him catch his breath. His grip tightened on her hand and his eyes glittered, but he did not move. He was taut and watchful, but utterly in control.

Whatever happened next was Magdala's own choice and she appreciated that more than he could know. She took a step back, willing the wild pace of her heart to slow, and smiled at him. "I thank you for your understanding, sir," she said, though her voice did not sound like her own. It was husky and sultry, a sign of her agitation, and she feared he would prove her expectations wrong.

But nay. Lothair held her gaze for long moments, as if he could not look away from her, as if he did not wish to leave her. The moment stretched long, Magdala scarce daring to breathe lest the spell be broken. She realized she wanted it to go on and on and on.

But Lothair abruptly bowed again and strode from the garden

with crisp steps, as if he could not wait to leave. He moved more quickly and quietly than Magdala might have expected possible.

Certainly more quickly than she might hope.

She watched the gate close behind him, surprised to feel a little bereft when she was alone, even though she had originally desired as much. She bent to her task again, reviewing all that he had said and not said, striving to understand her fascination with him.

How could she trust a man whose thoughts were so hidden, a man whose intentions she could not guess? Magdala did not know, but she did trust Lothair of Sutherland. He had been honest with her about the Lord de Tulley's prospects and she had felt confident even alone in his company. That was utterly new for her—previously, the sole man with whom she was at ease in solitude was the Lord de Tulley. Men, Magdala knew well, could not be trusted to consider the desires of any save themselves.

Save Lothair. He possessed restraint, a rare trait in her experience —and one that Magdala admired. She recalled the strength of his hand, holding hers so gently, the touch of his lips upon her hand, the feel of his cheek beneath her own lips. She shivered, feeling both hot and cold at the same time, a simmer awakening within her that made her anxious to see him again. He could have taken whatever he desired of her, overwhelming her with his greater strength, but she would wager that the possibility had not even occurred to him.

He was a man of honor, to be sure.

While Magdala was a liar. She winced at that truth, knowing that a confession would do little to earn Lothair's regard.

Perhaps it did not matter. Doubtless he would depart after the Lord de Tulley granted him a reward, and Magdala would never see him again.

That was sufficient to make her sigh with newfound longing.

Some moments later, Magdala heard hoofbeats and a familiar shout from the road below. She recognized Niall's voice, which meant the party from Annossy was arriving. No doubt Niall would bend his full attention upon charming her. She would be obliged to be as merry as Heloise could be. Magdala halfway wished she would miss the feast.

But she did not wish to miss the presentation of Lothair's reward. What would it be? Would the Lord de Tulley's choice prompt the taciturn warrior to smile?

More importantly, would it convince Lothair of Sutherland to linger?

~

LOTHAIR WAS BEGUILED.

In the garden, he had glimpsed another side of Heloise, one he found infinitely more appealing than the maiden he had met previously. In the garden, she had been quiet and thoughtful, practical and unafraid to soil her hands. Her maintenance of the calendula border was a triumph—the plants were lush and in full bloom, as healthy as any such flowers he had ever seen. That required patience and diligence—and her curiosity about the plants had prompted him to speak more than was his inclination. He sensed that she would learn quickly and that made him wish to teach her more.

Not just because knowledge should be shared.

He could not reconcile her labor with the maiden he had encountered before. He could not deny that she had seemed content in the garden and its tranquility, but this surprised him completely. She might have been alone for all the attention she had granted him at first.

She might have been another maiden entirely.

He was relieved that she was no fool. He was glad that she understood Tulley to be dying, but intrigued that her fear was for the loss of his company. Her manner hinted that she was not concerned with the old lord's fortune or his holding, but with the man himself. Lothair could not help but admire that. He tired of greed and found her manner a welcome change from his experience of recent years. Her life would change, perhaps radically, in the old lord's absence, but that did not seem to be the reason that she wished him to remain vigorous.

Perhaps she would be obliged to return to Idelstein with her brother. Perhaps the Lord de Tulley had summoned that man to send his niece home.

She would miss the garden, Lothair was certain.

Still, he could make little sense of her comment that tending the calendula had been her responsibility. She had tried to soften the claim after it was uttered, but Lothair thought she had spoken the truth first. In what realm would a nobleman's daughter be given such a mundane task? Lothair could not say, but he was intrigued.

The lady was a riddle, and he found puzzles irresistible.

By the time he savored a quick meal in the kitchens with Calum then continued to the stables, their horses had been tended. Quinn and Niall had arrived as well and the former comrades greeted each other heartily.

Quinn was as temperate in his manner as ever—he had never been one to leap to conclusions—but there was a new satisfaction about him. He had auburn hair and amber eyes that seemed to glow when some matter seized his attention. Niall teased him for he had gained a little girth in the happiness of his match with Melissande, but Quinn only laughed with pleasure. Niall was as handsome and charming as ever and, with his fair hair and blue eyes, even the kitchen maids made a good survey of him. He winked at one, sending her away with a blush, and grinned when Quinn bade him to mind his manners.

"We are the Lord de Tulley's guests," Quinn said quietly. "Do not get a child upon one of the maids this night."

"And why should I not, if she welcomes me?" Niall retorted, unrepentant. "I might learn something of this keep that is of use to you. Women know details of import."

Quinn gave the younger knight a quelling glance. "It is not for information that you seduce them, but for pleasure."

"And I ensure theirs as well." Niall turned away from Quinn's forbidding expression. "It is good to see you returned, Lothair. How far had you journeyed before you were summoned back?"

"Provins."

"Ah, there must have been an apothecary there!" Quinn said and Lothair nodded.

"With knowledge to share." Niall shook his head. "No woman's charms can compare." He glanced over Lothair's shoulder to the portal, then bowed low. "Although truly, the beauty of Lady Heloise von Idelstein must rouse you from your studies."

Lothair turned to find the maiden in question on the threshold, her eyes alight as she smiled in welcome. "And here is Sir Silver-Tongue, the most enchanting rogue in all of Christendom," she said lightly, which prompted Niall's laughter. This was the lady Lothair recalled, though he was not so delighted by her return as Niall seemed to be.

"I am loyal only to you, my lady," he vowed, sweeping a bow. "For there is not another lady who can compare."

"That must explain why you pursue me with vigor and diligence," she charged with a smile. "You are a scoundrel, sir, but one whose company is too delightful to be denied."

"I am glad again to be your company, my lady, for my days are desolate without you."

She laughed. "One day, sir, you will lose your heart in truth, Sir Niall. I wonder what you will do without it to offer to all and sundry."

"I have lost it already, fair Heloise, if you would but accept it as a token."

"Perhaps later," she said, her gaze flicking to Lothair and thence to Quinn. "Welcome, sir, to Château Tulley. My uncle sends word that he awaits your company in the hall." She surveyed Lothair then gestured to the darkening sky when his heart skipped. "The hall grows cold in the evening. You might be appreciative of your cloak, sir. I know I shall fetch mine." She turned, indicating the way with a flick of her hand and they followed.

Calum hastened behind Lothair, carrying both of their cloaks, and

Lothair donned his on the threshold of the hall. The youth had brought the lighter one and Lothair found himself glad of it. The stone emanated a chill, to be sure. The lady left them for a moment, returning with a fur-lined cloak moments later, and took her place at the board, on her uncle's left.

Quinn sat on the old lord's right hand, Lothair beside him, Niall beside the lady. Once again, she was laughing merrily, trading quips with Niall, her manner feeding an annoyance that surprised Lothair with its vigor.

'Twas as if she was two different maidens. Or as if the one in the garden had been an illusion. Lothair could not understand it. Just as he recalled, Heloise apparently required the attention of every soul in proximity and would do whatever was necessary to ensure that was so.

What had happened to the quiet lady in the garden? Lothair was surprised by how much he wished for her return.

He only half-listened to Quinn's accounting of all that had changed at Annossy—the salient point was that Bayard, Quinn's son by Melissande, was the most clever and vigorous babe ever born. Lothair was relieved that Melissande's delivery of the child had evidently been without incident, though Quinn did not notice his reaction. Niall had eyes only for Lady Heloise, and it irked Lothair that she laughed so merrily at the most pathetic jests he had ever heard. He had little chance to join the conversation and told himself that he had no wish to do so.

But for once in his life, it did not suit Lothair to be ignored.

Nay, he was disgruntled.

He listened and he watched and he wondered whether he had imagined the lady's change of manner. Perhaps she had simply been tired.

Perhaps she chose not to expend her charm upon him.

The meal was hearty, though, and the meat as plentiful as the wine. It had been a long time since Lothair had savored such a feast and he appreciated it fully.

He watched as the châtelain brought each dish to the Lord de Tulley first and a servant, a man of some forty summers or so, tasted it before the old lord did as much. He was reminded of potentates in the south, who evidently lived in dread of poison, and wondered at the Lord de Tulley's choice.

Had someone tried to kill him previously? Or was his caution an old habit?

Lothair told himself that it was not his place to be curious.

Calum's eyes were shining as he aided in the service of the meal, and truly that youth could eat for an army when the fare was good. A younger boy served at the table and Lothair heard him addressed as Quentin. This dark-haired boy with the somber gaze, then, would be the miller's son. He spoke to the boy, asking after his training, and Quentin was nigh as garrulous as Calum once encouraged.

There were two more tables of knights and warriors obviously sworn to the service of the holding and Lothair eyed them with an increment of curiosity. Their numbers were as he might have expected for a keep of this size and they looked to be able warriors.

When the meal was done, Lothair looked up to find the Lord de Tulley watching him avidly. The board was removed and a pair of minstrels began to play, music lilting across the hall even as the men in service to the keep began to regale each other with tales. Lothair heard a mix of languages, a familiar experience in his travels.

The older man beckoned and Lothair went to him. He bowed deeply as the minstrels fell silent and the men halted their conversations to watch. Clearly he was to gain his reward.

"I would thank you again, sir, for your generosity…" he began, but Tulley waved him to silence.

"On your knee," he instructed, his tone gruff. "I would grant your reward before sleep overcomes me." His brows rose and his eyes twinkled. "Such a substantial meal leads to a predictable result in these times."

Lothair dropped to one knee before the older man and bowed his head. They might have been alone in the hall for the dearth of conversation.

The Lord de Tulley cleared his throat, then his voice rang out with surprising vigor. "I thank you, Lothair of Sutherland, for sharing your knowledge with the miller's wife so that I was healed from my illness. I credit you with my recovery and would bestow a boon upon you in gratitude, for a man of merit does not forget his debts." The Lord de Tulley coughed and that servant patted him on the back before he managed to continue. "I bestow upon you the post of Captain of the Guard for Château Tulley."

Lothair looked up in surprise and saw the ring of keys offered by the older man. "But I had not meant to stay," he said before he thought of a more diplomatic way to refuse.

The Lord de Tulley's eyes glinted. "Surely this will change your thinking."

"But it was the miller's wife who made the potion. Surely she should be rewarded."

"She has been. Her grandson has come here to train as a knight, which was her request." The Lord de Tulley gestured and the dark-haired boy bowed. "I fully expect you to embark upon his training immediately. Quentin will be your responsibility, as well as the defense of the keep itself." The lord jingled the keys impatiently.

Mere hours before, Lothair would not have been tempted. His plan had been to leave battle behind him and to focus upon his studies in healing. He realized that it had been no coincidence that the Lord de Tulley had commanded Heloise to show him the garden.

For access to that garden, Lothair would do a great deal.

And truly, it could not be for long. The older man was not well, and whoever claimed his holding would bring his own Captain of the Guard.

"I thank you, sir. Your generosity is beyond every expectation."

"Then you accept?"

"I accept."

Quinn applauded heartily. "What excellent tidings. We shall be glad to have you close by again, Lothair."

"Indeed," Niall agreed. "If we could convince our four comrades to turn around, we could all be reunited here at Tulley again."

The Lord de Tulley himself harumphed. "I have no need of more knights wandering my lands, seeking trouble," he complained, then offered his hand with the signet ring upon it to Lothair. "I will have your pledge, sir."

Lothair swore obeisance to the Lord de Tulley, kissing the lord's signet ring, then presenting his sword to the older man. He was given the ring of keys and a pin for his cloak, emblazoned with the insignia of Tulley as a physical sign of his rank. Calum fastened the pin for him, fairly bursting with pride that his knight should see such an honor. Conversation broke out in the hall again and the minstrels resumed their tune.

Lothair rose to his feet at the Lord de Tulley's invitation, his cloak swirling around his knees. "I will serve you loyally, sir."

"I know it well," that man said. He pointed to the spot beside himself with an imperious gesture. Quinn was quick to vacate it, tactfully drawing both Heloise and Niall away, purportedly to better attend the minstrels. "Sit here now. I would talk to you."

Lothair did as bidden, assuming the lord had some advice about the defense of the keep or its idiosyncrasies. The older man gestured for more wine and music, and the servants hastened to the kitchens for their own repast. Lothair watched as Quinn smiled slightly at one of Niall's jests, interesting himself in the conversation of the other two.

"You watch my niece," the Lord de Tulley said, his voice low.

"I wager most men do," Lothair said.

The older man snorted. "Most are enthralled by her." He eyed Lothair. "I think you are not."

"I am intrigued by her, sir."

"Intrigued? And why is that?"

Lothair saw no reason to hide the truth. Indeed, it seemed the older man expected no less and he was a man inclined to speaking plainly. "Her manner was very different in the garden, sir. I wonder which is the true Heloise."

"Neither," that man replied, his voice low and hot. Lothair glanced at him with surprise. "This maiden is not Heloise," he continued with conviction.

Lothair was astonished. He looked at the laughing maiden, then back to the lord with his shrewd gaze. It was difficult to imagine that the Lord de Tulley might be mistaken, for he was keen of wit, but his claim made little sense.

"You doubt me," he said, sitting back in his great chair as if amused.

"I simply wonder, sir, how that can be."

The Lord de Tulley tapped his cup and waited until it was refilled, and the servant had moved away. "Let me tell you of Heloise von Idelstein," he began softly. "My niece is the middle child of my sister and her husband, now both deceased. Her older brother Herbert has inherited the holding. He is a little less nobly inclined than I would prefer, but he will serve Idelstein well enough. There were two daughters. Heloise, the older daughter, was always a merry and pretty child, utterly charming and willful in most matters. She came twice to visit Tulley before this most recent arrival, the last time about ten years ago when my sister brought her here. She showed a love of the hunt on that visit. Her aim was excellent and her skill with a falcon impressive. She favored my sister in that. The youngest child, also a girl, is Hildegarde. A solemn creature and in many ways Heloise's very opposite, but I suspect the most clever of the three."

Lothair nodded, sipped his wine and listened.

"I have never trusted Herbert to act for the advantage of any person save himself, for he is like his father in that. When my sister and her husband died in quick succession, I invited Heloise here. I had not seen her in a decade but I suspected I could make a better match for her than her brother would. The tone of Herbert's reply indicated to me that I was correct in that. So, just before the Yule two years ago, Heloise arrived." The Lord de Tulley inclined his head to the merry maiden at the board. "At least, *this* maiden arrived, dressed as Heloise. I thought she had changed. I thought it was the work of a decade upon a maiden, and dismissed my first impression. Still, my niece possessed a dimple, a deep one below the corner of her mouth, and this maiden does not have one. Does a dimple disappear? It might. I cannot say for certain. So, I arranged for a hunt, the better to please my guest. Surely what one favors does not change with time." He fell silent, frowning.

"She was not pleased," Lothair guessed.

The Lord de Tulley flicked him a glance. "She was terrified. She could not keep the falcon upon her fist, she could not loose an arrow with any accuracy, her seat on the horse was less than I recall and she was as pale as snow when the first hare was taken. One of the boys had to feed her falcon, for she could not bring herself to offer it the liver."

"She might have lost her taste for the sport."

"Nay. I think it was the first time she had ever ridden to hunt." Tulley nodded at his own conclusion, his gaze fixed on the maiden. "I believe she is not Heloise. In fact, I am certain of it. From that day, I watched and waited, wishing to discern her plan. Is she a thief? Is she an assassin sent by Herbert to hurry me on my way?" He shook his head, apparently mystified, and Lothair thought of the taster again. "But she has been here two and a half years and nothing has been stolen. Nothing has been damaged and I have not been assaulted. In fact, it was because of her efforts that I survived my illness this past winter. She asked all my vassals for aid and sent runners in every direction. Such was her urgency that all obeyed her. Any potion would have come too late otherwise. No one could ask for greater devotion or selflessness. She was an angel of mercy." He raised his brows. "She has, however, always found an excuse to avoid the hunt."

Lothair pondered this revelation. "But who else could she be?"

"That is my question." The Lord de Tulley nodded. "And so, as Captain of the Guard for Château Tulley, I grant you an additional commission. No door will be closed to you. I would ask you to take advantage of that and discover three things for me: What happened to Heloise? Who is this maiden? And what does she desire at Tulley?"

"I am not certain, sir, that I have the skill for unveiling such secrets."

"Do you not?" The Lord de Tulley cackled. "Consider that if you were to court a lady's affections, you might expect the surrender of some of her hidden truths. She might confide in you." He nodded, convinced of his own words. "Women do."

"Alas, I have no such ability to charm, sir." The very notion of courting this lady sent an unwelcome tide of heat through Lothair but he knew his own limitations.

"I ask you to learn the truth for me, and if you do, my reward will be a generous one." The older man fixed a bright gaze on Lothair. "What do you say?"

Lothair could not possibly accept the offer, though he knew his new lord would not be pleased. "I will not deceive any lady with regard to my intentions," he said stiffly. "It would be unkind at the least to feign a suit where there could be none."

"Why can there not be one? You might come to love her in truth."

"It would surely be inappropriate for a Captain of the Guard to court your niece."

The Lord de Tulley waved away this concern. "Since she is not Heloise, any match would not be unfitting." The older man turned a shrewd glance upon Lothair. "Unless you have a royal legacy of which I am unaware."

"Nay, sir."

The Lord de Tulley studied him, his gaze hot. "Unveiling her truth would earn a reward from me."

"Still, sir, I cannot follow your strategy." Lothair held the older man's gaze and felt the weight of that man's will upon him. But he would not do as much. It did not matter who the maiden was in truth. It struck him as a cruel deception and he would not undertake it.

"You are principled."

"I strive to be, sir."

"Will you endeavor to discover the truth by any other means? By observation, for example?"

"I will try, sir."

"No man can ask for more," the Lord de Tulley ceded in poor temper. "We will meet each midday in the solar and you will tell me in privacy what you have learned. No doubt you will have questions about the keep, as well. We shall say that is why we confer."

"Of course, sir."

Lothair found his gaze upon Heloise, who laughed merrily, turning her attention first upon Quinn and then upon Niall. Quinn responded politely, his thoughts clearly at Annossy with Melissande, but Niall responded to her with enthusiasm.

When the older man dismissed him, Lothair returned to his fellows and sat opposite Quinn, gesturing for a cup of ale. The lady went to her uncle, ensuring his comfort.

Lothair watched the ale being poured, well aware of Quinn's scrutiny.

"All is well?" that man asked quietly.

"Very well. This post is most unexpected."

"It is a fine keep with solid fortifications," Quinn said. "An admirable fortress."

"And you had no other assignment or opportunity," Niall said, predictably disinterested in Lothair's plan to learn. Quinn and Lothair sipped their ale contentedly, watching Heloise tease Niall who had followed her to the old lord's side.

"I have more tidings for you," the Lord de Tulley said suddenly, gesturing for the minstrel to fall silent. "I am so gratified to have a new Captain of the Guard that I nigh forgot to share this news." He rose to his feet, a little unsteady, and gripped the cane he had not used before.

Heloise was quick to move to his side and take his elbow, her manner solicitous. Lothair did not think she feigned her affection for the older man, whatever other falsehoods she told. "You must be tired after this day," she said. "I will help you to the solar, Uncle."

"Not yet, child, not yet." Tulley patted her hand then raised his voice. "I am most glad to have Lothair in my service in time to ensure that all is as it should be before my guests arrive."

"Guests, Uncle?" Heloise asked. "Who do you anticipate will arrive?"

"Your brother, of course." Tulley looked toward the company and so he must have missed Heloise's expression of dismay. It did not last long, but Lothair saw it and wondered at its import. "I have had word from Herbert that he intends to visit. Will it not be a fine occasion to see him again?"

"Most fine, Uncle," Heloise said as there was a smattering of applause from the company. She did not look convinced of her own claim, though.

The Lord de Tulley was correct. Herbert would know this maiden was not his sister and she dreaded the revelation.

But who *was* she?

Did Herbert know?

CHAPTER 3

*H*erbert!

Magdala could not imagine a worse candidate to reveal her secret. She had no doubt that Heloise's older brother would recognize her and she also knew that he would not be quick to reveal her. Nay, Herbert would want his price to keep silent. Even a short period of time in that household left Magdala certain of what his price would be.

She helped the Lord de Tulley to his chamber where Felix would aid him to bed. That man had served Tulley for decades and when she had realized that the older man had need of assistance with washing and dressing, Felix had been the inevitable choice. He was a quiet and competent man of some forty summers, a man who saw matters resolved and did not gossip. He also indulged the older man's concern with the prospect of being poisoned, an eventuality Magdala could not imagine. Magdala liked that no one beyond herself and Felix knew the full details of Tulley's infirmities. The old lord would not have wanted it otherwise.

As usual, she exchanged but a few words with Felix, kissed the old lord goodnight, then left them together in the solar. Hot water had already been brought and Felix had lit the brazier earlier to ensure that the solar was warm. It was a pleasant summer evening, but old bones felt a chill where Magdala did not.

Although that last revelation left her chilled. Herbert. Here. She wondered how soon and knew it would be too soon if he came in a decade.

She hesitated on the stairs, unwilling to return to the hall and the necessity of pretending to be as lively as Heloise. She had to think. The key to the garden hung from her belt. She turned away from the hall and walked quickly to her refuge.

The night air was not so cool that she required her cloak and she left it by the portal. Indeed, it was a relief after the heat of the hall and the solar. She opened the gate and stepped into the garden, taking a deep breath of the scent of flowers. The moon's silvery light made the garden look completely different than it did in daylight. The white flowers seemed to glow in the darkness and there were moths flitting from plant to plant. She simply stood by the reservoir and looked up at the moon, wondering what she should do.

She could not be here at Tulley when Herbert arrived.

The gate creaked and she spun to see a man step into the garden. For a moment, she feared her thoughts had brought Herbert in haste and her heart leapt.

Then she saw that it was Lothair, the moonlight making his hair even more pale and glinting on his chain mail. He paused, his gaze finding hers. "It is not my intention to disturb you, my lady."

"You do not," she said with a smile. "I think the garden can be shared."

He walked toward her slowly. "But you did not think as much earlier this day."

"Perhaps you changed my thinking."

He moved closer and paused beside her, still and somehow reassuring. This man would never change. He would never be influenced by another. He would never act ignobly. He would seldom be swayed from his path.

She wondered what he thought of the Lord de Tulley's reward.

"You must have had no immediate plans," she guessed, and his pale gaze flicked to meet hers. His question was so obvious that he did not utter it. "Because you accepted the post here. You could not have anticipated that he would offer it, but your acceptance indicates you had no alternative scheme."

He nodded. "He knew the garden would tempt me to stay."

Magdala smiled. "He probably did."

"Without this—" Lothair gestured "—I would have refused."

"Then you mean to study the plants here."

"Many I recognize. Some I do not. There will be someone who knows more of them."

"I suppose you may consider it your garden now. There will be a key on the ring granted to you."

He lifted the keys and let them drop through his fingers, his expression inscrutable. "I would not claim your refuge, my lady. As you say, it can be shared." He considered her, his intensity making her drop her own gaze shyly. "I could teach you of the plants."

She shook her head, though his offer was tempting. "I will not be here."

He ignored her comment, reaching for a white cluster of blossoms. "Sweet cicely," he murmured, brushing his fingertips across the surface. "In the sunlight, these blooms will be alive with bees and other insects."

"Yes. I have seen as much." Magdala wondered whether he had heard her or whether he was simply ignoring her declaration. "Do you know the convent of Ste. Radegund?"

She earned a sharp glance for that. "Should I?"

"You came from Outremer, through the pass at Beauvoir." She pointed toward the south and he nodded. "It is said to be beyond the pass, not far from the road. I have never been there but they speak of it in the village."

His eyes narrowed in consideration and she guessed that he was recalling the road. "There was a foundation, though we did not halt there. Why do you ask?"

Magdala took a breath. "Because I would go there. Would you escort me to its gates?"

Again, she felt the weight of his scrutiny. "You would join the cloister?" He sounded puzzled.

She nodded, for she was convinced she had little choice. "It is time."

Lothair's brows rose. "Others might say it was too soon."

"How so?"

"It is often older widows who take such vows by choice." He waited then, his silence and patience more compelling than a direct query.

"Perhaps I have a calling."

His sidelong glance was quick and bright. "I think not."

"Perhaps I have little choice."

"As the beloved niece of Lord de Tulley?" Lothair shook his head. "You will never lack for any comfort so long as that man draws breath."

"But that will not be for long, as we both know," Magdala said quietly, then she fell silent. She felt the need to depart before Herbert's arrival, yet clearly she would have to flee alone. She straightened and met his gaze. "Thank you for your concern, sir. I will find a solution alone." She made to step past Lothair but his hand landed on her elbow, drawing her to a halt. When she looked up, she found his gaze so bright that she could not look away.

"It is because Herbert comes."

"Herbert?" Magdala protested before she could stop herself. "Not Herbert."

"Your voice rises when you tell a falsehood." Lothair spoke as calmly as if he discussed the weather. There was no accusation in his tone. "Why do you fear Herbert? He is your own brother."

She could not tell him, could not utter the words aloud, but she did not have to. Magdala caught her breath and averted her gaze, then tugged her elbow from the knight's gentle grasp. "I fear I detain you from your reunion with friends. Forgive me, sir."

He released her readily and she strove to keep from running from the garden. "There is some matter between you," Lothair guessed just as she reached the gate, and Magdala could not keep herself from glancing back at him. "One you would not revisit." He shrugged. "If you fear that he will turn Tulley against you, I tell you, my lady, that cannot be done."

"Not that," Magdala confessed, though she was not equally convinced that the old lord would not be swayed. He was a warrior and a man of his word, blunt, but he would be merciless with any who deceived him.

Still Lothair waited for an explanation. "You may confide in me," he said in a low growl.

Magdala could not halt her steps and found herself returning to Lothair's side. She knew he would share whatever she confided in the Lord de Tulley and she could not turn that man against his own nephew. But still, it was enticing to have the chance to gain an ally. "I fear to be alone with Herbert, and I know that he will contrive it to be so at some point in his visit here."

"Why?"

"I cannot speak of it."

Lothair scrutinized her so intently that she could barely hold his gaze. Just when she feared he had guessed the truth, he frowned and turned away. "And so you would abandon all comfort for the remainder of your days, in anticipation of one potential moment alone with your brother?" Lothair shook his head. "I think you have more wit than that, my lady." He raised a hand before she could protest. "You are not undefended in this hall, after all."

"Aye, I fear I am."

He shook his head, closing the distance between them with one step. He looked so powerful and protective, so convinced of his own abilities, that Magdala found herself reassured simply by his proximity. "Nay, my lady," he said in a low rumble, his eyes fairly glowing with intent. "As Captain of the Guard, the safety of all within these walls is my responsibility." And he dropped to one knee before her, as if to pledge himself to her service, as Magdala stared at him in wonder. "I will defend you with my own life if necessary. I swear it." His words were filled with conviction and she believed that he truly would sacrifice his life, if necessary to ensure her safety.

Magdala's heart leapt—then it raced. He could not know how potent she found his words, and how much she wished to confide in him as a result.

"You do not know the truth of it," she whispered.

"I need not. You are the Lord de Tulley's niece." He caught her hand and kissed the one plain ring she wore, his breath warm against her skin. His gentle touch made her shiver yet also awakened a yearning within her. She looked down at the fair gold of his hair, the breadth of his shoulders, the strength held in check out of respect for her, and she was tempted.

But the ring had been Heloise's ring, one that she wore every day, a token surrendered to Magdala to support her disguise. It was a reminder to be sure.

There could be no truth between herself and this knight, for sharing the truth would see her cast from the gates. Who would believe a maid over the word of a lord like Herbert? Once her secret was revealed, she truly would be undefended.

She would flee before Herbert arrived.

"You do not trust me," he murmured and she realized he was studying her.

Magdala shook her head, unable to confess more. "I thank you, sir," she said, folding her hands around his own. His skin was warm, his fingers calloused, his surprise evident. He seemed to be at a loss for words. Or perhaps he had simply said all that he intended to utter. He watched her, eyes glittering, taut in preparation for something Magdala could not name.

On impulse, she bent and kissed his cheek again, finding tremendous reassurance in his manner. Then she looked into his eyes and was snared by the heat she found there, by an astonishing light of desire.

It seemed there was more they had in common than she had realized.

The very air stilled the garden as they stared at each other, the wind banished, the stars bright overhead. Magdala stared into his eyes and hoped for what she would never have, an honorable man sworn to defend her, a noble knight as husband and champion.

But she knew that could never be.

Nay, this man was not for her, and she must leave Tulley alone.

SHE WAS SO VULNERABLE, so fearful, that Lothair would have said anything to reassure her. This was the sorcery commanded by this maiden, that she could coax words from his lips so that he was loquacious instead of taciturn. She could provoke him to pledge himself to her, and promise more than he should, even knowing that she had deceived the Lord de Tulley, even with the uncertainty of her true name. More, she tempted Lothair as he had not been tempted in many years, and when she pulled her hand from his, he feared that she would do some rash deed.

He let her retreat, stifling his urges, wishing he could win her trust. He felt he had come so close to winning her confession, though that had not been his scheme. He had only wished to reassure her.

Should he escort her to the convent?

Would she flee there alone before he could ask the Lord de Tulley's counsel the next midday? He could not bear the notion of her alone on the road, for he had seen much of what could happen to solitary travelers.

She left the garden with rapid steps before he could think of the words that might persuade her to stay. Lothair stared after her, like a man in a dream, and wondered whether it was folly indeed to take the Lord de Tulley's commission. This woman might be a fraud, a woman so practiced in deception that she could change her apparent nature to suit her ends. She might be using him for her own purposes, whatever they might be. He certainly was not accustomed to the wiles of women. He could not let her know how readily she might enslave him to her will, not without being certain of her true nature and scheme.

But Lothair had told her the truth. He would defend her to his very last, and not just for the sake of the Lord de Tulley. He surveyed the garden and suspected that no matter how the matter was resolved, he would not regret the loss of anything he surrendered to this lady.

Aye, even to know her was perilous.

To linger at Tulley was folly.

But Lothair would regret naught, even if she destroyed him utterly.

The garden was not the temptation that had convinced him to accept. He wondered whether the Lord de Tulley knew as much.

Lothair was troubled, but not so distracted that he did not confirm which of the keys would open the gate to the garden. He secured the portal for the night, taking one lingering look at the garden, knowing it was not the sole detail of interest within these walls.

Then he descended to the bailey, spoke with the ostler and was shown to his chamber over the stables. An entire chamber of his own, with a bed and a mattress of straw, several windows and space for his trunk. Calum was there, fairly bouncing with his satisfaction over the arrangements, though Lothair did not listen to the youth's chatter. He praised him for his labor, bade him be still lest he make himself ill, and heard of the considerable meal that the youth had consumed. He learned that Quinn and Niall had retired already, even as he disrobed for the night. He strove to make a plan to familiarize himself with his duties and his new home, but he kept seeing the fear in those wondrous green eyes and feeling the potent need to protect the maiden.

His thoughts were consumed with the lady and her riddles.

Aye, the mystery of the maiden who claimed to be Heloise—but was not—kept Lothair awake long into the night and that was no good portent for his future at Château Tulley.

THE LORD DE Tulley was coughing when Lothair arrived at midday to consult with that man in his chambers. Lothair heard the older man's distress from the corridor and quickened his footsteps. He rapped on the door, but there was no response. He could hear a servant striving to soothe the older man, and the racking sound of that cough.

He considered protocol, then abandoned it, opening the door and striding to the older man's side. A hard tap between the Lord de Tulley's shoulders made that man choke and then fall silent. The older man looked up at Lothair, his eyes rimmed with red and his face pale. Lothair could feel how slender the lord had become, for the bones on his back were prominent.

"Not long now," the Lord de Tulley said gruffly, then nodded a dismissal at the servant. That man lingered for a moment, uncertain that he should leave his lord alone.

"I will remain with him," Lothair said. "Ask my squire for the blue vial."

"Do as much, Felix."

The servant nodded and bowed, then quickly vanished from the room.

"Another elixir?" the lord demanded.

"There is no magic in it," Lothair confessed. "It is a mixture to soothe the throat, with a base of honey. I can make more of it with access to your garden."

"What you need is there?"

Lothair nodded.

The older man waved a hand. "Use whatsoever you will, and teach Heloise, if you will."

"Aye." Lothair was surprised that the Lord de Tulley called her by that name, but then she appeared in the doorway as he helped the lord to his great chair.

"Uncle! You are unwell again?"

"The bread caught in my throat, no more than that," the lord insisted, though Lothair saw that his so-called niece was not deceived.

"You eat too quickly in the morning, Uncle," she said, granting Lothair a quick glance that revealed this was a fiction to save the older man's pride.

"I am hungry. It is no crime."

"Of course not." She was fetching a heavier robe, completely at ease in his chamber. The one she chose was lined with fur and she tugged it over the lord's shoulders, helping him to slide his arms into the sleeves. He nestled down into it with satisfaction as she found his fur-lined boots and knelt before him to put them on his feet. "And then you get cold because you do not let Felix dress you with sufficient speed," she chided gently. The sound of her voice clearly reassured the older man, who almost smiled as he watched her.

"You fuss overmuch," he complained.

She kissed his cheek. "And you would miss it if I did not."

Lothair saw that it was true enough.

"Away with you then," the Lord de Tulley said briskly and Lothair saw that she was surprised. "I must speak to Lothair of his new duties and such details are unfit for a maiden's ears."

"I have heard of the defense of Tulley before," she protested, her gaze flicking between the pair of them. Did she guess that the old lord knew her deception?

"And I will not be defied, even by the prettiest maiden who ever crossed the borders of Tulley," he retorted, wagging his finger playfully.

She smiled and blushed a little even as he pretended to scowl at her. "Whatsoever you desire, Uncle, is my will."

"Aye and so it should be."

The pair smiled at each other.

"Go," the Lord de Tulley said. "You must have some indulgence to occupy yourself."

She looked at Lothair and he knew she wished him to take note of her words. "I will tend the garden, sir, that the weeds might be diminished for your new healer's labor."

"Mind you do not kill the helpful plants!" the Lord de Tulley said, his voice rising.

She flushed again but paused to look back. "Perhaps I might be given direction, at Sir Lothair's convenience."

Lothair bowed to her, his heart leaping at the prospect of time alone in her company again. "I should be delighted to advise you," he said, and was rewarded by her quick smile. Then she was gone, her sapphire gown swirling behind her, both men looking after her with admiration.

"A veritable gem," the older man said with a sigh and Lothair found himself nodding agreement. "I cannot believe she is a deceiver, but she has deceived me, to be sure. What have you learned?"

WOMEN, in the view of Niall MacGillivray, were fickle, frivolous, and impossible to comprehend entirely. Indeed, mystery was a major part of their allure. He loved naught better than a woman who kept him guessing—unless it was a beauteous woman who did as much. If she was clever, in addition to those attributes, he would find her irresistible.

For a while.

But that interval would be glorious indeed.

Heloise von Idelstein was the pinnacle of all such maidens Niall had encountered. A beauty beyond compare, quick of wit, graceful and kind, she also confused him completely. Never had a woman held his attention so securely for so long, and he would not have been the man he was if he had not been determined to satisfy his desire for once and for all.

And soon.

It was unseemly for a woman to possess such a hold over him, and his pursuit of this particular lady had endured too long.

Worse, when he came from Annossy, specifically insisting upon his inclusion in the party the better to claim the prize he believed he had earned, the lady became changeable.

Niall could make no sense of it. She greeted him with indifference, she charmed him utterly at dinner, then she vanished from the hall with nary a word of parting. He had hoped that she might have retired to some private corner in anticipation of his pursuit, but nay. As far as he could determine, she had gone to her uncle, and thence to her own chamber for the night.

Offering not so much as a kiss for his trouble.

He even had crept from the hall, hoping to find her alone in the garden she favored, only to find her offering a kiss to Lothair. Lothair! There was a sign of desperation on her part.

Niall lay awake in the stables much of the night, considering his choices, seeking a possible explanation for the lady's changed favor.

Had he insulted her? Niall was certain he had not.

Had he failed to compliment her? Niall knew he had not.

Did she tire of his attentions? He could not imagine that situation.

Had she received tidings of his deeds beyond these very walls? Niall winced in the darkness. She might have heard of his seduction of the ostler's daughter at Sayerne.

Aye, and she might have become aware of his persistent flattery of the pretty shepherdess who lived in the hills beyond Annossy. Lady Melissande might have been fulsome in sharing her observations.

Niall grimaced. Heloise might somehow have learned of the wife of the knight who had returned from the east with her husband, but succumbed to Niall's charms in the inn at Beauvoir the month before.

He smiled in recollection of that merry night, the husband snoring in an adjacent chamber, the wife—ah, what a passionate delight she had been. He did not even recall her name, but he had a garter from her as a token of that happy interlude. He had no regrets, to be sure.

Was Heloise one of those maidens who believed that a man should grant his regard exclusively to her? Niall suspected that she might be, as tedious a trait as that was. All the same, his ardor for her was undiminished, and would not fade until he had sampled her sweetness.

A mere kiss would not suffice. Lothair had had that much, after all.

He was neither knave nor cur, to his own thinking, for the seduction would be their own secret. He had held his tongue when many another conquest had subsequently wed, without her newfound husband realizing that she was a maiden no more—much less that he could blame Niall MacGillivray for claiming what had been promised to him alone.

Niall simply was not wrought for matrimony. He knew his own nature sufficiently well to see the truth. So long as there was an infinite variety of women in the world, he could never commit himself to solely one—and to pledge oneself to a lady, then betray that trust by seducing others was simply not possible for him. Niall might possess many traits, not all of which were admirable, but he was not a liar. His word was his bond.

The pretty tales he told to alluring maidens were promises not pledges.

They did not count.

He feared that Heloise believed they *did* count. He feared that she wished for him to swear to her only. That could not be, but Niall intended to satisfy his curiosity—and ensure the lady's pleasure, too. She would only lose her maidenhead once. To his thinking, the matter should be done well, to pave the way for future intimacies.

He was the man for the task.

He had only to persuade her.

He rose the next morning with purpose, for he knew that Quinn would not linger at Tulley. Heloise did not appear in the hall, so Niall sought her out. He checked the kitchens and the storage rooms, then asked Rose, always a willing confederate, to check the lady's chamber.

All for naught.

He checked the stables and even walked the main street of the town, thinking she might have had an errand. It was late morning by the time he realized his own folly. The most convenient place to find Heloise would be the garden, for she was the sole one who ever entered that place. They would be alone there, which was ideal. He strode quickly back into the keep, aware that time was passing, and climbed the stairs with haste.

To Niall's satisfaction, the gate to the garden was unlocked and the lady herself was tending the flowers. She had her back to the portal, and was crouched down, intent upon her task. Niall admired the neat indent of her waist, revealed by the tight lacing of her kirtle. Her fair hair was burnished gold in the midday sunlight, flowing over her shoulders in a gleaming river. Her hands were slightly tanned, long and elegant, and he smiled in anticipation of feeling her caress upon his skin.

He pushed a hand through his hair, straightened his shoulders, then stepped into the garden. When she did not look up, he cleared his throat, summoning his best smile. "Good morning, my lady," he said and she glanced over her shoulder in surprise.

"Oh!" She straightened and stood, clasping her hands together before herself.

Another man might have thought the lady's expression had changed slightly, as if she were disappointed in the identity of her visitor, as if—perhaps—she had awaited another man, but Niall knew there was no man in this entire holding who had greater allure than himself.

Her smile was not as bright as Niall might have hoped, a sign that he had understood her vexation rightly.

All he had to do was dismiss her doubts, a task he knew he would accomplish readily.

"Good morning, sir," she said, lowering her gaze demurely.

Ah, she would be shy this day! She wished to be reassured and to be coaxed. Perhaps she desired a conquest. Niall was prepared to say or do whatever was necessary to claim his boon.

He let his smile broaden and stepped toward the lady, intent upon charming her into submission with all haste.

~

MAGDALA COULD HAVE CURSED ALOUD when Niall MacGillivray entered the garden. He was the last man she wished to see and she heartily regretted any modicum of encouragement she had ever offered him.

Worse, it was clear that he had expectations.

Her ploy to await Lothair alone in the garden had gone badly awry, to be sure.

Aye, she should have locked the gate. Lothair had a key, after all.

She forced a smile as the knight drew near, not wanting to insult one of Tulley's guests. Niall was handsome, more handsome than any man Magdala had ever known, and it should have been pleasing to have his attention. The difficulty was that Niall was convinced of his own merit beyond all others, and seemingly believed that all maidens should fall to his feet in surrender. She had jested with him from the outset because Heloise would have liked him well. She also recognized his heart would never be engaged and the risk of any obligation low. But as his expectations had become more evident, she had wanted to deny him his desire, as a matter of principle. No man should gain his every wish with so little effort.

The sole possession Magdala had was her chastity, and she would not surrender it lightly, as if it proved to be of no import at all. It was her only chance of an honorable marriage—and even then, if her identity was revealed, the chances of any match were low.

She stood near the reservoir, letting the knight come to her instead of meeting him partway across the garden. She had been savoring the quiet of the garden amidst the turmoil of her concerns, but strove to hide how much she resented Niall's interruption.

She could not quell her annoyance. Would Niall's presence keep Lothair away?

Niall walked toward her with long strides, fairly swaggering, doubtless granting her time to admire him. He was a finely wrought man, there could be no disputing that, with his wavy dark gold hair and twinkling blue eyes. His ready smile and quick wit had doubtless enchanted a hundred maidens, but Magdala could only wonder whether he held any concern for any matter beyond his own comfort and pleasure.

Another woman's heart might have fluttered when Niall bowed low before her, sweeping out one arm, as he made to kiss her hand. Magdala merely watched him and wished he could have looked her in the eye and told her the truth of his desire.

Then she could have refused, and the game would be over.

But no, he would flatter and tease first, endeavoring to make her feel special when she was no more than the most recent lady to have snared his attention.

Was she the most recent? It had been over a year since they had first met. Magdala bit back a smile, guessing there had been at least a dozen women to succumb to his charms in that interval.

"I fear you have missed my presence in recent weeks," he said.

"You need not have concerns on that account," she said sweetly, noting how quickly he met her gaze. "I have ample responsibilities and amusement."

His eyes twinkled as he smiled. "But surely there is some company that you prefer over others?"

"Surely there is," she assured him, granting him a moment to believe that he knew her thoughts before continuing. "But my uncle, sadly, does not welcome companionship as much as was previously the case. He has more need of rest in these times."

Niall's smile faded. "You prefer to be with the old lord, to sit beside a sickbed? Surely that is only a jest." He winked. "Do you take me to task for ignoring you, my lady? Would you have me punished for my inattention?"

She shook her head. "Of course not. I simply prefer to show my gratitude to the man who has treated me well. I *like* my uncle."

"Better than me?"

She smiled to soften her words. "He tells the truth more often."

Niall did not care for this comment, for his eyes narrowed a little and his charm faltered. "But he lingers in his chamber at this hour."

"It is true. He does not descend to the hall until the afternoon."

That smile returned. "Then you are without companionship, and I could not allow that to be. Let me entertain you, my lady, in whatever way you wish, to better pass the time until your uncle is prepared to enjoy your company."

"You need not do as much. Surely you have other duties."

"None so pressing as the cultivation of your smile."

Magdala managed to refrain from a groan. "I am content at my task here."

"But you are alone! Surely you need not suffer so."

"There is no sufferance in solitude when one has interests to pursue."

"If one's interest is conversation, then there must be hardship in solitude."

"But if one's interest is contemplation, then solitude is sweet beyond all."

"But what would you contemplate?"

"Whatever I desire. My perusals are my own." She gestured. "I find great satisfaction in removing the weeds so that the flowers show to advantage."

"You are a flower that should be shown to advantage." He moved closer and caught her hand. "You should be admired, my lady, and treasured..." He pressed his lips against her palm, planting a kiss there then glancing up at her through his lashes. He made the gesture with such surety that she knew he had done it hundreds of times.

Nay, she did not trust him a whit.

She pulled her hand away and crouched down beside the calendula again. "Treasured?" She laughed lightly. "I have no wish to be locked away in a counting room." She began to pull weeds with gusto, casting them on the ground between them.

The knight stepped around her to approach from her other side. "Nay, you should repose upon a bed of silken pillows and be fed the choicest morsels by hand."

She looked up at him. "Doubtless I should do as much in my sheerest chemise, or perhaps nude."

His smile flashed. "If that is your inclination."

"And what is yours, sir?"

"To cherish you, my lady." He dropped to one knee beside her and cupped her face in his hand. "To honor you, and to love you."

Magdala was so astonished at his touch that she did not pull away.

And then it was too late, for Niall moved with unholy speed. He leaned forward, slanted his mouth across hers and kissed her.

Magdala was shocked.

This was no chaste kiss nor even a sweet one, but a claiming of her mouth with obvious intent to have yet more. Magdala gave a little cry and twisted away from him, only to lose her balance and tumble to the ground. He immediately lowered himself over her, pinning her to the ground as if she had fallen to invite his embrace.

"Finally, there is sincerity between us, my lady!" He captured her mouth once again before she could protest. Magdala felt his tongue against her own and his fingers in her hair. His knee slid between her own, the cloth of her kirtle obstructing his progress, and Magdala panicked.

In that moment, she was in another keep at another time, another man atop her, and once again, she fought with all her might.

CHAPTER 4

"What have you learned of the maiden?" the Lord de Tulley demanded.

Lothair bent closer to confide more quietly in the older man. He was uncertain how far the servant had gone. "That she fears the arrival of Herbert."

"Why?"

Lothair shrugged. "She was prepared to retire to the convent of Ste. Radegund to avoid him."

"Nay!" The Lord de Tulley was visibly outraged. "Nonsense!"

"I fear not, sir. She asked me to escort her there."

"You declined?"

"Aye, but I sensed that she might attempt the journey alone."

"But it is several day's ride, and over the pass. She could not travel so far alone, even if she did ride. Walking, the journey might take her a fortnight." The Lord de Tulley sputtered in his justifiable outrage. Lothair was glad that they were in agreement about the perils that might confront the lady if she made such a choice. "There is no telling what manner of knights and warriors might be upon that road, never mind vagabonds and thieves and mercenaries. She would have to halt for the night repeatedly, and even in the hall of the Lord de Beauvoir,

I could not be confident of her safety. She would not have the coin to pay for her own protection!"

"And she will not ask for it either, I wager."

The Lord de Tulley flung out a hand. "And that does not even account for the donation that would have to be made for her acceptance into the establishment." He shook his head grimly. "Nay, this plan is folly indeed. You must stop her."

"Her fear of Herbert must be great."

"Aye, for he will recognize immediately that she is not Heloise." Lothair frowned.

"Well?" The Lord de Tulley demanded. "What do you suspect?"

"I wonder if it is more than that."

"You think he knows who she is in truth?"

Lothair chose his words. "I think she may fear his actions in her presence."

"Ah." Tulley drummed his fingers on the arm of his chair, his brows drawn together. "Do you think he has despoiled her?"

The irksome words hung in the air between the two men for a long moment.

"She fears him and his arrival," Lothair said finally. "Her terror was potent, indeed. I would guess that there is more than the revelation of a secret at root."

Tulley nodded. "If he has not despoiled her, then he has tried." He raised a hand when Lothair might have softened the accusation. "I know my nephew and his appetites. Such a deed would not surprise me. It hints to me that she has been a servant in that household, for he is the manner of man to prey upon those women who are undefended."

The very suggestion outraged Lothair, though he did not speak.

"Your eyes flash fire," Tulley said with a chuckle. "Aye, you see her allure as well."

"I vowed to defend her so she would not flee the keep."

"A pledge of protection?"

Lothair straightened. "In the post you have bestowed upon me, sir, it is my duty to defend all within these walls."

The old man's eyes glinted with unexpected mischief. "Of course. Of course. I should not have expected a knight of such experience as yourself to be snared by the charms of a woman of mysterious origin and one inclined to deception."

Lothair was spared from the need to reply by the arrival of the servant again. Felix brought a steaming cup of hot broth, a measure of which Lothair heartily approved, and also the blue vial. "I trust this is the one you desire, sir," he said, bowing to Lothair as he presented it. "Your squire said you would need these, as well." He removed Lothair's mortar and pestle from his purse as well as a measure of honey in a cup.

Truly, Calum had learned something in his days of journeying with Lothair. He nodded approval and asked the servant to keep the broth warm as he quickly prepared the mixture that would soothe the Lord de Tulley. It was only three herbs, dried and ground together, each useful on its own but more potent in unison than the sum of the parts. He mixed the ground herbs with the honey and offered a measure of it to Tulley.

"This much, before each meal and again at night."

"I would take more to feel greater improvement."

"This much, before each meal and again at night," Lothair repeated.

The Lord de Tulley gestured and his manservant consumed the measure. Lothair realized with a shock at the implication of Felix taking the mixture first. He strove to disguise that he was insulted by the notion that he might intend to poison his new liege lord, but his charge's eyes glinted.

The Lord de Tulley turned over a sand clock, the servant standing before him as they both waited to see the results of his ingestion.

This practice clearly was routine, and more seriously followed when the substance to be consumed was for the Lord de Tulley only.

"I cannot be too careful and Felix has volunteered to aid me in this matter," the Lord de Tulley confided, when the sand had run to the bottom. The servant showed no ill effects or even concern. He granted Lothair a smile of reassurance. "All is not resolved to my satisfaction as yet." The Lord de Tulley took a spoon and dipped it into the honey mixture, loading a similar measure onto it for himself. He consumed it, then shook the spoon at Lothair. "Then and only then will I be sufficiently satisfied to leave this realm."

Lothair did not tell the older man that the choice might not be his to make. It seemed a tactless detail to note, especially in the presence of a man who clearly believed that all should follow his desire. He watched Tulley take a breath and exhale, and heard that the obstruction was already lessened, just as anticipated. Felix was visibly relieved by his lord's improvement and busily heated a cup of the broth over the brazier, filling the chamber with the rich scent of it.

"You approve?" Tulley asked Lothair, gesturing to the broth.

"It is ideal for you."

Once again, Felix tasted of the broth first. Once again, the sand clock was turned and once again, the chamber was silent as the grains fell steadily. All three of them watched the progress of the sand, then the Lord de Tulley accepted a bowl of the broth. He sipped of it and smacked his lips.

"You must learn the details," he said to Lothair, continuing their previous conversation.

Lothair glanced at Felix, who acted as if he did not hear their words, though the conversation had to be audible to him. "I am not in that individual's confidence," he said with care.

Tulley smiled. "But you will be." Again, he shook the spoon in Lothair's direction. "Make a point of it." He punctuated that command with a hard look, then began to speak of Lothair's duties.

He referred to a north gate that Lothair had not realized was there and a rumor that it was not consistently secured. Evidently the former Captain of the Guard had not been diligent in this matter and Lothair took note of that implied warning. The Lord de Tulley reviewed a list of the men under his command and provided a summary of their experience, as well as a description of every steed in the stables. His memory was impressive, to be sure. This was followed by a demand for a full inventory of the armory before they met the next day at the same time.

His thoughts churning with details, Lothair left the lord's solar. Before descending to the hall, he hesitated by the entrance to the garden. Of course, he would need more horehound, fennel and marjoram, and he suspected that all three could be found in the garden. They were hardly herbs and grew even when left untended. But the true reason he stopped was that the gate was unlocked and he knew only one person in the household frequented the garden.

She had said she would be there.

Although Lothair told himself that it would only be polite to tell the lady of her uncle's progress, the way his heart leapt at the prospect of seeing her made it clear that the tale was no more than an excuse.

He could also have insisted to himself that he was following the Lord de Tulley's order in gaining the lady's confidence, but the simple truth was that Lothair could not sacrifice any opportunity to be alone with her.

And she had requested his instruction.

Lothair had not taken more than two steps into the sunlit garden when he realized that the lady known as Heloise was not alone. He might have turned around and left her to be kissed by Niall MacGillivray, particularly as the pair of them were entangled on the stone path with an intimacy better suited to a bed chamber.

'Twas the way the lady battled against Niall that changed Lothair's view of what he saw.

This union was not a willing one, not on the lady's part, which meant there was but one deed to do.

MAGDALA TWISTED AWAY from Niall's unwelcome kiss and struck at the knight's face. He swore with surprise and recoiled, evading the brunt of her blow.

"Heloise!" he said, apparently astonished that anyone could decline the favor of his salute.

He did not move, though. His arms were braced on either side of her, trapping her beneath him, and Magdala had to escape. She struggled against him, digging her elbow into his ribs. Sadly, there was a hauberk between them and she winced at the pain that shot through her arm. Her jab went unnoticed by the knight.

"Let me go!" she insisted.

"But a kiss from your sweet lips, Lady Heloise, and I will be your servant forevermore," he said smoothly.

Magdala doubted that. "I decline!" she said, then punched him in the nose.

This time, she did not miss. The crack of Niall's nose gave her tremendous satisfaction, as did the spurt of his blood. He swore but she raised her knee hard, liking that the hauberk did not defend him at that angle. He roared in protest when she kicked him, his eyes flashed with rare fury—then his weight was abruptly hauled away from her.

Niall was cast across the path with haste and another man stepped between them to glare down upon the offending knight. There was no mistaking the fair hair or considerable stature of Lothair, nor the disapproval that emanated from him.

Magdala had never been so glad to see another being in her life.

Niall's eyes were wide with astonishment, blood running freely from his nose, yet he immediately struggled to his feet and strove to explain himself. Indeed, he spoke with more haste than she had ever heard from him before, and his words fairly tumbled from his mouth.

Perhaps he feared the grim knight as well.

"Lothair! You clearly have mistaken the state of affection between the lady and me. Matters are not as they might appear with a casual glance..."

Magdala wished she could kick him again. She glowered at him as she sat up, brushing off her hands and her skirt.

"Silence," Lothair said with grim authority and Niall stammered for a moment before he did as instructed. Lothair then gallantly offered his hand to Magdala. "The lady shall explain what transpired here and no other." She placed her hand in his, aware of how she trembled inwardly when his hand closed over her own. Lothair lifted her to her feet as readily as if she weighed nothing at all.

Then he fixed that piercing gaze upon her, his scrutiny so intent that she could barely hold his gaze.

"Are you injured?" he asked softly, his apparent concern making her throat tighten.

"Of course, she is not injured," Niall said heartily. "I am the one who has been assaulted and for no good cause, to my thinking. Who could imagine there might be so much blood? And my nose may be broken! The lady, I assure you, welcomed me…"

Lothair lifted a hand, gesturing the other knight to silence again. "My lady?"

"I am hale," she said, smiling a little to reassure him. "Surprised, but uninjured. I thank you for your timely arrival."

Lothair held her gaze and nodded once, as if relieved. It was curious how she felt she understood his meaning even when he did not speak—and that she trusted him all the more for his reticence. Men, it seemed, often spoke a great deal when they meant very little, as Niall was inclined to do, and a weighty nod went much further in reassuring her than any lecture of his own good intent might have done.

"I hope that I did not interrupt a welcome interlude," Lothair continued, his gaze searching hers.

"Of course, you did!" Niall said but the other knight did not so much as glance at him. "A small misunderstanding with regards to timing, perhaps, but there is no ill will between Heloise and me. I would scarce assault the lord's own niece!"

Magdala was aware that Lothair waited for her explanation. "I did not invite such a salute," she said with conviction. "And if my words were interpreted thus, then I apologize to this knight for any misunderstanding."

"The apology is not yours to make, my lady," Lothair said, turning his gaze upon Niall expectantly. "A knight is charged with the defense of those weaker than himself."

Niall scowled before he forced a smile. "And my heartfelt apology is offered, though truly I cannot see how I might have erred."

Magdala caught her breath.

"Do you suggest that the niece of the Lord de Tulley uses the trick of a whore to deceive you, only to show you in poor light?"

It was a veritable lecture from this man and Magdala wondered at that. He spoke tightly but with great control. His entire body was tense and she saw that one fist was clenched. Was this how fury manifested in this warrior of such composure?

She could not help but be glad that he was stirred to anger on her behalf.

"Lothair!" Niall protested. "You know that I never demand of a lady what she is not willing to surrender."

"It looked as if your choices had altered."

Niall flicked a hot look at Heloise, then bowed to her again. "I apologize if my attentions were not desired," he said stiffly. "Though truly you might have suggested as much far sooner than this."

"Still you blame the lady for your own error," Lothair said with quiet heat. "It gives your apology the flavor of an accusation."

"That was not my intent."

"Undoubtedly."

The two knights glared at each other. "It seems my presence is unwelcome," Niall said, clearly hoping that he would be corrected. When no one spoke, he retreated from the garden, sparing one parting glance at Heloise before he vanished into the keep.

Magdala exhaled with relief, realizing that Lothair still held her hand. "I thank you again, sir."

"I told you that you could rely upon me," he said and she had to look away from his vivid gaze. He seemed to be lit with an inner fire, one that conjured a matching heat within herself.

"His conclusion was not entirely undeserved," she confessed. "I have enjoyed his jests and companionship in the hall." She took a breath. "He might have taken encouragement from that."

"Yet he should not have presumed upon you."

"You should not be too harsh upon him."

"You should not be too kind."

"You are the one who has been kind, sir," Magdala said, then smiled at him. She felt his attention sharpen and feared that she had only encouraged a view that she was no better than a harlot. She retreated and lowered her gaze, drawing her hand from his grip. It felt suddenly very warm in the sunlight, and Magdala feigned concern with the state of her kirtle. She frowned at Niall's blood on her sleeve.

"Cold water," Lothair said quietly. "And before it dries."

He was right, of course, and she knew that solution, as well, but she had been too agitated to think clearly. She dared to look up to find his expression inscrutable again.

She looked over the garden, uncertain of what to say and yet unwilling to leave.

"I believe your uncle would favor your companionship at this moment," Lothair said. "I have just reported to him and he was inclined to talk."

He had read her thoughts but, in this instance, it was a relief. Magdala was glad to have a ready suggestion presented to her. "I thank you for telling me as much. I never know when it would be best to visit him, but I do enjoy his company."

Lothair offered his hand to her and once again, Magdala slid her fingers into his warm grasp. He escorted her from the garden as if she were a queen, waiting for her to secure the portal, then accompanied her to the solar. He did not speak again.

He also did not leave until the lord had welcomed her and expressed himself glad of her presence. Magdala wondered whether

Lothair realized her uncertainty. She smiled and took a seat before the old lord, grateful again when Lothair suggested that she might rub an ointment onto Tulley's back.

"It awakens a heat in the skin, which will aid your recovery," he said, then excused himself. He returned moments later with a small vessel filled with unguent. He showed Magdala how much to use. "Once a day, in the afternoon, would be ideal."

The Lord de Tulley did not argue with this counsel but wrestled with the tie of his chemise. Magdala was unknotting it for him when she heard the door to the solar close softly. She felt Lothair's absence as keenly as his presence, but strove to hide her reaction from the old lord's bright gaze.

She reminded herself that she was safe.

At least until Herbert arrived.

LOTHAIR WAS SIMMERING EVEN when he found Quinn in the bailey with Niall. There was no doubt that the younger knight had confided in the Lord d'Annossy, and had contrived to share the tale to ensure that his own innocence was to be believed. Lothair saw consideration in Quinn's gaze, though, and knew that Niall had not been wholly believed.

They both knew his inclinations too well, it seemed.

Lothair was livid, both that a maiden had been assaulted in the keep that was now beneath his command, but also that so far as Niall knew, she was the niece of the Lord de Tulley himself. If ever a woman should have been left untouched, one of that rank and standing should be in such company! Worse again, Lothair had only just pledged himself specifically to the lady's defense before his own comrade strove to abuse her.

If she had not broken Niall's nose herself, Lothair might have been inclined to do the honors.

Niall had successfully halted the flow of blood, but he was

touching his face carefully and wincing at intervals. His nose was already swelling. In another man, the situation might adversely influence his amorous endeavors, but Lothair had no doubt Niall would use the injury to gain sympathy from some credulous maiden—or more than one.

Perhaps he should sustain an injury that would be less readily ignored.

"You will leave," Lothair said to Niall by way of greeting, halting before the pair of knights. "And you will do as much immediately, so that you make Annossy before dark."

Niall was clearly incredulous. "You cannot cast me from the gates for such a minor misunderstanding…"

"I can, as Captain of the Guard, and I do, as a knight sworn to defend all within these walls, particularly the Lord de Tulley and his family." Lothair folded his arms across his chest. "I will wait while you saddle your horse, then escort you to the gates." He felt rather than saw Quinn's brows rise.

"You cannot do this! She invited it!" Niall argued, casting out his hands. "It is the oldest ploy known for a lady of supposed virtue to encourage a seduction."

Supposed virtue? Lothair found himself bristling and Niall retreated a step from him.

"How so?" Quinn asked.

"She fluttered her lashes at me," Niall said, doing as much with his own as if to mimic the lady. He lifted the back of his hand to his brow and cast his glance skyward. "Then she appeared to feel faint." He made a gasp that was almost a moan. "Then she fell backward so slowly that I was obviously intended to catch her." He straightened and winked. "And once she was in my arms, what else was I to do but kiss her?"

"Aid her to regain her balance and step away?" Lothair suggested.

Niall rolled his eyes. "I did not force my interest upon her. I know women. I *understand* women. I know what she wanted."

"Though she did not let you give it to her, curiously enough."

"Nay, she did not." Niall scowled.

Quinn peered at Niall's swollen nose. "Her objection seems to have been most emphatic."

"And that was not the worst of it," Niall confided, gesturing lower.

Quinn bit back a smile even as Lothair felt a curious satisfaction in that confession. "One can only salute her vigor," Quinn said mildly.

Niall exhaled, sounding like his horse. He nodded at Lothair. "Perhaps she knew that you approached, and that was the cause of her sudden shyness."

"Why?"

"Because you would feel compelled to tell her uncle of her wayward manners. You are inclined to honor and duty. She might recognize that side of your nature even by now. But she deceived us both." He nodded to Quinn, inviting that knight's agreement. "You saw her at the board last night. She could not turn her attention from me for a moment. She was enthralled with me." He held his finger and thumb an increment apart. "I was *this* close to triumph, save for Lothair's intervention."

That he should still believe his attentions were welcome was outrageous—and a hint that Niall might resume his attempt at conquest.

"Lady Heloise is the niece of the lord and a maiden to be defended," Lothair snapped. "You are a knave and cur to even think of despoiling her while a guest in her uncle's home." He heard his voice rising but could not halt it. "She is not some goat girl in need of an interlude in the meadow!"

Quinn's brows rose and he eyed Lothair in surprise, doubtless noting his companion's volubility.

Instead of being daunted, Niall smiled. "A veritable lecture from the man of few words," he said, his manner knowing. "It seems I have competition for the lady's favor."

"Nay," Lothair began to protest, but Niall did not let him continue.

"She stirs you to eloquence," that knight said with conviction. "And that is a rare accomplishment." He brushed off the front of

Lothair's tabard, so confident in his conclusion that Lothair again felt an inclination to violence. "I see now why you accepted this post, though you always said you had no desire to become the Captain of the Guard of any lord. The lady is the true prize you seek, and why not?" Niall shook a finger at him. "But you err, my friend. You would wed her, rather than simply savoring her. Folly, my friend. Nuptial vows are folly!"

"You had no intention of seeking her hand?" Lothair was shocked to hear Niall say as much outright, though he could not understand why he would be. Niall never spent more than one night with any woman, and often his interest was sated within an hour.

"I have no desire for a bride, and no means to support a wife." Niall shook his head readily. "That is no cause to live like a monk, however."

"But a maiden of privilege..." Lothair forced himself to say, well aware that he was uncertain of the lady's lineage.

"Has desires as strong as any other woman," Niall concluded cheerfully. "We would have shared a merry interval, to be sure." He shook a finger at Lothair. "And one I would never have sought without her encouragement. If you seek that lady's favor, guard yourself against her charm. She has a way of changing her tale, and might even leave *you* with the appearance of wrongdoing." He turned to Quinn. "Do you leave this day for Annossy?"

"Aye, but I must confer with the Lord de Tulley first."

"Then I will leave the keep, as invited, and await you in the tavern below. A cup of ale might soothe my wounded pride."

"Or the attention of a maid in that establishment," Quinn said and Niall grinned, unrepentant.

He bowed elaborately to Lothair, then spun away from the pair and headed into the shadows of the stables. He called for a squire and began to whistle, his failed conquest nigh forgotten already.

"Doubtless I will find him between some other maiden's thighs when I would ride out," Quinn murmured, rolling his eyes.

Lothair was not prepared to jest about the incident as yet.

He could only consider Niall's assertion that the lady was deceptive. It was true that the maiden who called herself Heloise was an imposter, at least in the Lord de Tulley's view. She had been quick to excuse Niall's amorous venture, as well, though the knight had frightened her, taking responsibility for her own part in his false expectations. He wondered whether any of this particular lady's words might be believed.

And how he might be certain whether to trust her assertions or not.

He had to complete Tulley's quest, to be sure, unveil her true identity and her motives, in order to be sure.

How might he persuade her to confide in him?

MAGDALA MISSED LADY HELOISE.

She felt the loss of her former lady often but on this day, when Niall had nigh forced himself upon her and she had no one to share her concerns, she missed Heloise yet more. That lady had been sure of her choices and saw her way clearly, while Magdala always feared the worst. On this day, she wondered how much the Lord de Tulley had seen from his vantage point, what he might decide as a result, whether her time at Château Tulley came to an end independent of her desire.

Where would she go?

What would she do?

Lothair had declined to escort her to the convent and the incident with Niall made her dread a solitary journey.

Heloise would have known what to do.

Heloise would have contrived a plan and ensured its success. Heloise had been confident and fearless. Magdala turned the gold ring on her finger and fretted. It was the difference between being born to abundance and naught at all.

The Lord de Tulley dismissed all from the great hall when he finally descended from his chambers, insisting that he would confer with Quinn, Lord d'Annossy, alone. Magdala did not wish to leave the keep and stroll through the town, as often she did, not with Niall undoubtedly in close proximity. She descended to the stables, only to find Lothair occupied in his review of the armory and its inventory. She was not even certain he noticed her, which said much for his concentration upon his new duties. Even his squire was busy, hastening back and forth at his knight's command. Heloise knew she was only in the way and retreated to her chamber.

She stood at the window and eyed the ribbon of road that unfurled to the north. Her innards clenched at the prospect of Herbert's arrival.

Any exchange would be worse, far worse, than the day she had encountered Gaultier de Lonvaux by accident in the village of Tulley. On that day, she had nearly been revealed. That handsome knight had seen Magdala before she had been aware of his presence. A former suitor of Heloise's and a stranger to Magdala, he had mistaken Magdala for her former mistress. Mercifully, Heloise had spoken of the man, and Magdala had been able to respond with sufficient authority to convince him that she truly was Heloise.

Her heart had raced as she had left him, though, and she had remained within the keep for some days, fearful of encountering the knight again. Later, she had learned that Gaultier had ridden for Annossy, and had been relieved. Magdala felt that she had had a near escape.

But she would not be so fortunate again, not with Herbert. Herbert would not ride for Annossy or depart from Tulley until he claimed his desire, whatever it might be. She feared that might be the old lord's demise and the seizure of Tulley's seal.

God in Heaven, what if that fiend insisted upon having her aid in that scheme? Magdala clenched her fists, terrified of him having such power over her.

It would be better, far better, to be abused herself than to be compelled to betray the old lord who had treated her with kindness.

She would not do it.

Which meant she had to eliminate Herbert's potential hold over her, and before he arrived.

She had to confess the truth to the Lord de Tulley.

There was naught for it. That was the sole way to diminish Herbert's power.

Her heart faltered at the prospect even as she acknowledged its inevitable truth.

Could she confess the truth outright to the Lord de Tulley? The revelation might adversely affect his well-being. Older people did not accept surprises well and he was not as strong as he would have others believed. Magdala took a steadying breath that she, or her tale, could cause him harm.

Indeed, he might not even believe any accusation she made against Herbert. She was not certain he was fond of his nephew, but a blood tie could not be ignored. Families stood together, regardless of the details—at least she had learned as much from Lady Heloise.

Who else could she confide in first?

Not Felix or the châtelain or anyone else beholden to Tulley. They would simply hasten to the old lord and surrender the truth without concern for his welfare. It would make for a worse surprise.

Perhaps she should have gone to Annossy to ask the aid of Melissande, Lady d'Annossy–but she would have been near Niall then. In addition, Melissande still believed her to be Heloise. Melissande would be recovered from her son's delivery by now and might ask Magdala to hunt with her again.

Magdala shuddered at the prospect. The one time that she had ridden to hunt with the old lord, she had struggled to hide her aversion because Heloise had adored the hunt. Magdala was not certain of her own success, but the old lord had abandoned the hunt soon after that day, and she had been able to make the excuse of remaining at the keep to ensure his comfort.

In all of Château Tulley, there was only Lothair.

She would have to confide in the taciturn knight, so that she could request his counsel about telling the old lord the truth. As a healer, Lothair might have recommendations about timing. He might have a potion to calm the older man, the better that he accepted the tidings. That was an encouraging possibility.

Magdala was convinced that he would aid her, not only to keep his pledge to best serve the Lord de Tulley but in defense of the truth.

Lothair it would be.

All that remained was choosing the moment.

Magdala left her chamber to seek him out, hoping against hope that Lothair would be occupied no longer.

Alas, she was doomed to disappointment. She lingered, perhaps longer than was sensible, but he was instructing Quentin in the use of a knife, Calum fast by his side. When Quinn appeared from the hall, she left to ensure her uncle's comfort, pausing in the kitchen to verify that all was in order for the evening meal. She went to the bailey again, but Lothair had vanished into the stables. She heard the sound of his voice and knew he was occupied. Knowing her presence was unusual and might not be welcome, she left the bailey with reluctance, wondering whether she imagined the weight of Lothair's gaze upon her.

Perhaps he would seek her out in the garden.

She could only hope.

CHAPTER 5

hy had the maiden come to the bailey?

Twice?

Lothair could not explain her presence, nor had he been able to excuse himself from his obligations without causing commentary. The second time she came, he had been reviewing the inventory of the armory and the state of all weapons within it, making a scheme with the blacksmith and the armorer for maintenance and repairs. The men now under his command awaited him, in order to make themselves known to him and to swear to him. He could not set all aside to serve a lady's whim!

At first, he feared the Lord de Tulley must have fallen ill, but the lady had not interrupted his task. Then Quinn had come from the hall, confiding that the old lord was as sharp as ever. Quinn further said that the Lord de Tulley had retired to his chambers, so Lothair had continued with the task of inventorying all within the stables and armory. He had no doubt his new lord would have questions for him when they met again, which he fully anticipated would be at the evening meal.

Indeed, he admired that the Lord de Tulley remembered so many details of his responsibilities and could manage his domain so well from the solar. A man could only hope to be so quick of wit at such an advanced age.

Quinn departed once his destrier was saddled and the two warriors embraced, Quinn offering his congratulations again. He invited Lothair to visit Annossy and Lothair agreed, though he had no notion when that might be. As soon as his former comrade had departed, Lothair returned to speak with the warriors and knights in service to the holding. Their experience was considerable and their knowledge of the keep itself welcome. He was surprised when it was time for the evening meal.

Lothair had protested earlier that he could eat with the other men in service rather than at the high table, but the Lord de Tulley had insisted otherwise. There had been a hint that he might learn more from the maiden, but Lothair could not see how that might be achieved with the lord himself sitting between them. Calum, of course, was thrilled to once again aid with serving the meal.

"What do you think you will eat on this night, sir?" the youth demanded as they entered the great hall. "Venison again? Boar? Perhaps hare in a sauce?"

"We shall eat what is offered and be glad of it."

"So you always say, sir, but I was glad indeed of a dish other than eels last night. A stew of venison with pepper in the sauce! 'Twas a marvel."

The dish had been most savory.

"And eggs in sauce, and a tart, as well," Calum enthused. "Then pears poached in wine with saffron. Do they feast like kings each night at this abode, sir?"

"I cannot say."

"I could die contented if there were no more eels presented to me," Calum continued. "If my father had told me that I would eat my weight in eels twice over on this journey, I might have remained at home and foregone the adventure."

Lothair smiled, for Calum had been most intent upon accompanying him. He did not believe that even the prospect of eels would have deterred the youth. "I doubt as much," he said.

Lothair, though he would not say as much lest he encourage Calum, was not any more fond of eels than his squire.

"I was curious, to be sure, and intent upon adventure, sir, but *eels*." Calum sighed. "Smoked eels, salted eels, boiled eels, roasted eels, stuffed eels, eels with sauce or without. I would be happy indeed to never eat an eel again."

Lothair thought such a situation unlikely, and truly even eels were better than naught at all. "There is not always fish for a holy day when one is far from the sea."

"Then perhaps one should remain by the sea," the youth countered cheerfully. "Think of all the various fishes we consumed at home! Halibut and cod and herring from the sea, fresh or salted, as well as salmon from the river. *Salmon*, sir. How long has it been since we tasted salmon?"

"Long indeed."

"And now it will be longer yet, for you have taken this post." The youth sighed. "I would be glad to see home again, would you not, sir, and not solely for the salmon?"

Lothair was not convinced he would ever see Scotland again, but he was saved from making a reply by the sound of a shuffle descending the stairs. He gestured to Calum to stir the fire to greater vigor, then turned and stood tall, his hands behind his back. The other warriors in the hall stood as well, several slipping through the portal at the last moment to take their places. Lothair eyed the late-comers, knowing a glance could make a difference as well as a chastisement.

The Lord de Tulley came into view, leaning heavily on his cane, the maiden holding his other arm. On this night, she was garbed in deepest blue, a hue that favored her mightily, and Lothair watched her approach with admiration. She flicked the barest glance his way, almost smiled, then returned her attention to the older man.

"Fuss, fuss, fuss," the Lord de Tulley complained as he gained the floor. "I am not so infirm as that."

"But the stairs are steep and the light is dim, Uncle. I fear to fall myself, so appreciate your arm."

The Lord de Tulley snorted, a gleam lighting his eyes. "And you, sir, how was your day?"

"Most interesting, my lord." Lothair bowed. "Château Tulley is magnificent."

The old lord grunted an agreement. "You have completed the inventory of the armory?"

"Indeed, sir, and all is as anticipated."

"The men?"

"A fine contingent, sir."

"Ha! But you will improve them."

"I have some ideas, my lord."

The Lord de Tulley settled into his seat with a sigh, smiling as Heloise tucked furs and robes around him. "'Tis not the dead of winter yet, child," he said, but the way he touched her hand was affectionate.

"Still the stones hold a chill, it seems to me."

"Then it is good that you shall sit upon my left, closer to the fire."

"Aye, Uncle."

"Take this pelt for your shoulders."

"Thank you, Uncle." She smiled and kissed his cheek, her move making the old lord beam with pleasure.

"You smell of sunshine and plants," he said to her. "Were you in the garden?"

"As always in the afternoon, Uncle," she replied, casting another quick glance at Lothair as she took her place.

Had she expected him to come to her there?

Had he not been so occupied, Lothair might have done as much.

Perhaps, on the morrow…

At the lord's gesture, Lothair took his place, Calum standing behind him attentively. The men took their places and the serving of the meal commenced.

"What is your name, boy?" the Lord de Tulley demanded of Calum. "You must have arrived with Lothair."

The youth stepped forward and bowed as gracefully as a courier to an emperor. "Aye, my lord. I am Calum, sir, youngest son of Angus, Mormaer of Moray, and his lady wife, the daughter of Lulach."

"You are far from home."

"Indeed, sir. My father ordered me to squire for my lord Lothair, and so I journeyed first to France and thence to Outremer with that knight upon crusade."

The Lord de Tulley studied Lothair. "Moray is not far from Sutherland, as I understand."

"It is not, sir," Lothair replied steadily. "I was fortunate to know the patronage of Angus, the Mormaer of Moray."

"At the price of training his son," Tulley commented and Lothair only nodded. He was well aware that the lady listened intently. "Moray, Heloise, is at the north of Scotland, south of the area the Norse called Sutherland. Both are well beyond England and far to the north of France."

"So distant, Uncle?"

"So very far."

The soup was brought from the kitchens and Calum, to Lothair's relief, did a neat job of serving him after the lord and lady had been served by the boy from the kitchens.

"Leek," the old lord said with satisfaction after Felix had tasted it first. "Good and hot. Give my regards to Antoine."

When the boy had returned to the kitchens and a measure of the soup had been consumed, the Lord de Tulley turned back to Lothair. "But I had understood that the warriors in those northern lands were not knights?"

"Nay, sir, they are not. In France, I found a patron in my lord Angus' former comrade at Montvieux."

"That is south of Paris," the Lord de Tulley informed the lady. The old lord frowned. "You had a companion from there in Outremer."

"Amaury de Montvieux, to be sure."

"Son and heir of a magnificent holding," Calum contributed cheerfully, earning a glance from Lothair that prompted him to flush and retreat. He should have remained silent, but his enthusiasm seemed to amuse the old lord.

"You, boy," the Lord de Tulley said sternly to the squire. The twinkle in his eyes belied his fierce manner. "You will need to learn to hold your tongue, lest you surrender the secrets of your lord knight, or make trouble by sharing what you hear at the board while you serve."

"Aye, sir." Calum bowed low, as if a deeper bow showed more contrition.

The Lord de Tulley bit back a smile.

Lothair concentrated on his soup.

"And what of the horses?" the older man demanded when the stew was carried into the hall. It was more richly aromatic than any concoction with eels might have been. Boar this time, he wagered, with a different sauce than the night before.

Felix stepped forward to taste the stew.

Lothair heard Calum's stomach growl in appreciation from behind him.

The lady laughed under her breath and the old lord grunted.

"Let him fetch a bowl and eat by the fire once we are served," the Lord de Tulley said gruffly. "Just the once, boy. Do not imagine that it will become a habit."

"I thank you, sir! Is that *boar*?"

"It is, indeed, boy, and best consumed while very hot. Antoine uses a mix of spices in the sauce to make it a meal fit for a king."

"It surely seems to be, sir," Calum said with an enthusiasm he clearly could not restrain. "Indeed, in two nights here at Château Tulley, I have seen finer fare than we enjoyed in the entirety of our journey these past years."

"Pilgrims and crusaders do not journey to Outremer for the fare," the Lord de Tulley said sternly.

"Of course not, my lord, but good fare, rather than simply a sufficient measure, can make all the difference in the merit of one's day."

The old man chuckled. Lothair shook his head and the lady laughed. He looked up to find her eyes sparkling and her gaze fixed upon him.

"Never have knight and squire been so opposite in manner," she said and Lothair felt the back of his neck heat.

"My lord Lothair says I talk overmuch," Calum confided in the lady, startling both lord and lady. "When he speaks at all. But how can one smell such a fine stew and not show an appreciation for the finest of fares? I cannot remain silent, sir, before such bounty."

"He cannot remain silent at all," Lothair said beneath his breath, feeling a surge of pleasure when both lord and lady laughed heartily.

Calum flushed and spoke no more, then the Lord de Tulley waved a finger at him, indicating that he should fill his bowl. "Eat, boy, while it is hot."

Calum did not have to be invited to do as much twice.

And Lothair was obliged to speak more than was his wont, for the Lord de Tulley wished for his views on every blade in the armory. Their number was so great that it took the entire meal to review them, then the old lord dismissed his warriors and the lady.

"I will hear a blunt assessment of the men, and you, Heloise, will not know of such blunt details."

"But, Uncle…"

"It would be unseemly. Go to your chamber and send Felix to me."

The lady stood, her dissatisfaction with the situation clear, then kissed the old lord's hand and departed in a swirl of skirts. Lothair could not help but watch her leave.

On the morrow, he would seek her out, no matter what the demands upon him. He became aware of the old lord's expectant expression, dismissed a very satisfied Calum, and began to confer with his liege lord about the men in the keep.

His thoughts, though, followed a certain maiden. What had she wished to tell him, if anything? Lothair could not deny that he wanted very much to know.

~

UNCERTAINTY KEPT Magdala from sleeping that night. She disliked her conundrum. Each passing moment made her fear that she erred in planning to reveal her truth or alternatively that she would have no opportunity to confess her secret.

What if Herbert arrived at first light?

What if he arrived during the night?

What if Lothair did not believe her? How she wished she had been able to speak to him this day. She had not the audacity to seek him out at night, though she wagered he had been given the chamber above the stables, previously occupied by the former Captain of the Guard.

She tossed and turned on her down-filled mattress. Her plump pillows offered her no comfort. She was alternatively too cold and too hot, her thoughts spinning, her agitation inescapable.

Finally, she rose from bed and paced the chamber, unaware of the chill of the floor beneath her bare feet. She looked out the window, opening the shutters to peer over the ramparts and the sleeping town beneath, but on this night, the sight granted no tranquility. She considered her predicament from all sides, and still she found no better solution than telling the truth.

Lothair might reveal her to the Lord de Tulley—she fully expected he would, given that he had sworn a pledge to the older man—and the older man might cast her out for her deception. She would have an increment of time, then, to flee to the convent beyond the mountain pass and evade Herbert yet again.

Magdala could only hope it was long enough.

Perhaps Lothair would even accompany her there, or at least ensure her safe journey, after her confession. He might do as much out of duty or compassion, or even at the Lord de Tulley's command. Magdala hated that she could not be certain of the result.

Entering the convent had little appeal, but Magdala saw no other option. Indeed, she would not linger over the telling of her tale.

The truth it must be, she resolved as the sun rose, and she would surrender it this very morning. At least in the convent, she would still draw breath. She had no confidence that Herbert would allow that to be.

~

LOTHAIR ROSE, washed and dressed at the dawn, prepared to undertake his duties. Indeed, there was much to be learned in this keep and he found himself intrigued by it. Calum tended him in uncharacteristic silence—proving the difficulty of indulging in a rich meat stew with enthusiasm after years of meagre fare. Lothair suspected his squire might appreciate a short nap on this particular morning and was inclined to be indulgent.

He left Calum with a hauberk to polish, an excuse which could be readily ignored, then strode into the stables. The horses were stirring, the ostler rousing a pair of young grooms to bring water to the horses. A farrier led a palfrey into the bailey for a closer examination of her hooves, and sunlight shone through the open portal into the shadowed stables beyond. Once again, he was struck by the affluence of this holding, how well it was equipped and the number of servants who ensured that all was well. The stables at Château Tulley were a fine facility, to Lothair's view, spacious and clean.

On this day, he meant to inventory the steeds. Lothair entered the cool shadows, conscious of the curious glances of the horses. Several nickered and more than one twitched its ears, a sign that he was not the first to pass them by this morning. Indeed, he sensed a presence in the stables that did not belong there. He halted and listened, aware of the slight scent of a lady's skin.

She was in the stables at this early hour, unless he missed his guess.

Lothair took a step forward and spotted her in the shadows. She stood by a stall that was empty, adjacent to the one occupied by Sleipnir. Her agitation was evident, despite her obvious attempt to disguise it, and he recalled the Lord de Tulley's confession that she did not like to ride to hunt.

Perhaps she did not like horses either.

What then was of sufficient import to drive her into the stables?

She watched him, awaiting his approach, her uncertainty clear.

"My lady," he said and inclined his head to her.

"Sir!" To Lothair's surprise, she darted toward him and placed a hand upon his arm. "I must confide in you," she whispered, her gaze rising to his. "And in a place where none might hear my words."

This was what he sought! "You might have summoned me."

"I guessed you would be here. I strove to confide in you yesterday but you were occupied."

"Why did you await me here?"

She gestured to Sleipnir, who watched with open curiosity. "I know that knights value their steeds, so it seemed reasonable that you would visit him each day."

"And so I do," Lothair said, moving to rub Sleipnir's ears. The beast accepted the apple he had brought, but did not avert his attention from the lady. "We might ride out," he suggested, ensuring his tone was light.

"Nay!" the lady protested, retreating a step in apparent horror before recovering herself. "It is difficult to confer while riding."

More importantly, she did not like to ride. He was certain that the Lord de Tulley was correct in that.

"Then we might walk," he suggested. "You might show me those establishments of interest in the town." Still she hesitated.

She glanced toward the bailey, her decision made. "There is a village beyond the lower gates," she said. "It lies beneath the authority of the Lord de Tulley, as well, and you should know it."

Lothair inclined his head. "I welcome your instruction, my lady."

"More than that, I find myself in a quandary, sir, and I must confide in you in the hope of setting matters to rights." The hesitation in her tone made Lothair wonder what she would admit—or how much.

"Indeed? I welcome your confidence."

"I thought you would," she said, glancing up pointedly as the ostler and grooms entered the stables.

Lothair gestured and she left the stables ahead of him. It was said that greater beauty came from deeds and words than appearances, and he wondered at the truth of her nature. Was she deceptive for some base reason? Or was there good cause for her pretense at being Tulley's niece? The old lord seemed inclined to think well of her and so was Lothair.

Was he merely seduced by her beauty? Lothair thought not—he had not been so susceptible before.

They walked together through the bailey and thence gates of the keep, with nary a word passing between them. Had he ever known a woman who could hold her tongue so long as this? Aye, she was a lady of mysteries, to be sure, and Lothair knew himself to be intrigued.

As they passed under the portcullis, Lothair nodded to the gate-keeper, taking visible note of that man's laconic manner. He was relieved to see the effect of his daunting expression. The guard straightened immediately and gripped the hilt of his sword with greater diligence.

"Goodness," the lady said softly. "Your disapproval *is* fearsome."

Lothair did not argue the matter. She knew little of how fearsome he could be. "He is wary of the new commander. It is only good sense on his part."

"But are you fearsome in truth?" she asked with rare persistence. "I would wager that you are."

"All men who have ridden to war can be." He felt the weight of her gaze upon him and wondered whether his words would halt her confession.

They continued down the sloping road that twisted around the steep mound that supported the keep. Buildings clustered on either side of the road and there were sounds of activity from behind their doors. Some windows and doors were open to the morning breeze and once again, he was struck by how tranquil and orderly Tulley was. The residents were confident in their safety. They were reasonably affluent and well-fed. He heard occasional laughter and liked that this place should be his home, even for a short interval.

"You admire this place," his companion said finally and Lothair nodded.

"It makes admirable use of a natural formation of the land. Tulley could not readily be taken by force."

"Then it is an impregnable fortress?"

Lothair shook his head. "Deception would be required, but all fortresses are vulnerable to that."

"Deception," she repeated, her words low and thoughtful.

He wondered at that. "A spy within the walls," he continued, as if she had not understood him—though he knew she had. "A man, or woman, who has gained trust but is not worthy of it. It takes little to steal a key, to grant a sleeping potion to a guard, to distract a sentry, if the intention is there."

God in Heaven, but this woman's very presence made him loquacious! He strove to remain silent after that long–an unnecessary–explanation.

"But surely a sentry would not be readily distracted from his duties," she suggested and Lothair had to reply, lest she think him rude.

"Some are readily so." He might have halted there but she lifted her gaze to his, inviting him to continue. Such was the power of her glance that he did as much and readily. "Standing sentry is dull labor. Any diversion may be granted more attention than it deserves."

"To the peril of those being guarded."

"Indeed."

"You said a man or a woman might be the culprit."

"Aye." He dared to glance toward her, only to find her intent upon the ground before her feet. Did she strive to hide her thoughts or merely be certain of her footing?

"Do you make an implication, sir?" Her tone was teasing but her gaze was watchful.

"Nay. Women are excellent spies, as a rule. That is the sum of my meaning."

She glanced up, as if he had caught her at some crime. "Truly?"

"Truly."

Her eyes narrowed. "Because it is our nature to be deceptive?"

There was peril in agreement to that query, to be sure. Lothair shook his head. "Because many men are foolish. They believe a woman could not have the wits to trick them, or to have the desire to betray another."

"But *you* believe women to be capable of deception?"

"I believe women to be capable of whatever they desire to do, good or ill."

"Is that due to your experience in Outremer?"

He shook his head again. "Experience, to be sure, but not solely in Outremer. People are much the same, wherever they make their homes or find themselves to be, and women are not so different from men in their natures and inclinations, despite the differences in our forms."

She seemed to be consider this, winding a tendril of her hair around her fingertip as she walked beside him, a space between them as was appropriate.

What was she thinking?

And why did he desire so very much to know?

For someone inclined to make a confession, she did not hasten to it. Why not?

Though, truly, Lothair had no objections to more of this maiden's company. Even the Lord de Tulley could not complain of his absence from the stables, for that man had charged Lothair to learn the lady's secrets.

"You will know the tavern, I wager," she said, gesturing to that establishment. She indicated another building as they passed it. "And of course, someone will have directed you to the armorer near the gates of the keep."

Lothair nodded, his impatience growing with her reticence.

The lady granted him a smile as if she sensed his mood, which he thought securely hidden. Once again, she might have been Heloise. "Here then is the market, though this is not a market day. The butchers are always there, in the shade, the eel monger beside them, the miller and the baker opposite in the sunshine, and all other victuals in between. The brewster can be found at the tavern, selling her wares before the door." She indicated a smaller alley that curved away from the main path. "The weavers and dyers ply their trade in this area, as do the bootmakers and leatherworkers. There is also a scribe near that small chapel who will write a letter as required."

"I write my own," Lothair said, assuming she thought him unlettered, and she turned to face him. There was an admiring light in her eyes, one that could make a man forget himself.

"Not just a knight but a scholar, as well."

"My mentor judged it best that a man be able to keep his own books, to ensure he would not be cheated."

"Your mentor was a landholder then?"

"Aye."

"A relation? I know that many men are trained for their spurs by an uncle."

She was curious, to be sure. Lothair again shook his head, marveling at how much—and how readily—he confided in this maiden. He sensed that she tested him, though there was little she could do with such information as he surrendered. It was more important to win her trust, and thence her own confession.

"A leader who took a liking to me," he admitted. "I was fortunate in his sponsorship."

"The Mormaer of Moray," she repeated, as if she did not know the meaning of the words.

"Aye. A mormaer is a great steward and Moray is one of the seven regions of Alba."

"And Sutherland is one of them, as well?"

"With Caithness."

"I shall need a map."

"I could draw you one."

She smiled but did not accept his offer. "I understand there is great expense in training a warrior."

"Aye." Lothair was relieved to find his usual taciturn manner returning to him.

The lady strolled onward. The sun was becoming warmer and the town was rousing itself. Lothair smelled bread baking and heard women calling to each other. Dogs barked and children shouted as they played. He heard a rooster call, one that had missed the sunrise by a goodly measure.

When they reached the base of the mount, there was another gate barring the road, this one with a more formidable barrier and two men to watch over it. Their posture was more alert, to his satisfaction, and they looked to be formidable.

They bowed immediately to Lothair, impassive at their posts. He spoke to them for a moment or two, asking their view of the vigor of the gate, then ordered it opened that he might walk toward the village with the lady. They clearly recognized her as well and bowed to her, before following his order. The gates were well-tended, neither a creak or a squeak from setting them in motion, and he approved of the heartiness of the lock upon them.

The mountains rose to the south, snow upon their distant peaks, forming a natural border. The road forked some distance from the keep: he knew that one path led to the pass at Beauvoir and the other headed north toward France and points beyond. Lothair looked upward, certain that the sky was not so brilliantly blue in any other location, nor the air so crisp and invigorating.

He realized then that the lady was watching him.

"You like this holding, though it is not your home," she said with surety.

"It will be so, so long as I am here."

"Will you not miss another place? Sutherland. Or Moray. The land where you were raised?"

"There is naught for me in either place."

She tilted her head to study him, hearing what he had not said. "Never or no longer?"

"You ask many questions, my lady."

She flushed prettily. "I am curious about you. Is that not reasonable?"

"Reasonable enough, but you must expect a measure of curiosity on my part as well."

"Yet you show none."

"The fact that I do not declare any curiosity does not mean I have none."

"Yet any curiosity is so well hidden that it might not exist. I wager, sir, that you keep secrets well."

"It has been said before."

She spun to face him, stepping into his path, her eyes bright with challenge. "Would you keep my secret as well as your own?"

"That would depend upon the secret."

She scrutinized him, then nodded and turned away, leaving him with the sense that he had lost something of merit. "Because your pledge to my uncle is of greater import than any promise made to a lady," she said. "I understand."

They had reached a bridge over a quick cold stream. Lothair halted and looked back toward the keep, having little interest in continuing to the village on the far bank this morn. "If you desire privacy for a confession, my lady, this location is ideal," he said, feeling his words were overly blunt.

She took no insult, but granted him a smile that warmed him to his toes. "And you would prompt me to share the tale, the sooner that you might return to your own labor."

"I would not criticize you, my lady."

"Yet I have admitted little as yet. You remind me as much in a most tactful way." She took a breath, her hands clasped together before herself, her gaze rising to the now-distant keep. She was so lovely that Lothair could only stare, welcoming the opportunity to do as much unobserved. Then she lifted her gaze to his so abruptly that he was snared and could not look away. The back of his neck heated as she held his gaze. "You are patient. That is rare in a warrior and a trait to be admired. A keeper of secrets and a diplomat."

"Do you suggest that you are neither?" He meant to tease her a little, for her manner was suddenly solemn, and was pleased when her eyes glowed with pleasure.

"I can keep a secret as well as you, sir, and I have kept a considerable one since my arrival at Tulley. Though it was my intention to confess it to you this morning, I find it difficult to know where to begin."

To Lothair's thinking, there had been considerable opportunity to make that choice.

Perhaps she had another ploy. Perhaps she did not mean to share a tale at all, but only to lure him away from his duties.

He glanced toward the keep towering above them, wondering, then back to the lady, his decision made. He inclined his head to her. "Sadly, I have responsibilities this morn, my lady, and can linger no longer. Perhaps your tale would be better told another time."

He had no expectation she would do as much, but turned to retrace his steps.

He did not manage three steps before she spoke.

"I am not Heloise," she declared and Lothair glanced back in surprise. Her gaze was so steady that he would not have doubted her assertion, even without Tulley's suspicion. "And Herbert will recognize the truth as soon as he sees me."

"Because he would recognize his own sister?"

She shook her head slowly. "Worse, he will know me as Heloise's maid."

And there it was, the two of the three details that the Lord de Tulley had asked him to discover.

Could Lothair learn yet more?

CHAPTER 6

$\mathscr{L}$othair did not believe her.

Of all the possibilities Magdala had imagined, this had not been one of them. She could not think of any other interpretation of his complete impassivity, though. His was a blank stare, as if she had spoken in another language entirely.

How could he be skeptical? What reason would she have, if she were Heloise in truth, to confess otherwise?

Her outrage loosened Magdala's tongue as naught else could have done. When she told him the entire tale, he could not fail to be convinced of its truth, to be sure.

He would have it all, and with haste.

He had not even moved toward her, but held his ground, several steps away, his gaze fixed upon her, as inscrutable as ever. Magdala closed the distance between them with purpose. "I have surprised you," she said for it was more likely to win his favor than an accusation of his unmerited skepticism.

He shrugged, admitting naught at all.

"Or perhaps you do not believe me," she suggested, hearing the hard edge in her own tone.

"It seems an unlikely tale," he said simply, then began to walk back toward the gates as if he would leave her behind. "Surely *someone* would have known." His pace was more crisp than it had been before, as if he hastened back to his duties, but Magdala kept step with him.

"Aye, I might have expected as much myself, but I do not contrive a tale," she insisted. "I cannot imagine how such a tale might benefit me, if it *were* a tale." Her voice rose despite her resolve to remain calm. "It is the truth!"

"How could such an exchange occur?" Lothair asked. "Someone would have noticed the difference, to be sure."

Magdala shook her head with vigor. "Nay, not the way Lady Heloise arranged matters."

There was a moment of silence, then to her relief, he spoke. "Tell me," he invited.

She heard the doubt in his voice, but at least he was listening. She would take whatever opportunity she had to set matters to rights, now that she had decided to tell the truth.

"We traded places for the journey," she said and once she began to explain, it was easier to continue than she might have anticipated. "It was the practice of Lady Heloise's mother, Lady Verena, the better to ensure her own safety, and Lady Heloise did the same. The notion was that the lady would be assaulted, not the maid."

To her gratification, Lothair's brows rose, as if this shocked him. "A most perilous situation for the maid. Yet you agreed?"

"I had no choice. 'Twas one of my obligations. I was glad, though, that my lady was disinclined to leave Idelstein often."

Lothair made a sound of disapproval that Magdala found heartening. If he could have any concern for her welfare, then his support was not entirely lost.

She took a steadying breath. "When my lady chose to embark upon this journey to Tulley, we retired to her chamber together, and at her direction, we each donned the other's garments. We were hooded and veiled when we left the chamber, so none might see our faces and guess the truth. I was as skeptical as you of the scheme's success, but she was right. No one looked keenly at us. They assumed our names by our garb."

Lothair slowed his pace slightly, to Magdala's relief. She was obliged to take three steps for every two of his and appreciated the concession.

"This then was the first time you were so disguised?" he asked

"For me. I do not doubt that Lady Heloise had done as much with other maids before. I had only been at Idelstein two years, and Lady Heloise's parents had died the year before. Her brother, Lord Herbert, had assumed the lordship after his father's demise. Then my lady decided that she had to visit Tulley for the Yule."

"Had she a reason?"

"If she did, I did not know of it. She was somewhat inclined to be impulsive, as perhaps might be expected of one of her high birth." Magdala felt Lothair's gaze land upon her and heard the query he did not utter. "She could have whatsoever she desired. She had only to name an item to have it in her possession. I can well imagine that such circumstance might make one willful."

He nodded. "But still, I cannot believe that no one saw through the disguise."

"There was a strong resemblance between us. I have oft wondered whether that was why Lady Verena chose me over all the others."

She knew Lothair had noticed her choice of words, for he cast a quick sidelong glance her way. But she would recount this tale first.

"We left Idelstein with three warriors to defend us," Magdala continued. "Lady Heloise told me it would take a week or so to reach our destination. I had no notion, for I had never journeyed so far. We rode in a closed cart together, the hope being that our party would not appear to be so rich as to attract attention from thieves." She took a breath. "The ploy was not a success. We were followed from the village of Brennenburg. Do you know it?"

Lothair shook his head.

"It is two days' journey from Idelstein, the last village on the eastern periphery of the Grimwald forest. The road through the forest concerned the man-at-arms who had responsibility for our party. Ranulf was a man of some forty summers, a warrior proven and true. My lady spoke lightly of brigands and thieves, of peril ahead, teasing him for his concerns which she evidently thought unwarranted. Ranulf said naught at all, but he was grim. His manner ensured that I slept little that night in Brennenburg. We left the tavern at dawn in order to ensure that we would be through the forest by the time the light faded, at his insistence." She faltered to silence, not wanting to recall that day.

"The days would be short in December."

"Aye. They were." She nodded and gathered her resolve, vaguely aware that she had clenched one fist. "Ranulf vowed that we would be in the town of Grimwald, to the west of the forest, by mid-afternoon."

"He had served long with Idelstein?"

"Longer than me. He was an experienced warrior, a knight who had been in service at Idelstein for many years. Lady Heloise said she had known him as a child." She flicked a glance at Lothair and risked an additional confession "You remind me of him in your manner. He was quiet, but he listened well. He was a fearsome warrior, as I soon learned, and a man whose honor was absolute." She grimaced. "I liked him."

Was Lothair pleased by the comparison? Magdala could not tell.

"Ranulf drove the cart that day while we remained hidden inside, with one guard riding ahead and one behind. I dared to hope that all would proceed well when naught went awry by midday. Lady Heloise even fell asleep." She frowned. "But I knew when Ranulf urged the horses to greater speed that we were pursued."

Magdala's words spilled forth, mirroring both the haste of events and her own agitation in recalling them. "The road in the forest is not as level as might be best, for the roots of the old trees grow across it. We did not go far before the cart hit something and tipped, fairly spilling us onto the ground. Lady Heloise awakened with a scream. I learned later that we had collided with a stump and one wheel had come loose from the cart. In that moment, I knew only that all was upended and confused. I heard a horse whinny and the pounding of hoofbeats, the sound of men shouting and that of swords being unsheathed. Lady Heloise shrieked and Ranulf swore."

"You were beset."

She nodded quickly. "By the time we were free of the cart, the guard behind had been cut down and lay bleeding on the ground. He did not move. I remember staring at him, unable to believe that he was dead. His horse was gone. The guard who had ridden before us was battling with a pair of ruffians. Ranulf defended us with vigor, backing us into a tree behind him. There were four of them, brigands all, and they were ruthless."

"Did you see their faces?"

"Nay, they wore helmets."

Lothair nodded thoughtfully.

"When the guard who had ridden before us was cut down, Lady Heloise lunged toward him. I do not know what she believed she might do. I can only think that she was frightened and concerned for his welfare—though truly, he was already dead. The brigands seized her and when she struggled—" She fell silent then and her throat worked, leaving her uncertain whether she could recount the rest of the tale.

Lothair touched her elbow to recall her to this moment and to her surprise, his expression was less stern. "You saw her die," he guessed gently, holding her elbow as if he would support her.

Magdala nodded in gratitude. "I saw her assaulted and I saw her fall. 'Twas quick at least. They thought she was the maid and that her demise would encourage me, the lady, to surrender all of my wealth. I called a surrender and a cessation of bloodshed. I cast all her jewels at them and the coin, as well. I scarce was aware of my own deeds. There was only Lady Heloise, on the path, bleeding. She looked to be asleep but she did not move and there was a dark puddle beneath her."

She trembled, hearing her voice turn husky, and Lothair drew her a little closer to his side. Magdala found herself yearning to welcome whatever consolation he might offer—though this warrior might offer none at all. "When they saw there was naught more, they attacked Ranulf and left him wounded on the path, then fled with all the wealth." She closed her eyes, seeing Ranulf's astonished expression as his own blood flowed over his hands. Even in recollection, the sight sickened her.

"Leaving you alone."

That was the salient point, to be sure. "Aye, there was another party behind us. The brigands may have fled then because they feared to be caught. That small company aided us. The gentleman was a baron whose name I did not attend, and he took command of all. God in heaven, but his aid was most welcome. He knew precisely what to do when I did not. His men repaired the wheel of the cart and retrieved the two horses that had not been taken by the brigands. They tended the injuries of Ranulf and gathered our dead for us. He was so very kind. The cart was heavily burdened when we continued the journey, but we would not have made the village of Grimwald that day without their aid and escort. The baron paid for our shelter and meal at the tavern, so great was his compassion." She bowed her head. "I meant to thank him in the morning and learn his name, but his party had departed at first light."

"And the dead?"

"They are buried in the churchyard in Grimwald village. I had forgotten during the attack that Lady Heloise always kept a coin in the sole of each shoe. I found them later that night at the tavern, when we were safe." She caught her breath, blaming herself yet again for the omission. "If only I had remembered them sooner," she whispered.

"Two coins would not have changed the result," Lothair said grimly.

She looked up at him, knowing this confession was the most important. "I failed my lady. There must have been something I could have done, something I did not do, that would have saved her."

"Nay." Lothair was utterly convinced of his view. "I suspect there was not."

"'Twas all so very quick, so very brutal. I had never seen the like." She shivered when he did not reply. "But I saw them buried, with those two coins," she continued. "So there was merit in that. The priest in the church at Grimwald declared the funds sufficient for the burial and for funeral masses to be sung. He said they would have a place in his churchyard to rest, and that their places would be marked, in case family wished to retrieve them. Ranulf insisted that we make haste to Château Tulley."

"You continued in the cart?"

She nodded once. "I had never ridden a horse before, but Lady Heloise loved to ride."

"And still Ranulf did not perceive your ruse?"

"Aye, he knew once he saw my face in the forest, but he bade me keep the secret until we reached Château Tulley. He thought those in Grimwald might disapprove of the maid continuing without her lady and I ceded to his counsel."

Lothair nodded slowly. "And there were no further incidents?"

"Nay, but something was amiss. I realized as much by the next night, but did not know what to do. Ranulf assured me that all was well, but he was flushed, uncommonly so. There was perspiration upon his brow, though the day was not warm."

"Ah," Lothair said as if he had guessed the reason.

"I asked but he insisted he would have aid once we arrived here at Tulley. He refused to halt elsewhere. There had to be an apothecary at Château Tulley, to my thinking, and I reasoned that he knew as much. I trusted his decision." She fell silent again.

"Three days?" Lothair asked.

Magdala sighed as she nodded agreement. "A veritable eternity."

"His wound was infected," Lothair said then, no query in his tone.

Magdala nodded. "So I learned."

"Where is he now?"

She gestured toward the village behind them and Lothair turned without comprehension. Of course, he would not know that the cemetery was in the village outside the walls.

"Ranulf died upon our arrival here and is buried in the village." She shook her head. "I could not believe that all had changed so very much in a mere week, that so many of those I knew and trusted should draw breath no more." She pursed her lips. "But then, that is the way of matters. I call it my curse. All those I hold in affection die."

Lothair's expression was forbidding, which was not what Magdala had expected.

"What is amiss?"

His brows rose. "The sole other witness of the attack died before he could share the tale."

Magdala felt a chill inside her. "Aye, but I did not contrive it to be so."

"You could have. A wound is readily infected by one who knows such matters."

"I did not!"

"But you were taught the cultivation of calendula and perhaps more of the apothecary's arts." He did not grant her the chance to reply, but continued steadily. His tone had hardened and she sensed that she had lost a potential ally, against every expectation. "And you lied to the Lord de Tulley, and all others here these past years."

Again, Magdala felt her annoyance rise. "It was not a plan. We had reached a sanctuary. I meant to confess all to the Lord de Tulley, but when he seized my hands and praised God that I, Heloise, had been spared, I could not tell him the truth in that moment. His joy and relief were too great." She frowned at the ground as her voice softened. "He was so old and so much alone. I could not disappoint him."

"And once the lie was believed, it became harder to tell the truth."

She nodded. "I always meant to confide in him, in privacy. But I dreaded his anger, and I had nowhere to flee, and so it seemed easy to let the matter be for another day. After he was ill last winter, I saw his frailty and feared the shock might end his days." She looked up at him, appealing for his understanding, though she had little hope of gaining it. "I could not do that to him. I could not imperil him."

"You should have told him."

"I thought it kinder for him to believe a small lie that gave him joy."

Lothair's gaze hardened. "It is not a small lie to pretend you are his blood."

"Nay, it is not so small as that," Magdala had to cede, feeling her color rise. "Though it seemed as much at the time. I would tell him this very day if I could be certain that the tidings would not affect him adversely. Is there a remedy you might give him that will calm him for such a revelation?"

"I know of no such potion." Lothair spoke with finality. They approached the lower gate and passed through it in silence, Magdala fairly simmering with her frustration.

"I had hoped for some aid from you," she said when the guards would not be able to hear them. "Perhaps I should not have confided in you at all. Perhaps my trust was mislaid."

Lothair said naught at all, the cur.

"I will go to the convent this very day," Magdala concluded with heat and he looked at her with surprise. "I will journey there alone as no one is inclined to accompany me. I will not be at Château Tulley when Lord Herbert arrives." She eyed him, not troubling to hide her annoyance with him. She had confessed the truth and he had decided it was a falsehood. "Do you know when he is expected?"

Lothair shook his head.

She turned to glance back at the ribbon of road, the one that led to the Beauvoir Pass. "Then this very day will suffice." She inclined her head to Lothair crisply, then pivoted. "Good day to you, sir." She did not say farewell, though she was tempted to do as much. She marched toward the higher gate, already planning what she would take and what she would leave behind. Most of the items in Heloise's chamber were not hers to claim, but she would take the best boots and the warmest cloak as well as the few coins in her possession. Perhaps she could take a satchel of food from the kitchens. Perhaps she would survive to reach the convent.

Would they even accept her there? Magdala did not know, but she had no choices remaining.

A curse upon Lothair of Sutherland, who might have made all the difference to her future, if he had only believed her!

Nay, a curse upon all men.

Magdala had no intention of glancing back or even of acknowledging the existence of the new Captain of the Guard at Château Tulley, but he said the one thing that could have brought her to a halt.

"What then is your name?"

SHE COULD NOT LEAVE! Not alone. The old lord would be furious. Lothair dreaded that if he let the maiden leave his sight in this moment, he might never see her again. He doubted that she would reach the convent in safety, yet he could neither abandon his post to accompany her nor assign a man to do as much when she had deceived the Lord de Tulley. Even if she did reach the convent, he would never see her again, and that prospect troubled him.

Could he convince the Lord de Tulley to allow her to stay?

But then, what about Lord Herbert? What would that man do upon his arrival? Her very concern made Lothair uneasy.

He had to ensure she remained within the walls until that conference was completed.

So, he asked her name.

To his delight, she turned back, her surprise evident.

"Why?" she asked with an increment of suspicion that he believed he deserved.

He shrugged and her lips tightened.

"The nuns called me Magdala."

Magdala. Lothair repeated it in his thoughts, thinking it suited her better than Heloise. But the nuns named her? "Your parents did not give you a name?"

"I do not know. I was surrendered to the abbey as an infant, in possession of naught but an empty belly. I was left at the door." She bowed her head, ashamed of her history, and Lothair's heart twisted.

It was not unlike his own.

"God in heaven," he whispered.

"I do not remember," she said with a smile, as if she would reassure him. "I was raised there so it was the only place I knew."

"Was the expectation that you would one day take your vows?"

She shook her head. "Nay, for I had no donation to make to the foundation to see me kept. The expectation was that I would remain there to labor, so the nuns could pray."

"Those who fight, those who work and those who pray," Lothair recited under his breath. She was not bitter or resentful about any of this. It had been her fortune and she did not even see its lack. In his experience, that said much of her nature and all of it good.

"A life of prayer is an indulgence in a way, a service done by widows and friars sworn to the Lord's service. I worked in the garden and in the kitchens, until Lady Verena came in search of a maid for her daughter."

Lothair watched her straighten.

"She chose me, though I know not why. The abbess bade me be glad, though I was not. I walked behind her cart, for my garb was plain and I was of lesser birth than she. I had naught. My feet were bare. My dress was worn."

Lothair knew that Lady Verena must have been lavishly dressed. There was still a measure of awe in Magdala's tone.

"That was four summers ago. I still remember her beauty and the gems upon her fingers. She might have been a queen come to visit. And Idelstein was beyond magnificent." She sighed, undoubtedly oblivious to the sympathy welling within him for her.

Lothair could not stifle his sense that Magdala deserved better than what she had known in this life. Indeed, he could not blame her for savoring the luxuries of Château Tulley, if she had chosen to do so, but in truth it had been her kindness for the old lord that had compelled her to hold her tongue.

With sudden ferocity, he wanted to ensure that she never faced such a situation again. He wanted to show her what it was like to have someone upon whom she could rely. Lothair was startled to realize that he was more than prepared to be that person. He knew what a difference it had made to him for the Mormaer to claim him, almost as another son. That act had anchored Lothair's life and fed his confidence in a wondrous way. He would not be the man he was this day without the patronage of Calum's father.

'Twas within his power to change Magdala's life for the better, simply with an offer for her hand. He did not doubt that she would be a good partner, and something within him heated at the notion of her as his wife.

It was madness. He had no intent to wed again.

She held him spellbound!

Magdala was undeterred by his silence and continued her tale. "And then she died the following winter, for no treatment made a difference. The priest said that wealth could not buy all matters of import. Her husband, Lord George, died the following winter, then Herbert became Lord Idelstein, as you know." She looked up, her gaze clear.

Lothair could not silence his suspicions. "Do you think Lord Herbert had aught to do with his sister's death?"

Magdala was visibly startled. "Nay! How could he have done?"

"He might have hired the brigands."

Magdala was shocked by the very suggestion and turned to face him. "To what purpose? She was his sister and one of the last of his family." She shook her head. "Nay, he is not a kind man, but that is not his manner of wickedness."

"What *is* his manner of wickedness?"

"He wants what he wants and, like Lady Heloise, he has never been denied his will." She shrugged. "But he held Idelstein before Lady Heloise's demise. The treasury was his. There was naught Lady Heloise might have added to his power."

Lothair, though, was not convinced. He averted his gaze, his brow yet furrowed. Did Lord Herbert have a secret? Had his sister guessed it? Lothair could not help but note that mother and father had died in quick succession, thereby clearing the path for their oldest son to inherit Idelstein and its wealth. Why had no treatment aided Lady Verena in her illness? Had any been offered? Why had Lord George died so soon afterward?

Lothair had seen enough wickedness in his days to immediately think of poison—and truly such a suspicion would explain the Lord de Tulley's task for Felix. If the Lord de Tulley's grandmother had known of the helpful plants, it made sense that his sister—who had been the mother of both Herbert and Heloise—might have had some knowledge as well. Did daughters of the house take cuttings from the garden with them when they wed? Lothair had heard the like often from those with an apothecary's skill.

How much of the garden's secrets did the Lord de Tulley and his family know?

Magdala had been shocked by his question, but he knew that men would do much to gain a holding, a title and a treasury. Her surprise, at least, indicated that Lady Heloise had not confided in her maid, if she had known a secret of her brother's.

Of course, it might not matter. If Lord Herbert believed that Magdala knew his secret, he might act upon that suspicion, whether it was true or not. A man with such a secret might not risk exposure.

In silence, they continued up the steep road to the keep, Lothair's thoughts churning.

When had any woman prompted him to be so protective? It was curious, for Lothair suspected that Magdala had fended for herself for much of her life, but there was an innocence about her that made him want to defend her from all the ills in the world.

Or maybe just from Lord Herbert.

They were passing the tavern when a man stepped from the shadows within into the sunlight. He was a warrior, tall and broad, dark of hair. Lothair would have paid little notice to him, save adding him to a mental inventory of fighting men within Tulley's walls.

Magdala scarce glanced his way, but the man smiled, taking a step back to survey her.

"Good day, my lady," he said with the pleasure of one who unexpectedly encounters an old friend.

Magdala then looked at him and started visibly, her expression changing utterly as she eyed the man. He bowed low before her as she stared. "Good day," she stammered, then hastened toward the keep as if she fled an assailant. Lothair caught up to her with an effort, noting that she was pale, as if she had seen a ghost.

"Do you know him?"

"I thought as much but it cannot be," she said, glancing back with a shiver. "He reminds me of someone I once knew, no more than that."

Lothair looked back but the man had vanished from view.

Mallory.

Magdala had been certain that it was Mallory before her, as merry and handsome as she recalled him to be—if risen from the grave.

For the man could not be Mallory. Mallory was dead and resting in the graveyard in Grimwald. Mallory had been the first cut down by the brigands who had attacked their party and killed Lady Heloise.

Yet she could have sworn it was Mallory before her.

And he had seemed to recognize her.

It made no sense. How could Mallory be alive and at Château Tulley? The warrior had to be a stranger, one who meant to charm her, no more than that. She had simply seen a resemblance to Mallory because her thoughts were full of that man's final day.

The explanation, though utterly rational, did little to dismiss her unease. Perhaps it was all the events of the day that conspired to upset her, from the reliving of that adventure in recounting it, to the surety that her time here at Tulley had come to an end. She was alone again, but likely would not survive the journey to the convent. She was aware of the knight strolling beside her, of his composure and his watchfulness, but she had no more to confess to him.

She was not entirely certain he believed her, and that was a disappointment.

To her surprise, Lothair halted in the bailey and turned to face her.

"Swear to me that you will not leave this day," he demanded, as if that was utterly reasonable on his part.

Magdala bristled for he had clearly guessed her intent. "Why should I?"

He flicked a glance at the tower above them. "Because there may be another choice."

"You will tell him."

"I am obliged to surrender all tidings to my liege lord."

Magdala took a deep breath. Lothair would meet with the Lord de Tulley at midday. She would have one last interlude with the older man. Another woman might have decided to plea for mercy or to argue her case, but Magdala would simply behave as she always had.

"Promise me, Magdala."

The sound of her name upon his lips was alluring to be sure, his deep voice making her name sound exotic and lovely. His gaze bored into hers, the blue hue of his eyes vivid and clear, as if he would compel her to agree by force of his will.

"One day," she agreed, feeling a wave of relief that she would not have to venture through the gates alone this day. "But I do not see what other solution you might contrive…"

Lothair held up a finger for her silence and she bit back her protest.

One day.

She turned away, well aware that the knight watched her go. When she glanced back, he inclined his head to her then returned to his duties, as if she had not bared her soul to him at all. Magdala watched him speak to the ostler, uncertain as to why she felt such a profound relief.

The secret had burdened her and even sharing it with Lothair had lessened its weight. She looked up at the tower above her and wondered whether the Lord de Tulley truly would be so upset by her confession.

She could tell him now.

But she dared not take the risk.

She was a coward. She would rub his back with Lothair's unguent. She would visit the garden one last time this afternoon and she would sit politely at the board this night. She would leave the telling of her secret to Lothair.

And on the morrow, she would flee at first light.

THE LORD DE Tulley wondered at what he had witnessed in the bailey below. He had seen the maiden leave with Lothair and was impatient to know what that knight had learned from her. He had also seen their final exchange, what had looked like an entreaty on the part of the knight, and that intrigued him mightily. The Lord de Tulley was not accustomed to being cursed with curiosity so he did not accept the change well.

The maiden appeared with reasonable speed, though it seemed like an eternity to the old lord. Felix left them alone together. The shutters had been opened to admit the sunlight, though the brazier still burned hot near the Lord de Tulley. She reminded him of the unguent, as if naught had changed, and her manner relieved the older man. He leaned forward at her instruction, bracing his elbows on a table and complaining about the posture—until she began to rub it into his back. He caught his breath at the fire it lit beneath his skin, then closed his eyes as that heat spread through his body. It had a pleasant if bracing scent and his skin tingled with its application.

"Lothair said it would ease your discomfort and warm you."

"It does that."

She rubbed more of the unguent into his skin and his curiosity became nigh unbearable.

"You admire him," the Lord de Tulley said, his words softly uttered.

"Who?" she asked, though she had to know.

The Lord de Tulley smiled, knowing she could not see as much. "My new Captain of the Guard, of course."

She flushed, just a little, but her lips set with something that might have been annoyance. Good. "He seems a very honorable knight, though his thoughts are difficult to discern."

"Mmm. Not so hard upon the eyes, either."

"I would not know, my lord."

"Would you not?" He chuckled and watched her flush yet more.

"It would not be fitting for me to look upon any man." Her blush belied her words.

"You should look upon this one," Tulley growled.

She did not reply to that but continued to rub his back. The unguent was potent and pleasing, and her hands were both strong and soft. He might have dozed in contentment if he had not been so determined to know of their conversation. How could he ask? Would she tell him the truth?

"You are fortunate to have such an apothecary in your service," she said finally.

"A woman would be fortunate to have such a man by her side."

"Do you strive to make a match for me?" she asked, as if outraged.

The old lord chuckled. "What if I did?"

He thought she might reply in kind, but she frowned instead. She drew up his chemise and turned away, washing her hands with more attention than was required. "I doubt I shall ever wed," she said with such care that he knew he had found a matter of import.

The Lord de Tulley harrumphed. "And why is that? Do you fear to surrender to a spouse's authority? Do you dread the prospect of bearing children?"

She smiled, but it was not a merry expression. "I am happy, just as matters are."

Tulley straightened and tied his own chemise, gesturing to his tabard so that she would fetch it for him. She put it over his head, as efficient as any squire, and he stood as she laced the sides. She brought his belt, knowing he watched her, but frowned at the task of fastening the buckle as if it required all her attention. The Lord de Tulley watched her closely.

"I was at the window yesterday," he said softly and she looked up warily. "I wished to see whether Lothair sought you in the garden or not."

"He did."

"But he did not find you alone."

Magdala shook her head.

"Am I right that his arrival was timely?"

She nodded again. "And much appreciated."

Tulley studied her, then nodded once. "You could do worse," he said simply and she flushed again. "That is a fine ointment."

"Aye, I feel it in my hands, as well." She was closing the small crockery pot with the unguent inside when she looked up suddenly, clearly having realized the import of his words. "Worse," she echoed and the Lord de Tulley grinned at her.

She parted her lips, her eyes brightening with the intent of demanding an explanation—and he knew what question it would be —just as Felix knocked upon the door, then entered with Lothair. The knight barely glanced at the lady, as sure a sign of his interest as Tulley could hope to see, while the maiden looked at Lothair only after she had retreated to the door. Her expression was thoughtful and when she met Tulley's gaze again, he nodded reassurance.

Aye, all would end well, and soon.

CHAPTER 7

Magdala was so shaken that she did not see the corridor before her very eyes.

The Lord de Tulley had said that she could do *worse* than to take Lothair as a husband.

But if he believed her to be Heloise, why did he not expect her to wed *better*? Lothair was a knight and a crusader, but he possessed neither title nor wealth, and Magdala knew that ambitions had been high for Lady Heloise's match.

The Lord de Tulley *knew*.

How long had it been since the older man had guessed the truth?

Was it possible that he had known her secret all along?

Had he ever been deceived?

Magdala felt a fool then for not confiding the truth in him, but on the other hand, he had not admitted to her that he was aware she was not Heloise.

She had reached the garden before she wondered whether the Lord de Tulley had possessed a scheme all along. She had seen him guide people to a hidden goal before, moving them like pieces upon a chess board, often while they were unaware of his intentions. She glanced back toward the solar.

Surely not. Surely he would not contrive to arrange her future? Why should he, if he knew she was not Heloise?

But Magdala could not dismiss the notion, not when she recalled his questions this day about her reaction to Lothair. It was characteristic of the older man to meddle thus in the lives of those beneath his hand, always to the greater good of all involved.

What would she do if her marriage to Lothair was proposed, or arranged?

What would Lothair do? She could not imagine that knight would desire a wife. Perhaps the Lord de Tulley's scheme would never come to fruition. Perhaps this time, the old lord had erred in the making of his plan.

"YOU HAVE DONE WELL," the Lord de Tulley said when Lothair had shared Magdala's confession. He sighed. "And Heloise is dead after all. I had hoped otherwise."

"What other outcome might there have been?"

The older man smiled. "That she had fled with a lover and asked her maid to provide a tale. I would not have been surprised. Heloise had a tendency to desire her own choice above all others, and I recall my sister complaining of her daughter's encouragement of undeserving courtiers. If she had decided she loved one and his suit had been denied, she might have contrived such a scheme." He shook his head. "She was not inclined to be denied."

Lothair considered the possibility even as he was glad not to have met that maiden. While he appreciated resolve, he did not admire willfulness. "That might yet be the case."

"You did not believe Magdala?"

"I did, but she has lied to you and others for several years."

The Lord de Tulley made a sound of disgust. "But I never believed her! Nay, you cannot insist that she is an accomplished liar. I think her eyes reveal the truth." The older man peered at him, eyes twinkling. "Perhaps you did not look closely enough at them."

"Perhaps not. We were walking and she stared at the road as she spoke."

The old lord nodded. "An established ploy. She is not witless, that is for certain. Magdala," he said. "An intriguing name."

"What of this Ranulf?"

"He was a warrior accompanying Heloise's party, though he was nigh mad with fever upon arrival here. His wound was so filled with poison that naught could be done to save him. It is true that he died. That very day of her arrival, I believe."

Lothair frowned.

"What troubles you in this?"

"With his demise, there is no other survivor to either confirm or deny the lady's account of events."

"What else might have occurred?"

"She might have been in league with the brigands."

The Lord de Tulley shook his head. "Then she should have left these walls long ago instead of lingering."

"She intended to leave this very day, alone, purportedly to retire to the convent of Ste. Radegund."

The old lord regarded him warily. "You are suspicious of her."

"She lived with nuns who knew of the healing arts. Who knows what she might have learned?"

"Speak plainly!"

"It is a small thing to coax infection in an injury."

"How so?"

"Dirt, my lord, of a most pungent kind can fatally poison a wound."

"You speak of night soil."

Lothair nodded. "Readily available and easily added while a wounded man sleeps, it would ensure his death."

"But to what point?"

"Perhaps she waited for you to die, sir. Perhaps she hoped for a legacy. Has she not lived at ease here these two years?"

The old lord studied Lothair for long moments, his eyes glittering, then shook his head. "I do not believe it. Do you?"

Lothair considered his impressions of the lady. "Nay," he admitted, shaking his head. "But I might be beguiled."

Tulley laughed at that. "You? Beguiled? I cannot accept the possibility." He shook a crooked finger at the knight. "But still, you have completed only two thirds of the task assigned to you. You tell me the fate of Heloise, and I shall seek confirmation of that. What of Magdala's intention within my walls? I must have all the tale before you gain your reward."

"I do not have need of a reward, my lord. I am sworn to your service."

"And I keep my pledges, sir. I promised a reward for such information and I will grant it." The old man smiled. "When you succeed." He arched a brow. "*If* you succeed."

"And what shall I tell the lady in the meantime, sir?"

"Did she not promise to linger one more day?"

"Aye, sir."

"That will suffice for my purposes." The old lord gestured with impatience to a small trunk set against the far wall. Lothair retrieved it for him and set it on the table. It was sturdy and made of good oak, straps of leather bound about it, and a lock upon the lid. The Lord de Tulley sorted through the keys he removed from his purse and set a large brass one into the keyhole.

The lock turned with a resolute click and the old lord turned the trunk toward Lothair.

"Open it," he instructed, a knowing glint in his eyes.

Lothair wondered what might be within this treasury, but there was little to be gained in speculation. He opened the lid and stared at the contents in surprise.

A book reposed within, one bound with leather. He assumed it was a Bible, copied and bound by skilled monks in some foundation over the course of years. Though he had seen such volumes once or twice, he had never yet touched one. The others had been studded with gems, their coverings embellished like jewelry. This one was comparatively plan. At the Lord de Tulley's nod, he lifted it free of the trunk with care and set it upon the table before the older man.

The Lord de Tulley nodded, running his fingertips across the volume. "This belonged to my mother," he said. "And to her mother before her." He shot a glance at Lothair from beneath his bristling brows. "Do you know what it is?"

"A Bible?" Lothair guessed, but the Lord de Tulley shook his head.

"It is more important to me than that. The counsel within this volume is practical and useful." He opened the cover and ran a fingertip beneath the line of script on the vellum. "Can you read?"

Lothair nodded and the Lord de Tulley gestured to the book. Lothair leaned closer and read the line of script. "*The Capitulare de Villis,*" he read. He spoke slowly because the style of the script was less familiar to him and he could not read it easily. It was only after he had said the words aloud that he realized what was before him.

"Aye," said the Lord de Tulley, noting his expression with satisfaction. "It is a copy of the compilation made for Charlemagne about the government of his royal estates." He turned the pages with care to a passage that looked to have been consulted often. There was another sheet of vellum inserted there, not bound into the book, like a marker of goodly size. Tulley began to read. "*It is our wish that they should have in their gardens all kinds of plants: lily, roses, fenugreek, costmary, sage, rue, southernwood...*" He paused and looked up. "An inventory of plants for a garden of useful plants, a collection fit to ensure both the needs of the apothecary and the kitchen."

"*'The names of the apples are gozmaringa, geroldinda, crevedella, spriauca; there are sweet ones, bitter ones, those that keep well, those that are to be eaten straightaway, and early ones,'*" Lothair said, recalling the text.

"You know it!"

"It was read to me once, by an apothecary in a monastery whom I consulted. It is a most venerable source." Lothair eyed the book with a yearning he was not accustomed to experiencing. A week with such a volume would teach him much, to be sure.

"My grandmother took the veil as a maiden and was inclined to be of service to those around her. My grandfather had seen her once and could not forget her. It took him a decade to persuade her to leave the foundation and become his wife, and she only agreed upon her own terms."

"She did not wish to wed him?"

"She believed she had a calling and that it would be a defiance of God's will to abandon it." The older man's fingertips trailed across the book. "The foundation, however, was interested in the donation he was prepared to make to them, and she was urged to accept him. She offered a list to him, certain he would not collect all of the items."

"She negotiated."

"She was a clever woman, much concerned with the wisdom of books and the useful plants. She was the one who planned and planted the garden that Magdala admires so much. This book was one of her requirements, as was the copy of *De Materia Medica*." He paused and watched Lothair, his expression shrewd.

Lothair was so astonished that he could not disguise his surprise. "The work of Pedanius Dioscurides, the Greek physician in the Roman army, almost a thousand years ago?"

The Lord de Tulley nodded. "Doubtless, she thought she had set the goal too high, but my grandfather was not a man to be deterred." He pointed to the small chest and Lothair realized there was another book within it, one he had not seen because the dark leather of the cover was nigh the same hue as the interior of the chest. At the lord's gesture, he removed the volume with care, staring at it with wonder and awe, then opened it at random. To his further surprise, the text was legible to him, though he knew that the original had been written in Greek.

"This is Latin," he said.

"Aye, my grandmother did not read Greek." The Lord de Tulley sat back, smiling with satisfaction as he watched Lothair's reaction.

Lothair could not believe that he held such a precious volume in his hands. The page before him illustrated dill with its tall stalks and yellow flowers, the very plant he had weeded the day before in the garden here at Château Tulley. *Anethum* in Latin. *Polpum* to Dioscurides. A remedy for discomfort after eating, for a rash on the privates, for treatment of a headache. A plant with a welcome heat and a savory addition to a sauce as well. He recalled all he had been taught about this one plant, conjuring a list, then realized that the Lord de Tulley watched him closely.

He straightened and closed the book with an effort. "A marvel," he said, putting the book down. Truly, he learned much of his own capacity for desire at Château Tulley.

"And one of interest to you." The Lord de Tulley replaced the smaller volume in the chest and Lothair could not tear his gaze from it. What would he give for a day with that volume? The Lord de Tulley added the other atop it, then closed and locked the chest. The key vanished into his purse. "I would make you an offer, Lothair of Sutherland," he said softly. "If you agree to my suggestion this night at the board, I shall ensure that you have sufficient time alone with both of these volumes to read them through."

Lothair had the urge to recoil from such terms. That they were mysterious could not be a good sign. "What would you demand of me, sir?"

The Lord de Tulley smiled. "We will make an exchange. What I desire in exchange for what you desire. It is simplicity itself." His gaze hardened. "Swear to me that you will agree."

Lothair shook his head. "I cannot, not until I know what you will ask."

The Lord de Tulley patted the locked trunk. "Even for such a prize?"

"Even so, my lord."

"Well, then, consider the reward when I name my price. I will keep my pledge if you agree."

Their gazes locked for a moment, Lothair wondering whether his sense that the older man would have him make a bargain with a demon, then the Lord de Tulley closed his eyes. "Send Felix to me, if you would," he said, leaning back in his chair as if suddenly exhausted. He opened his eyes, which were vividly blue. "And think upon the prize this night before you decline. You would have to journey far to find another such copy of this volume, and do far more than I will ask to gain access to it."

Lothair bowed and left the older man, finding his servant just outside the door. He marched down the corridor, unsettled as he had seldom been. The reward was considerable. What would the Lord de Tulley ask of him? Lothair could not help but believe that it was something he would be otherwise inclined to decline.

What would he do?

How would he endure the remainder of the day in such uncertainty?

He noticed that the gate to the garden stood open and guessed who might be in that space. He paused at the portal and looked into the garden, its bounty glorious in the sunshine, and watched the maiden who steadily weeded the calendula border. She had her back to him, and he wondered what she was thinking. It made sense to him that she would spend time in this place, which he knew she favored, before she left Château Tulley for good.

He did not like that she was in distress, and he liked the old lord's manner even less. Though he had accepted the responsibility here willingly, he felt cornered in a way he did not find pleasing.

What of the lady? She had few choices herself.

Once she left these walls, he would never see her again.

The truth of that troubled him more than he knew it should.

She glanced up in that moment, as if she had sensed his perusal. To his pleasure, she neither turned away nor frowned, but straightened. There was some uncertainty in her expression and he realized she must wonder at the Lord de Tulley's reaction to her confession.

Perhaps he could set her concerns at ease.

It was an excuse and Lothair knew as much, but still he entered the garden and strode toward the lady.

MAGDALA COULD NOT LEAVE, not when all was so close to fruition!

The Lord de Tulley could not countenance her departure, for if the maiden left, he could not ensure her future. But Lothair declined to promise, which left more uncertainty than the Lord de Tulley might have preferred.

People, he was convinced, had become far more vexing than in the days of his youth.

The Lord de Tulley had been certain that he had offered the right inducement, but in the silence of the solar and the absence of the two he would see together, he wondered whether he had overlooked the most obvious temptation. He had offered the security of a post in his household, the freedom to peruse the garden and even to consult the books in his possession, but as the Lord de Tulley pondered the matter, he considered whether Lothair's sole desire might already be the lady herself. He had thought the intended couple needed time to be convinced of the merit of his own view, but it was possible he was mistaken.

If so, the solution was simplicity itself, for the Lord de Tulley was never adverse to insisting that a match be made.

MAGDALA HAD the definite sense that Lothair was shaken. She could not have named the difference in his appearance, for he appeared as inscrutable and decisive as ever, but there was something in his manner that gave her the impression that he had been shocked.

She would have wagered that did not occur often.

What had the Lord de Tulley said to him?

"You told him," she said when Lothair halted before her.

"Aye." He frowned then, his gaze rising to hers. "You need not fear for his welfare."

Relief surged through Magdala. The Lord de Tulley *had* known. Why had he allowed her ruse to continue? She realized that Lothair awaited her reply. "But you are troubled all the same."

"He insisted that I make a pledge to him."

"Have you not already made one?"

"Aye, but another." The prospect clearly troubled Lothair. "I could not swear to it, despite the temptation offered, not without knowing his intentions."

What would the Lord de Tulley wish for Lothair to do? Magdala could not imagine, but she knew it would not be immoral or wicked. "You do not trust him," she ventured and he nodded.

"I do not know him."

"I have watched him these two years," she said. "And I trust him utterly."

That intrigued the knight. She could see as much by the way his gaze sharpened upon her.

She continued. "He likes to make matters right for those beneath his hand. He likes to shape their futures and ensure their happiness."

"I am *not* beneath his hand."

"Are you not? I thought you had pledged fealty to him."

Lothair frowned. He crouched down and began to pull weeds, his gestures quick and impatient as was not usually the case. Whatever the old lord had said to him had been vexing, to be sure. "How?" he demanded after a moment.

"He has great conviction in the merit of marriage."

"Yet he is unwed himself."

"Aye. I have wondered about that. But he arranged the match of your comrade, Quinn de Sayerne, and the lady, Melissande d'Annossy."

Lothair flicked a glance at her. "I thought they were previously acquainted, due to their family holdings being adjacent."

"You thought your comrade returned to find his lady still enamored of him?" Magdala asked and he nodded once. "Hardly that. They did not know each other and she despised his father. She argued mightily with the Lord de Tulley, but he would not bend. He offered Lord Quinn the seal to Sayerne only if they wed and produced a son within a year." She watched Lothair's brows rise and anticipated his next question. "He already had claimed the seal to Annossy upon the death of Lady Melissande's father, and granted it upon their nuptials to Lord Quinn. The lady, I believe, had hoped to hold it herself."

"Neither had a choice," Lothair said softly, as if this detail was of great import.

"They were wed immediately, both simmering with the injustice of it all. And yet, within months, their match was a merry one, and now neither can imagine his or her days without the other."

"A happy coincidence?"

"A scheme," Magdala said with a firm shake of his head. "The Lord de Tulley schemes for all beneath his hand with the intent of ensuring the welfare of each and every one."

"You trust his counsel." Lothair seemed surprised by this.

"He is perceptive and knows much of people." She considered this for a moment. "I believe he has a talent for seeing precisely what a person could achieve with a measure of aid."

"Indeed."

"He would not have welcomed the miller's son, Quentin, if he had not known that the boy would have an aptitude for a knight's trade."

Lothair nodded. "The boy is most enthused and shows promise with a blade."

"And he will be happy when he completes his training, perhaps so content that he would pledge service to Tulley. The Lord de Tulley's sound judgement brings bounty to his holding."

"There have been other instances," Lothair guessed.

"Dozens of them even in my short time here, from the expulsion of those he believes unworthy, to the breaking of betrothals he deems unsuitable, to the negotiation of alliances. He was the one who proposed the match between your comrade Rolfe de Viandin and

Lord Quinn's sister, Annelise, a bond they both battled against yet made on their own."

"Then whose happiness would he intend to achieve with this wager?"

"Perhaps yours."

His gaze lingered upon her, his gaze so bright that Magdala could not take a breath.

She tried to disguise her awareness of that by rising to her feet and brushing off her skirts. "I shall miss this place, to be sure, but perhaps there is a similar garden at Ste. Radegund." She was keenly aware that Lothair straightened and stood beside her, looking down upon her.

"You do mean to leave, then."

"At first light." She shrugged. "Perhaps he will chastise me at the board this night, which is fair." She wondered though, whether he would even mention the matter, having guessed the truth previously.

"You do not fear him?"

Magdala shook her head with complete confidence. "I misled him about my name, but I tended him in his illness and have endeavored to act as a good niece or daughter would. If he knew that I was not Heloise and did not cast me out, he may be annoyed, but he will not be vengeful." She straightened with a smile of amusement. "I do not doubt that I will hear his view on the matter and in some detail, though."

A glow lit in Lothair's eyes and he almost smiled at her. "You are fond of him."

"I know him. His tongue may be sharp but his heart is good." She looked across the garden, considering. "Perhaps I will seek him out before the meal, and invite him to share his view in private. He might prefer that." She turned to the watchful knight on impulse. "I remember the drying of the calendula petals, but not the other ingredients of the mixture made of them. I did dry a quantity of them this year and Felix has complained of a slight rash. Would you tell me how to mix it for him?"

It would not hurt to perform one last kindness before she left

Tulley for good and she was glad when Lothair inclined his head in agreement.

∿

FELIX ADMITTED Magdala to the solar quietly, then retreated as was his habit. She stood for a long moment by the portal, studying the older man. The Lord de Tulley appeared to be asleep in his chair, his chin fallen to his chest. In slumber, he appeared much older and more frail than she knew him to be, and her heart clenched tightly that his days might be drawing to an end.

She crossed the chamber on silent feet, placing another fur over his shoulders. He started, and glared up at her, almost as if he did not recognize her, then his lips tightened.

"You lied to me," he said flatly.

"I did," Magdala admitted. "Though it was not my intention to do as much."

"A lie is a lie. You told me you were Heloise."

"Nay, I never did. You called me Heloise when I arrived and I was so glad to be within the walls of such a fortification that I did not correct you. Then Ranulf had to be tended."

"Then Ranulf died," the Lord de Tulley supplied.

"And then, it seemed late to confess the truth."

"It was!"

"I admit it. Each day, I thought to tell you and each day, I could not find the words. Then you were ill last winter and I feared that confessing the truth might shock you overmuch..."

"I am more robust than that!"

"Perhaps." Magdala folded her arms across her chest to regard him with affection. "But we shall not know the truth of that, sir, for you were not fooled."

He smiled, caught in his own deception, and they eyed each other for a long moment. "That is no credit to you," he finally said.

"Nay, but it might be said that you deceived me, by not confessing that you had discerned the truth. And so we are equal in our trickery and perhaps that is sufficient to each forgive the other."

He glared at her, his eyes the fierce blue she knew so well. His very brows seemed to bristle in his annoyance and his lips nigh disappeared. "You call me a liar?"

"I call you perceptive, sir, and a man who keeps his own counsel."

The Lord de Tulley laughed suddenly, his gaze twinkling. "I had not realized your tongue was so gilded as this."

"Perhaps I have learned some skills here at Château Tulley."

"Perhaps you know how best to reconcile with an old man, by telling him what he wishes to hear."

"Perhaps I have told you the truth, in all matters but my name."

He shook a finger at her. "And there you revealed yourself, for never was there a maiden so different from my niece, Heloise." He patted the seat beside him in invitation, a sign that she had been forgiven. Magdala smiled in her relief and knew he noticed.

"How did you know?"

"Do you not recall when we rode to hunt?"

She shuddered. "Only the once and it was sufficient."

"Daily could not be sufficient for Heloise," he asserted.

"I remember."

"She could not have changed so much as that, even in those years."

"That was the first week I was here."

He nodded, his expression becoming smug. "Aye. Felix knew within moments."

"Truly? How?"

"He was startled by your concern for Ranulf and thought it unlike the maiden he recalled." The Lord de Tulley nodded in recollection. "He told me that first day that he feared you were not Lady Heloise. He had anticipated that she would demand a hot bath and a clean chamber, that she would wish for another maid and a change of garments, as well as a fine meal with all haste." He granted her a hard look. "She considered herself and her own comforts, and naught else." He reached out and took her hand. "Your nature is much kinder. You asked only for a piece of bread, and that after Ranulf had been tended."

"I have not had the opportunity to think only of myself."

"And thus you are a finer maiden as a result." He squeezed her hand. "Magdala."

"Aye, sir."

He nodded approval. "A fine name." He sighed. "But I will continue to call you Heloise for the moment, as will Lothair."

"If you so wish, sir."

He leaned back his head and closed his eyes, his hand still clasping her own. She thought he might have dozed off, but he spoke suddenly. "Where is she?"

"The priest in Grimwald village was to bury her in the churchyard there, though, of course, he believes she is me."

"And the two knights who fell in the forest?"

"They, too, rest there. Gideon and Mallory." She frowned, recalling the curious resemblance between Mallory and the man who had stepped into the road earlier this day.

A coincidence, to be sure. She had seen Mallory in him because she had been recalling that day.

"All must be set to rights," the Lord de Tulley said. He shivered then and opened his eyes. "I feel chilled on this day. Is there more of that unguent?"

"Of course, my lord." Magdala rose and fetched the small pot, returning to help him to remove his chemise. She rubbed the preparation into his back and shoulders, feeling its welcome heat beneath her own hands. He sighed and leaned forward, putting his head on his folded arms. She felt his breathing slow and his skin warm.

"I will share a scheme at the board this night," he said some moments later, when she had thought he might not speak at all. "I would ask you to consider its merit well."

"Of course."

He wagged a finger, his speech slowing as if he would doze. "Do not decline with haste, Magdala. Consider it first."

"You know that I will," Magdala assured him but the old lord scoffed softly before he began to snore.

What did he mean to propose?

CALUM FAIRLY SCAMPERED up the stairs to the great hall before Lothair. The youth had spent the afternoon sparring with Quentin and evidently was even more hungry than was typical. "Do you think there will be meat again, sir?" he asked, his hope clear from his shining eyes. "Three nights in a row?"

"Perhaps."

"That stew last eve was a marvel. I could have eaten twice as much and easily."

"Temperance is key to governing temptation," Lothair found himself saying, repeating the axiom favored by his patron and Calum's father. The squire clearly recognized it, for he laughed aloud, but Lothair did not smile.

His own temperance was stretched thin, his dreams filled with the intriguing Magdala. The lady not only possessed many charms but just as many mysteries. Never had he yearned to unfurl the secrets of another with greater vigor—or been tempted to win their surrender by any possible means.

The Lord de Tulley could not know that the lady tempted Lothair far more than the book, which said much of his interest in her.

"I shall not become plump, sir, not when I fight so hard each day."

"You did well sparring this day."

"A spar? 'Twas a battle, to be sure, and that move you taught us both—well! Such a feint and so smoothly delivered. I have seldom seen such finesse, sir, and I fear that neither of us did your example credit."

"You will learn."

"I will practice, sir, each and every day, and Quentin says he will do as much as well. I like him. He has an enthusiasm almost equal to my own, though I believe I fight better."

"You talk more," Lothair could not refrain from noting.

Calum laughed again. "Perhaps I have more to say! He wished to know of Outremer and of the places we have seen. He has never been on a ship! Can you imagine?"

"Readily, as there are no bodies of water in the vicinity of Tulley."

"And he knew naught of dousing. I wager he could not find water with ease as I did so often on our travels."

Calum did have a remarkable talent for finding water and that skill had aided their company more than once in those hot climes. "Doubtless he would best you at tasks in a mill."

"Oh, I should ask him of that. Do you think we might journey to Annossy to see the grain being ground? I should like to see how it is done, and how it differs from the pressing of oil from olives. And they make wine there, as well, Quentin says, some of the best in this region. I should like to see it all!"

"It will depend upon the Lord de Tulley's will."

"Aye, sir, but you might persuade him. He seems to favor your counsel…"

Lothair halted at the threshold to the great hall and gave the squire an imperious glance. When that did not stem the tide of words, he touched a fingertip to his lips.

Calum sighed and smiled. "Aye, sir. I will be quiet in the hall. I know the Lord de Tulley does not approve of comments from those who serve at the board, for I was told as much this morning in the kitchens."

"And yet…" Lothair murmured. They were crossing the floor, Calum a pace behind him, and still the youth chattered. The Lord de Tulley was already seated in his great chair and the fire was blazing at his elbow. Magdala was arranging furs over his lap. She wore the crimson kirtle this night and Lothair could not help but appreciate her beauty.

"You stare, sir," she whispered when he bowed before her, but she flushed in a way that made him believe she did not mind.

"I think this hue flatters you well," he said. "I but admire."

Truly, he gained the graces of a courtier in her presence and found himself embarrassed by his own flattery of her after the words were uttered.

Their gazes clung, her lips parting as she stared at him and desire unfurled within Lothair with a vigor that was troubling. She flushed then, her manner becoming flustered as if she had seen the direction of his thoughts, and he realized the Lord de Tulley was watching him with an indulgent smile. Something about the older man's expression roused a suspicion within Lothair, for he sensed that a scheme was about to be revealed—and that he had been assigned a part within it.

To what would the older man have him agree? He had offered temptation, to be sure, and a considerable one. Lothair suspected the concession would not be a small one. How would he decline it without giving insult?

Magdala might not be the only one leaving Château Tulley at first light.

He was uneasy as he took his place, and could not fail to note that Magdala appeared to share his trepidation. What did she know of the Lord de Tulley's plans? Had the older man confided in her? If not, her manner offered no encouragement.

"Felix, summon the household, if you will," the Lord de Tulley said. "I have an announcement to make this evening." His servant bowed and vanished from the great hall on fleet feet. Lothair glanced at Magdala, noting how she bit the ripe curve of her bottom lip.

He wagered that she did not know the scheme but she dreaded it, as Lothair did.

That was a poor portent, indeed.

CHAPTER 8

The household took an eon to gather, to Lothair's thinking. The knights and guards were already in the hall for the evening meal, but even the sentries and squires were summoned from the stables. The ostler and his grooms were roused from their evening meal in the kitchens. No less than six maids who labored in the hall and kitchens appeared, their aprons stained from their labor, their expressions puzzled and manners expectant. The cook, the baker and the saucemaker, arrived together, all striving to disguise the fact that they were disgruntled to be summoned so close to the serving of the meal. The châtelain appeared last, taking his place beside Felix, and that pair bowed in unison.

"I have good cause to interrupt your duties," the Lord de Tulley said. "For I have tidings to share with all of you. My niece, Heloise, will wed my new Captain of the Guard, Lothair of Sutherland, and you will all partake of the feast."

There was a moment of astonished silence in the hall. Then the women cooed with delight and there was applause from the company as well as a few cheers. More than one shouted their congratulations and Magdala flushed crimson even as her gaze dropped to her hands in her lap.

This was what the older man had wished Lothair to accept.

This was the price of access to those precious tomes.

Lothair was surprised by the war of instincts within him. He was stunned first and foremost by the tide of yearning launched by the suggestion. He *wanted* to take this maiden's hand—indeed, the very idea had already occurred to him, and this despite his own expectation that he would never wed again. But he heartily disliked having a price upon the transaction. He wanted to wed the lady for herself. He did not want to be offered a bargain or an inducement, as if she was not worthy of his admiration on her own. He certainly did not wish for that arrangement to be a secret withheld from her, for he had no doubt that she would unravel the truth in time, and would despise him for his choice.

All would turn sour between them as a result of such a revelation and he knew it well.

That was no good basis for a match, and indeed, such a secret would doom any marriage.

Lothair could not agree, and worse, he could not remain silent— no matter the price of the Lord de Tulley's displeasure.

He stood and all turned to him, falling silent. Doubtless his expression was forbidding, for he heartily disapproved of the old lord's choice.

"Nay," Lothair said crisply. "I regret that I cannot accept this edict, sir."

He saw the Lord de Tulley's eyes flash and watched that man's expression turn to outrage. Doubtless few had the audacity to defy him.

Lothair had been so concerned with the implications that he was late to realize that the lady was watching him closely. Before he could say a word to make amends, Magdala averted her gaze, her lips tightening even as she clenched her hands together before herself.

Then she stood, turning a glance upon him so cold that he nigh shivered.

"I fear this knight is not inclined to accept your surprise, Uncle," she said with composure, but he heard the thrum of anger beneath her words.

She was insulted. Lothair had erred in his protest, though it was right in itself, his manner of making it was lacking.

Doubtless a man more inclined to charm would have found a better way to express what had to be said.

"Perhaps you fail to understand the honor I offer to you," the Lord de Tulley said, his manner indignant. "A mere three days you have been beneath my roof and I would welcome you into my own family. Do not show such disdain for what is offered, sir!"

There was a murmur through the household at this, for it *was* a marvel.

If not precisely true. Magdala was not of the Lord de Tulley's family, though only they three were aware of that truth. Lothair felt the back of his neck heat, but he would not dishonor this maiden for any price.

Not even for the opportunity to peruse those volumes at leisure.

"I greatly appreciate the honor, but regret that I cannot accept it."

Before Lothair could decide how best to repair his error, Magdala caught her breath and turned away. She left the great hall with quick steps and did not look back.

The silence in the hall was complete after her departure, then the company erupted in excited speculation. The Lord de Tulley dismissed them with a wave of his hand and fixed Lothair with a glare. "You defy me," he said in a furious undertone.

"You insult the lady without cause," Lothair said stiffly, taking his seat again with reluctance.

The older man studied him. His features softened, as if he were amused, though Lothair could find no humor in the situation.

"She will leave Tulley now," Lothair continued in frustration. "She will leave at first light or before, putting herself in peril in her attempt to reach sanctuary at the convent of Ste. Radegund."

The Lord de Tulley settled back in his great chair, his eyes gleaming. "Then you know what is at stake," he said under his breath. "I grant you the task of convincing the maiden of the merit of this scheme." He raised his brows. "Perhaps she has fled to the sanctuary of the garden she loves so well."

Lothair rose to his feet again, knowing he had been dismissed, uncertain how he would gain Magdala's agreement.

The older man was clearly untroubled by any prospect of Lothair's failure. He beckoned to his châtelain. "Thomas, please ensure that the meal is served shortly. I do not doubt that all will have returned to the board by then with happy tidings to share."

Lothair bowed and excused himself, aware that the entire household watched and speculated, as he marched from the hall. He went directly to the garden, knowing as well as the Lord de Tulley that he would find Magdala there.

He expected that she would anticipate his arrival, but she was not there. The garden was empty. As he turned from the locked gate, he heard a minute sound from far above him.

A key turning in a lock.

The lady had retreated to her chamber, the one place he could not give chase.

Lothair doubted that was an accident. Nay, she made her view of him and this scheme clear. He had to contrive a plan to stop her from leaving in the morning, though he had no notion what she might find persuasive.

Never had Lothair so wished for an increment of charm as he did on this eve.

Nay, the truth would have to suffice.

MAGDALA WAS FUMING.

As much as she appreciated Lothair's fondness for honesty and the truth, she could not enjoy the fact that he found the notion of wedding her so unacceptable. Was she a loathsome lady, ugly and misshapen? Nay! Was she a shrew with a sharp tongue? Nay! Was she too ancient to grant him a child? Nay again. She was penniless, to be sure, but he was scarcely a king's son in his own right.

She might have concluded that he had no affection for women, but the heat that occasionally lit his gaze when he studied her hinted otherwise. Nay, he simply did not desire her, not even when the Lord de Tulley endorsed the match.

Perhaps he had surrendered his heart to another. Magdala stared out the window, frowning at the distant mountain peaks. Why did she strive to find a noble excuse for his reticence? He could simply be a cur and a knave, a man who might have wed her if she had truly been the Lord de Tulley's niece and potentially an heiress, but thought himself too fine for an orphaned maid of uncertain parentage.

She had erred in trusting him with her own truth, to be sure.

But would she desire a husband who had wed her for a birthright she did not possess, who had accepted her under false pretenses? Nay and nay again.

Then why did his rejection burn so? He was but a man, yet another of many who might not desire her.

The difference was that she desired Lothair. She was fool enough to dream of such a man by her side, a man upon whom she could rely, a man whose honor was unimpeachable, a man of integrity and honor. Even now, she sighed a little in recollection of his resolve.

He had a reason for declining her, of that she had no doubt. Magdala also suspected she would not like the reason, for a man such as Lothair would be practical and pragmatic. What had she to offer a spouse? She might bear a child to him, but she might not. Beyond that, there was only her own self, and that, she knew, had never been sufficient for anyone. Even Lady Verena had chosen her because of her resemblance to that lady's own daughter, Heloise, not because of her diligence in completing her assigned tasks or her cheerful nature.

There could be no further reprieve from the convent and though she feared the journey, she feared Lord Herbert more. Magdala surveyed the chamber, acknowledging that nothing in it was truly her own. She would wear the simplest and sturdiest of her collection of garments, the heaviest and warmest cloak and the newest, plainest boots. She would take some bread from the kitchen, perhaps some apples and a bit of hard cheese, some provisions that would not be missed.

She would leave Heloise's little ring behind, as well as all else of value, for none of it belonged to her. She would not be called a thief as well as an orphan.

Her resolve was made when there was a knock at the door and she jumped that any would trouble her in her chamber. It was Rose, the older maid from the kitchens, and Magdala admitted her with reluctance. Rose was a gossip and surely sought some tidings from Magdala that she could share.

"I have brought you something to eat," that woman said. "At the Lord de Tulley's suggestion." It was chicken in a savory stew, with bread and fruit alongside, as well as some boiled eggs. Magdala might have insisted she could not eat on this night, but some of the offering would travel well.

"I thank you, Rose, for your kindness," she said, letting the woman enter.

Rose carried the tray to a trunk, and fussed over it, clearly lingering. "You should know, my lady, that all in the hall are most distressed by the rudeness of the new Captain of the Guard this night," she said, shaking out a napkin. "Why, who might imagine a knight could be so proud, even one returned from crusade, as to decline the hand of the Lord de Tulley's own niece? Who does he expect to wed? The Queen of France? The Emperor's daughter?" Rose laughed at the very prospect. "I tell you, such pride can only bring misfortune upon any soul, and you should be glad your life is not to be bound to his."

"Thank you, Rose."

The older woman looked around the chamber. "You know that you could summon a maid to aid you. There are girls in the village who would be glad of the opportunity to serve. Therese was only

with you for a few months before her son came and no one understood why you did not demand a replacement for her services."

"I am content to manage on my own."

The older woman surveyed her. "There was a time when you
could not have enough servants fluttering about."

"I have changed, Rose," Magdala acknowledged. "I thank you for
the meal."

"I suppose it makes a measure of sense," that woman continued.
"Seeing your little maid killed before your very eyes must have been
troubling."

"It was."

"And you having insisted that she take your place." Rose shook her
head, but her gaze was knowing. "I wager you feel some responsibility
for her demise, the poor girl."

"Who would not? Good night, Rose," Magdala said, refusing to rise
to the older woman's comments.

Rose hesitated for a moment before she went to the door, then
paused on the threshold. "If you have need of anything else, my lady,
you have only to call."

"I thank you again, Rose," Magdala said firmly, then locked the
door after the other woman had departed. She would eat the stew and
save the rest. Even as she sat down with purpose, she wondered. How
far was it to the convent? She supposed she would have to walk for
days.

She would take the few coins she possessed, and put them in her
shoes as Lady Heloise had done.

～

LOTHAIR DID NOT SLEEP.

He sat on the edge of his bed, elbows braced on his knees and
considered how best to ensure Magdala's safety. The sole way was to
wed her, but he would not blame her if she declined again.

He had to tell her the truth.

141

Calum snored contentedly, having regaled Lothair with a full description of the chicken stew and eggs poached in wine served at the board that night. He also had sung the better part of a ballad offered by a minstrel, which had entertained the Lord de Tulley mightily, by his account.

A cock crowed when it was yet dark, the one kept by the ostler's wife, which was reliable indeed. The sky was yet dark, but Lothair rose and left his chamber, silently progressing to the empty bailey. He had remained garbed so that he would not have to awaken Calum. He watched with approval as the sentries changed their shifts, as efficient as ever but newly silent at his own orders, even as he crossed the bailey. The gates to the town were not yet open and he waited in the shadows there, hoping against hope that Magdala did not know another means out of the keep.

She did not, to Lothair's great relief.

He suspected he was the sole one who knew the identity of the lady in plain garb with her hood drawn over her hair. She emerged from the kitchens with a satchel, wearing sturdy boots, just as the gatekeeper raised the portcullis. Lothair followed her through the gates and saw her shoulders stiffen at the sound of his boots.

She spun to face him, fury lighting her eyes. "Do not imagine that I will speak with you this morn."

"I do not, but I would speak with you before you depart."

"I will not listen."

"I will follow you and speak in the hope that some of my words will be heard."

"What can you possibly say? Why would you trouble yourself to do as much?"

"Because you do not know the truth and I have a great conviction in the power of the truth to cause change."

She looked over her shoulder then, intrigued despite herself, and Lothair dared to be encouraged. She frowned and averted her gaze again.

"You would journey to the convent alone," he ventured.

"My choices can be of no import to you."

"But they are, my lady. I would ensure your welfare and safety."

"Then you might have accepted my hand." There was hurt in her tone.

"I could not, not without truth between us."

She spun to confront him then, one hand upon her hip, defiance in her eyes. "What secret do you possess, sir? Have you another name, one hidden from all? Have you a dark past, filled with infamous deeds and disrepute?" She did not believe her own words, Lothair could hear as much.

Nay, she thought he had found her lacking, and nothing could have been further from the truth.

He had to make this right, no matter the price to his pride.

"I refused because the Lord de Tulley offered an incentive to me to take your hand, and I found that to be a vulgar notion."

She turned away again. "Why? People make such wagers all the time."

"But I would not see you deceived. A marriage must be anchored upon truth to succeed."

Her tone softened a little. "You truly believe as much?"

"I do. You would learn of his offer in time, I am certain, and the revelation can only be unwelcome. He might even tell you of it when it suits his scheme." His voice hardened along with his expression. "And I will not have you believe that I accepted your hand to ensure my own gain."

Magdala studied him. "What a curious man you are," she said softly and Lothair felt his neck heat. He was spared the obligation of replying because she continued, her eyes bright with curiosity. "What did he offer?"

"You are not insulted?"

She smiled, if only briefly, and even that glimpse made his heart skip. "Who would not wish to know their price?"

Lothair could respect that. "Yesterday, he asked me to pledge that I would agree to whatsoever he proposed last eve."

"Without knowing what it might be?"

Lothair nodded. "And in exchange, he would grant me access to an ancient volume of the healing arts in his possession. A rare tome, to be sure." He frowned. "I declined to make that vow, for I was uncertain of his intentions."

"But you wished to examine the volume?"

"Aye." He spoke with resolve, but could not entirely disguise the echo of his yearning. He continued, his tone turning rueful. "Already, he knows me well. The hook was baited well."

Magdala eyed him for a moment, then continued upon her way to the lower gates. "Then why did you decline?"

Lothair's reply was low and hot, so fiercely uttered that even he was surprised. "Because you deserve better than a husband bought to accept your hand."

The lady, though, seemed to be amused. "You feel strongly of the matter."

"I do."

"It is a fine sentiment, sir, but you must recall that I am not Lady Heloise or the Lord de Tulley's niece. I am a mere orphan of no legacy or lineage."

"You are a maiden of much merit," Lothair replied. "Any man would be fortunate to have you by his side."

"But you declined."

He pushed a hand through his hair and marched beside her for long moments, choosing his words. He was seldom so agitated as this, and it confounded him. Magdala, however, seemed content to grant him all the time he needed.

At least until they reached the lower gates. Then she would walk through them and vanish. His innards clenched at the very prospect.

They passed the tavern and he noted that there was more activity in the street as the sun rose. "I have little to offer a wife, save my own self and my skills," he confessed finally.

"I have no more to offer a husband," she replied. "Those who knew the truth of our respective circumstances would call this a fortunate match for me." She spoke dispassionately, as if they discussed strangers, but Lothair was far from indifferent to the topic of their conversation.

"But I must have truth in marriage," he continued. "And now you know the price offered by the Lord de Tulley to encourage my agreement."

"And now that there is truth between us, what is your inclination, sir?"

Lothair shook his head. "Nay, my lady, you name it amiss. The sole question is *your* inclination." He dared to catch her hand in his, pulling her to a stop beside him. She looked up at him, curiosity in her gaze and he wanted the chance to encourage her to regard him with a far warmer response. "I will wed you as he decrees, and I will honor our match until the end of my days, even if the Lord de Tulley does not fulfill his promise. The choice, though, must be yours." She looked down at their hands and he was certain she would decline.

"He means to achieve a goal," she said softly. "He means to ensure that I do not leave the keep, and also that I feel myself defended." She raised her gaze to Lothair's again and studied him. "And he means to guarantee that you remain here, as well. Is there a reason you might depart otherwise?"

Lothair shook his head. "Why should he care?"

"Because he ensures the welfare of all beneath his hand. Because he believes our match would be a fitting one. Because he trusts you to defend his objectives at any price." She inhaled and he again sensed her fear. "Because something will occur when Lord Herbert arrives, and he wishes both of us to be present at that moment."

"Perhaps he fears the intentions of his nephew."

"How so and why?"

Lothair chose to confide his suspicions. It was cursedly easy to speak with this lady, to be certain. "Lady Verena and her husband died in quick succession, clearing the path for Lord Herbert to gain his inheritance. I have wondered if their demises were encouraged, and whether Lady Heloise knew something about that, something to the disadvantage of her brother."

Magdala caught her breath. "She was on her way here and might have shared the tale with the Lord de Tulley."

"Who would have ensured that justice was served, I wager."

"Of course, he would have done. Although I cannot believe that Lord Herbert would be so vile."

"I thought you distrusted him."

She flushed. "I do, but not to such an extent." Before Lothair could question that, Magdala clutched his hand. "You do not think the Lord de Tulley is in danger?"

Lothair eyed her, impressed that she could be so concerned for the older man, then shook his head. "And you would defend him, though he toys with your fate. You are loyal, my lady."

"He knew my truth all along but treated me well." She smiled. "My loyalty is earned."

And she would never surrender it. Kind, loyal and thoughtful of others, if ever there had been a woman fit to claim Lothair's heart, truly she stood before him. "Choose, my lady. I entreat you."

"You would have me after all?"

"I would be honored to have your hand in mine." It was true, but he saw surprise in her eyes. "I simply could not swear as much before you knew the fullness of the tale."

She smiled at him so suddenly that he was dazzled and could not look away from her relief.

"Then I propose, sir, that we comply with the Lord de Tulley's scheme." Her eyes shone, a sight so alluring that Lothair seized the moment to convince her of his admiration. He caught her close, lifting her in his arms to capture her lips sweetly beneath his own. He felt her hesitation and belatedly recalled her experience with Niall—but then she melted against him, her mouth opening to his in glorious surrender, her fingers sliding up his chest to rest against his jaw.

To call their embrace a kiss could only discount its power.

Lothair was stirred beyond all expectation—not just to desire but to a protectiveness that was more vehement than any he had known before. Not only had Magdala confided in him, her very manner ensuring that he trusted her word utterly, but she offered a kiss to sear his very soul.

He was utterly seduced.

He could not recall an interval or an exchange with Aileen that had so addled his thoughts and confounded him—and certainly not a kiss. He was seldom so overwhelmed by emotion that he forgot himself, and never due to a woman's caress.

But Magdala had changed that.

Lothair scarce knew her. This should have concerned him mightily. It should have made him cautious, if not wary, of a maiden who kindled such a fire within him.

Yet he did not care.

The realization should have prompted him to break his kiss, rather than deepen it, but Magdala was irresistible. This was a precarious situation for a man of reason and a knight such as himself. And what of the future? Would one night abed see him sated and his reason restored? Or would he be in thrall to this mysterious lady forevermore?

Even that notion did not stir him to saddle his steed and ride away from temptation.

Instead, he lifted his head, smiling at the sparkle in her eyes and the flush in her cheeks. He brushed his lips across hers gently, unable to deny himself one more taste. She sighed and leaned against him, so content that he could have carried her back to his chamber above the stables that very moment.

"I am glad," she whispered. "I did not wish to walk that road alone."

"And now you do not have to," he said, hearing that his own voice was husky. Aware that the town bustled to wakefulness around them and that more than one curious glance was being bestowed upon them, he took Magdala's hand and led her back to the keep, to give the Lord de Tulley the tidings that man expected.

If his heart was singing, no one need know of it.

~

MAGDALA HAD no notion that a kiss could be so stirring or so enthralling. She had no idea that such a caress could stir her with such vigor. She was nigh dizzy when Lothair lifted his head and though she noted a gleam of satisfaction in his eyes, the man remained as inscrutable as ever. Had he not found their embrace potent?

Or was he accustomed to sharing such embraces? For Magdala, his kiss was a revelation and a promise of future pleasure. If this was what could be conjured between two people and readily, then what she had known of men was less than half the tale.

She could not wait to learn more, from Lothair.

They walked back to the keep in companionable silence, her hand secure within his own. She was aware of a shiver of awareness thrumming through her veins but he might have been untouched by their embrace.

What would it be like to stir this man to passion? What would it be like to see him abandon himself to sensation? Magdala wished very much to know. To be sure, there had been a hunger in his kiss, but it had been tempered and controlled. Perhaps that had been part of its sorcery, for she knew that he would have halted at the most subtle sign from her. She felt empowered in his embrace, alluring and desired.

That only made her anticipate learning more.

The Lord de Tulley was clearly content to see them arrive together. He sat in his chemise and robes in the solar, sipping of a hot brew prepared by Felix, who stood behind his chair. Lothair waited by the portal in characteristic silence, letting Magdala explain that they had agreed to wed after all.

The old man beamed at her.

"You smile only because you won your way," Magdala accused

him, her tone teasing. Indeed, her heart was lighter than it had been in a long while. To remain at Château Tulley was her greatest desire: to do as much as Lothair's wife and the truth known to all three of them was beyond her dreams.

The older man chuckled. "There is satisfaction to be had in that, to be sure," he admitted. His gaze brightened. "You will fare well together, I believe. I have arranged many a match in my time but this may be the one with the most promise."

Lothair did not smile, but then Magdala no longer expected as much of him. There was a contentment in his manner, though she could not have precisely named what granted that impression.

Perhaps she came to know him better. The notion prompted her own smile.

"And what of Magdala's name?" Lothair asked.

"What of it?"

"When will you reveal the truth to the household?"

"Not soon," the Lord de Tulley said, to Magdala's surprise.

"But before the nuptials, certainly," she protested.

The older man shook his head. "I must witness Herbert's expression in the moment that he realizes the truth. There can be no chance of him learning that Heloise is dead before he appears before me."

"Do you know when he will arrive?" Magdala asked, disliking this edict and feeling Lothair's disapproval of it.

"Nay." The Lord de Tulley was untroubled. He finished his tonic and set the cup aside. "I would rest, Felix. The nuptials will be three days hence and I leave the arrangements in your hands, Magdala." He fixed Lothair with a look when that man did not move. "Have you no duties this day?"

"What of the lady's name?" that man repeated. "When will you reveal it?"

"In my chosen time!" the old lord said with impatience. "You wed the maiden not her name. I will have this secret kept until I decree that the truth be revealed." He snorted. "If ever I do. Is that understood?"

"I would not like to deceive my comrades," Lothair insisted and Magdala saw that this was the root of his concern. There must be trust and honesty between men who have fought together, and she could appreciate that he would not like to hide a truth from them.

The Lord de Tulley waved this objection away. "They are deceived already and none the wiser for it. I see no cause for confession, not before Herbert's arrival, and if I recall correctly, my word is law in this holding." He glared at both of them in turn and Magdala knew he would not be swayed.

"Of course, sir," she said and bent to kiss his hand before leaving him.

"Stay," the old lord insisted. "I would have some of that unguent on my back again before I rest."

Lothair's expression was inscrutable but Magdala was certain she could sense his disapproval. Was that about her lingering in the solar, or the lord's decision not to reveal her name?

"Use a little less," he advised as she retrieved the jar.

She showed him how much she would use. "Is there a risk with it?"

His lips drew to a thin line. "I will tell you of it later." His gaze clung to hers, as if there was something he would say but could not find the words. Before he managed to do as much, the Lord de Tulley dismissed him tersely.

Magdala watched him go, resolving in that moment to seek him out at earliest convenience.

"You mean to wed a stubborn man," the Lord de Tulley said under his breath once the door was closed.

Magdala smiled, not willing to have her relief diminished. "Perhaps that bodes well for my future," she replied lightly. "For I have grown accustomed to such men. I should not know what to do with one who ceded to me in all matters."

The Lord de Tulley laughed aloud, his good humor restored as surely as Magdala's own had been.

Wed and in three days time! Magdala could not believe all had come so right.

CHAPTER 9

*L*othair did not deign to wait upon the Lord de Tulley at midday. He was irked with the older man, disliking that he would be obliged to deceive his former comrades. He spent the morning drilling the sentries and reviewing the smith's work in maintaining the armory, then supervised Quentin and Calum's sparring. At midday, Felix appeared in the bailey and he braced himself for a reprimand.

Instead, the Lord de Tulley's favored servant offered a familiar chest to him.

At Lothair's nod, they retired to his chamber over the stables and Lothair threw open the shutters to admit the sunlight. He moved the single table beneath the window and watched as Felix placed the chest upon it, unlocked it and displayed the contents to Lothair.

"My lord requests that you summon me when you have finished your reading for the day," that man said. "He would see this secured in the treasury each night."

"Of course," Lothair agreed, unable to believe his good fortune.

Felix left, murmuring to someone at the door and Lothair assumed that Calum came to him. Instead, it was Magdala that stepped into his chamber, her eyes alight with curiosity. She looked at him with unexpected interest, then crossed to the chest. "This is it then," she said. "The prize for which you have sold your soul." She spoke lightly and he could tell that she was not pleased to see it in his possession already.

"I had no notion he would send it to me."

"Today or ever?"

"Ever."

"He promised, did he not?"

"And I defied him." Lothair's hand rose of its own volition to the edge of the chest. "I fully expected him to withhold it."

She was watching him but when he glanced at her, she averted her gaze, conjuring the small vial of the unguent from the folds of her skirts. "It is almost gone. I wondered if you would teach me to mix it."

"I would if you knew more." He continued before she could respond, for he had seen the flash of her eyes. "I had a teacher most strict about access to poisons, and I follow his model. It is too easy to err and the implications are not small."

"Poisons?"

He unlocked his own chest of ingredients and set several on the table beside the chest. "There are many herbs that can kill in one quantity but are helpful in lesser amounts. You will have noticed the heat that mixture makes beneath your hands."

She nodded, her eyes alight with curiosity. "Of course."

"That comes from wolf's bane, also called aconite."

"Monkshood," she said. "It has a blue flower in late summer."

"The very one." He opened a small bottle and showed her the powder within it. "The root must be dried then ground to a powder."

She considered the few powders he had set out in bottles. "So many look the same."

"So it is of import to clearly label them." He indicated where he had done as much, then wondered whether she could read. "Learn its scent but do not inhale of it."

She did as instructed, then grimaced. "It is sharp. And hot."

"On the skin, in small quantities, it warms the skin and dulls the pain as it is absorbed. When ingested, and in larger quantities, it burns from within. It is a quick and efficient poison, with no antidote."

Magdala returned the bottle to him with the respect it deserved. "That powder looks similar."

"Ground from the dried paste harvested from the seed pod of the sleeping poppy. Also poison, but slower."

"How so?"

"A small amount encourages drowsiness. A larger dose conjures sleep and dreams. A yet larger dose provokes a slumber with no awakening." He lifted the bottle of poppy powder. "If one was to choose how to end one's days in haste, I would select the poppy powder over the wolf's bane."

"One would simply fall asleep and never wake," she guessed and Lothair nodded. "And now you have the book to peruse. I will not detain you from your studies."

Curiously, he could not tell if this troubled her or not. He felt awkward that he had been granted this inducement and that she was witness to it, but truly, her expression was so impassive that he could not guess her thoughts.

He did not know what to say, so he mixed the unguent as she watched, reminded her to be cautious of its quantity, then watched in silence as she left. She granted him a polite smile from the portal and then she was gone.

Yet Lothair felt that somehow he had erred and mightily.

MAGDALA REMINDED herself that she had never expected to be wed at all, much less to be placing her hand in that of a knight and crusader. She had never thought she would have a husband at all, let alone one whose kiss set her very soul afire. She was accustomed to being found useful, even attractive, and should have been glad that Lothair spoke to her as if she was a person of sense.

Still, it was irksome to be aware of her price.

She bade herself forget it and be glad of her good fortune, yet she could not. The abbess had always said that good fortune led to greed, and Magdala had never understood the caution until now. It was true that she had unexpectedly gained many blessings, but as the abbess had warned, that made her wish for even more.

She wanted to be Lothair's wife and partner in every possible way. Perhaps that would come in time. Perhaps it would not, but she would do her best and hope it might suffice.

The next few days passed swiftly for Magdala, for there was so much to do. Two of the women in the village had been retained by the Lord de Tulley to embellish Magdala's finest gown, there being a lack of silk available soon enough for the creation of a new one. Her favored red kirtle was whisked away to be embroidered with gold. The women also were charged to make silk slippers for her, embroidered with gold, and a fine new girdle of gold. A lovely veil was hemmed for her, woven of silk as fine as gossamer, and a golden circlet was made by the goldsmith for her own. Two more women sewed new linen chemises for the couple, their needles flying late into the night.

The Lord de Tulley granted Magdala the crucifix she had often worn in the past at his insistence, making it her own. Lothair, she knew, was instructed to choose a ring from the treasury, though she would not see it before the ceremony.

She did not doubt that Lothair's squire, Calum, was busily ensuring that his knight would look his best. Invitations were dispatched to Beauvoir, to Annossy and to Sayerne, and provisions were acquired. The kitchens were bustling, Antoine shouting all the day long. Lothair led a company to hunt each morning, reporting to the Lord de Tulley on his return of their success. The rushes in the hall were changed, the chapel was cleaned, and the other chamber alongside Magdala's own was swept and aired for the guests. It was resolved that Lothair would join her in her chamber after their vows were exchanged and his former comrades would share his chamber over the stables. The other finer room would be granted to the Lord de Beauvoir and his wife.

The days were filled with the bustle of preparations, both for the feast and the arrival of the guests, but the evenings were Magdala's favored time. She found an excuse to seek out Lothair each midday and several times found him in his chamber with the book. He explained more the role of those herbs he carried and she prepared the calendula ointment under his instruction.

Felix professed himself well pleased by the results and the Lord de Tulley beamed that she undertook the tasks favored by his mother and grandmother. One afternoon, she and Lothair conferred in the garden, a rare day when the Lord de Tulley descended there to savor the sunlight. Lothair identified most of the plants and reviewed their placement, the Lord de Tulley recalling various details as they wrought a plan to see it all returned to rights.

At the board each night, she sat between Lothair and the Lord de Tulley, listening as they discussed details of the keep—which most often meant that the older man instructed the younger on the history of his holding. Lothair kissed Magdala's hand each evening before he left the hall, and it might have been said that her dreams of those nights were the sweetest she had ever known.

Indeed, for once in all her days, Magdala dared to believe that all would be well.

As MUCH AS Lothair wished to reveal Magdala's name to his former comrades, the Lord de Tulley would not be swayed. What game did the old lord play with them all? Never had Lothair felt so much that he was snared in a trap for the amusement of another, and he did not like that sense at all.

He also did not like being any part of a deception, however small, and did not know how he would greet his friends. Quinn would not have taken issue with that, for so long as Lothair was content with his match, so was Quinn.

Niall, however, was another matter. The swelling in that man's nose had diminished markedly by the time their party arrived from Annossy, and the bruising was turning from deep purple to an unfortunate hue of green. Lothair might have checked the healing of the nose, but Niall seemed intent upon having an argument. Truly, the injury gave him a rakish and reckless air, and Lothair could not doubt he had already used it to advantage.

Magdala barely glanced at the other knight, much to Niall's dissatisfaction, and vanished into the great hall with Melissande, Berthe and the two infants.

"You have fared well for yourself," Niall said when the four of them took their leisure together in the stables. Quinn, Niall and Bayard had all requested a bath, and the tub had been rolled into a corner of the stables for their use.

Their squires had been dismissed once the tub was filled and Lothair had ensured that there was no one to heed their conversation. He even abandoned his own hauberk, sending Calum to polish it for the nuptials, while he spoke with his friends in chemise and chausses. The air was filled with steam but the atmosphere less convivial than might have been hoped.

As ever, they had chosen to ignore rank and cast the dice instead for first use of the water. Bayard had won and Quinn had already teased him that he always won, so he must somehow cheat. A friendly dispute had ensued, and they might have been in Outremer again, so familiar was their camaraderie.

So too was Bayard's long bath. That man was as disinclined to hasten as ever, ducking his head into the water and splashing with satisfaction. The way he savored the hot water made Lothair suspect it would be cold long before the other two knights had the opportunity to use it—but that was not a new experience either. He sent word to the kitchens that they would need more hot water. Quinn stood in his chemise and boots, tolerant of the other man as ever, while Niall wore only his chausses and fairly seethed with impatience.

It was not the bath that truly troubled Niall, though.

He cast Lothair a glare when Lothair did not reply. "But a matter of days in the château and you, of all men, are chosen to wed the Lord de Tulley's sole niece!"

"You of all men," Bayard echoed. "There is an insult I should not let pass."

"Indeed," Quinn agreed. "Why not Lothair?"

"Hasten yourself," Niall urged Bayard, who smiled and sank slowly below the surface of the bath, blowing bubbles all the while. "But *why* Lothair?" he demanded when it was clear that Bayard no longer listened. "Already you are Captain of the Guard of a formidable holding, but now you will have an heiress to wife, as well."

"She may not be an heiress," Lothair said but Niall scoffed.

"Next Niall will insist it is not fair," Bayard said to Quinn, emerging from the water. "But life is seldom fair."

Quinn nodded, watching the exchange with bright eyes.

"I suppose you will insist that 'tis love that guides your hand," Niall said, propping his hands on his hips, his tone filled with challenge.

Surely he would not insist upon a duel.

"The lady *is* admirable," Quinn said, clearly trying to soothe the tension between the two knights. "Any man might lose his heart to her."

"Save a man who is reputed to be without one," Niall retorted.

"A beauty of considerable charm," Bayard agreed, reaching for a cloth. "We should celebrate Lothair's good fortune." He rubbed his chin. "Do you think I have need of a shave?" he asked Quinn.

"You always have need of a shave, in my view," that man said.

"Aye." Bayard's dark brows rose. "Given my swarthy good looks."

Quinn laughed and Bayard splashed some water at him.

"She was stolen from me!" Niall roared as if they had said naught. "Nigh two years I spent diligently courting this maiden, softening her reserve, awakening her to the possibilities..."

Bayard scoffed in his turn. "You do not teach *all* women of desire, Niall."

"Perhaps you courted her so long without results because her heart was not stirred," Quinn suggested, earning a dark glance from Niall.

"Perhaps someone else has seized the prize without earning it, cheating me of my reward."

"The Lord de Tulley decreed the match," Lothair said.

Bayard chuckled and splashed in the tub. "Perhaps you should have endeavored to charm him instead of the lady," he jested, but Niall did not smile.

"You might have declined the honor," he said to Lothair, who felt the back of his neck heating.

"I had no such inclination," he confessed. "And the lady seemed content."

"Woo hoo!" Bayard crowed. "The truth is revealed! Lothair had already noticed the lady." He dropped his voice to a conspiratorial whisper. "Was that why you returned from Provins with such haste?"

"The Lord de Tulley invited me to return," Lothair said stiffly.

"Because of your concoction," Bayard recalled. "Perhaps you taught the miller's wife how to make it as part of a scheme to be rewarded by the Lord de Tulley."

Lothair glared at him. "That would be a plan beyond all expectation."

"Though the Lord de Tulley is aged and often has had a cough in winter," Quinn noted. That man smiled. "But I cannot believe that you anticipated this lady might become your wife, no matter what favor you did for the lord."

"I could not have so conspired it and would not have done," Lothair said with heat. "She is a fine lady, a maiden of honor and integrity, and I am beyond fortunate in this match."

Quinn raised his brows. "So fortunate as to be fulsome," he murmured.

"Again," Niall noted, his dissatisfaction apparently dismissed by this.

All three knights studied Lothair openly.

"You do not mention her beauty," Bayard teased. "Are you unaware of it?"

"I have noticed, of course, that she is most comely." Lothair's neck might have been on fire.

"Comely?" Niall echoed, flinging out his hands. "She is a beauty!"

Lothair continued, his manner stony. "But that was not the reason I accepted her hand."

"Why did you, then?" Niall asked. "If it was neither her beauty nor her fortune that tempted you, what made you agree to wed her?"

Lothair opened his mouth and closed it again, well aware that his friends watched him closely. He frowned and cleared his throat. "I like her." Saying it once made it easier to declare the truth again. "I like her well."

They were astonished to momentary silence.

"What has that to do with the matter?" Niall asked, apparently perplexed.

"Who would willingly join his life to that of a person he despised?" Lothair asked. Niall shook his head and hastened to Bayard to hurry, as if Lothair was incomprehensible. Lothair cleared his throat. "And it occurred to me that a lady of such gentle manner and beauty might have need of protection."

Niall spun to face him. "She had no need of protection from me." He pointed a finger at Lothair. "Was that why you interrupted us? Because you had schemed even then to claim her for your own?"

"Scheme! I had no scheme." Lothair knew his expression was grim. "I interrupted because the lady had need of aid."

"She welcomed my embrace!" Niall protested.

"Aye, I could tell by the way she broke your nose," Lothair said and Bayard laughed.

"She was the one who did as much? Ha, I like her better already."

Niall granted the other warrior a dark glance. "It was a misunderstanding."

"And one of such import that even you, with your gilded tongue, could not put right," Quinn noted.

"His gilded tongue might have been the issue," Bayard whispered wickedly. "Not every maiden wishes to make its acquaintance." He wagged his tongue at Niall, who dove toward him laughing. The pair tussled over the side of the tub until Bayard hauled Niall into the water. That man landed in the tub with a splash and a bellow, then they wrestled in truth as the water spilled over the edges. When they began to laugh, Lothair knew that Niall's customary mood had been restored.

"It is her loss," that man said, pushing Bayard under the surface playfully. "She missed her chance to enjoy me."

"Doubtless she prays even now in gratitude for her escape," Bayard said, his tone taunting. "Besides, would the goat girl not miss you if you wed an heiress?"

"Wed? Who spoke of my nuptials?"

"What of the brewster's daughter? Or the widow of that cloth-monger? Or…"

Niall pushed his former comrade beneath the surface again as they laughed together.

Lothair realized belatedly that Quinn was watching him closely. "I hope you did not feel compelled to wed against your will?"

"Nay. Never that."

"But I understood you never meant to wed again," Quinn said quietly.

"I never meant to wed the first time," Lothair confessed. "This time, at least, it is my choice."

There were a dozen other details that Lothair could have confessed, but he was bound by Tulley's dictate to keep Magdala's secret. He also did not think it wise to reveal the precarious state of the Lord de Tulley's health to one of that man's vassals, even if they were friends, though he was tempted to confide in Quinn.

That knight studied him in silence for a long moment, then nodded, clapping his hand on Lothair's shoulder as he turned to the others. "I, for one, am glad that Lothair has been persuaded to take a bride. I believe he and the lady will be well suited to each other and I will be glad indeed to know he is close at hand." He turned back to Lothair with a smile. "You must come to visit at Annossy when the Lord de Tulley allows as much."

"I thank you," Lothair said, unable to speculate when that might be.

Certainly not before Herbert's anticipated arrival.

MAGDALA SCARCE SLEPT the night before the nuptials, so great was her anticipation. She awakened to a perfect summer's day, the sky so clear and blue that a cloud would not dare to mar it. The women came from the village to aid her with the kirtle, which was the finest garment that ever she had seen. Her thanks were so heartfelt that the one woman wiped away a tear, while the other could not suppress her smile.

The Lord de Tulley was outside her door when she opened it, his eyes glinting as he surveyed her. The women fluttered past her like birds, daunted by his presence, but he smiled and bade Felix to see their fee paid. He winked at the loyal servant when the women had bowed and retreated and Magdala smiled at him.

"You mean to see them paid more generously than they expected."

"And why should I not?" he said, bowing over her hand. "This is a day of celebration, and I would have all share in my joy."

"One might think you had contrived this match long ago," she teased, taking his elbow as they began down the stairs.

"And where is it writ that I did not?" he demanded gruffly, chortling at her sidelong glance of surprise. "I know who should be together," he continued. "I always have. When Lothair of Sutherland left, I wished I had a reason to summon his return, for I sensed that you and he would fare well together."

"You said naught of this to me."

"If I had, you would not have heard me, so occupied were you in holding the attention of that scoundrel Niall MacGillivray."

"Heloise would have adored him."

"Aye, which is no good endorsement, to be sure."

"Sir!" she protested and he chuckled at her outrage.

"Do not fear for his future. There will be a maiden for him, but not you, my child. The lady who desires the heart of that knight will have a battle to claim it securely, to be sure." He patted her hand as they reached the hall. "Nay, I would see you with a stalwart man, one who would never give you any cause for doubt. You have borne sufficient uncertainty already in your days."

His words warmed Magdala's heart and she kissed his cheek in gratitude. Her salute was witnessed by many in the hall who beamed with approval.

They approached the chapel and Magdala saw Lothair standing by the door, awaiting her. His mail was polished to brilliance, and his tabard seemed a deeper hue of green than she recalled. She gazed upon him with a strange mix of anticipation and conviction in her heart. He was speaking to Quinn, who stood behind him, but turned as he sensed her presence. Their gazes locked and held, and it seemed she could not draw a full breath. Then Lothair smiled as never she had seen him smile before, the expression softening his features and making him look both younger and more handsome.

"Good day, sir," she said, her words breathless when she and the Lord de Tulley halted before him.

"It is a good day, my lady," Lothair said with quiet conviction, taking her hand in his. "It may, indeed, be the very best day of all."

Magdala blinked in surprise that this man, of all men, should find such fine words.

Quinn chuckled at her reaction and Lothair's neck reddened.

The Lord de Tulley harrumphed and relinquished Magdala's hand. "Make haste about it," he said to the priest. "I cannot stand in this draft forever."

"Oh, sir, they have brought your chair," Magdala said, having instructed that should be done.

Felix appeared behind the older man with the chair in question, and placed it as close as possible to the church door. The Lord de Tulley sank into it with relief.

"I still see no cause for delay," he said gruffly, and Magdala bent to kiss his cheek.

"Nor do I, sir." She looked into his eyes. "I thank you," she whispered and he snorted, gesturing to the priest to begin.

Magdala turned and placed her other hand upon Lothair's, staring into his eyes as the priest made the blessing. The exchange of their vows was profoundly moving to Magdala, and a reminder of her remarkable good fortune. She felt that time stood still as she faced the man who would be her husband for all time. Then Lothair lifted her left hand in his, holding a ring between his finger and thumb as he placed it above each of her fingers in turn.

"In the name of the Father, the Son and the Holy Spirit," he said, then slid the wide golden band onto her ring finger. "Amen."

"Amen," Magdala whispered, her heart in her throat.

But was she wed to Lothair in truth? The priest had called her Heloise.

Uncertainty rose within Magdala but she did not know who might answer her doubt. For once she and Lothair consummated their match, her maidenhead would be gone, whether they were truly wed or not.

Perhaps she worried over naught at all.

The doors were flung open and they were ushered into the chapel for the Mass. Laughter broke out among the company when they returned to the great hall. A cask of wine was opened and one of ale, the minstrels began to play, and the new couple were offered congratulations by all in attendance. The Lord de Tulley sank into his great chair to watch with obvious satisfaction.

Magdala noticed the glint in the older man's eyes as she accepted the good wishes of those in attendance and a cup of Annossy wine.

"What is amiss?" Lothair murmured, the weight of his hand upon the back of her waist sending a thrill through her. His touch felt possessive and reminded her of their one kiss, filling her with anticipation for the night ahead.

She also liked that he had noticed her concern.

She turned to him, finding herself almost in his arms, and the company hooted approval, evidently concluding that they would kiss. "Are we wed in truth?" she whispered as Lothair bent and brushed his mouth across hers, a tantalizing sensation that left her wanting more of his touch.

"Why would we not be?" he breathed, apparently unable to tear his gaze from hers.

Magdala knew he was not fascinated with her. "But the priest called me Heloise."

"And you are my wife, no matter your name." Lothair lowered his head and claimed her lips in a long slow kiss. Magdala closed her eyes and found herself clinging to his tunic as she was swept away by sensation.

"I will ensure there is no doubt, my lady," Lothair murmured against her temple, his hand sweeping up the length of her back. Relief flooded through her, though she did not know what he might do. "I vow it to you."

And even though she had no notion what he might do or say, Magdala trusted him.

Lothair spun her before him, his unexpected move making Magdala laugh with delight. Her view of the company swirled, but her attention was snared by one face at the back.

Mallory!

Nay, it was the man who resembled him.

Again.

When Lothair placed her hand upon his elbow and guided her across the hall, Magdala glanced back, hoping to catch a glimpse of that man again. A longer look might dismiss her impression that the guard from Idelstein yet lived and breathed, but she could not spy him in the company again.

Had he even been there?

Had her eyes played a trick upon her?

Then the Lord de Tulley waved for the meal to be served and she was so occupied that she forgot the mysterious man once again.

ONCE AGAIN, Lothair resented the Lord de Tulley's instruction. It was unfair that Magdala fretted about the verity of their vows, and he saw no cause for her to be so troubled. Why could they not have revealed her deception and forgiven it? Why could he not have wed Magdala before all, instead of Heloise?

He had no intention of letting the match be dissolved, which meant he had to dismiss her fears.

Fortunately, he knew how he might do as much, though he could not act until they were alone together.

At the Lord de Tulley's summons, there was a fanfare from the minstrels and a line of servants entered the hall, evidently having come from the kitchens. Each in the line carried a platter or a large bowl, a procession of fine food worthy of a great celebration, and the smell was sufficient to make more than one stomach growl in anticipation. The company applauded with enthusiasm and Magdala clearly joined in their approval. There was a roast boar, as well as both a swan and a peacock dressed in their own feathers, and all the bounty of the recent hunt. There were pies and tarts, eggs in sauce, stews and breads and every manner of indulgence.

"This for a niece!" the Lord de Beauvoir declared with delight. "Imagine, Lady Heloise, if you were my old comrade's own daughter! The abundance would be astonishing."

The Lord de Tulley snorted, but his expression was indulgent. He patted Magdala's hand even as he turned to eye the procession drawing close to the high table. "I expect a son within the year, my dear," he said softly, command underlying his tone.

Lothair saw that she was untroubled by this request, though it was one that sent a jolt of fear through him. Was this the root of it then? The old lord wanted children at Château Tulley? But any children of Magdala and Lothair would share no blood with the old lord. It made little sense, but then, men in their dotage often had fancies—and Lothair could not blame any man who was enchanted by Magdala.

Not when he was utterly beguiled himself.

A child, though. He strove to forget that long-ago night and hide his concern.

"I shall do my best, sir," Magdala replied to the old lord's obvious satisfaction.

The Lord de Tulley and the Lord de Beauvoir began to talk of old times, Lady Beauvoir sitting silently between them, her gaze darting from one man to the other unless it was upon the board.

"A quiet woman," Lothair said to Magdala and she smiled up at him.

"Always," she confided. "I am not certain I would recognize her voice if I heard it." She smiled and his heart warmed at the sight. He placed his hand upon the back of her waist, liking that they were to share a trencher. Quinn and Melissande were seated to his left, while Niall sat with the company.

The platter of roast boar was brought first to the Lord de Tulley by Calum and another boy. The platter was too large for either to carry it alone, though the gleam of anticipation in Calum's eyes was utterly predictable.

The cook himself, Antoine, followed the platter and carved it before them all, placing choice pieces on the trencher of the Lord de Tulley first, then on that of Lothair and Magdala. Of course, Felix tasted from the old lord's trencher before that man consumed a bite, but no one in the hall seemed overly concerned by this routine caution. The merriment gained in volume as the meal was served and both ale and wine flowed, and Lothair strove to enjoy the festivities.

In truth, he wanted only to have Magdala alone, the better to set her concerns to rest, but patience was the key on this night.

CHAPTER 10

Magdala's heart was racing as she and Lothair were seen to her chamber by what seemed to be the entire household. His expression was inscrutable, though she glanced his way repeatedly in the hope of discerning some emotion. The most she could have guessed of his mood was that he was tolerant of the enthusiasm of the others. He had said little at dinner, beyond advising that Calum exercise restraint.

She had spoken with Melissande, though she had been concerned that she might make an error as she did not know the extent of that lady's relations with Heloise. It was irksome to continue the ruse but she had been glad of Lothair's presence and attentiveness. His touch steadied her and fed her confidence that all would be well.

At the foot of the stairs, in the hall, he offered his hand to her and she had placed hers atop it. He had nodded slightly and they began their ascent together, the chattering household gathered behind them. Even the Lord de Tulley himself followed, his cane thumping on each step.

Magdala counted the steps. Lothair said naught at all to her, though she could feel the warmth emanating from him. For her part, she was chilled to the bone.

A wedding night.

More importantly, a consummation. Her uncertainties rose with every step. It was inevitable, necessary, and just moments away. Had that kiss been an exception or would she feel thus with him each time? She could not help but think of Herbert and even of Niall, though truly she wished to think of her lord husband. Magdala wished he might have climbed the stairs more slowly. It was too soon that they reached the next floor and she could see her own door. Two maids from the kitchens flanked that opening and Magdala realized the candles had been lit in the chamber already. The maids were beaming with excitement.

Lothair swept her ahead of him to enter the room and she considered, for a moment, the merit of refusing to cross the threshold. He had every right to carry her into the chamber if she did not proceed by her own choice, and claim her thus however he so close. She wanted to be wed to him—she simply wished to be certain of the law before her maidenhead was lost.

But he had promised her.

She had to trust him in this moment.

Magdala swallowed and entered the room, her agitation such that she was blind to the changes there. She saw only the blur of golden light from dozens of beeswax candles and felt their heat. Her gaze slipped over the bed, now adorned with new linens, the drapes pulled back to grant a view to all.

Lothair kissed her hand and she caught his intent glance before she was surrounded by jovial women. It seemed a dozen busy hands removed her finery with relentless ease and she was powerless to halt them. It would have been rude to protest but it was unsettling to be disrobed so quickly.

She looked up to see that Lothair was similarly besieged. He caught her gaze and almost smiled, that steady look alone sufficient to calm her.

Her girdle was set aside, the veil and circlet beside it, her kirtle folded, her slippers removed along with her stockings. Her hair was unbraided and combed out, then a maid with a merry twinkle in her eye unfastened the lace on her chemise. The women laughed.

Magdala was turned to face Lothair, only to find that he, too, wore only his chemise. His hung to his knees while hers swept the floor, but both garments were wrought of white linen and newly made for this day.

With the encouragement of the company, they stepped toward each other as one. Lothair caught her hands in his and bent to kiss her, so sweet and potent an embrace that her fears melted away.

All would be well. She tasted his promise in his slow kiss.

The women escorted Magdala to one side of the bed, whispering encouragement behind her, while the men urged Lothair to the other side of the bed. The linens were drawn back and they climbed onto the plump mattress as one. It had been her bed for as long as she had been at Château Tulley, but Magdala had always slept in the middle, alone. It was curious to have Lothair's heat beside her, to be compelled to remain on one side, to be aware of his weight dipping the mattress as if even the bed would compel her into his embrace.

There was a rap of a cane as the Lord de Tulley approached the bed, his eyes glinting and a rare smile upon his lips. "May your match be blessed each day and each night," he said, and Magdala lowered her gaze as she flushed. She saw Lothair's strong hand close over her own and caught her breath. She felt herself tremble and knew he would not miss her reaction. She swallowed and turned her hand so that she could grasp his fingers.

Lothair gave her hand a squeeze, so slowly and deliberately that she believed he understood.

"A son within the year is usually the Lord de Tulley's edict," Quinn said and his wife laughed.

"I have made it known," the old lord said and there was laughter aplenty.

The priest blessed them and the bed, then the curtains were unbound at the sides and allowed to close. Magdala exhaled in relief as shadows closed around them. There was only a view over the foot of the bed, toward the door, and the last thing she saw before Lothair's fingers rose to her chin was the old lord's nod of satisfaction.

Then Lothair turned her face toward him. His gaze locked with hers, his scrutiny searching, then he shook his head slightly as if to tease her—and he smiled. "I salute you, my lady wife," he whispered, his voice so low that only she would hear his words, and then he touched his lips to hers so sweetly that her heart thundered.

She had expected a possessive and demanding kiss this time, but his embrace was so gentle that her fears seemed foolish. When he broke their kiss, her heart was racing and he studied her for a moment before he turned away.

He surveyed those gathered, with their expectant expressions, then spoke with finality. "You will close the portal behind yourselves." There was a flutter of protest, but Lothair continued with authority. "My lady will find her satisfaction in privacy or not at all."

Magdala saw the Lord de Tulley nod approval, then he was the first to depart. He mustered the others out of the chamber, encouraging them to hasten, then reached himself to close the portal.

Magdala saw him wink, the old devil.

She heard the sound of a key being turned in the lock, then watched in amazement as the key was slipped beneath the door with sufficient force that it only halted when it had traveled half the distance to the bed.

And then she was alone with Lothair, in her bed, in candlelit silence.

~

"THEY ARE GONE," Lothair said, his fingertip beneath her chin again. "And now we begin in truth. What is this of vows?"

"The priest called me Heloise," Magdala repeated. "Which must mean that we are not wed."

"I say that we are, and before witnesses, but we can improve upon that." He rose from the bed and beckoned to her. Magdala joined him, uncertain of his intention but trusting him. "Marriage is the sole sacrament that requires only God as witness," he said, taking her hands in his. "And so, we shall pledge each to the other, here in the sight of God."

Magdala was delighted by the suggestion. "You do not think me foolish?"

"I do not wish you to have any doubt that you are my lady wife," he said with a surety that made her heart glow. Then he repeated the vows they had exchanged earlier, his gaze clinging to hers. Magdala repeated hers as well. Lothair even removed the ring from her finger and repeated the incantation before seating it upon her finger once more.

Magdala was relieved in truth.

"Better?" he asked softly.

They were standing toe to toe in their chemises, bathed in the light of dozens of candles. The air was warm with the scent of beeswax and Magdala could not help but smile in her relief. "Aye," she said simply, unable to summon another word. Her throat was tight, the moment seemingly portentous.

"What do you fear of this night?" he asked, his manner so intent that she believed he truly wished to know.

"All of it."

Lothair shook his head. "Nay, there is a precise detail that concerns you. You have kissed me with enthusiasm before."

"Because I knew there would only be a kiss."

"But on this night?"

"There must be more. I know it well." She caught her breath. "There must be."

"And what do you know of it?"

"Little good."

Lothair let his fingertips trail down her neck and over her shoulder. "Do you fear being touched?" His caress was light and obviously intended to reassure her.

Magdala was surprised that it did, to an extent. She actually preferred the warmth of his fingertips against her bare neck to the sensation of them through her chemise. She swallowed and shook her head. "I do not fear being touched like that."

He watched his hand slide down her forearm and she caught her breath when his fingertips passed the end of her sleeve. She shivered in pleasure at the brush of them against the bare skin on the back of her hand. He traced the shape of each finger with his own fingertip as she watched, intrigued, then he closed his hand over hers. "And like that?"

"I do not mind." When he did not speak, she continued. "That feels as if you shelter me."

He nodded and moved his attention to her other hand, tracing the outline of the ring he had placed upon her finger with a light stroke.

"Why do men not wear a ring?"

He flicked a very blue glance at her. "I will wear one if you wish it."

His words sent an unexpected surge of pleasure through her. "Truly?"

"Truly. I have a fondness for harmony, in which each party speaks of his or her desire."

"Why?"

"It is always best. In a company of men, there is only a true union if all speak of their needs and desires with honesty. A marriage must be the same to my thinking." He watched the path of his fingertip. "It must be a partnership, in which each of us confesses his or her preference, in which we choose our path together."

"As I told you of my concern."

"Precisely thus," he said with satisfaction. "I am glad you told me." He nodded, his hair gilded by the light. On impulse, she reached and pushed it back from his cheek, her heart fluttering when he smiled at her.

"You never told me whether you would stay until he breathes his last."

"Nay, but why the concern now?"

"I would not abandon him," she confessed and he nodded agreement.

"There are places I could go to learn more, but there is no urgency in the matter. There is much to be learned here." He lifted her hand to his lips and kissed her palm, folding her fingers over the hot imprint of his mouth upon her skin. His gaze was warm. "We do not need to decide as yet."

Magdala stared into his eyes, amazed by his words. "We? You would not simply choose and tell me what we will do?"

"I see no cause for such authority." His features softened a little. "And if we are to make each other content, then we must know of each other's desires."

Make each other content.

"I know what your desire must be on this night," she said with haste.

He lifted that hand to her cheek, cupping her face in his hand. His hand was large and warm, and again, Magdala felt cherished. "And it is my obligation to ensure that your desire is as mine this night," he whispered, much to her astonishment. "Tell me, Magdala, if I do anything that feeds your fear."

She nodded, her throat tight.

He leaned closer, moving so slowly that she could evade him if she so wished, but Magdala recalled the beguiling kisses he had given her before and did not move. Her hand clenched in her agitation, but she neither retreated nor fled. Indeed, she held his gaze and her breath, watching as he eased ever closer—and only gave the merest sigh when Lothair's mouth closed over her own in a sweetly persuasive kiss.

Aye, this man could entice the most reluctant of brides to welcome his touch.

And Magdala believed that whatever reluctance she might have possessed would be utterly dismissed.

She could not wait to see it done.

~

HAD MAGDALA BEEN ABUSED PREVIOUSLY? Lothair would have guessed as much, though perhaps she had only been told fearsome tales of the union of man and wife. She had lived in an abbey, after all, and women often sought counsel there for unwanted pregnancies.

The Lord de Tulley had made it clear that he expected a child of this union and there was solely one way to guarantee that outcome—but that was not what motivated Lothair on this night.

Nay, he desired his bride. He wanted her to savor their night together, to meet him in passion, to welcome him on this night and all future nights of their union.

He wanted to begin well.

The strange thing was that on this night, in this moment, against every expectation, Lothair found himself recalling Aileen.

His first wife had been a widow on the night of their nuptials while he had known little of seduction and romance. He had understood how to attain his own satisfaction, but much less of conjuring a lady's pleasure. Aileen had taught him to seduce her sweetly, guiding and correcting his impulses, instructing him in matters intimate. And though their match had been arranged and one of duty instead of affection, Lothair was uncommonly glad of that tutelage on this night.

He wanted Magdala to welcome his touch. He wanted to see her reach the pinnacle of pleasure and he wanted to banish the uncertainty from her gaze. He was glad beyond belief of Aileen's tutelage

The key was to begin slowly and gently.

Lothair let his fingertips trail across Magdala's bare skin, then down her arm again, listening to her all the while. She was breathing quickly and there was a tremor beneath her skin, one that hinted at her history. She might have been a frightened foal ready to bolt, and he knew that if he moved too quickly, she might flee from him forever.

The key to the chamber was on the floor at the foot of the bed. He did not retrieve or move it, knowing she was aware of its presence, guessing that she was reassured by the availability of escape. When he had repeated his caress of her arms, she exhaled shakily, and he dared to kiss her sweetly once again. This time, her mouth softened a little beneath his own, though he did not yet feast upon her.

His seduction would be tender, languorous, unhurried.

He kissed her cheek, her ear, and her neck, moving aside the chemise with his teeth so that he could kiss her bare shoulder. He looked up to find her smiling, though still wary. He pushed his hand through her hair, letting its silken strands run over his fingers and watching it spill from his grip. Then he did as much again, noting that the second time he made a gesture, she was less fearful of his intentions. The third time, he raised his hand to her nape, his grip filled with the shining softness of her hair, and bent to claim her lush mouth once more.

This time, Magdala closed her eyes and parted her lips, arching her back slightly. Lothair dared to prolong the kiss, savoring the softness of her sweet mouth, exploring her a little more than he had before. She made a sound of entreaty that enflamed him, but Lothair did not surrender to temptation—yet. He raised his other hand to her chin and held her head captive, kissing her lingeringly but not for too long. Her eyes were shining and her cheeks flushed when he broke their kiss. He glanced down at her and reached for the tie of her chemise, tugging it completely loose so that the linen fell away from her breasts.

They were spectacular, high and ripely curved, pale as alabaster with nipples as hard and red as rubies. There was encouragement in the response of her body to his touch and he welcomed that minute sign. Lothair raised his hand to cup one breast, the chemise trapped between his hand and her skin, then kissed her again. When she leaned against him and he smelled the welcome heat of her arousal, he teased that nipple with his thumb, rubbing it back and forth across the peak until she moaned into his kiss.

He bent then, ducking his head through the opening of her

chemise and capturing that nipple in his mouth. She jumped a little, then made a sound that might have been a purr of pleasure. He worried the nipple to a taut bead, then suckled it, flicking it with his tongue and savoring her gasp of delight. When she wavered on her feet, he scooped her into his arms and carried her back to the bed, liking how she continued to kiss him, trusting him and her body's reactions an increment more with each passing moment. He left the draperies open so that they were bathed in candlelight, ensuring that there would be no surprises. His hand swept down to her knee, and he felt the warmth of bare skin beneath his palm. He slid his hand up her thigh, astonished by her softness, then eased his fingers between her thighs so that she gasped aloud.

She was slick and hot, so aroused that one touch sent fire through him. He forced himself to continue slowly, though, and touched her with care, for this pleasure was all new for her. He felt her shudder and drew her close, capturing her mouth in a sweet kiss of reassurance as his fingers caressed her with persuasive power. She clutched his shoulders, whispering his name when he lifted his head and staring at him, so soft and alluring that he wanted her with a ferocity that stunned him.

"What do you fear?" he asked again, his voice husky.

"Being forced," she admitted this time.

Lothair shook his head. "Never." There was conviction in his vow and he saw in her eyes that she believed him. His fingers moved against her and she gasped aloud, then smiled a little.

"You would have me beg for satisfaction," she accused lightly, though it was not entirely a jest.

"I would urge you to ask me for whatever you wish of me," he said. "This union should offer pleasure to both of us and obligation to neither."

Magdala sobered, studying him with what might have been surprise. "You mean that."

"I do." He leaned closer and touched his lips to her ear, loving how she shivered when he whispered to her.

"Then tell me what you would have of me," she whispered.

"I would like to put my mouth upon you," Lothair confessed, feeling her surprise. "I would like to give you pleasure there as well. It will not hurt, I vow it to you, but you may like it well." When he pulled away slightly, her eyes were glittering and her cheeks flushed.

"I should never have thought you so wicked, sir."

"It is never wicked for a man to please his wife."

His words clearly pleased her, for she smiled and parted her thighs a little more. Her blush deepened. "I do not know what to do," she admitted and his heart clenched.

"You have only to enjoy," he vowed, then eased her chemise up to her waist. He looked upon her and could not believe his good fortune, to have a wife so beautifully wrought, and one whose nature filled him with satisfaction. He prayed silently that their match would be a long one, and vowed to do his part to make it happy. He then eased down the length of the lady, inhaled deeply of her beguiling scent, then kissed her in that most intimate of places.

Magdala caught her breath. She tensed. And then her hands slid across his shoulders as she succumbed to his caress so completely that Lothair was humbled. She fell back against the mattress with a little moan of pleasure that might have been the most alluring sound Lothair had ever heard.

She trusted him, and that was the greatest gift of this day.

He would ensure that she did not regret that choice.

Magdala was both hot and shivery at the same time. Lothair awakened a need within her that she already found irresistible. The weight of his hands upon her, the warmth of his skin, the smooth leisure of his every gesture, all combined to make her feel safe in his embrace. The sensations he conjured from within her were thrilling and almost overwhelming, yet she understood they were but a hint of what could be.

When she watched him look upon her, her own blood fairly simmering, she was filled with anticipation at the sight of his satisfaction. His eyes were glowing and he moved with purpose as he lowered himself over her. She felt his breath upon her, then the heat of his mouth, then the enticing stroke of his tongue—and she was lost to both pleasure and sensation.

Time might have halted in the chamber as Lothair kindled her passion. His every caress awakened her to a higher level of delight, his patience meant that she could succumb to the lesson he was determined to teach. She felt a demand grow within her and knew he summoned it apurpose. He guided it and cajoled it, driving it toward a peak—then retreated to let it slow to a simmer again. Over and over, he summoned her response with surety and confidence, as if she were a lyre he was destined to play more beautifully than anyone else.

And in doing so, he taught her to trust both her impulse and his mastery of it, to heed her inclinations and even follow them to newfound territory.

She knew the moment he chose to summon the tempest within her and unleash it. He moved with greater deliberation and purpose, fairly demanding a response she was powerless to withhold. She knew that she moaned, that she twisted beneath him like a wanton, that her fingers tangled in his hair. She demanded more in an incoherent whisper laced with need. She did not care: she only wanted more and more. Lothair teased and touched her, he caressed her with a surety she could not deny, and she found herself clutching at him, demanding more than the beguiling caress of his tongue—though she did not know what it might be.

He smiled then as she writhed beneath him, a sign of his own satisfaction in what he wrought within her. He was giving her pleasure and proud to know as much. He touched her more vigorously then, his fingers replacing his tongue, his mouth closing over hers with a wicked and glorious heat. The tumult rose within her with sudden heat, conjured and commanded by him. She felt as if she stretched for the very stars, her heart thundering, her body aching for a satisfaction she could not define—then with a single bold caress, he cast her into an abyss of sensation that made her shout aloud.

Fire might have spurted from her fingertips in that moment and she would not have been surprised. The heat raged through her like an inferno, searing her from head to toe and leaving her gasping in its wake. She strove to catch her breath and opened her eyes to find Lothair beside her, his weight braced on his elbows as he watched her with a smile. He had also cast aside his chemise and she swallowed that his skin was bare so close beside her.

"Your eyes glow," she whispered. "Did you find pleasure in that feat?"

"I found pleasure in your delight," he said, winding a curl of her hair around a finger and kissing it. The gesture was so whimsical and unexpected that she did not know what to say. She felt pinned to the spot by his hot gaze and could not summon a word to her lips. "Would you finish the deed, my lady?" he asked, his voice deep, and she could only shake her head without comprehension.

Lothair rolled to his back, at ease with his body as she was not. She supposed it was like his arsenal of weapons, another tool he would use at will to gain his objective.

There were women who did as much, she knew, women like Lady Heloise.

But Magdala did not wish to think of Lady Heloise this night. This was *her* wedding night.

Curious, knowing that she flushed crimson, Magdala sat up and surveyed him. Never had she seen a man nude, but even so, she knew that she looked upon a most uncommon man. Lothair was all muscled strength, tanned and powerful, lean and vigorous. There was a considerable dusting of fair hair upon his body, not least of which was the tangle of curls upon his chest. His nipples were flat and dark, and she could see evidence of more than one healed wound. He lay there, eyes glittering, watching and waiting, letting her choose how to proceed.

She could not look upon that part of him, not yet, but when he was so immobile, she could consider the possibility. She reached out and let her fingertip land upon his nipple, mimicking how he had touched her. She felt her eyes widen when the nipple tightened beneath her fingers. His gaze had darkened and he had sobered, but still he did not move.

He was taut, holding his own power in check.

For her.

Never had there been a greater gift.

Magdala caressed him with increasing audacity, fascinated that his body responded precisely as hers had done. On impulse, she leaned over him and kissed his nipple as he had kissed hers. Her hair fell against his chest in a tumble and she saw him raise a hand to bury his fingers in it. She felt him catch his breath, then saw his other hand clutch at the linens, as if he strove to control his body's urges.

The very possibility that she could shake this warrior's restraint, that she could lay siege to his control over his desire, was more than sufficient encouragement. Magdala ran her tongue across that nipple, watching as his nostrils flared. She kissed and teased it, suckling it as he had teased her own, and coaxing it to a taut peak. She felt the skip of his heart. She felt the heat from his body and was aware of the growing tension within him.

Because she summoned his storm, just as he had invited hers.

That was a potent realization and one that made Magdala even bolder.

When Lothair emitted a low growl of satisfaction, she slid her hand down his belly, meeting his gaze as she touched him for the first time. He was hard and large and he inhaled sharply even at her light caress.

"Magdala!" He whispered her name as reverently as a benediction and she could do naught but tear her gaze from his and look upon him.

His manhood was enormous and daunting for all of that. She knelt beside him and cast off her chemise, then reached out to brush her fingertips across his strength. He moaned from the depths of his being beneath her touch. Evidently her caress was both temptation and torment, as his had been to her, and that kindled her own desire anew.

When he trembled mightily, she knew that she held him in thrall—and she loved it. She watched as her fingertips trailed up and down his strength, her caress becoming more bold. Did he become larger before her eyes? He caught her hand in his and wrapped her fingers around himself, showing her how to move her hand and give him pleasure. Magdala was intrigued by the magnitude of his response.

"I do not know what to do," she confessed and he moved like quicksilver to catch her around the waist. He lifted her easily above him and she straddled him, smiling down at him as he lowered her atop him. Her hair fell around her shoulders and he looked at her with an awe that melted her reservations.

"You might be an angel come to smite me," he said and she laughed.

"You cannot be my lord husband," she teased. "He would never speak thus."

"Any man would speak thus before such beauty," he said roughly, then reached between them to guide their union. He watched her, his eyes glittering with need, and once again she admired his discipline and restraint.

"You move slowly," she whispered.

"I would not injure you for any price," he said, his teeth gritted, and Magdala could only smile. She felt him against her, then the heat of him eased inside her. She gasped and Lothair might have halted but she laid her hands upon his chest and drove herself against him so that he was suddenly within her. The sensation made her cry out but she shook her head when he froze.

"Now, 'tis begun," she said, her voice shaking. "You must finish what has been started, sir."

His expression softened and he reached to place a fingertip on her lips. "Lothair," he corrected and she smiled beneath the weight of his finger.

"Lothair," she echoed, then smiled. He smiled at her then gathered her into his embrace, his fingers in her hair as he kissed her sweetly. He slowly moved deeper, caressing and kissing her as he buried himself inside her. Indeed, time might have halted then, for there was only Lothair, his heat and his strength, the glitter of his eyes.

"Speak to me, Magdala," he entreated, his voice husky.

"I think this a moment for deeds, not words, sir." She exhaled, accustoming herself to the feel of him, then moved. Once again, she had the satisfaction of both surprising him and provoking a reaction from this taciturn man. He swore softly and shook, his obvious pleasure making her smile. He studied her expression, his own smile dawning anew as they moved together and found their rhythm.

It was glorious, so intimate, so much more magical than she had ever imagined it might be. This was a far cry from Herbert grabbing and fondling her, intent only upon his own satisfaction. This might have required a different name, for it was beguiling beyond belief. Magdala had never felt such a union with another, had never thought two hearts might truly beat as one. But as her confidence grew, she moved with greater insistence and Lothair grew taut beneath her, even as her own reaction stirred again. He gripped her hands and she sat up taller, their fingers interlocked as she rode him with greater and greater urgency, lost in the glow of his eyes.

She felt beautiful and powerful, a woman in command of her pleasure and even that of the warrior who could not tear his gaze from hers. She smiled at him and tossed her hair, reveling in her ability to give him pleasure.

Suddenly, Lothair's grip tightened upon her hands and his eyes flashed with fire. He rolled his hips suddenly, driving himself against her so that once again Magdala felt the tumult race through her. She cried out, consumed by the fire he commanded within her, even as Lothair roared with his own release and caught her close. His arms were locked around her, his breath hot on her shoulder, and she felt the thunder of his heart against her own. He was atop her, though he had been beneath, but Magdala felt cherished.

Sheltered.

He cradled her against his chest, his fingers spearing into her hair, and she felt replete in a way she had never experienced before. He kissed her then, softly and sweetly, lingeringly, and she kissed him back with delight.

"What do you fear?" he whispered again, his breath against her ear.

"Naught when I am with you," Magdala replied, because it was true.

To be wed to a man of honor and a knight was a fine fate, to be sure, and more than she had ever hoped might be her destiny. But after this night, Magdala found herself thinking of love and affection. Once she would have been content to place her hand in that of a man like Lothair. Once security would have been sufficient to sate her, a home and a hearth, a husband, even sons and daughters.

But now that she was Lothair's wife, Magdala also wished for love.

CHAPTER 11

*S*he was glorious.

And Lothair was the most fortunate man ever born.

He lifted Magdala in his arms like the precious treasure she was, not wanting to release her. He rose from the bed, easing the draperies open as he carried her into the chilly chamber. She shivered and he held her close as he sat on a small stool, balancing her on his lap. "The floor is cold," he said, then washed her gently. She leaned against his chest, her hair spilling over her shoulders and her sole adornment. She was flushed and drowsy, her lips swollen a little and her manner languorous.

If it had not been her first time, if she had not been so very tight, he would have been unable to resist taking her again. As it was, there was more blood than he expected, the truth of it making him fear she had been hurt.

She straightened at the blood on the cloth, staring at it. She had not seen the linens, then.

"We are wed in truth then," she said and he could not guess her thoughts.

"Does that not please you?"

What would he do if she spurned him? If she left him? If she was discontent with him by her side? Lothair would do whatsoever was necessary to change her thinking, to prove his merit, to win her loyalty.

To his relief, though, she smiled at him, those eyes glinting with satisfaction.

"It does, sir." She studied him, her manner playful. "And you?"

"Lothair," he corrected quietly, needing to hear her say his name in this moment.

"Lothair," she repeated and he was astonished by how much pleasure a single word could grant.

He was shaken by her influence over him already, despite how little they truly knew of each other, and yet, he could not regret a single detail. They had a lifetime to unfurl each other's secrets and learn each other's histories.

He carried her back to the bed, wrapping her in his cloak while he removed the stained linens. Doubtless, the Lord de Tulley would demand the proof of the consummation. She rose with purpose to spread fresh linens on the mattress, and he liked that she was so practical. They might not always know such comfort as was offered at Château Tulley, given his trade, but he sensed that Magdala would not complain.

She donned her chemise as he tugged on his own and he watched with satisfaction as she braided her hair into a single plait. He got into the bed beside her, amazed that this was his place, drawing the drapes and pulling her against his warmth. Magdala curled against him contentedly. Her buttocks were in his lap, her sweet curves in his arms and the soft silk of her hair against his face. He took a deep breath of her beguiling scent and knew there was nowhere else he wished to be.

"Sleep well, my lady," he murmured, unable to resist the impulse to press a kiss into her hair.

There was humor in her voice when she replied, though she sounded sleepy as well. "No doubt the Lord de Tulley will offer new challenges in the morning."

Lothair felt suddenly awake. "Aye?"

"He has a look about him," she admitted then yawned. "Though I may sleep to noon and miss whatever surprise he means to launch."

Lothair braced himself upon his elbow to look down at her, but her breathing was already becoming slower. "What manner of look?"

"Like a man with a scheme," she said, her voice even more sleepy. "I have seen that expression often enough to recognize its import." She raised a hand, gesturing vaguely with a finger. "He has a plan, to be sure."

"What manner of scheme?" he asked but Magdala was asleep.

If the Lord de Tulley had another scheme for Lothair like that man's insistence upon him taking a bride, Lothair could have no issue with that. He wrapped himself around Magdala from behind. She gave a contented sigh and made a little wriggle of her hips that almost distracted him from the need for sleep—but not quite.

A scheme.

What did the old lord contrive?

Lothair was still awake, considering the possibilities, when he heard footsteps in the corridor. They were stealthy, but quick. Someone was in a hurry, but why at such an hour?

He rolled over and opened the drapes around the bed, seeing two shadows in the gap beneath the door to Magdala's chamber. He eased from the bed, closing the draperies again even as Magdala rolled into the warm hollow left by his body. She sighed contentment but did not awaken.

Lothair crept toward the door, intent upon surprising whoever was there, then another shadow appeared beside the two feet. "My lord?" Calum whispered and Lothair realized that the youth was trying to peer beneath the portal.

"Calum?" Lothair replied in a whisper. "Do not disturb the lady."

"Nay, my lord." Calum whispered. "But there is revelry in the town, sir, perhaps on account of the ale given by the Lord de Tulley to all on this day. Lord d'Annossy bade me fetch you before all goes awry."

Revelry. Lothair could imagine the effect of the Lord de Tulley's generosity this evening.

Duty called.

Lothair found his boots and his robe, his tabard and his belt, casting them on with haste. He would have to arm himself in his own chambers before riding out to calm whatever turmoil had erupted. He seized the key from the middle of the floor and unlocked the portal, glanced back once at the bed with regret, then left the sanctuary of his lady's chamber.

He locked the door behind himself and slid the key beneath the gap once more, then hastened after Calum to the stairs.

MAGDALA AWAKENED ALONE.

The mattress was cold beside her. Even before she opened the drapes on the bed, she knew Lothair was gone. Still, it was a surprise to find no sign of him. His every garment was gone, as if he had never been in her chamber and she wondered for a moment if she had dreamed the night before. Then she rolled over and smelled his skin upon the linens, the very scent sending a joyous heat through her.

It had happened.

They were wed in truth. She rolled to her back and smiled as she recalled every touch, every glance, the low thrum of his voice as they pledged to each other here alone. Such a man. She was fortunate beyond belief and she would ensure he never regretted that he had acquiesced to the Lord de Tulley's command.

And honesty between them. What a gift. She liked that he had confessed the Lord de Tulley's inducement before accepting her hand, and thought that could only be a good portent for their shared future. Aye, he was a man of honor and that suited her well.

The morning sunlight was forcing its way between the shutters and she was washing when someone tapped gently at the door. The key gleamed on the floor, but it was in a different spot than she recalled.

Lothair had left and secured the door behind himself, leaving her the key so that she would not be disturbed. Magdala smiled at his protective nature.

"My lady?" It was Felix. She recognized his voice and hastened to pick up the key, fearing that something was amiss with the Lord de Tulley.

"Is the Lord de Tulley well?" she asked as she slipped the key into the lock.

"Hale and hearty," Felix replied, his eyes widening when the portal swung open. Magdala clutched the front of her chemise and dropped her gaze, realizing that her braid had become unfurled and her new chemise was beyond sheer. Felix cleared his throat and addressed the corner of her chamber. "My lord requests the linens, however." The servant kept his gaze averted. "He would secure them, but prefers not to have them paraded before the company."

"As do I, Felix. I thank you." Magdala pointed to where Lothair had left them, folded neatly in anticipation of this request. Felix retrieved them and retreated with a bow. He cleared his throat again. "You look to be most pleased, my lady, and I hope that is so."

"Thank you, Felix."

"All within the hall will be glad if you are content, but I would be particularly so."

"I am, Felix. Thank you again."

"And I may confide as much in the Lord de Tulley?"

Magdala blushed. "Aye, Felix."

He bowed. "Lady Melissande and her companion break their fast in the hall. My lord suggested you might join them in his stead."

"Of course, Felix. I will be pleased to do as much."

He bowed and hastened in the direction of the solar. Magdala was closing the door when she heard the Lord de Tulley bellow a demand, satisfaction evident in his tone for any who knew him well. She smiled, and hastened to bathe and dress, lest Lady d'Annossy felt neglected.

Melissande had been born to wealth and position, as the sole and much indulged heiress to Annossy. Truth be told, Magdala found the other woman's competence and confidence somewhat intimidating—if anyone were to catch out her falsehood about being Heloise, it would be Melissande. Not only had that lady known Heloise and ridden to hunt with her in the past, but she knew all the details of an aristocratic lady's life that Magdala did not.

She descended to the hall, wishing yet again that the Lord de Tulley would permit the confession of the truth. She disliked that these women did not know her name. The two were admiring Melissande and Quinn's infant son, and their husbands were not to be seen. Berthe, Magdala suspected, would deliver of a child herself during the winter, though no one had mentioned as much as yet.

Berthe had been Melissande's maid, until the return of the company of knights with Quinn to Sayerne. The Lord de Tulley had insisted that Melissande and Quinn make a match, as Magdala had explained to Lothair, but in the meantime, Berthe had lost her heart to Quinn's companion, Bayard de Neuville. That man was a warrior as well but not a knight, a younger son and man-at-arms who had joined the crusades to seek his fortune. He had found it with his comrade, Quinn, who had appointed Bayard to administer Sayerne while he governed neighboring Annossy, the legacy of his lady wife and the greater holding.

The infant was named Bayard in honor of that friendship and was a healthy child, a detail made clear by his vigorous wail.

"He is hungry, too, Clotilde," Melissande said with a smile, surrendering her son to the nursemaid. The infant quieted as soon as he was offered her breast, and Clotilde carried him away, singing softly to him as he nursed.

"Berthe has shared fine tidings with me this morn," Melissande said after the women had exchanged greetings. "She and Bayard anticipate a child of their own before the spring."

Berthe smiled and curved a protective hand over her belly. "Given the tales I have heard of Sir Lothair's expertise, I am most glad of his return to Tulley."

"How so?" Magdala took her place. "I know he has an interest in the healing arts."

"But he has been particular in gathering knowledge of the arrival of children," Berthe supplied. Magdala looked up in surprise to find Melissande nodding agreement.

"Quinn told me of Lothair aiding in the arrival of a babe in Outremer. They should have ridden on, but Lothair would not leave the lady in her distress. Her husband was most skeptical but the lady was in such anguish that she begged his indulgence. The child, it seemed, was tangled in the cord and could not emerge from the womb." She spread honeycomb on her bread. "If it had not been for Lothair's intervention, they might both have died, as Quinn told it."

"Did he not tell you this tale?" Berthe asked, smiling when Magdala shook her head. "My Bayard nigh told me every tale that showed him to advantage when he sought my favor, and a few more besides. That man could boast of awakening in the morning, as if that was a feat." They laughed easily together, Berthe evidently having no quibble with this trait of her husband's.

Magdala broke her fast quietly, feeling a glow of pride in Lothair's reticence. She liked that he had aided others for the sake of that alone, and had not sought approval or praise for giving assistance where he could.

"Do you know how the companions met?" Melissande asked and Magdala shook her head.

"The man tells you naught at all!" Berthe laughed and Magdala felt herself flush.

"We have not known each other long," she said.

"And you have a lifetime to learn all his secrets," Melissande said, granting Berthe a quelling glance which made no difference at all to the younger woman's manner.

"I should ask him all the questions in your place," Berthe confided. "A woman cannot know enough of her husband."

"Even if it is not all the truth?" Melissande teased and Berthe laughed.

"Aye, I do not believe all that Bayard tells me."

"While I can trust in every word surrendered by my husband." Both women looked to be content with their lot. Magdala had to admit that she was curious about Lothair and his past, and she hoped he would share more detail in time.

He had been more talkative of late than she might have anticipated.

"They met when my Quinn was injured," Melissande continued. "He had been imprisoned by Saracens, captured in battle at the siege of Antioch. His wound sustained in that battle did not heal well."

"Despite the aid of my Bayard," Berthe contributed. "He was convinced they would perish in that stronghold, though by his telling he did not share his doubts with Quinn."

"But three of the other knights at that battle took note of their capture and schemed for their release."

"Luc and Thierry Douglas," Berthe supplied as she cut a fresh plum into pieces. "Along with Rolfe de Viandin."

Magdala recognized these names as being among the company of knights who had become such close friends and comrades. She had met the first two and heard tales of the third.

"They attacked the prison, surprising the captors, and gained the release of many knights."

"But then the tide turned against them, for Quinn was so injured that he could not run."

"And they would not leave him behind."

"They thought they all would be doomed, though they fought on valiantly, despite the odds."

"Until Lothair the Viking came," the women concluded in unison, their words delighting Magdala.

"He fought with a vengeance," Berthe said, jabbing the air with her eating knife as if it was a knight's sword. "He scattered their foes left and right, ensuring their escape from that stronghold, and taking them out of peril."

Magdala was not astonished that Lothair should be so courageous, but she felt foolish that she had no awareness of the tale.

"He did not even tell you of this?" Berthe demanded and Magdala was obliged to shake her head.

"Perhaps he does not wish to remember such battles," she said.

Berthe wagged her knife at Magdala. "But he must have told you how he saved Lord Quinn's life, drawing the infection from his wound, healing it and ensuring that he recovered his former strength. His diligence and skill were worthy of a bard's tale, as I heard it."

"I am indebted to him forever," Melissande said, a tear in her eye. "I cannot imagine never having had Quinn in my life."

"Or your bed," Berthe teased and her former lady flushed crimson.

But she did not deny the charge.

"You have wed a knight of considerable skill, Heloise," Melissande said. "But do not be surprised if every woman in Tulley requests his attendance when she delivers a child."

Magdala was not certain of her opinion of that possibility, though she suspected she would be glad of Lothair's expertise in her own time. Meanwhile, her companions agreed that the Lord and Lady Beauvoir were unlikely to appear before midday. They were speaking of their homes and details Magdala did not know when Calum appeared.

He halted before her and bowed deeply. "Good morning to you, my lady."

"And to you, Calum."

"My lord Lothair sends his apologies to you, for duty detains him in the village."

"Is something amiss?" Magdala felt the curiosity of the other two ladies as their conversation fell silent.

"No more than an enthusiastic consumption of the Lord de Tulley's ale," the youth confided and Magdala's companions laughed lightly. The squire's eyes twinkled. "I wager that a night in the dungeons will be sobering for even those who were most indulgent. My lord regrets his early departure and hopes for your understanding of his absence."

Magdala smiled, guessing that Lothair had not offered so fulsome an explanation or apology. "I thank you, Calum, for these tidings. Doubtless I shall see him later this day."

"Doubtless, my lady." The youth bowed deeply again then pivoted crisply to leave the hall.

Melissande leaned closer. "Surely all was well last night?" she asked.

"Surely you were satisfied?" Berthe said, her manner more blunt.

"Aye." Magdala felt herself blushing. "I did not know fully what to expect but all was well."

Berthe laughed heartily. "Aye, one would expect a man so learned to know best how to please his lady wife. From Bayard's tales, all of those comrades savored the favors of the whores in Outremer."

"Berthe!" Melissande chided.

"Though not Lord Quinn, of course, a man of great temperance," Berthe corrected.

Melissande smiled. "Take no heed of her, Heloise," she advised. "She tells tales with just as much enthusiasm as her husband." Berthe laughed but Calum interjected.

"My lady, you err in the matter of my lord Lothair as well," Calum said, making the three of them realize he had not departed from the hall as yet. He returned to the high table with a confident step and smiled at Magdala. "He was not one to savor the companionship of whores. I have served him these nine years and I would know."

Magdala smiled at this endorsement. "I thank you, Calum."

"It would have been his wife who taught him such skill in amorous matters, my lady."

Melissande caught her breath. Berthe looked between Magdala and Calum, her eyes wide.

Magdala was sufficiently astounded that it took her a moment to find her voice. "His wife?" she finally managed to ask.

"Aye, my lady. My lord Lothair wed my sister." The youth spoke with complete confidence, clearly untroubled by this detail. He smiled at Magdala. "I suppose you did not know."

His *wife*.

LOTHAIR WAS EXHAUSTED. He dispatched the last of the merrymakers to the dungeon, securing the trap door after him, and ran a hand over his eyes. Some of the prisoners shouted insults, their words slurred, but already half of them had to be asleep.

He could only be envious of that state.

He sent Calum to give his apologies to Magdala, then returned to the bailey where Quinn and Niall laughed together.

"The Lord de Tulley's ale was potent, indeed," Quinn said with a smile.

"And there was plenty of it," Niall agreed.

"I thank you for your assistance," Lothair said. "Matters were concluded more quickly with two more to aid us." He made a mental list of those sentries and guards who had failed to respond to his summons, knowing full well that the lord's ale was responsible for that, as well.

There would be admonitions, but not overly stern ones.

He spared a glance at the keep looming above them and acknowledged that one matter, at least, had gone well.

"Quite a nuptial night," Quinn said as if he had read Lothair's thoughts. "I hope the interruption was not too early."

Niall did not have time to make an observation that Lothair deserved his fate, nor Lothair to reassure his friend before the door to the hall flew open and Magdala herself appeared.

She marched toward him, eyes flashing and her veil flying behind her. She looked magnificent, garbed this day in blue silk as dark as the twilight sky. Her hair was demurely covered by the veil, a mark of her changed status, and she wore a plain circlet of gold. His innards clenched that this beauty was his own bride, then she halted before him, fairly breathing fire.

"You, sir, have deceived me!" she charged and for a moment he could not comprehend her outrage.

Lothair frowned. "I?"

"You." She glared at him, then poked his chest with one finger. "Calum tells me you wed his sister."

Lothair glanced toward his squire who had followed her from the hall. The youth looked curious, not sheepish. He had been followed by the ladies wed to his companions, but they appeared to be shocked.

"Aye," Lothair acknowledged, wondering at the cause of this reaction to a simple truth. Of what import if he was widowed?

Magdala's eyes flashed. "Oh! And you did not see fit to tell me of this before we exchanged our own nuptial vows?"

"Nay," Lothair said with caution.

She flung out her hands. "Whyever not? What madness seized your wits that you failed to confess a matter of such importance?"

"It was not relevant," he admitted, which did nothing at all to improve her mood.

Color flared in her cheeks. "You outrage me, sir. I was prepared to accept your reticence and your reluctance to surrender any detail of your life. I thought you a taciturn man, one who would confide in me in time, but I never wagered that you were a rogue and a scoundrel..."

"My lady," Lothair protested against this assault on his nature.

She held up a shaking finger. "You have deceived not only me but the Lord de Tulley in this matter and the price for such a deed will be high, you may be sure."

"But Magdala," he dropped his voice to a whisper for his appeal, but his use of her name made no difference at all. Indeed, he could see her tears rising and truly felt like the cur she accused him of being.

Save that he had no understanding of why she was so vexed.

She lowered her voice to a hiss, ensuring that only he could hear her words. "I had *naught* save my virtue. Naught! No dowry. No lineage. No reason for a man to take my hand in his, save my maiden-head. And now it is gone, sir, surrendered to deception and I, I know not what I shall do." Her first tear fell then, sliding down her cheek. Lothair lifted a hand to wipe it away, but she spun from him, striding out of the bailey with vigor and slamming the portal to the hall behind herself.

He realized that his former comrades eyed him with astonish-ment, that their wives were scandalized and that more than one member of Tulley's guard regarded him with suspicion. Even the sentries upon the walls had heard her outburst, it was clear, and watched warily for his response.

It was only then that Lothair understood what had transpired. "Calum, why did you tell my lady wife of this?"

"I believed she knew, sir."

"But you did mention that Aileen is dead, did you not?"

The squire's eyes widened with dismay and there was Lothair's reply.

"God in Heaven," Melissande whispered in her relief and the two ladies embraced. Niall clapped Lothair on the back and Quinn shook his head. Calum looked between them, then. His eyes widened in sudden dismay.

Lothair for his part could not imagine how he would begin to make this right.

Honesty, he decided. Honesty could be the sole course. Magdala had asked to know more of him, and soon she would.

It was his sole chance.

Wretch and cur!

Magdala retreated from the astonished stares of Lady Melissande and Berthe, knowing the women would have questions aplenty for her. The last thing she desired was to confide in another.

How could Lothair have so betrayed her trust?

How could he have neglected to mention such a critical detail.

Married.

Magdala hastened up the stairs, knowing that she needed solitude most of all. If she went to the solar, the Lord de Tulley would demand to know what ailed her. If she retreated to her chamber, someone would rouse her for some cause or other.

There was only the garden. She unlocked the gate, then secured it behind herself, not wishing to be disturbed at any price. She had to pace the perimeter several times to calm herself sufficiently to settle at any task. She had only just crouched down beside the bed where Lothair had identified the sweet cicely when she heard a key in the lock of the gate.

Of course, he had a key. She closed her eyes in exasperation for she had forgotten as much.

But there was not one word Lothair could say to her to explain his error. There was not a single explanation that could make all come aright. A man could not be wed to two women at once, which meant her marriage vows, coming second, were void. Her hand began to tremble as she pulled small plants with vigor, not caring if they were weeds or not.

She heard him lock the gate behind himself. Of course, he proceeded with care for he was not so witless as that.

She heard his footsteps as he approached and braced herself for some appeal. It would all be futile. Mere words could not make this right. She blinked back her tears, refusing to so much as glance his way.

Not relevant.

The fiend.

She felt Lothair's warmth as he crouched beside her, was aware of the weight of his gaze upon her. Still she did not look up or acknowledge his presence. She pulled plants with savage force, not caring for her hands or nails, nor even if she mired her skirt.

"Magdala."

Oh, he said her name thus and her heart fluttered but she would not be swayed. Doubtless even he could find a pretty lie to win her favor again, but Magdala was adamant. She would not be swayed. She would have to retreat to the convent after all...

"Aileen is dead."

She spun to face him in her surprise, only to find him watching her closely. He nodded once, his sincerity absolute. "She has been dead these nine years." He lifted a fair brow. "Calum neglected to mention that detail, I believe."

"You are not wed?" Magdala had to hear it again.

"I *was* wed. I am a widower and have been for some years."

Magdala exhaled, shaken and relieved. A widower. She felt a little foolish that she had not imagined that possibility. She returned to her task, not knowing what to say. She expected Lothair to depart then, to keep his midday meeting with the Lord de Tulley, but he indicated a small plant that was growing in profusion in the bed.

"Mint," he said. "Ever enthusiastic in its desire to claim more territory." He indicated how it had propagated beneath the shadow of the sweet cicely and began to pull it out.

"But useful for an ailing stomach," Magdala said.

"And for application to sores and wounds, when pounded with sulphur and vinegar," he said. "But one can have too much of it."

"There is a bed of it near the reservoir."

"Doubtless the source of the seeds that rooted here." He cleared his throat. "I believe the original plan was that the culinary herbs should be there, closest to the portal, and I would suggest that we strive to confine them there."

Magdala blinked at this lecture but said naught at all.

"Another variant of mint," he said long moments later. "Though this one belongs with the lady's mantle."

Magdala recalled that it was for women's woes. "How so?"

He turned a sprig of it in his fingers. "Pennyroyal. Some believe it aids in preventing conception."

Why did he tell her this? Did he not wish for them to have a child? Magdala could make no sense of it but she would not ask.

She was still irked with him.

They worked together in silence and Magdala found herself reassured by the rhythm of the labor, as well as the tranquil strength of Lothair's presence. She was certain he had duties and knew he would excuse himself shortly.

To her surprise, he began to speak, his gaze fixed upon the garden bed.

"I was wed, as Calum confessed, to his older sister, Aileen. I had no intention of taking a bride. A warrior whose blade is for hire does not enjoy the comfort of a keep of his own, with a fire on the hearth, as might be best for a wife and family. I knew my trade might require me to follow a leader to another land and such upheavals are not the best for a family."

Magdala was certain she had never heard Lothair utter so many words in sequence. She dared not comment, though, lest he halt the tale.

He lifted a fair brow. "My trade also can result in the abrupt end of one's days, as had occurred with the lady's husband."

There was a detail of import.

"The match was arranged," she guessed, reassured by this confession.

"It was ordered by the Mormaer of Moray, the father of both Aileen and Calum, and my patron. The lady had recently been widowed and was with child by her late husband's seed. My patron feared for her welfare and perhaps also for that of the infant. There was turmoil in the land in those days, to be sure, and her husband had been a man with both wealth and enemies."

A noblewoman, daughter of his patron. Calum was a handsome youth and his sister must have been alluring as well. Magdala could imagine the grace and confidence of such a lady, born to privilege, who doubtless had been affluent in her own right after the death of her spouse. "What was she like?" She had to ask.

Lothair shook his head. "A tempest and a whirlwind both. A lady who knew her own desire and was fearless in its pursuit. I wager she might have continued the campaign launched by her lord husband, or at the very least, ruled his holdings with authority and skill, but her father forbade it. How they argued, so similar they were in temperament." He fell silent for a moment, surely regretting the loss of such a magnificent wife. "She died in the delivery of that child. A boy, who also died." His lips drawing to a taut line. "I could not believe that a woman so fierce and so resolute could pass from this world so young."

Magdala felt a lump rise in her throat.

"Her death was why I left Moray."

Because he had loved her.

Magdala was so certain of it that she knew that would be his next confession—but it was not.

"Aileen changed the course of my life, not once but twice, for she died while I could only watch. There was not a single thing I could do to aid her. The midwife had come from the village and I rode to the next village for another. Together, they could not save her, and I have never felt so powerless in all my days." His voice hardened with resolve as he continued. "I decided then that I must learn the skills of an apothecary and also seek knowledge beyond the lands I knew. No one there could save her, but someone somewhere had to have the learning that might make the difference."

"What did your patron think of this choice?"

"He was displeased, to be sure." Lothair's gaze collided with her own. "He had planned for me to serve him for the duration. He is not unlike the Lord de Tulley in his conviction that his way alone will suffice, and his interest in both crusade and healing was minimal."

Despite herself, Magdala smiled. She recognized, though, that Lothair had a resolve of his own. "But you would not be swayed."

"It was right, Magdala." Lothair took a breath. "I accepted the Mormaer's son as my squire and rode for Jerusalem, partly as penance for my failure to aid my lady wife but mostly to seek knowledge. I studied wherever I could, learning from those who practiced the healing arts, adding to my understanding virtually each day."

Magdala nodded. "And so you are both warrior and healer."

"Aye. Because of Aileen."

His debt to that lady was considerable to be sure, and she heard a rare heat in his words. "You will always be indebted to her, I wager," she said, striving to keep her tone light.

"Never more than last night."

Magdala met his gaze in confusion, disliking the sound of that. "You thought of her last night?"

A rare smile curved Lothair's lips and Magdala could not tear her gaze away. He leaned closer, dropping his voice to a whisper that made her toes curl in her slippers. His eyes glinted and she was certain she had never seen a more alluring man in all her days. "Because Aileen taught me how best to please a lady," he confessed. "And I was uncommonly glad last night that I had the ability to set your fears at rest. I wanted our first night to be a success, Magdala, a beginning upon which we might build a future."

"It was," she managed to say, feeling that her cheeks were aflame. She smiled when his gaze dropped to her lips and caught her breath in anticipation. Lothair studied her then leaned closer, gently brushing his mouth across her own. Magdala heard herself sigh with contentment, then he stood, gathering her into his arms and lifting her to her feet. She stood within his embrace, feeling far more content than she had just moments before.

Indeed, she was thinking of the night ahead and the pleasures they might share abed. Her expression might have shown as much, for Lothair's eyes shone.

"Dare I hope that I am forgiven?" he whispered and she smiled.

"You know you are, sir. I am sorry that I was so distressed. I should have asked."

"You could not have anticipated such a detail. I should have told you sooner."

"You have become quite fulsome, sir," she teased, watching his smile broaden.

"What is your sorcery that gives you such power, my lady wife?" he mused, as if he expected no reply.

"I possess no sorcery."

"Nay? Then how is it that you alone can compel me to explain myself or share tales of my past?" He bestowed a slow and seductive kiss upon her, one that nigh banished her thoughts. "How is it that only your distress can cause me such dismay?"

She eyed him, wanting to believe him with all her heart.

"I have never known the like, Magdala." He shook his head. "It cannot be of no import to care so much for the goodwill of another. I have dared to believe it might be a good portent for our shared future."

"You would try to charm me, sir," she protested.

He lifted a brow. "Do you mistake me for a man like Niall MacGillivray?"

"Never that."

"Never that," he agreed with feeling. His gaze clung to hers. "I would never do you disservice, my lady, and if I err or you believe I have, I entreat you to demand an explanation of me first."

"I never thought you would answer my queries."

"Yet another mark of your sorcery," he said and she laughed, stretching to her toes for another celebratory kiss.

CHAPTER 12

*L*othair had seldom felt relief of such magnitude. He had not cared how much he had to confess to Magdala to prompt both her forgiveness and her smile, and he was triumphant in achieving both. He left her in the garden, her manner much more content, and climbed the stairs to the solar to confer with the Lord de Tulley at midday.

He was halfway there before he realized he had never before confided so much in another person. That made his steps pause. Surely, he would not be deceived as his father had been?

He looked back, uneasy at the prospect. Nay, not by Magdala.

Nay.

"Are you wed to another?" the Lord de Tulley asked by way of greeting. He peered at Lothair from his chair, his expression forbidding.

"I was wed, my lord, but my wife died nine years ago."

The Lord de Tulley harrumphed. "Then this is why Magdala forgave you," he said, brows bristling. "I saw from the window and thought she had lost her wits."

"Nay, sir, she did not."

"And you, doubtless, did not become a man who could charm the birds from the trees." The older man nodded with satisfaction at a mystery solved. "I should have known that it would be the truth that would satisfy her."

"Aye, sir. My wife is a lady of good sense."

The older man's eyes twinkled. "So much so that you are become garrulous."

Lothair did not reply, for he tired of all those around him making comments about his loquaciousness. It was true that he routinely said little and it was true that he had spoken more to Magdala than any person in the sum of his years—perhaps more than to all people in the sum of his years—but they might find another detail of interest to comment upon.

"You glower at me but it is true, is it not?"

Lothair inclined his head.

The Lord de Tulley laughed and dismissed Felix with a wave of his hand. He asked after the disturbance in the village and Lothair's handling of it, the number of villagers in the dungeon and their names, then provided some history of those individuals. The Lord de Tulley suspected that one was the instigator, for that man was fond of making mischief, though the older man said there was no harm in him truly. This matched Lothair's own suspicions and they agreed that man would spend an additional day in the dungeon after the release of his fellows, and face the Lord de Tulley at his next court. They then discussed the guests and their comfort.

"And they intend to depart when?"

"The Lord Beaupoint indicated that he and his party would leave on the morrow, at first light, while I believe the Lord d'Annossy intends to linger another day."

The Lord de Tulley nodded. "And you will ride to Grimwald on the morrow."

Lothair was startled. He would? But one look at the older man revealed that he had planned to surprise his Captain of the Guard, and Lothair could only dislike that he had succeeded so well. "Why?"

"I must have the remains recovered from those graves," the lord confessed. "And you are the sole one who can be trusted. Take whosoever you will with you, but depart early and return with all haste." He sat back, his lips set with resolve. "My niece will be laid to rest here at Tulley, as she deserves. Felix will grant you sufficient coin from my coffers for your expenses. Be sure to confirm your party to me this evening and I will make the calculation."

Lothair, however, was not so quick to agree. It was time, to his thinking, that the Lord de Tulley had someone to challenge his edicts —and that he ceased to consider all within his holding as so many chess pieces to be moved at will.

"With respect, my lord," he said with quiet vehemence. "The remains have been there more than two years."

The Lord de Tulley turned a sharp glance upon him. "What of it?"

"They may wait a few days longer, the better that your guests do not suspect that anything is amiss."

The Lord de Tulley glared.

Lothair held his gaze unflinchingly.

"How many more days?" the older man demanded.

"I would have a week with my lady wife," Lothair said. "The guests will have departed by then." He did not wish to meet Magdala abed quickly, for she needed time to heal, but perhaps by the third night, she might welcome him again.

The Lord de Tulley scowled. "It cannot be thus."

"You were the one to insist upon a child within the year."

The older man shook his head. "Impossible! You do not understand the extent of my planning. There cannot be such a delay."

Lothair felt his eyes narrow. "What plan, sir?"

"You will learn the details when you need to know them. Nay, you must depart upon the morrow, at first light."

Lothair let the silence stretch long between them, doubting that the older man missed his displeasure with the order.

"Then I would have a different concession," he finally said.

"Do you think we negotiate?" the Lord de Tulley demanded, eyes flashing. "I have a plan. You have a part within it. You are my

Captain of the Guard and you will do as I instruct, with no further defiance."

"Nay," Lothair said with resolve. "My greater responsibility is to my lady wife and I will ensure her welfare before all other matters."

The Lord de Tulley sat back, his expression changing from annoyance to consideration. "What would you have of me?"

"Your permission for me to share my lady's name with my former comrades, the better to ensure the lady's security in my absence."

"She is safe in my abode! She has been thus nigh three years."

"Yet I will see her defended in my absence in my own way," Lothair insisted, his voice hard. "I would ask, sir, that you might invite the Lord and Lady d'Annossy to remain as your guests until my return. I will ask Niall MacGillivray to accompany me on your errand, along with Sir Gerald."

The Lord de Tulley's expression turned shrewd. "You would have companions you can trust."

"Aye, my lord."

"And if I refuse?"

Lothair straightened. "The lady and I will depart for Provins at first light." He had no notion how he might convince Magdala of the merit of this choice, but they could not remain subject to every whim of the Lord de Tulley, not without knowing that man's motives.

"You are pledged to my service!" the older man hissed.

"And I will abandon it, if you do not see fit to heed my counsel."

The two men glared at each other, a veritable battle of wills that was interrupted by the arrival of the lady herself.

WHAT WAS AMISS?

Magdala had discerned the Lord de Tulley's vexation from the stairs and had been surprised to hear Lothair's firm tones in reply. Though it was time to rub the unguent into the older man's back, she was hesitant to interrupt a dispute.

But what could they argue about?

She tapped on the door to the solar and opened it without waiting, immediately feeling the charge of anger in the chamber. Lothair stepped away from the Lord de Tulley, turning to look out the window, his posture so straight that she guessed he was furious. The Lord de Tulley was fuming, picking up items from the table before him and putting them down again, flicking poisonous glances at the apparently indifferent Lothair.

"What is amiss?" Magdala asked and Felix rolled his eyes, retreating with evident relief at the Lord de Tulley's dismissive gesture.

The Lord de Tulley exhaled in annoyance when the door closed behind Felix.

"And you?" the older man asked, turning to Magdala. "What do you know of this outrageous notion?"

"Notion?" she echoed, looking between the two men in confusion.

"That you should leave for Provins with your husband, against my express wishes, for he declines to do as I have commanded him to do!" The Lord de Tulley fell back in his chair after this tirade, his fury undiminished.

Lothair did not move, turn, or explain his position. Indeed, he folded his arms across his chest and Magdala recalled his confession that he had defied the Mormaer, Calum's father, when he did not agree with that man's plan.

"And what was your command, sir?" Magdala asked, fetching the unguent as if nothing unusual transpired.

"That my Captain of the Guard should ride to Grimwald and bring my niece home."

"Her home would be Idelstein," Lothair said tightly.

Magdala could not imagine that Lothair would find this task so objectionable as appearances would indicate. She could appreciate, though, that he might not like being ordered to undertake such a journey like a lowly servant.

"And when did you instruct him to undertake this journey?" she asked mildly.

"I bade him depart on the morrow at first light."

Magdala was surprised. "It is three days ride to Grimwald," she said, speaking with a temperance she did not feel. She was aware that Lothair heeded her quiet words and also that losing her temper with the old lord would gain naught. "If not a little more, plus the return journey." She opened the small jar, then plucked at the Lord de Tulley's chemise. "Would you truly dispatch my new husband for a week or more so soon after our nuptials?"

"I order as I see fit!" the older man bellowed, spinning to point a finger at Lothair. "And this man, this man upon whom I have bestowed so much favor in so short a time, he dares to demand more!"

"Did he?" Lothair glanced over his shoulder, his gaze still simmering, and Magdala smiled at him. "I confess, sir, that I can find no fault with a knight who has the audacity to speak his mind. Even if such a confession is not convenient to you, it speaks of honesty and valor." The older man harrumphed. "I thought, sir, that you appreciated men with thoughts of their own." She saw some of the tension ease from Lothair's shoulders before he turned back to the window again.

The Lord de Tulley seized her hand. "But he vowed to take you from me," he said, sounding much more frail than she knew him to be.

He strove to turn her to his view, to be sure.

"I doubt as much, sir," she said, tugging up the hem of his chemise. He resisted for a moment, but when she smoothed the unguent on his back, he leaned over the table.

"You should know, my lady, that I requested a week in your company before such departure," Lothair said.

"Impossible," the old lord murmured.

"And was declined," Lothair continued. "I then asked that your safety might be ensured by the Lord d'Annossy remaining longer as a guest, on the condition that he, Sir Niall, Sir Bayard and their wives were told your name."

"Impossible," the old lord insisted.

"In the face of such rigid insistence upon one path and one path only, I suggested that we would leave on the morrow for Provins."

"Oh!" Magdala had mixed feelings, for she did not wish to leave the old lord or the security of the heavy walls of Château Tulley. She did admire, though, that Lothair had challenged his lord, and on her behalf. She saw, too, that he was resolute.

"And what say you, Magdala, now that you know his temerity?"

"I believe, sir, that my lord husband knows better in such matters than I do, and I am content to follow his dictate."

"I suppose you will tell me that a lady should have greater loyalty to her husband than to her guardian."

"I have always understood matters should be thus."

The Lord de Tulley snorted, but there was indulgence in the sound. "To the left, if you please," he said, his tone more serene.

Magdala had a curious sense that she had succeeded in a test.

She felt the tension ease in Lothair and risked a glance in his direction. He was watchful but beyond that she could not guess his thoughts.

Was he pleased by her support of his view? The silence in the solar no longer simmered with tension, though it was not as tranquil as it might have been. Magdala rubbed the unguent into the Lord de Tulley's back until it was completely absorbed, then pulled down his chemise. He seemed to be dozing as she closed the jar and washed her hands, and she saw Lothair turn from the window. Of course, his expression was inscrutable.

"You may tell them," the Lord de Tulley said to him. "But no others."

"Agreed," Lothair said.

"First light," the older man insisted.

"Earlier yet," Lothair replied, his gaze locking with Magdala's. "For the sooner we depart, the sooner we will return."

The Lord de Tulley harrumphed again and waved a dismissal. Lothair opened the portal for Magdala and Felix slipped through it to tend his lord. They descended the stairs together in silence and she wondered again at his thoughts. Was he as disappointed as she?

"And so you are to be sent away," she said, not disguising her disappointment.

Lothair closed his hand over hers and squeezed it. "You may trust Quinn completely," he said when she might have hoped for a sweeter confession but she nodded understanding.

"I thank you for that," she said. "I have feared to make an error in their presence."

He turned a very blue glance upon her. "Honesty is always best, my lady."

Magdala smiled and he studied her for a long moment, then excused himself, kissing her hand before he returned to his duties.

Why did the Lord de Tulley wish to send Lothair away? If his reason was as stated, why could the errand not wait?

OF COURSE, his former comrades were surprised by the revelation, but the confession vastly improved relations between Lothair and Niall.

"Still a beauty, but not an heiress," Niall said with cheer, congratulating Lothair as he had not before.

Lothair rolled his eyes. "You did not intend to wed her."

"Of course not."

"But no longer a maiden," Quinn noted. "I believe the lady has lost her allure for Niall."

"That would be for the best," Lothair said grimly and Niall grinned at him.

"You might find me another lady."

"You manage to find enough of them yourself," Lothair retorted and they laughed together, as easy as once they had been. "I would ask you to accompany me on the Lord de Tulley's errand."

"Aha!" Bayard said. "Not so trusting of Niall as all of that."

"That is not my concern," Lothair insisted, though his friends teased him mightily all the same. When he could continue, he did as much. "I would you, Quinn, to remain here as a guest with your lady wife while I am gone, for I would take both Niall and Sir Gerald with me."

"You fear some trouble?"

"The Lord de Tulley insists that his nephew will arrive, though I know not when."

"Of what import is that?" Bayard asked.

"My lady distrusts him."

"That is sufficient cause for me," Quinn said with a nod.

"When do we ride out? In the morning?"

"Nay, earlier," Lothair said. "Before the dawn." He cast a glance upward to the window of Magdala's chamber, wishing she might be recovered from their first night and knowing it would be too soon. He would have liked to have spent even a few hours in her bed, but knew the temptation might be too much for him.

He would take a nap in the stables once all was prepared for their departure, and look forward to the moment of his own return.

MAGDALA WAS aware of the bustle of preparations in the stable and the bailey for his departure. The Lord and Lady de Beauvoir departed in the afternoon, as did Bayard and his wife, Berthe. She dined quietly with Lady Melissande, expecting Lothair and Quinn but they did not come to the board. The Lord de Tulley had remained in his chamber with Felix, and the hall was particularly empty. Lady Melissande made a jest about all those who had celebrated so heartily the night before being in need of rest. They had retired early, and Magdala had hoped for Lothair's arrival in her chambers.

But he did not come.

The candles burned low, the bailey became quiet, darkness descended and still he did not come to her. She could see no signs of movement below, only the sentries on the walls, and could not hear even the distant echo of his voice. She thought of his confession in the garden that day and wondered whether he feared he had confided too much in her.

She thought of his wife and his obvious love for her and sighed. Aileen. Somehow it was worse to know that lady's name.

Somehow it was disappointing to believe that their nuptial night had been no more than a duty to him.

Or perhaps he feared that she might be lost in childbirth. Was that why he told her of the pennyroyal? Magdala did not know and Lothair was not there to be asked.

She extinguished the candles except for one, wishing for his company and his touch, and feared she would not know either soon.

She waited to no avail.

And finally, Magdala surrendered. She pinched out the wick of the last candle, drew the drapes around the bed and retired alone.

She was still awake when the horses mustered in the bailey in the darkness before the dawn, but she did not go to the window to look upon them.

Lothair had not come to her and that seemed a bad portent indeed.

IT WAS curious that doing the right thing could leave a man feeling like a knave.

Lothair felt that he had been unkind to Magdala, though he knew he had chosen rightly in letting her heal. He supposed he might have spoken to her of his decision, but he was not one who initiated discussions, particularly ones of such intimate matters, and would not have known where to begin. No doubt he would have stammered to silence and she would have studied him, mystified, leaving him to feel like a fool as well as a knave.

Nay, all would be set to rights upon his return to Château Tulley.

He had told her of Aileen and resolved that misunderstanding, and she had supported his view in his challenge to the Lord de Tulley. Rationally, Lothair knew they began well.

But for the first time in a very long time—perhaps ever—he feared that reason might not be sufficient.

He spurred his steed to greater speed, cutting their nightly rest short, determined to return to his lady wife as soon as that might be achieved.

~

ON THE SECOND DAY, Lothair's small party was obliged to leave the road for an approaching entourage. The other travelers did not progress with particular haste, nor did they form their company in an organized manner. Four wagons and at least a dozen horses comprised the group, which straggled over the width of the road. They could have ridden two abreast, with the wagons between the horses, but instead they claimed the entire width of the road. Lothair counted six knights among the considerable company.

"Aristocrats," Niall muttered beneath his breath as their own five steeds waited impatiently by the side of the road for the sprawling company to pass. "Nary a concern for another."

Lothair chafed to ride on, his destrier stomping with impatience to run.

A plump man of an age with Lothair, with fair hair and a cloak lined with thick fur, spared them a disparaging glance as he passed. Though he was not dressed as richly as might be, his garb was well wrought and his manner imperious. He surveyed Lothair's company with disdain, offered no greeting, and did not hasten his party— though he had to have seen how his party inconvenienced their own.

"Do you recognize the insignia?" Lothair asked when the largest and most ornate of the wagons drew abreast of them. Truly, he was unfamiliar with the nobility of this region and did not care overmuch.

Niall shook his head, but Sir Gerald cleared his throat. "It is the mark of Idelstein, sir, and I believe that man may be its lord."

Lothair peered after the other man with alarm. "Lord Herbert von Idelstein?"

"Aye, sir, the very one." Gerald smiled. "I daresay your wife will be gladdened to see her brother arrive at Château Tulley. Was he not anticipated there?"

Gerald had not been admitted to the secret of Magdala's name and the other two knights exchanged a glance.

"Aye, the Lord de Tulley mentioned as much," Lothair said with a calmness of manner he did not feel.

He should have asked why Magdala disliked this man so much.

Should he return to Tulley and risk the Lord de Tulley's wrath? Would Magdala have need of his aid? Surely not, with Quinn in residence?

Lothair watched the last of the party pass them, snared in indecision. He felt Niall watching him closely as he weighed his choices. On the one hand, his duty was to serve the will of the Lord de Tulley, who had dispatched him on an errand to Grimwald. On the other, he trusted Magdala's concern about Herbert.

He reminded himself that Quinn would defend her.

Still he hesitated. "How far yet to Grimwald?" he asked Gerald.

"Less than a day, sir. We have made markedly good time thus far." He grinned. "But then, it is clear that you would return to your new wife with speed, and who could blame you for such an impulse, sir?"

Aye, Lothair had ridden with the purpose he had learned in Outremer, and knew this knight found it an ordeal. In contrast, the other party ambled on its way, Herbert clearly feeling no haste to reach his uncle's abode.

"Then we shall make better time," Lothair said, gathering the reins as his decision was made. "I would reach Grimwald before we rest this night, the better that we might ride back to Tulley on the morrow." He did not wait for Gerald to express doubt of this scheme. He knew it would be a long day for all of them, and the horses as well, but he could not suppress his sense that his presence would be needed at Tulley with all haste.

Niall made no comment but gave his steed his spurs, his agreement evident by his choice.

~

HERBERT VON IDELSTEIN arrived at Château Tulley with all the pomp and pageantry of an emperor on the fifth day after Lothair's departure.

The days and nights had stretched long for Magdala, though she had tried to keep herself diverted. Lady Melissande was determined to improve her riding skills and she spent part of each morning with a palfrey in the bailey. The tale, contrived by Lady Melissande, was that Heloise had experienced a bad fall and needed to regain her confidence in the saddle. Magdala doubted if that lady had realized how much of a challenge that would prove to be. She was not at ease with horses, but hoped that familiarity would improve that.

Herbert's retinue included two dozen pages and squires, six knights on destriers, each accompanied by at least one palfrey and squire, and no less than four wagons loaded with his trunks. Herbert himself rode in the middle of the procession, waving to those villagers who stood watching in wonder, as if he was a conqueror come to claim his due.

The Lord de Tulley could not have missed the implication any more than Magdala.

Magdala stood by the older man at the window of the solar, watching the approach of Herbert's company. She silently wished Lothair greater speed. She could not imagine that he would return in less than two days and she feared Herbert's scheme.

She held the older man's elbow as he peered out the window of the solar, leaning more heavily upon his cane than upon her. His lips were drawn to a taut line and his brow was furrowed as he eyed the length of Herbert's procession.

"His party will claim the road all the way from one gate to the other," the older man muttered, then granted Magdala a piercing glance. "It seems he arrives with the intention of lingering long."

Magdala did not doubt Herbert's ambitions but she said naught.

Tulley eyed her and harrumphed before turning from the window. "I will wear my new tabard this night, Felix, the one that the lady embroidered so artfully for me."

Magdala bit back a smile. That tabard, wrought of silk of deep blue, was heavily embroidered with the insignia of Tulley. Around the hem were the emblems of all the holdings sworn to Tulley, each coached in silver thread. It was a glittering and impressive garment, if she did admit as much herself, and she had been amazed that each time she had shown her work to the old lord, he had insisted that she add yet more embellishment.

Now she understood that he had prepared for this meeting.

"You had best not stand in the sunlight, sir," she said mildly. "No one will be able to look upon you in your majesty."

He grinned at that, a mischievous smile that prompted Magdala to conclude that the Lord de Tulley had been a handsome rogue in his time.

She smiled back at him, intending to leave him to his garb, but Tulley scowled. "Stay," he instructed, the single word a command that could not be denied. "Herbert can wait upon me for a while yet. I will not descend to the hall until the evening meal."

"But he should be greeted."

"Quinn can manage the details," the Lord de Tulley said with a wave of his hand. "And his wife can be most charming when receiving a guest. I am glad that they were convinced to linger." He granted her a bright glance. "Your husband was right in that, but do not tell him as much. He may become vain in his own judgement."

"His judgement is good, though, sir. I wager I will tell him."

He coughed at this but did not protest.

Magdala frowned, knowing that as Heloise, she should greet Herbert as well. "I should change my own kirtle, then."

The Lord de Tulley smiled at her and seized her hand. "You will not face him alone. It is evident that he will recognize you and if I know Herbert as well as I believe I do, he will seek to find some advantage in his knowledge. Leave him to the Lord and Lady d'Annossy."

"As you wish, sir."

"Sir," he echoed, his tone testy. "Why do you no longer call me Uncle?"

Magdala exchanged a glance with Felix, who seemed to be struggling to hide a smile. "Because you are not my uncle, sir, and all in this chamber know as much."

"But I liked it," the Lord de Tulley replied with impatience. "And with Herbert arrived, you must maintain the ruse. I insist that you call me Uncle again."

"Even though there are those in the hall who know the ruse?"

"Even so. I should have liked to have had a niece I could rely upon, and I should have liked that you would be that niece." He peered at her. "Have you another uncle to claim your affection?"

"Nay, sir."

He cast her a stern glance. "Then I insist upon it."

Magdala bowed. "Aye, *Uncle*."

And the Lord de Tulley smiled in satisfaction. He gestured vaguely to the unguent for his back and Magdala retrieved it. He sat down as had become his custom and leaned on the table as she pulled up his chemise. She gathered the right increment of the unguent on her fingers and began to massage it into his skin, marveling yet again at the warmth it emanated.

How remarkable that a plant could yield a cure in one measure and a poison in another.

The Lord de Tulley sighed contentment as Felix laid out his garments for the evening meal.

"Why did you not wed and have children of your own?" Magdala asked.

The older man scoffed. "There is no guarantee that marriage will result in children."

"There is not," she agreed. "But I ask more after your own inclination. I should have imagined that a knight of your stature with such a holding as Tulley would have been sought after."

The Lord de Tulley shook his head. "I was the youngest son of three. There was no hope of my inheriting so much as a millstone. I was sent to an uncle to earn my spurs, as was appropriate, and he, as my patron, granted my spurs, my sword and my horse to me."

"And what then?"

"Tournaments," the older man acknowledged. "Not as they are now, though. Nay, there was peril in accepting a challenge in those times, and fewer rules. Many men of my acquaintance did not survive long in that pursuit without dire injury." He stretched out his knee and it creaked as always it did. "A bad fall granted me that souvenir."

"A choice of the intrepid, then?"

"A choice of those with naught to lose," the Lord de Tulley said sadly. He sighed. "I lost my heart at a tournament, a large one that drew combatants from far and wide. If I had claimed the prize, I might have asked for the lady's hand, but alas, I was bested by her own brother."

"How unfortunate."

"Unfortunate? My loss was planned, Magdala. It might have been a game of chess, contrived to ensure my failure."

"But why?"

"To dismiss my suit, of course. The lady was not unwelcoming, but her family wished for a better alliance than the third son of Tulley." He shook his head and she wondered if that lady had held his heart captive all these years.

She could imagine that he might be one to be loyal to a memory.

"Who did she wed?" she asked long moments later.

"She did not. She declined to accept another match, by all reports."

"And what became of her?"

"I know that she fled her father's abode when he was determined to see her wed. She must have taken refuge somewhere, but I never found tell of her. Perhaps she, like Heloise, encountered villains on the road and met with an untimely end." His voice hardened. "I have never uncovered the truth, though it has not been for lack of effort."

Magdala understood that his fortunes had changed and he had sought his love. "What happened to your brothers?"

"Godwyn was killed at the hunt, gored by a boar he insisted upon facing alone and on foot." The Lord de Tulley shook his head. "He was proud and confident, certain that he could defeat any foe. The wound festered, defying the intervention of any healer. It took him two weeks to die."

Magdala understood that his passing could not have been pleasant. She rubbed the unguent into the Lord de Tulley's shoulder. "He was the oldest?"

"Aye. Godwyn always expected matters to follow his choice and they often did." The Lord de Tulley chuckled. "He infuriated my next oldest brother, Ulric, besting him in all pursuits with apparent ease." He sobered. "Godwyn had wed young and had one son, Henrik. He had seen eighteen summers when Godwyn died and the seal fell to his hand." The Lord de Tulley shook his head. "Too young for such responsibilities. He fairly emptied the treasury in his pursuit of pleasure, but no one could chastise him. I tried and was cast out of my birthplace for the effort."

"Your nephew banned you from Tulley?"

"Aye, the impertinent knave. My other brother, Ulric, a man more inclined to scholarship than warfare, had no desire to wed himself, but he arranged the match of our sole sister, Verena, to the eldest son of the Lord von Idelstein. That was considered to be a brilliant match and was heartily celebrated in both holdings. Even Henrik approved." He smiled a little. "Verena was less happy with it, but they had a son within a year, so it could not have been so horrific."

Magdala had barely known the Lord von Idelstein for he had died shortly after her arrival at that keep. "What was he like?"

The Lord de Tulley shrugged. "George was not one I admired or would have trusted, but he was shrewd and he was wealthy. She had every comfort there, to be sure."

Magdala remembered Lothair's concerns. "Did she take seeds from your grandmother's garden for her own?"

"Aye, she did! Curious that you should think of that." He peered at her. "You must have seen it."

"Aye, but I never worked within it. It was secured most of the time. Lady Heloise was not fond of time spent in the tranquility of a garden."

"Nay, more a merry dance or an arriving company of warriors."

Magdala nodded agreement. "It was much smaller than the garden here and less gracious in its design. It was more like a kitchen garden than the one in the cloister at the abbey."

"And this one resembles the abbey more?"

"It does. Perhaps that is why I like it so well."

"You were happy there."

"I was content, but then, I knew nothing else."

The older man straightened and granted her a bright glance. "Do you regret that you left it?"

Magdala shook her head, feeling her flush begin as the old man's eyes glinted. "Not now," she said and he grinned.

"Aye, you would never have shared a bed with Lothair there," he teased and her cheeks burned. There was a fanfare from the bailey below and they looked toward the window as one.

"I have a notion, Magdala, that you and I should greet Herbert here," the old lord said and she wondered what he planned.

"Aye, Uncle?"

"Aye." The Lord de Tulley frowned at the boots Felix was polishing. "Nay, the new ones from Paris," he instructed and the servant hastened to fetch them.

They were already buffed to a sheen, but Felix polished them again.

The Lord de Tulley, meanwhile, stood, leaning upon his cane. Magdala helped him to don the glorious tabard, lacing the sides for him as he fussed over it. She fastened his belt around his waist, giving the ornate silver buckle a stroke of admiration. Magdala combed the length of his hair, a veritable crown of gleaming silver, and even dared to adjust his bushy brows. He flicked a hot blue glance at her for her audacity, but he looked well and she knew he knew it.

"The red cloak," he said to Felix. "The one with the lining of wolf fur." The cloak was fastened to his shoulder with a large gold pin set with garnets, then he sat down heavily again. He gestured for the ebony stick and turned a proud glance upon Magdala. "Well?"

"Your magnificence might stun your guest to silence," Magdala said.

"One can only hope," Tulley said beneath his breath. "Herbert is cursedly inclined to be fulsome, particularly when he wishes for something. He cannot be here for any other reason."

"You invited him, did you not?"

"He has declined my invitation before. Nay, he accepted it because it fit with his own objectives." He offered his hand to her, eliminating Magdala's faint hope that she might be able to delay this meeting. "I like the blue on you," he said with approval. "I wish Lothair was here to see you thus."

"He could not be, Uncle, for you sent him away."

The old man laughed, taking no offense. "And you are disappointed," he said shrewdly.

Magdala tried to smile. "Perhaps any lady would miss her new husband if they shared but one night together."

"Perhaps his errand will better ensure your future," the Lord de Tulley retorted. "I know a thing or two about men and their merit. Trust me in this matter." He rapped his cane upon the floor and rose to his feet, even as footsteps sounded on the stairs. Lady Melissande's voice carried through the portal, then Herbert's low reply.

Magdala lifted her chin and held the Lord de Tulley's elbow, making it look as if he supported her and not the other way around.

"Ah, child, you are a gift beyond expectation," he growled with affection as the door opened and Herbert was admitted to the solar.

CHAPTER 13

*L*othair was so surprised that he scarce understood the words of the priest at Grimwald. "No one died?" he repeated, certain that he was too tired in this moment.

They had managed to arrive in the village of Grimwald on the morning of the third day after their departure from Tulley. They rode directly to the small chapel. All three of them were exhausted and their horses more so, but Lothair could not dismiss his sense that something would soon go awry.

If it had not already done as much.

This, however, he had not expected.

The priest looked to be discomfited. "That is correct, sir."

"But we were told that a lady and two warriors were buried here, after that Lady Heloise von Idelstein was attacked in Grimwald forest," Niall insisted.

"It would have been more than two years ago, before the Yule," Lothair supplied. "There was a maid and another guard with them, who survived the assault. They were escorted here by a baron and his party, who happened upon them in the forest while they were under attack." He felt Niall eye him in surprise and recognized again

222

Magdala's influence upon him. He would deliver a treatise to gain her favor, and do yet more to defend her cause.

The priest winced. "They arrived as you say, sir, but there was no funeral."

"The lady said she paid two coins for the burial and funeral masses."

The priest dropped his gaze. "And I took it, for the payment was fair. But in the morning, there were no corpses to be dressed and buried. That baron told me it had been a jest."

"A jest?" Niall echoed.

"And you did not return the coin to the lady who had paid it?"

"I tried to, sir, but she and her guardian had departed by the time I located the inn they had chosen."

Niall and Lothair exchanged a glance.

"He was injured and I understood that they sought a healer to tend his wounds." The priest shrugged. "It was all most strange. I thought for the duration of the day that the jest had been played upon me, but there were no corpses to be found. I added the coin to the donations for orphans, for I knew the names of none of them."

"Not even the baron?"

The priest shook his head. "I did not recognize him, or his insignia. He was a handsome man, with a merry manner, to be sure, with sufficient affluence to have half a dozen horses and guards to his name."

"And this is all you knew of him?" Lothair asked but the priest shrugged.

"A jest," Niall repeated again, shaking his head. "Does this mean that Lady Heloise is not dead?"

Lothair could not say. He scanned the chapel, his thoughts flying. "If not, perhaps we might find her."

"If not, surely she would have appeared at Idelstein or Tulley by now?" Niall asked and Lothair had to acknowledge that his comrade was right.

"I wish we knew more of the baron. Do you think the tavern keeper might recall him?"

"I doubt as much, sir," the priest said. "I do not believe he stayed there."

Lothair felt his eyes narrow. "He rode through the whole of Grimwald forest, then did not linger overnight at the tavern."

"There was some suggestion of a need for haste," the priest said, frowning in recollection. "Perhaps an ill relation awaiting them? I am sorry but I do not recall the details well."

Lothair had turned away, wondering where to start when the priest called after him.

"His wife was most gracious. I remember that. And such a beautiful woman."

Lothair glanced back. "What did she look like?"

"Oh, she could not have seen twenty summers, and her hair was of a glorious golden hue. She was lovely beyond belief and so devoted to him. Indeed, I recall that they were in quite high spirits after their jest for they embraced multiple times, even in my presence. She apologized so prettily for drawing me into her ruse." He raised a finger. "And what skill she had with a horse! I would wager that she was a better rider even than her lord husband. One does not often see a lady who rides so very well."

"Heloise," Lothair whispered and Niall nodded agreement.

The Lord de Tulley would be most interested in these tidings.

The question remained: where was the lady now? Lothair feared he could guess the truth, though he had no cause to believe Heloise would arrive at Tulley now.

Herbert was there, which was cause enough for haste.

Lothair could not dismiss his sense that every moment might be of import.

～

"Uncle!" Herbert declared, his charm as excessive and untrustworthy as ever. "How hale you look! I believe you have grown younger in my absence."

Magdala suppressed a shiver as she eyed the new arrival, noting Herbert appeared as confident as ever. The gold glittered on his embroidered tabard, the expanse of cloth required to contain his person more than considerable.

Herbert was garbed as a nobleman, with neither hauberk nor breastplate, his legs encased in dark hose that did not manage to diminish the appearance of his bulk. He wore a great chain around his neck with a medallion marked with the insignia of Idelstein, which also appeared on his gold signet ring. His hair was longer than Magdala recalled, curling upon his shoulders in its mingled shades of gold, but when he bowed, she saw the gleam of bare skin on the top of his head.

She heard Tulley snort but strove to remain impassive herself.

Perhaps she learned a feat or two from Lothair.

"And your tongue has silvered," the Lord de Tulley said, his tone grumpy.

Herbert laughed, his gaze darting around the solar. Did he assess the value of every item within it? Magdala would have wagered as much. He stepped toward the older man before being granted permission to do as much and made to seize Tulley's hand. The Lord de Tulley recoiled slightly and Herbert's eyes narrowed. "I meant only to kiss your ring, Uncle," he said. "My intention was not to startle you."

"And yet I was startled all the same." Tulley rapped his walking stick and Herbert retreated.

The Lord de Tulley waved and the Lord and Lady d'Annossy retreated. "A moment!" he cried and the portal was closed, securing uncle, nephew, Felix and Magdala in the solar together.

Herbert considered Magdala, a familiar hunger lighting his eyes as he surveyed her. "And my dear sister, Heloise," he said, almost chortling when he uttered her name. "I believe you are even more beautiful than I recall." He swept a low bow and Magdala managed to hold her ground, though she ensured that her hands were occupied in aiding the old lord, lest this fiend see fit to touch her.

"You are too kind, sir," she contented herself with saying.

The older man's eyes narrowed, but Magdala noticed that he was tiring. He was leaning upon her more heavily. "Come, Uncle. Your chair is near the brazier, just as you prefer. Perhaps Herbert might speak with you there."

The Lord de Tulley nodded his assent and she aided him to his chair, well aware that Herbert watched avidly. Was he calculating the days the older lord had yet to live? Was he anticipating the fall of Tulley's seal into his own outstretched hand?

Was Lothair right that he might have encouraged his parents' demise? If so, he might have similar plans for the Lord de Tulley. Magdala bristled at the very possibility, determined to defend the older man from such indignity.

"It seems that life at Tulley suits you well, sister."

"Perhaps it is marriage that suits the lady well," the Lord de Tulley said gruffly and Magdala turned in time to see Herbert frown in surprise. His gaze was upon her left hand where Lothair's ring glinted and she saw his eyes narrow. Did he recognize it? Magdala knew that the Lord de Tulley had given it to Lothair, and in this moment, she wondered if the ring had a greater import.

"Is that your grandmother's ring?" Herbert asked, his voice strained.

"And who better to wear it than my oldest niece?" the Lord de Tulley demanded. "I suppose you have some compliment to make and we had best see it done." He settled back in his chair, bracing his hands upon the arms and glaring at Herbert. Magdala might have tucked the furs over his lap but he granted her such a fierce look that she retreated.

It was not the most welcoming of receptions, but Herbert was not deterred. Felix stood slightly behind the Lord de Tulley, his hands behind his back.

Magdala had the curious sense that something was about to happen.

The door closed and the sounds of the newly arrived party rose from the bailey. Magdala heard horses stamping and their trap jingling, as well as Quinn's decisive commands.

"And who have you wed, sister dear?" Herbert asked her. "Some knight errant who lost his heart at a glance? Or was your match a particularly advantageous one to be so arranged by our beloved uncle?"

"I have wed a knight and crusader named Lothair of Sutherland."

Herbert blinked. "I have never heard of him," he said, as if he knew the reputation of every man in all of Christendom. "Has he a holding and a fortune?"

Magdala shook her head. "Not to my understanding." She turned to the Lord de Tulley. "Uncle?"

The older man claimed her hand. "His merit is in his nature," he said with resolve.

Herbert continued to look astonished and Magdala sensed that the older lord was enjoying his nephew's discomfiture.

"And where is this most fortunate of men?" Herbert asked finally. "Did I encounter him upon my arrival and fail to give him the greeting he is due?"

"He is my Captain of the Guard," the Lord de Tulley repeated, his tone impatient. "And thus he has ridden out at my command. His errand is of no import to you, so you need not trouble yourself to ask of it."

Herbert's brows rose. "I but strove to make conversation, Uncle."

The Lord de Tulley harrumphed. "Do you consider yourself greeted now?"

"Not by half, Uncle." Herbert smiled. "Do you not wish to know what gift I have brought you?"

The Lord de Tulley straightened, to Magdala's surprise, and leaned forward. "I wager I will dislike it."

"I wager otherwise, Uncle." Herbert opened the door with a

flourish and snapped his fingers. Someone stepped quickly to attention and surrendered a small chest to him. He dismissed the servant with an impatient gesture and shut the door again, carrying the chest to the Lord de Tulley on the flats of his hands. He bowed again, surrendering the chest.

The Lord de Tulley accepted it with some suspicion, then opened it warily. Magdala could see that the interior was filled with dried fruit that she did not recognize.

"Ah!" said the Lord de Tulley, as if both pleased and surprised.

"I recalled your affection for figs, Uncle, and dispatched a messenger to find some for you when I realized I would be coming to Château Tulley. These were acquired from the finest vendor of foodstuffs in Venice, a man whose wares are sought out by kings and emperors, and that was the cause of my delay in attending you. The best fare does require some patience at times."

"Figs!" the Lord de Tulley said with delight and licked his lips. "Are you fond of figs, Heloise?"

Magdala had no notion for she had never seen the fruit before. "I do not, I fear. But then, you will not feel compelled to share your treat with anyone."

"You used to love them," Herbert said, his tone wicked as if he would catch her out.

"Aye, but one's tastes do change over time," she replied sweetly.

Herbert laughed, though the sound was not merry. He turned back to the Lord de Tulley. "You must taste one, Uncle, and let me know whether they were worth the journey and the price."

"You speak aright. I have not tasted a fig in so long, and just the scent of them arouses my anticipation." The older man snapped his fingers and Felix stepped forward. "This looks to be a fine plump one," the Lord de Tulley said and Felix obediently chose that one.

"What is this?" Herbert demanded in outrage.

"A precaution," the Lord de Tulley said firmly.

"You have a food taster?" Herbert asked. "What caused this change in your routine? Has someone deigned to risk your life, Uncle?" His gaze flicked to Magdala, his fury clear, and his very manner made her glad of this precaution.

Perhaps Lothair was right.

The Lord de Tulley waved his nephew to silence and waited expectantly.

"A most intriguing scent," Felix said. "But then, I have never eaten a fig." He put the fruit in his mouth and chewed steadily, standing beside the old lord's chair as that man watched.

"I cannot imagine what I have done to deserve such a response to my gift," Herbert huffed.

"Uncle's digestion has become delicate," Magdala began to explain. "And thus Felix…"

But before she could finish, Felix made a strange choking sound. He had just swallowed the fig and raised a hand to his mouth. Magdala thought perhaps it had caught in his throat, but his eyes opened wide. He shook so hard that he fell to his knees, then collapsed upon the floor, convulsing. She raced toward him as he arched his back, shuddered, then became limp.

"Felix!" she cried but the Lord de Tulley seized her arm and drew her away from the fallen man. His strength was far greater than she might have anticipated and his fingers dug into her shoulder.

"You cannot aid him now. He has been poisoned!"

"Poisoned?" Herbert echoed.

"I know the signs well enough," the Lord de Tulley said grimly. "Look upon him! Already he breathes his last."

Magdala could not believe it. "But, Uncle, are you certain that nothing can be done for Felix?" she insisted. "I have not the skill of Lothair but surely I could try to help."

"Leave him be! Can you not see that he does not draw breath any longer? I cannot bear to see such loyalty so wickedly compensated." The Lord de Tulley shook his head, then rose majestically to his feet as he roared for the châtelain. "Thomas!" He bellowed. "Felix has been poisoned by my nephew's gift!"

Herbert looked to be both agitated and flustered. If she had not seen the truth with her own eyes, Magdala might have thought him as surprised as she. It appeared he could feign innocence better than she had believed.

Perhaps he had sufficient practice.

"But Uncle, there was naught amiss with the figs." Herbert reached for the chest. "I shall verify their good state with all haste…"

The Lord de Tulley's cane came down on Herbert's hand with a loud crack, and that man winced at the blow even as he pulled his hand away. His features were ashen now and his eyes wide.

"As if I would heed your request, varlet and cur, to have the proof eliminated," the Lord de Tulley said with more hostility than Magdala had ever seen him show. He waved his cane at his nephew who retreated toward the door. "You are no more than a scheming knave who would steal my holding from beneath me. I knew always that you were interested solely in your own comfort and reward, but this —*this* is an insult beyond all endurance! That you could arrive here and as a guest in my abode attempt to end my days is abominable and reprehensible beyond all else. Leave my chamber and my hall immediately!"

"But, Uncle…"

The Lord de Tulley roared as the châtelain appeared in the doorway.

Even the customary calm of Thomas had been ruffled and he swallowed visibly when his gaze fell upon Felix. He crossed himself hastily. "Sir, if I may just…"

"Leave him be!" shouted the Lord de Tulley. "Is it not sufficient that a man of such merit lies dead? Must we submit him to indignities after his demise?" He took a step forward and pointed his walking stick at Herbert. Magdala eyed Felix, wondering whether she had seen him move a little.

A twitch perhaps after he expired.

"Lord d'Annossy!" shouted the Lord de Tulley. "I demand that you hurl this blackguard from the gates! Clear my chambers of all these intruders. I would be alone to mourn the loss of Felix." He caught his breath then, as if overwhelmed, and Magdala placed a hand upon his arm. He covered her hand with his and she was not surprised to feel him trembling.

"Heloise," Herbert hissed. "Encourage Uncle to see reason, if you please."

All eyes turned to Magdala and she saw the threat in Herbert's stare. She lifted her chin. "I think it most reasonable to deny a welcome to any man who has tried to poison the Lord de Tulley. Surely, brother, you cannot expect otherwise?"

Their gazes locked and held, Herbert's filled with venom.

"Ah! A lady of good sense," the Lord de Tulley said. "Who could complain of her counsel? At least I have one person left in my household I can trust absolutely."

"Uncle," Magdala chided gently. "You have many. Thomas has served you for countless years." She nodded toward the châtelain who inclined his head, his gaze trailing to the fallen Felix.

Herbert stepped forward again and his tone was hard when he spoke. "Uncle, there is a detail you should know about my sister..."

"Out of my chamber, fiend!" The Lord de Tulley took a hasty step backward and stumbled. It nigh toppled Magdala to catch him before he fell and ensure that he landed in his chair safely. He frothed and fumed, rapping his cane upon the floor and glaring at Herbert as if that man had pushed him. "Get out!"

Quinn appeared then, looking most fearsome in his armor, no less because he was followed by three knights sworn to Tulley. Herbert was quickly escorted from the chamber, despite his protests, and the door closed behind them.

The Lord de Tulley raised Magdala's hand to his lips and kissed her knuckles. "You will leave me, child," he said, sounding tired beyond all. "Thomas will attend this unpleasant task. If you might speak to the priest in the village about a funeral mass for Felix two days hence." He sighed. "He will rest in the chapel here in the keep on the morrow that those in the household can pray for his soul. And Antoine will have to be advised, for there can be no meat until the day after the funeral." He sighed then, looking so much older than his years that he might have wilted in place.

"If you are certain, Uncle."

"I am, child. I am weary beyond all. Leave me be this night and the morrow, but on the day of the service, I should appreciate your aid."

"Shall I take the figs?"

"Nay! I would not risk you."

"I will not eat one, not now."

The Lord de Tulley shook his head with vigor. "Thomas will ensure there is no risk of another consuming them."

That man nodded to her. Magdala kissed the cheek of the Lord de Tulley, surveyed the fallen Felix, and left the solar, unable to dismiss her sense that she had overlooked some detail of import.

THE LORD DE Tulley waited until the sounds in the corridor had faded to silence. Then he reached for a fig in the same moment that Felix sat up.

"God in Heaven," Thomas whispered, then at Felix's glance, offered the other man a hand. "Are you raised from the dead?"

Felix chuckled. "Hardly that." The Lord de Tulley offered him a fig, which he accepted. "Was I convincing, my lord?" he asked, pushing a hand through his hair. He straightened his tabard fastidiously even as he consumed the fruit and with no ill effects.

"Perfect, Felix, as I had anticipated."

Thomas looked between the two of them in astonishment. "You contrived this?"

The Lord de Tulley nodded. "I knew Herbert would come. I contrived that he might arrive in the absence of Lothair." His lips drew to a thin line. "I also anticipated that he would have a scheme to claim the seal of Tulley for his own. Instead, I struck first and he is discredited. My plan will proceed most admirably."

"Which plan is that, sir?" Thomas asked.

But the old man only smiled contentedly. "Tell no one of this, Thomas. Felix will remain hidden here in the solar until all the details have fallen into place."

"We shall have need of a coffin for the burial, my lord," Thomas noted. He hesitated when he was offered a fig, then with the Lord de Tulley's nod of encouragement, reluctantly accepted one. He nibbled it with caution.

"Aye, and it will be filled with sand. Arrange the details, Thomas, if you please, and betray this confidence to no one."

"Of course not, my lord."

"And eat your fig. They are too good to be wasted."

Thomas obediently ate his fig, though his uncertainty over the wisdom of that was most clear. Only when he had swallowed it all did the Lord de Tulley nod his dismissal.

Thomas bustled away, securing the door behind himself. The Lord de Tulley helped himself to another fig. "They are quite delicious," he acknowledged. "Had he a more noble nature, I might feel guilt at falsely accusing my nephew."

"But it is his nature that prompted your choice," Felix noted.

"Aye, he would destroy Tulley and all within it, ravage the treasury and ensure only his own comfort. He might as well be Henrik's son and I have not rebuilt this holding to see it ruined yet again." The Lord de Tulley shook his head. "I cannot allow such a possibility. Let him be content with Idelstein. If Fortune smiles upon us, he will die young of his excesses and Hildegarde will regain the losses."

"Should you see to her match, sir?"

"Only if I live another few years. She is an uncommonly wise child. I do not fret for her in the absence of my counsel." The Lord de Tulley considered the chest, then chose another fig.

"You did not think, sir, that you could confide in Lady Magdala?"

"I hated to deceive her, Felix," the old lord acknowledged, chewing his fig thoughtfully. "But I dare not risk an untimely revelation, or the return of Herbert to the hall, not when my plan is so close to fulfillment. She would undoubtedly confide in Lothair, and he would tell his comrades, and I do not trust Niall MacGillivray to recall his place or hold his tongue."

"Of course, my lord."

"Worse, Lothair might insist upon seeing your corpse. That was why he had to be absent, Felix. That man would not have been deceived."

"Nay, my lord."

The Lord de Tulley gestured to the chest of figs, raising his brows.

Felix smiled. "Aye, sir, I do not mind if I have another."

And the two men, lord and servant, sat in the solar of Château Tulley, enjoying figs in companionable silence, confident in the success of the older man's scheme.

THE REMAINDER of the day passed in a blur of consultations and arrangements for Magdala and she slept poorly that night. Herbert had been escorted through the village and out the gates by Quinn and the knights in service to Tulley. His camp had been established beyond the village outside the gates, since he had protested to Quinn that he could not immediately undertake the journey to Idelstein. Quinn had agreed, though Magdala guessed his concern was for the horses and not for Herbert's comfort.

Lady Melissande had been of great assistance in deciding the details of the arrangements, once she had affirmed the number of years that Felix had served the Lord de Tulley. That lady had far more education than Magdala and an unerring sense of what was appropriate.

Magdala would have liked to have consulted with the Lord de Tulley, but that man remained in the solar, the portal barred to all but Thomas. The châtelain took the older man his meals and undoubtedly tidings of the hall, as well, but said little when he returned to the hall.

Thomas shook his head when Magdala asked and said the lord had taken to his bed, a most dire situation indeed.

Still, he shouted at Magdala when she knocked on the portal late that afternoon, dismissing her with characteristic impatience.

She returned to the hall, sensing again that she had overlooked some key detail, only to find Thomas awaiting her at the foot of the stairs.

"A message for you, my lady," he said primly. "From your lord brother."

"Oh!" Magdala hoped it was not a written missive, for she would be unable to read it. Heloise, of course, had learned to read but not Magdala.

Surely Herbert knew as much?

"He sent a messenger," Thomas said, gesturing to a young man who waited at the entry to the bailey. He was no more than a boy and looked to be harmless. He smiled at Magdala. "I understand that your brother would like to consult with you and your lord husband, whom he has invited to halt at his tent on his return to Tulley. Perhaps he would offer his felicitations upon your match."

"Lothair is there?" Magdala's heart skipped in anticipation of seeing him so soon. "He returns earlier than expected."

"Evidently. Perhaps he rode with great haste, my lady. The Lord de Tulley will be glad of his arrival before the funeral, to be sure."

The presence of Lothair was reassuring beyond all, for Magdala would never have responded to a summons from Herbert alone. She knew him too well for that. Thomas was watching her, as if he had a secret he wished to surrender, though she could not imagine what it might be. "But what does Lord Herbert wish to discuss?"

Thomas' lips tightened. "I would wager, my lady, that Lord Herbert is reluctant to lose the affection of the Lord de Tulley." He sniffed. "He may think himself falsely accused. Perhaps he means to appeal for your aid." His gaze clung to Magdala's and she wondered at his import.

Had someone else poisoned the figs? She could not think of how it might have been done, but then, Herbert would undoubtedly have surrendered the chest of fruit to someone for the journey. He might never have confirmed its state when he purchased it—and it was far too easy to believe that anyone might wish Herbert dead. His plan to grant the fruit to the Lord de Tulley might have been an impulse, or a plan confided in no one else.

Magdala found herself wanting to know Herbert's side of the tale. "I will go then, Thomas, and consult with my brother and husband. I thank you."

"Would you request another to accompany you, my lady?"

"Since my lord husband is already there, I would not compel any in the keep to abandon their task," she said with a smile. "I will fetch my cloak," she said to the boy who bowed deeply. He could not have seen ten summers and Magdala knew he could not overwhelm her.

Better yet, she would see Lothair soon.

LOTHAIR SLOWED his destrier to survey the valley at the foot of Tulley's mount. The fields were green in the summer sunlight and the village outside the walls looked both peaceful and prosperous. The road wound onward to the south, vanishing from view at intervals as it climbed to Beauvoir on the pass. The mountain peaks were dusted with snow even in this season. He admired the pennants flying from the towers of Tulley and felt a satisfaction at the sight.

For the first time in a long time, Lothair thought of some place—this place—as home. He knew that was because Magdala awaited him there, along with a list of duties, each and every one of which granted him purpose and satisfaction.

But it was the promise of Magdala that made his heart leap.

He eyed the camp outside the gates, closer to them than the village, and wondered at it. The insignia he now recognized as that of Idelstein was on the banners that fluttered over the camp, and the large central tent, round and wrought of silk, was made in the same colors.

"That was a run, to be sure," Niall said, halting his destrier beside Sleipnir. He patted the beast's side, which gleamed with perspiration, then grinned at their companion. "I will wager that Gerald has not seen the likes of it before."

"Nay, sir," that man said with a shake of his head. "You do not linger when you have a destination, sir, to be sure." The three boys on their palfreys halted behind the knights just as Gerald gave a low whistle. "So, the Lord von Idelstein arrived, despite his slow pace. I wonder how long he has been here."

"I wonder that he does not stay within the keep itself," Lothair said. "Is that customary?"

Gerald shrugged. "His party was larger this time. Perhaps the Lord de Tulley did not see fit to accommodate him."

Perhaps all was not well between uncle and nephew.

"I think I should greet him," Lothair said softly.

"And assess the numbers of his companions," Niall agreed in an undertone. They exchanged a glance and a nod.

"Gerald, you will remain outside the camp of the Lord von Idelstein, with the horses and the boys. Niall, I would have you at my back."

There was agreement and they rode on with purpose, the party dividing as Lothair had decreed. Calum caught the reins of Sleipnir as Lothair dismounted.

"You fear trouble?" Niall asked quietly.

"My lady wife distrusts Lord Herbert," Lothair explained in an undertone. "Though I do not as yet know why."

"'Tis sufficient warning for me," Niall said, dropping his hand to the hilt of his sword as they entered Herbert's camp.

❧

MAGDALA'S HEART was in her throat when she was ushered into the large central tent in Herbert's encampment. It was a large tent wrought of striped silk in the colors of Idelstein, a peak high in its middle. The sun shone through the silk, casting bands of light and shade over the interior. Herbert lounged on a chair before her, his small eyes gleaming with a satisfaction she thought undeserved.

Though the tent was richly furnished, the ground thick with carpets and trunks on all sides, she immediately saw that they two were alone.

"Where is Lothair?" she asked and Herbert smiled.

"Who can say? Not I."

Magdala spun to find the tent flap closed behind her and the silhouettes of two guards visible through the silk.

She turned again to find that Herbert had risen to his feet and approached her. She caught her breath to find him so close.

"We must confer, lovely Magdala," he said in a low voice.

"I see no reason to do as much."

"There was nothing wrong with the figs," Herbert insisted.

"You cannot be certain. Someone may have tried to poison you."

Herbert shook his head. "Impossible. I carried them with me. I ate four of them myself and rearranged the contents so they did not appear to be missing." He sighed. "They were remarkable figs, worth every penny of their cost." He raised a fist. "And they were *not* poisoned!"

Magdala jumped when he snatched at her, but not quickly enough. He seized her shoulders and lifted her to her toes. He had to weigh twice as much as she did, and Magdala realized too late that she was alone within his lair where none would come to her aid.

"You did this," he hissed. "I do not know how you managed the feat, but somehow you are responsible. You ensured that I lost the favor of my uncle, for your own nefarious means."

"I did not!"

He shook her, his grip tightening when she struggled against him.

"And you will repair the damage you have wrought, or I will tell him of *your* deception."

This was an empty threat, for Magdala knew the Lord de Tulley knew the truth.

Herbert, however, was unaware of that.

"And if I refuse?" she asked, wishing to hear the worst of it.

"Then I will tell him all of it. I will tell your lord husband that you are a fraud. I will ensure that you are revealed as the liar you are, as a humble lying maid who wishes for more than she deserves. I will see that you are cast out from Tulley in shame." He smiled and she almost shivered. "And then I will be there, Magdala, when you have no one to defend you, and I will take what you have so long denied me."

"He will not cast me out. He will never do as much!"

"There is a new fire in you, Magdala." Herbert's eyes gleamed. "I like that."

"Release me, sir!"

"Perhaps my uncle will become convinced that you poisoned the figs. I do not care what I have to say, Magdala, to regain the promise of my inheritance. You will soon learn that blood is of greatest import, and that the Lord de Tulley will not deny his own in favor of a scheming harlot."

"I am no harlot!"

"But who knows the truth, Magdala? I could tell him that you welcomed me, that you rutted with me and every other man at Idelstein. I will tell him of your unholy appetites and he will believe me." He claimed a lock of her hair and wound it quickly around his beringed finger, giving it a hard tug. She grasped the lock of hair and strove to pull it from his grip, without success. Indeed, he pulled her into his embrace.

"Do you still like to fight, Magdala?" Herbert asked in a dangerous whisper. "I remember you were spirited before. I have such fondness for overwhelming my conquests by force. The triumph is so much sweeter when it has been fairly won." He smiled then, a warning that she had no time to heed, for his ankle hooked around her own. She was tripped and fell, only to find Herbert atop her, his weight pinning her down. "Oh, that is so much better," he purred, bending to lick her ear so that she shuddered in revulsion. "See how you seduce me, you wanton harlot."

As previously, the pose awakened a panic within her. Magdala struggled against him and would have screamed, but he locked his mouth over hers in a demanding embrace that he would have called a kiss. His hand landed upon her breast and he squeezed so hard that she caught her breath, then he pinched the nipple savagely.

It pleased him to hurt her. Magdala had not forgotten that. She knew that struggling against him would only increase his satisfaction but she could not halt herself.

"Ah, Magdala," he whispered, rubbing himself against her as he locked one hand over her mouth to silence her. "Perhaps Uncle should be told that you came here to seduce me. How very wicked of you, a lady who has previously held his trust." His eyes gleamed. "I think you are unworthy and Uncle should know of it."

In response to that, Magdala bit his plump finger hard in the same moment that she drove her knee into his groin. Herbert was prepared for her retaliation, though, and he grinned in delight that she would battle him. He struck her across the face for her objection, then reached to pull up her skirts when she flinched. She fought with all her might, then Herbert abruptly froze.

Magdala opened her eyes to find Lothair standing over them, his sword drawn, his expression more grim than ever she had seen it. Herbert looked astonished and she realized the tip of her husband's sword was at the base of her assailant's skull.

"Lord Herbert von Idelstein, I assume," Lothair said, his voice as cold as ice. "I suggest you release my lady wife."

CHAPTER 14

This was the root of Magdala's fear. Lothair understood completely when he saw Herbert atop her, for there was no mistaking the terror that fueled her resistance. She feared this man because he had striven to abuse her before. She had battled Niall with such vigor because she had been reminded of a similar incident.

He did not know what ruse had brought her to this camp, but he was certain the situation had been contrived by the man before him.

It took all within him to refrain from slaughtering Herbert immediately. He was filled with a fury beyond anything he had felt before, a need to defend Magdala and drive the fear from her eyes that was all consuming and fierce.

That was before he saw the red mark on her cheek where she had been struck.

Niall cleared his throat from the portal, recalling Lothair to his senses.

Lothair exhaled and lifted his sword tip from the other man's neck. Herbert had the wits to abandon Magdala and rise to his feet. That Magdala's kirtle was around her hips, that there was a mark on her cheek from a blow and marks around her mouth from the weight of this fiend's hand only fueled Lothair's rage and need for retaliation.

He reminded himself that this was the nephew of his patron, and gained control of his reaction. He did not sheath his sword but kept it between himself and Herbert, even as he offered his other hand to Magdala.

"Sir, I can explain," she said quietly but the way her hand trembled within his own told Lothair all he needed to know.

Surely she did not believe he blamed her?

"You need not, my lady," he said tersely. "I believe I understand the situation well."

"But not all of it," she said. "Much has occurred in your absence. Lord Herbert has been dismissed from Château Tulley, as Felix died from sampling the figs brought to Uncle as a gift."

Lothair was surprised by this detail. He held Herbert's gaze steadily, liking how it unsettled the other man. "Felix is dead?"

"The funeral will be on the morrow, my lord. It is a tragedy beyond belief."

"I did not do it!" Herbert protested. He took a step forward, found Lothair's sword against his chest, and retreated with his hands raised. "It is a plot to discredit me, launched by this witch to claim my uncle's legacy in my stead. I am certain of it."

"Witch," Lothair echoed, the sword tip nudging the other man.

Herbert visibly ground his teeth. "Lady," he corrected with heat, eyes flashing even as he sneered the word.

Lothair spoke with a composure he did not feel. It took all within him to refrain from slicing this man to ribbons and leaving him to die slowly. "And have you proof to support this accusation against my wife?"

"Who else could have done it?" Herbert demanded. "There were only the four of us there, Uncle is hale, Felix is dead, and I did naught. It must have been her."

"But how?" Magdala asked. "I did not touch your gift."

"I cannot explain your treachery, save that I know you are a liar. You have proven to have a talent for deception." He took a step back and eyed Lothair, challenge in his expression. "I know secrets about your wife, sir, truths that would compel you to put her aside, if you only have the wits to heed me."

"There is naught you could tell me of my lady that would compel me to abandon her."

"You say that because you do not know her guile…"

Enough! The tip of Lothair's sword nicked Herbert's throat, drawing blood, and that man gasped. "I say that because it is true," Lothair replied calmly. There was a tension in his tone, one that he suspected his rival did not hear or appreciate. Indeed, he was close to losing his temper, a rare incident indeed. He retreated a step from the temptation of injuring Herbert, taking Magdala with him. "Alas, our conversation has reached its end. Godspeed to you, sir."

He backed away from the other man, considering him to be unpredictable especially when his displeasure was so evident. "God-speed?" Herbert echoed.

"You will be gone when the sun rises on the morrow," Lothair said, glancing back. "Or you will experience the hospitality of the Lord de Tulley's dungeons."

"You should heed me!" Herbert cried, but Lothair pivoted to duck under the flap that Niall held open, drawing Magdala toward the waiting horses.

"Sir," she began but he shook his head.

The very fact that she felt she had to explain any of that situation angered him anew with the injustices she had known. "Not now, my lady." He spoke tersely. Calum bowed when Lothair reached Sleipnir, and Lothair locked his hands around Magdala's waist. He saw her alarm and attributed it to his touch, so soon after Herbert's abuse.

He despaired silently of ever returning to her bed, but vowed to win her trust anew.

"I would only lift you to the horse," he said quietly and she shook her head.

"I would prefer to walk."

"It is far to the keep," he insisted, wanting only to see her safe and with all haste. "And you have been threatened."

She cast a glance over the destrier, which was a massive beast even of his own kind, and set her lips. He knew she lacked confidence in the saddle and did not wish to feed her fears, of either the horse or himself.

"I fear I will fall and that will mar your return," she said quietly, which was not unreasonable. Sleipnir was tall and broad, and a lady would be compelled to sit sideways. The road was steep and the footing uneven. She gripped his arm and met his gaze. "Ride with me?"

Lothair would never refuse her any request, much less one that would have her so close. He swung into the saddle and reached down to lift her before him. She was nigh in his lap, her sweet scent rising to torment him, his one arm tightly around her waist. He thought she might recoil, but to his relief, she leaned against him, wrapping one arm around his waist—though surely that could only be to steady herself—then leaned her cheek against his chest.

"He said you were there and proposed a meeting," she confessed, her voice shaking slightly. "I should never have gone otherwise."

"I am glad that I returned in time," he said tightly.

And Herbert called her a liar. He should have cut the fiend, slaughtered...

"As am I. Thank you, sir."

He turned the horse, urging Sleipnir to trot toward the lower gates.

Sir. She did not address him by his name. She did not even refer to him as her lord. He had been absent for days and his new wife did not miss him, save when she had need of a rescue.

Truly, Lothair had a task before himself to win this lady's trust.

They approached the lower gates and he wondered whether he had finally found the challenge that would test even his patience.

But the reward would be sweet indeed, if he could win it.

∾

IF MAGDALA HAD THOUGHT to celebrate Lothair's return in private, she was doomed to disappointment. Once again, she was reminded of a statue as they rode up the steep road through the village to the château at the summit. Though the man held her securely before himself, there was no tenderness or affection in his embrace. Indeed, he seemed to keep a resolute distance between them.

Did he believe she was soiled? There were men, she understood, who found women offensive who had known the touch of another man. Lothair might well be one of them, given his principles and high expectations.

Did he believe she had invited Herbert's advances? This was twice he had found her beneath another man, and he might lay the blame for that at her own feet.

She wanted nothing more than to talk to him, to share that honesty he had mentioned on the day of their nuptials, but he did not speak for the entire distance. When they reached the bailey, he swung from the saddle then lifted her to the ground, turning immediately to greet Quinn and the knights sworn to Tulley. She was nigh forgotten and abandoned as he spoke to his men and gathered tidings, though Niall bowed to her as he led the destriers to the stables.

She could not stand there alone, like a dog awaiting a kind word from its master, so she left the bailey and fairly marched through the hall. The Lord de Tulley was yet barricaded in his chamber, according to Thomas, who also anticipated that the gathering in the hall that evening might be more ribald than suited her tastes. Magdala understood that she was being warned away from Lothair's homecoming, and asked for her meal to be brought to her chamber. Her choice seemed to please Thomas much more than it did her.

She went to the garden then, having no taste for embroidery in her current mood. Her vexations faded as she brought an entire bed to order, and she began to hope that Lothair might seek her out.

He did not. When the sun had sunk and the air turned chilly, she heard the men shouting to each other in the bailey as they gathered for the evening meal. She retreated to her chamber, just as Thomas brought the Lord de Tulley's meal up the stairs. She was at the window when her own meal was delivered, though she had little interest in it. She ate a measure of it, straining her ears for some hint of Lothair's approach.

There was none.

She lit a candle and paced in her solitude, moving to the window some time later when the laughter of the men echoed in the bailey. She saw one who could only be Lothair there, shaking hands with his comrades and giving instruction to the sentries for the night. She was certain he would come to her then, but he vanished into the stables.

Doubtless his steed was of greater interest than his wife.

Magdala waited and watched, her temper rising as it became clear he had no intention of coming to her this night. Whyever not? If he thought her too soiled for his attention, then they should dissolve the marriage. He should ride on, cherishing the memory of his beloved dead wife, intent upon learning the skills that might have saved her life.

It was in that moment that Magdala realized how much she resented Aileen. Through no fault of her own, that woman had known Lothair first, she had captured his heart, she had granted him a quest that would last the remainder of his days, and she had ensured that no other lady might win his regard.

And that, Magdala realized, was what she desired beyond all else. Once she had believed she would be content with a husband and a home, with security and affection, but that had been before she had met this intriguing and infuriating knight. She loved Lothair as she had never loved another, as she would never love another, and she wished with all her heart that he might love her in return.

Why did she always yearn for what she could not possess?

But it burned that Lothair had no desire for her. It irked her that he could not see how well suited they were, each to the other, and it infuriated her that he abandoned his supposed goal of partnership and trust so readily.

He might be destined to leave her and Château Tulley behind.

But before he did, Magdala would make her view of his choice beyond clear. The hours passed and he did not come to her.

Which only meant that she must go to him.

～

LOTHAIR SANK LOWER in the bath, savoring the heat of it. His chamber over the stables was filled with steam and he had scrubbed the mire of his journey from his skin with satisfaction. Quinn, Niall and Melissande had chosen to ride back to Annossy and his chamber was his own again.

He was exhausted. He had been tired and he had been dirty. He had been welcomed by a hundred tasks awaiting his attention.

Calum had scrubbed his back and now the squire organized Lothair's belongings, waiting his own turn in the tub. Lothair lingered, soaking, wishing he could dissolve the influence of Magdala on his thoughts as readily as mud from the road.

Herbert had rekindled her fears. He was certain of that and as much as he wished to climb to her chamber and seduce her anew, he knew he had to proceed with caution.

"And you can read this?" Calum asked, returning once again to the book that Thomas had brought after the evening meal. It had been delivered to Lothair's chamber and he had recognized the small chest immediately. He had removed the book and opened it on the table before Thomas' approving gaze, knowing that his interest would be reported to the Lord de Tulley.

In truth, he had no interest in the volume. It was yet a marvel and a wonder, but its secrets could wait for another day.

The mystery of Magdala held Lothair in thrall. How could he ensure that she did not believe him to be like all other mean? He had no notion and for the first time in all his years, he regretted that he had not spent more time in the courtship of ladies.

"Aye," he replied to his squire.

"I can only look upon the pictures, but even they are not all recognizable to me."

"It is Latin," Lothair said.

"And so you can read this volume and decipher its secrets. What cures will you learn from its pages? I confess myself to be curious beyond all."

"Do not turn the pages so roughly," Lothair said. "Such an old volume is fragile."

"Aye, my lord." Calum turned a page with exaggerated care, eyes wide as he strove to understand what was written within it.

Lothair stood in the bath, knowing it was time to go to Magdala and strive to win her favor. He did not believe in his inevitable success, but perhaps inspiration would come to him in the moment.

He could only hope.

"If you are done with your labor, you can have the second water," he said to Calum.

The youth beamed at him. "I have sorted your weapons, sir, and will hone the dagger again on the morrow when I can better see the blade. Your hauberk has need of a polish, but again, it will be easier to see the dirt in the sunlight. Sleipnir has been brushed, watered and fed, and truly I think he is content to be back at Tulley again. The palfreys also are settled for the night and I asked the ostler to see to Abigail's back left shoe."

"I wager he will see to it on the morrow."

"Precisely, my lord." The youth hastened forward with a large cloth.

Lothair was just stepping out of the tub when someone knocked upon the door to his chamber. Who came to him at such an hour? Surely naught was amiss? "Enter!" he cried, reaching for the cloth.

He stared in astonishment when Magdala herself swept into the chamber. Her hair was unbound and a cloak was wrapped over her shoulders. Doubtless she held the front of it closed from inside, which prompted Lothair to conclude that she wore only a chemise beneath it. She wore sheepskin boots, so she must have come from her chamber in haste and he feared the import of that.

"My lady, what is amiss?"

"You, sir!" she asserted, her color rising when her gaze swept over his nudity. "At least, your absence is amiss," she said, averting her gaze as she blushed more deeply.

Lothair gestured and Calum bowed before leaving the chamber, his slowness in doing as much a clear indication that he wished to stay and hear whatever the lady had to say. Lothair glared at him when he lingered in the portal and the squire retreated, closing the door behind himself.

Doubtless he had his ear to the keyhole.

Lothair wrapped the cloth around his hips even as Magdala pointed at him. "You may avoid me and surely you did, but I will have my say and you will hear it." Her eyes were flashing and her words fell with uncommon speed, her vexation more than clear. For a moment, he could not comprehend that she was annoyed with him, much less why. "I will have you know, sir, the indignity you do to me in avoiding our marital bed. I did not expect love in marriage, but I expected an increment of respect."

Lothair straightened. "You have my utmost respect, my lady."

"And how would I know as much?" she demanded, flinging out her hands. Her robe opened at the front, revealing that he had been right about her wearing only a chemise. It was the sheer one from their nuptial night, the one that offered a hint of revealing shadows, and he was glad that the cloth hid some of his reaction to that temptation. "How would any in this household guess as much? You avoid me and my bed as if there is a contagion there." She spat this last with disgust.

Lothair made to speak but she took a step closer, shaking her finger at him. God in Heaven, but she was glorious. He had never seen her angry before, but it was almost worth vexing her to watch her chastise him so.

"You may love your dead wife beyond all and your heart may be securely in her keeping forever. You may even wish to avoid the possibility of seeing a woman die in childbirth again, but my views are of import as well in this match. I desire children! I desire a family and a home, and I would do whatever is necessary to conceive those children and bring them to light."

She thought he did not desire her?

She thought he avoided her for love of Aileen? Lothair opened his mouth to explain but Magdala shook her finger beneath his nose and continued her furious diatribe.

"You are the one who spoke of honesty and partnership and yet you do not ask about my wishes. You simply decide, as all men are wont to do, and expect me to be glad of your choices. I am *not*, sir."

He could smell her skin now and feel the heat rising from her. He thought of her bed and her within it, and wondered how she could doubt his enthusiasm.

Perhaps he should remove the cloth.

"I am embarrassed that my new husband does not come to me after he has been away for nigh a week. I am ashamed that there is so little desire in our match, and I do not know how I shall bear the gossiping of the maids in the kitchen after this night." She took a breath and raised her chin proudly, looking like a warrior princess come to slaughter him. Aye, she might smite him with a glance.

"I do not know why you wed me at all," she confessed and he heard the hurt he had not meant to inflict.

"My lady," he said, raising a hand to her. "We were not gone a week, because we rode with uncommon haste." She stared at him, her heart in her eyes. "The better than we might return sooner."

Her gaze fell then upon the book on the table and Lothair nigh groaned aloud at the poor timing of that. Magdala retreated a step and her gaze became cold.

"But you are reacquainted with your book already," she said with heat. "My apologies, sir. I see precisely why you wed me. So, now you have your prize to peruse and have no time for your new bride. I understand that all is exactly as you told me it was not." She spun and marched back to the door, then glanced over her shoulder at him. "It seems it was my folly to believe you and to trust you. You may laugh as you consult your volume of wisdom to know that I dared to love you. Now my heart is securely in your possession, though I doubt, sir, that you care for its burden."

Lothair heard himself gasp.

Magdala did not. She flung open the door, moving with such speed that Calum was surprised and stumbled backward in haste to move out of her path. She left with all the fury of a tempest and Lothair could only stare after her in amazement.

He suspected his mouth was open.

She loved him.

"She loves you," Calum whispered, evidently as surprised as his knight. He looked after the lady then back at Lothair, his manner expectant.

The youth was right. There was not a moment to waste.

"My chemise!" Lothair ordered, casting aside the cloth and drying himself quickly. "My boots, my tabard and belt. With haste, Calum. *With haste!*"

MAGDALA WOULD NOT WEEP.

She had been content with the Lord de Tulley before and she would be so again.

If he allowed her to stay.

On impulse, she unlocked the gate to the garden and entered that space. The air was still, the stones still radiating some heat from the day's sunshine. She took a deep breath of the scent of the flowers and watched a moth flit across the garden. There were clouds overhead, obscuring the stars, and she was glad of her cloak. She blinked back her tears as she walked the perimeter of the garden, looking at each plant in turn, repeating their names to herself.

She halfway thought that Lothair might follow her but the moments stretched long and there was no sign of him.

Of course not. He had his book.

One of the roses was in bud, its first blooms almost bursting forth and she paused to touch the ripening flower. Would Lothair return to Provins to study with that apothecary? Would he abandon Tulley now that she had been so forthright? She hated that the decision of how to proceed with her own life was not hers to make. As a wife, she had to wait for his choice—and she could not guess what it might be. She shook her head, impatient with her own whimsy. Poor Felix was dead. She should count her blessings and trust that the morrow would be brighter.

She turned with purpose, intending to retire, and froze. Lothair stood in the portal, inside the open gate, watching her. There was such anguish in his expression that he might have been a different man and she wondered what had caused him such pain.

She took a step toward him, unable to quell her impulse to aid, and that seemed to be all the encouragement he needed. He strode to her and caught her hands in his, his brow furrowed as he met her gaze.

"I never loved Aileen," he confessed, his words husky. "Ours was a match of convenience, ordered by her father to ensure her safety. We grew up together and there was no more than respect between us. She was a strong woman, fearless, even, resolute in gaining her way. She never ceded to any one, and her husband had been her match. They were fierce, they two, and volatile, relentless in their ambitions. Her very presence tired me, and I feared that she would never hold sufficient to satisfy. Her greed was beyond measure, and she possessed no ability to appreciate what she had gained, no less to count her blessings. I honored our match, for I had given my vow, and I disliked that she died as she did, but she gave me a purpose. She made no claim upon my heart."

"This must be of import to you," she said quietly, hoping to lighten his mood. "You deliver a veritable lecture."

He did not smile, though. "It is of the greatest import, my lady. My heart, it appears, awaited you, for you claimed it surely, the very moment I returned to Tulley. I had noticed you before, but you pretended to be Heloise then, a woman of charm and passing fancies. It was here, in this garden, when you asked me about the welfare of the Lord de Tulley, when you were kind and sweet and sincere that I knew myself to be lost."

Magdala wanted to believe him, but she had to be certain.

"You thought you found a hidden truth, then. Was that what intrigued you?"

"You intrigued me," he insisted. "Then the Lord de Tulley told me that you were an imposter and asked me to uncover your secret. I did not argue with him over the chance to spend time with you, to be sure and each day, I felt myself fall deeper in love."

"But you argued against wedding me."

"Because I did not wish you to believe I had done as much solely to gain access to that book."

"You had it earlier."

"The Lord de Tulley sent it to me." He shook his head. "Truly, I think sometimes that man wishes to create trouble between those of his household. It is most vexing how he chooses to be manipulative of others."

Magdala smiled a little, such was the measure of her reassurance. "I think he does cause trouble at times, when he believes people need to consider a truth they would rather not confront."

"Calum looked at it, not me. I was thinking of you while he complained that he could not read the text."

"But you did not come to me on the second night of our match. And you did not come this night."

"I saw that you had a fear of men. I guessed that some incident had occurred in your past, and after this day, I would wager that Herbert was your assailant. This was not the first time he strove to force himself upon you, I suspect."

Magdala bowed her head and nodded.

"And thus you responded with fear to Niall's advances."

"And thus you believe me soiled, or that I invited such trouble."

"Never!" he said with such heat that she was startled. He gripped her hands more tightly and she dared to meet his gaze. "My lady, the acts of others are not your responsibility. And worse, I would not have you feel compelled to fight me."

"It is not the same, sir. There is no similarity at all between such unwanted attention and your caress." She smiled a little, daring to hope. "I feel treasured when you touch me. You should have returned."

"I wanted to, with all my heart." He winced. "There was so much blood that first night, my lady. I feared I had injured you." Lothair shook his head. "I wished only to give you time to recover, then this day, I confess, I nigh injured Lord Herbert beyond repair. My anger was beyond measure that he should so assault you." He fell silent. "I would not follow that incident with another." His voice hardened. "I could not."

"And you would not," Magdala said. "For you have no unkindness in you."

He lifted a brow, his gaze steady. "I have ridden to war, my lady."

"But not in the bedchamber."

He almost smiled at that, his gaze falling to her hands. "I nearly killed him," he confessed. "Such was my fury to find you so beset." His gaze locked with hers, his own warming as she smiled at him. His fingertip rose to her cheek and when she saw him inhale, she knew there was yet a mark from Herbert's hand.

"I missed you," she confessed quietly. "Lothair."

He caught his breath. "And I have yearned for you more than I can say. I love you, Magdala," he continued and her heart leapt. "And though I am neither rich nor well-born, I will serve you until my dying day."

"You are a knight and a man of honor," Magdala said. "I never imagined I should be so fortunate as to wed a man of your ilk."

"And if you desire children, then we shall strive to do as much." He smiled crookedly at her. "Your wish is as my own. My desire is solely to be with you for all my days and nights."

Her joy complete, Magdala stepped into his embrace, sliding her arms around his neck as he gathered her close. "Your hair is yet wet from your bath," she whispered as he tightened his grip upon her.

"And you wear only a chemise beneath your cloak. You will become chilled."

"Then you had best warm me," she whispered wickedly before he claimed her lips in a sweet hot kiss, sending a welcome fire to her very toes.

He swung her into his arms without breaking his kiss and carried her from the garden, holding her captive in his embrace as he locked the gate behind them. The keep was almost silent around them, although someone snored in the great hall below. Lothair strode up the stairs, taking them three at a time, his urgency making Magdala smile and her own anticipation rise.

He shouldered open the door to her chamber, locking it behind them before he carried her to the bed. She was divested of her cloak and savored the weight of his hand sliding down her length in admiration, then he turned to light the candles in the chamber.

He shed his own garments with a speed that would have amused her in other circumstance, abandoning them on the floor as he turned toward the bed again. Magdala caught her breath, for she had wished to stir him to passion and it seemed she had succeeded. She surveyed him with anticipation, admiring his evident power. Never had a man been so perfectly wrought; never had one so strong tempered his caress with such tenderness. His chest and back were tanned, his body so taut that he was all sinew and strength. His eyes fairly glowed as he looked upon her and he moved closer with a measure of awe.

On impulse, she sat up and pulled her chemise over her head, casting it aside and baring herself to his view. He moved to the side of the bed and whispered her name, lifting one hand to her nape. He lifted her to his kiss and Magdala rose to her knees, wanting all he had to share. "I desire all you have to give, Lothair," she confessed. "I am not so fragile as you would believe."

"But..." he began to protest and she laid a finger across his mouth.

"Please me, sir," she whispered, then boldly replaced her fingertip with her lips. Lothair caught his breath then his arms closed around her. His kiss was filled with a new urgency, demanding more of her and granting far more pleasure than she might have believed possible.

Like a sorcerer, he conjured her response, sometimes playful and sometimes fierce. Gone was the gentle lover who had slowly coaxed her to join him: in his place was a warrior, with appetites and passions that would not readily be sated. More, he demanded that she meet him, touch for touch, by awakening a need within her beyond all expectation. Magdala burned like a woman claimed by a fever, and she found herself emboldened by her own passion. She had never imagined that mating could be so potent and she only wanted more.

Lothair's fingers speared into her hair during that first kiss, cradling her nape and holding her captive to his hungry kiss. Not only did his mouth close over hers, but his tongue flicked against hers, tantalizing and tempting her to join him. She opened her mouth to him, closing her eyes and surrendering to him, her trust complete. He groaned as he lifted her into his arms, his mouth plundering hers. One of his arms was locked around her waist and the other held her knees captive against his chest as he climbed onto the bed like a triumphant conqueror.

When she was perched in his lap, he did not release her or end their kiss, but continued to feast upon her mouth, even as he caught her knees in the hand of the arm around her waist. His other hand swept down her thigh, his thumb landing upon the most secret part of her with surety. His smooth caress made her gasp and he chuckled as he swallowed the sound, then his fingers eased within her in a most delightful and wicked way. His thumb tormented her, moving back and forth across her clitoris with a surety that nigh made her dizzy. She was captive to the pleasure he was determined to grant, and there was nowhere she wished more to be.

He teased her and tormented her until she could bear it no longer. She felt the tide rise within her and struggled to control it, but Lothair meant to release it. The tide overcame her, conjured and commanded by him, and Magdala cried out in her release. She shook from head to toe as he held her tightly, compelling her to ride the crest of pleasure until it was utterly spent.

"Lothair." She whispered his name with awe and studied him in wonder. "Is it always thus?"

"It may improve," he fairly growled and she could not wait. She watched his slow smile of satisfaction and the way it lit his eyes and her heart leapt that she should be so fortunate as to be wed to this man. She smiled back at him and he grinned outright, then cast her across the mattress as if she weighed naught at all. Lothair stretched out beside her, his expression revealing his contentment with that situation. He watched his own hand as he slid its weight over her breast, into the indent of her waist, across her belly and down her thigh.

Then he caught her hands in his and laced their fingers together, the sight of his satisfaction warming her all over again. He kissed her again and she returned his embrace hungrily, learning a little more with each passing moment and striving to torment him in her own turn. He moved atop her, his weight easing between her thighs as his gaze clung to hers. She saw his question before he could ask it and parted her legs to welcome him. He caught his breath, then settled his hardness against her softness with a contented smile that lit a glow within her.

This time, she felt a rising excitement and anticipation of the pleasure of their union. She wriggled beneath him and Lothair inhaled sharply, a sign that she took as encouragement to repeat her feat. She laughed when he swore softly and braced himself above her, his fingers twining into her hair again.

"Around my waist," he murmured, then bent to kiss her thoroughly as she followed his instruction. Her breasts collided with his chest, then were crushed beneath him, her nipples so taut that she shivered at the feel of his chest hair against them. Then he was at her portal, his grip tightening on her hands as he eased within her, and she felt once again that glorious sense of union. She felt him hesitate, for she knew she was yet tight, but she moved beneath his weight again and had the satisfaction of feeling him shudder.

He braced himself on his elbows then and looked down at her, his eyes glinting as he studied her. He was all golden power and heat and her heart thundered in her chest.

"Too fast?" he whispered and she heard the catch in his voice, a hint that he needed to claim her thus.

"Perfect," she said and he moved within her. "I like when your composure is lost," she confessed and he chuckled, moving with such vigor that she gasped aloud.

"I shall tempt you to lose yours again," he threatened and she could hardly wait.

"I cannot wait," she teased, unable to completely suppress her smile.

"I will make you wait, temptress, for then the satisfaction will be greater yet," he threatened and moved again, releasing her hands and sliding his beneath her buttocks. She found herself lifted against him even as she was snared beneath him, a glorious sensation of being both surrounded and filled. Better yet, in this posture, his strength rubbed against her in a most delicious way. She felt both claimed and possessed, and the fire in his eyes as he watched her was as potent as any of his kisses. She dragged her nails over his shoulders, loving that he held his power in check to better please her, and he buried himself within her once more.

"Magdala," he whispered, his voice husky, then bent to capture her mouth again. This kiss was all teeth and tongue, a fierce possession of her mouth that thrilled her to her marrow. He moved with greater vigor then as if he could not help himself, and she knew the torrent rose within him. She kissed him back with an echo of his own hunger, writhing beneath him with the surety that he would never injure her.

When he rolled to his back, carrying her with him, she seized his wrists and held them against the mattress as she rocked atop him. She rode him, knowing already how to deepen his ardor and she watched as his entire body became taut with need. His gaze burned into hers with such intensity that he might have seared her very soul, and still Magdala rode him harder, feeling a primal need to ensure that he thought of her and her alone when he imagined pleasures abed.

She moved faster and faster, snaring herself in her own spell so that her desire spiraled beyond control. There was only the power of the man beneath her, the heat they two conjured together, the fury of their passion—followed by the exquisite satisfaction of their mutual release. Magdala heard herself cry out, then Lothair roared, rolling her to her back to drive deeply within her one last time before he gained his release with potent shudder.

He kissed her again, slowly and languorously, a kiss that felt like a celebration in itself. "Magdala," he whispered again, then kissed the taut peak of her nipple with lazy satisfaction. "You may kill me in our own chamber," he said roughly and she could only laugh.

"Our chamber, sir?" she asked, playful in her relief. "Do you mean to abandon the room over the stables."

"Aye," he said with surety. "I will sleep only with my wife."

Magdala had no complaint with that scheme.

Lothair rose from the bed, carrying her with him as he crossed the chamber. He caught her against him with one arm, as if he did not wish to ever let her go, and poured a measure of water for washing. He perched on the stool and washed her himself, his gaze so hot that she blushed beneath his perusal.

He had a scheme, she was certain of it, but she did not care to protest. And when he abandoned the cloth, his hand easing between her thighs as he kissed her once again, Magdala was more than happy to surrender to sensation once more.

CHAPTER 15

She was a marvel.

Lothair could not believe how welcoming Magdala was, how honest and open she was in her response, how passionately she responded to his caress. He was amazed how her confidence grew and shaken by her ability to conjure his response. He loved to watch her crest the summit of pleasure and could not imagine he would ever tire of the way she caught her breath when he surprised her with a touch. She was flushed and soft, her eyes shining and her lips parted, as willing a partner as any man might desire.

She was his wife.

And she loved him.

His heart nigh burst with the surety of his good fortune and he felt compelled to ensure that she never regretted her acceptance of him.

He loved that she already began to tease him, that she laughed and smiled in her delight. He loved that she was impulsive and knew that with time, she would become an ever more dangerous threat to his concentration. He had known whores, of course, bored with their trade and utterly pragmatic about what pleasures were available for what price. Such transactions were indifferent at best and generally unsatisfactory. He had known Aileen, of course, but intimacy had been a duty to her, and a short-lived one in their marriage.

In contrast, Magdala's delight in her newfound discovery of sensation was more seductive than he could have imagined. It was enticing to surprise her with a different caress and to watch her eyes light as she became more bold with her own overtures. Lothair feared he might never sleep again, that this might be the price of his adoration of his wife.

And worse, he did not care.

He held her against him as she found her pleasure again, watching in fascination as her lips parted and her cheeks flushed. She was perfection, to be sure, and Lothair was engulfed by a tide of tenderness when she collapsed against his chest, her breath coming quickly.

She was so precious, a veritable gem he had been fortunate to claim.

"We shall never sleep," she whispered in echo of his own thoughts and he kissed her temple tenderly.

"Aye, we will," he said and washed her again, ensuring attention was not diverted this time. "We must," he added when he set her on her feet and fetched her chemise. "Felix's funeral is on the morrow."

She sobered at the reminder. "Poor man," she said. "It seems unkind that he should have died, serving his lord thus."

"It can be a fate of food tasters, to be sure."

Magdala frowned. "But there was something of it that was troubling. The Lord de Tulley would not let me try to aid Felix, nor even approach him. I thought I might induce him to expel the fig, but perhaps it was already too late."

Lothair looked up at this. "How quickly did he fall?"

"At once."

"Were there convulsions?"

She shook her head. "I thought a poison either caused the victim to convulse due to the pain or it lulled one to a sleep from which he or she would never awaken."

Lothair nodded. "You are not mistaken in this. I have understood poisons to act in one way or the other." He wondered then what had happened, but doubted he would learn. Perhaps there had been too much happening for accurate observation. Either way, Felix would be buried on the morrow, so he had died.

"And what of your errand?" she asked, retreating toward the bed as she tied the braid of her hair.

Lothair donned his chemise and tied the lace, unable to resist the impulse of catching her in his arms again. She kicked her feet, clearly not minding his choice, then laughed as he carried her around the chamber that she might extinguish the candles. He felt a profound satisfaction when he climbed into the bed with his lady wife and she pulled the bedding over them. As before, she nestled before him, her braid cast over his arm, her scent filling him with the sense of having come home.

"Tell me," she insisted, her voice already sleepy.

"There was no grave," he confessed.

She was awake then. She sat up to look at him, even in the darkness, and he could taste her outrage. "They took the coin from me and did not see my lady buried with honor?"

"Not that. The priest said the corpses vanished, and the lady returned to tell him that it had been a jest."

Magdala fell back onto the mattress beside him, and he could fairly hear her thoughts. "I did no such thing."

"It must have been Heloise," Lothair said. "The priest commented upon her embraces with the baron and her skill with a horse."

"Then she did not die?" Magdala was clearly thinking furiously. "But I was certain. I saw her fall. I saw the blood." Then she caught her breath.

"What is it?"

"But that explains why I thought I saw Mallory in the village. He did not die either!"

Now Lothair was the one to brace himself on his elbow to peer down at her. "Mallory was one of the guards in your party?" he guessed.

"He was the first to be struck down."

"When did you see him here?"

"The day we walked to the village and I told you my name," she said. "And again, he was in the great hall in the company on the day of our nuptials." He felt her shake her head. "I thought I erred, because he was dead. I thought I confused another man who resembled Mallory with Mallory himself."

"But Mallory is not dead," Lothair said, lying upon his back and staring at the canopy overhead.

"And he is here at Tulley," Magdala said, curling against his side. "He smiled at me," she further confessed, words that sent a chill through Lothair. He recalled that man hailing her, her surprise and the man's smile.

It had not been a smile to inspire trust.

Aye, if Mallory was here and he had defended Heloise in the past, Lothair would wager that Heloise herself was close.

What did she desire at Tulley? If she was of her brother's ilk, it could only be the Lord de Tulley's legacy.

"What are you thinking?" Magdala whispered.

"Only that we must devise her scheme in time," he said then kissed her temple. "Sleep, Magdala. We may need our wits for the morrow."

But Lothair knew that he would not himself sleep soon.

To his thinking, Heloise's presence could not bode well for Magdala, though he could not discern how she might be threatened anew.

Magdala awakened alone again, but she could hear Lothair and Calum beyond the draperies of the bed. It was obvious that Lothair strove to dress quietly so as to keep from awakening her, but Calum was pestering his knight with whispered questions about the funeral. Magdala smiled as she heard Lothair's patience thinning, marveling that she learned to discern the subtle clues in his tone.

It was just barely light and she called his name before he might leave the chamber. He dismissed Calum then parted the drapes, her heart leaping at the sight of him.

He bent and kissed her sweetly, which made everything within her leap anew. "It appears that Lord Herbert has need of some encouragement this morning."

"Do you ride out to him immediately?"

"I will wait until after the service, lest he remains reluctant."

Magdala nodded agreement that the honors for Felix should not be interrupted.

"Calum will move my belongings here during the service, if that suits you."

Magdala smiled. "It does." She sat up, liking how he caught his breath in anticipation of her kiss. Long moments passed and she thought she might convince him to join her again, then Calum cleared his throat from the portal. "I will see you in the hall," she whispered and he nodded once, his satisfaction clear.

She took her time dressing for the day, wanting to savor her newfound contentment. In the end, she chose the darker of her blue kirtles and chose not to wear a cloak. The day was overcast, the first such they had seen in a while, but she did not think it would rain before nightfall.

Magdala knocked on the door to the solar only to find that all was in disarray within that chamber. The Lord de Tulley might have had a tantrum, for the chaotic condition of his possessions and garments. Trunks were opened and the contents of chests cast upon the floor, his bed was unmade and he looked uncommonly unkempt.

Clearly, he missed the organization of Felix.

"We shall have to find you another servant," Magdala said soothingly, marveling all the while that he could cause such untidiness so quickly.

"I cannot find my hose," he complained. "I do not know where my black belt is to be found."

"It is here, Uncle." Magdala wondered that the loss of Felix had so disconcerted the older man. He seemed to be confused as he had not been before and more volatile than ever. She would have to encourage Thomas to solve the situation with haste.

"And where would I find a clean chemise? What of the tabard I wore yesterday?" His voice rose in vexation. "All must be right! I must honor the memory of my old friend and comrade."

"All will be well, Uncle. There is time." Magdala hastened around the chamber, glad that she knew his belongings well. He had washed and shaved alone, to her surprise, but she was glad of it. Felix had generally attended that task and she would not have liked to take a sharp blade to his chin when he was so unpredictable.

She found a clean chemise and aided him to don it, then his chausses and favored boots, polishing them as he dictated. He sat in his chair then while she combed out his hair, then aided him to don his tabard. She brushed it off and buckled his belt, placing his rings upon his fingers so that he would appear in his full splendor. She did not see his heavier cloak, the one lined with fur, and made to open the single trunk that was closed.

It might have been locked, yet this trunk had no lock. She struggled but could not move the lid at all. She was bending to peer at the latch when the Lord de Tulley cleared his throat. "We shall be late!" he cried, tapping his cane upon the floor.

"I would fetch your heavier cloak…"

"Not this day," he said with impatience. "The wind is warm. I will have that one, child. Hurry, hurry."

Magdala gave the trunk with its stubborn lid one last look, then went to his side, flicking the cloak over his shoulders. She fastened it with a great pin on his shoulder, ensuring that it fell properly, then smiled for him.

"Most regal, Uncle," she said and he kissed her cheek. His eyes were twinkling now, giving him that roguish look that was more reassuring than any other. "And we will not be late," she assured him.

Thomas appeared at the doorway as she had requested, though he seemed to be somewhat ill at ease with his task. He did not look the old lord in the eye, as far as Magdala could tell, though she supposed that they did not often touch each other. Thomas took the free arm of the Lord de Tulley to aid him on the stairs, while Magdala put her hand through his elbow on the side he carried his cane. He liked to have the appearance of escorting her, but she knew he could lean upon her if necessary.

The entire household was assembled in the hall, their expressions solemn and their eyes downcast. The Lord de Tulley left the hall first, followed by Magdala, then his household. In the bailey, the knights, guards and sentries sworn to Tulley were gathered, many mounted upon their horses. One held the stirrup of the Lord de Tulley's favored steed and Lothair helped the older man into the saddle. The Lord de Tulley looked most fine then, proud and noble, as six men carried the coffin from the chapel within the keep. They led the procession from the keep and through the gates, the Lord de Tulley following with Lothair behind. Magdala walked behind them, followed by those of the household who would attend. The squires and grooms, she noted, remained at the keep, as did the ostler and most of the sentries.

The streets were lined with villagers, all of whom crossed themselves when the coffin passed, then bowed low before the Lord de Tulley. In the saddlebags of the old lord's horse were the alms that would be distributed on his return to the keep. This procession, though, moved in silence down the winding road to the lower gates, the company swelling in numbers as many villagers joined the procession behind the household.

They reached the lower gates and passed through them, crossing to the village on the far bank of the river and to the church there. There were too many mourners for all to fit within the church, though Lothair assigned a man to guard the Lord de Tulley's horse during the service. The coffin was placed before the altar and the mass was sung for Felix. When the priest had given the blessing, they might have continued to the cemetery, but the Lord de Tulley stepped forward.

He raised a hand, then his voice. "I thank you, all of my comrades, villeins and vassals for joining me to mourn the loss of my loyal Felix. I would say something of this man I knew and trusted as a friend."

The company listened attentively.

"Felix came to Tulley as a boy and was accepted into service by my brother Godwyn. I do not know his origins, save that he came from the south and was an orphan. After the demise of Godwyn, Felix then served my nephew Henrik and was praised for his fastidious attention to detail." The Lord de Tulley shook his head in recollection. "I know that Henrik would not leave his chamber until Felix had pronounced himself satisfied with his choice of attire."

Magdala saw one smile in the company.

"As ever, gain comes with loss. Felix became my own manservant when Henrik died and Tulley came to my hand. I was grateful time and again for his detailed memory of people and past events, as well as his boundless knowledge of the realm of Tulley. I quickly came to rely upon his insight and recollection." The Lord de Tulley sighed. "Of late, he tasted food for me, testing for poison, a task for which he volunteered. It pains me to think that he lost his life in serving me this way." He turned and laid a hand upon the coffin, his voice husky. "Never was there such fidelity in a single man."

"Amen," said the priest softly.

The Lord de Tulley braced his hands upon his walking stick and considered the company. "And so, as you are gathered here this day, I will share a decision with you. As most of you know, Felix died in tasting fruit brought by my nephew Herbert as a gift for me, fruit that had been poisoned in an attempt to claim the holding of Tulley by nefarious means."

There were whispers in the assembly at this, but at a stern glance from the Lord de Tulley, they fell silent.

"Herbert is my sister's son, her sole son, and might reasonably have expected the legacy of Tulley as I have no children of my own. In this deed, though, he has discredited himself beyond redemption. I have cast him out of Tulley and banned him from my holdings now and forever." The Lord de Tulley straightened and frowned. Magdala wondered how much longer he could stand thus. "My sister Verena had three children by the Lord von Idelstein, Herbert and two daughters. The oldest daughter, Heloise, you all know well, for she has aided me much in recent years. The younger, Hildegarde, is yet a young maiden at Idelstein. I have chosen to ensure the stability of Tulley after my demise by naming an heir to follow me." There were murmured nods of approval at this course. "And so I decree that my heir shall be the husband of my niece, Lothair of Sutherland, my Captain of the Guard."

A whisper rippled through the assembly at that even as Magdala caught her breath. She saw Lothair straighten and knew he was surprised. She heard whispers of Lothair's marked good fortune, but she knew that no man deserved this honor more than her husband.

Even though she was not Heloise. This must have been why the Lord de Tulley had kept her name secret longer.

The Lord de Tulley offered his hand to Lothair, the signet ring gleaming upon it.

Lothair dropped to one knee before the older man and touched his lips to the ring. "You do me much honor, my lord, with your kindness and generosity. I shall do all within my powers to uphold the honor of this gift."

The Lord de Tulley smiled. "I know you will, sir," he said, lifting Lothair to his feet and shaking his hand. He beckoned then to Magdala, kissing both of her cheeks.

"Uncle, you stand overlong," she whispered and he chuckled.

"Aye, I do." He leaned on her then as the coffin was carried from the church, and let her support him as he followed it, even as the company murmured on all sides.

Magdala could not dismiss her sense that the older man was triumphant, as if a scheme had come to fruition, but she could not explain that sense at all.

~

CALUM ENJOYED a hearty breakfast in the kitchens, listening to all the gossip of the hall as he ate his fill. He returned to the chamber over the stables later than had been his plan, but wagered he could see all to rights before his lord knight's return. Indeed, the company was only just beginning to muster in the bailey, a small group of those sworn to the house waiting at the chapel to pay their respects. He could hear Lothair's voice but did not see his knight.

They would be in the great hall, no doubt, with the Lord de Tulley.

Calum whistled as he climbed the stairs to the chamber over the stables, then halted in surprise. The door to that chamber was ajar, as he knew it had not been.

He heard a rustling from within and drew closer with caution. To his surprise, his lady stood within the chamber, her back to him. She was wearing his knight's heavy cloak, the one with the fur lining, and had the hood raised. He could see a tendril of her fair hair but no more than that.

"Finally!" she said, turning slightly. How curious that she neither faced him nor called him by name, and that she seemed intent upon keeping her features obscured.

"My lady." Calum bowed, feeling in that moment that his knight's comments about the mysteries of ladies was well-deserved.

She wore the cloak that Calum knew had been left in this chamber overnight. What had she worn to arrive here? Only her chemise? He could not fathom her choice.

"I do not know the location of my lord Lothair," he said, but she made a dismissive gesture.

"That is of no import. I would have you bring my red dress kirtle here while we attend the funeral, the one I wore for our wedding, and my heavy cloak with the fur. I will change my garb before the midday meal."

"Here?" Calum asked in surprise.

"Here," she said, her voice filled with an uncharacteristic resolve.

Then she swept past him and fairly fled into the keep, leaving him wondering why she would not move the kirtle herself. He shook his head and began to pack his lord's belongings, doubting he would ever know the truth of it.

~

LOTHAIR WAS ASTONISHED by the honor granted to him by the Lord de Tulley. He also welcomed the challenge, not only of ensuring that all continued in Tulley as the older man desired, but of winning the support of all and sundry within its borders. He saw immediately that Magdala had not anticipated this development and did not doubt that there were those who would think it an injustice.

It would be best if Lord Herbert departed for Idelstein soon.

After the service, the company made to return to the keep and the village. Lothair summoned Gerald to accompany him, convinced that a show of force might only worsen any confrontation with Lord Herbert.

There was not a tremendous amount of activity within the visiting lord's camp, as if all within it slumbered late. Only one sentry challenged the two knights as they made their way to the central tent favored by Herbert, and that man stepped back as soon as he recognized Lothair.

"I thought your lord left this day," Lothair said to him and the man shrugged.

"He rises late, as is his wont. His sister arrived last eve with her husband and there were revels." The guard yawned. "No one expects to depart before midday."

Lothair and Gerald exchanged a glance.

"Were you…?" Gerald began and Lothair shook his head.

Was Heloise here? Was the guard Mallory her husband now?

He knew enough of that lady to be wary of what they might find.

He continued to Herbert's tent, Gerald fast behind. There was not a sound from within it, no conversation, no sounds of intimacy, not even a snore. Lothair hesitated, sensing that something was amiss, and silently drew his dagger. Gerald did the same, turning so that he might defend Lothair's back.

They advanced into the tent and the first thing that Lothair noticed was the smell. It was sufficiently foul that he grimaced and might have retreated. But he saw the disarray of Herbert's belongings, and he spotted a bare foot. The owner of that foot could only be lying on the ground, on his belly, and Lothair stepped closer, astonished that a man of such wealth would abandon the comfort of the bed he had brought with him.

But Herbert did not sleep. His back was arched and his eyes bulged, his expression was stricken. The source of the smell was evident from the waste that surrounded him.

"God in Heaven," Gerald whispered and turned away.

The dead man had ingested a powerful poison, it was clear. So great was the dose that even his stomach's attempt to void itself had not been sufficient. Lothair touched Herbert's throat, verified that there was no pulse, and noted the slight heat of his skin.

"It has not been long," he said as he straightened. He scanned the interior of the tent but there was no sign of any other person. He might have turned away, but he caught a whiff of a familiar odor, one that he would never mistake for anything else.

He bent over Herbert's corpse and inhaled more deeply.

Aconite.

That was when Lothair saw that Herbert's signet ring was gone.

Heloise was here!

MAGDALA HELPED the Lord de Tulley up the stairs, well aware that the older man had need of a respite after his exertions of the day. She asked Thomas to request some broth from Antoine for the Lord de Tulley when they crossed the hall, then they two continued to the solar.

"Are you pleased?" the older man asked yet again. "You will stay?"

"Of course, Uncle. Your generosity is most unexpected."

"And welcome?"

"How could it not be?"

He peered at her. "And your husband will agree?"

"We shall see," she said, removing his boots. "Perhaps we will discuss the matter at the board this night."

"I strive only to ensure your comfort and protection."

"I know, sir."

He leaned back in his chair, looking so frail that her heart clenched.

She kissed his cheek. "Let me fetch that broth."

He murmured an asset then seemed to doze.

Magdala hastened down the stairs with purpose, halting when she realized the door to her chamber was ajar. Calum must have neglected to secure it. She entered the room, saw that Lothair's belongings had been moved, then frowned that his chest of apothecary supplies was open. She stepped toward it and immediately sensed her error. She saw a flick of red and felt the air move behind her, then she was seized and a knife tip placed at her throat. The man was strong but she did not have to see his face to guess his identity.

Not when he turned her to face Lady Heloise, garbed in Magdala's own wedding dress.

Mallory.

Lady Heloise secured the portal then approached them again. She smiled and the familiar dimple appeared below the corner of her mouth. "You have done well, Magdala," Heloise whispered. "A husband and a legacy both."

Magdala saw the signet ring for Idelstein upon the lady's largest finger and guessed Herbert's fate. He would never have surrendered that prize willingly. "It looks as if you have one as well, my lady," she said and Heloise lifted her hand to admire the ring.

"The trouble with something fine is that it makes one yearn for a collection," she said, eyes glinting with familiar avarice. Though it was a similar sentiment to that of the abbess' warning, it sounded more sinister with Lady Heloise's phrasing.

Mallory laughed. "You would not wish to deprive Hildegarde," he said.

"Nay, my sister can have Idelstein, once I hold Tulley."

"The Lord de Tulley is yet hale," Magdala protested but Heloise's brows rose.

"Not for long," she said, then turned to Lothair's collection. She chose a vial, one that Magdala recognized, and Magdala's very blood ran cold.

"You would not do him injury," she protested.

"Nay, I will not." Heloise's smile was utterly untrustworthy. "You will do him injury, Magdala, for he alone will discern the difference between us. He will not drink any substance I bring him, to be sure, no matter what kirtle I wear."

There was a tap at the door, and Heloise gestured. Mallory dragged Magdala out of sight of the doorway, locking a hand over her mouth to silence her. The prick of his knife at her throat was sufficient to ensure her cooperation, especially as no one else was at risk.

Yet.

Heloise had raised the hood of Magdala's best cloak, hiding her features from view. There was only the splendor of the dress, which no one could mistake.

"The broth, as you requested, my lady," Thomas said with a bow, surrendering the small pot to her. "Your idea that you should take it to him is most sensible."

"Thank you," Heloise said, her voice somewhat muffled. Thomas might have lingered but she began to close the door and he retreated with reluctance. She waited, holding the vessel, until the sound of his steps faded upon the stairs.

Then she put the pot upon the table, opened the container of poppy powder and poured it all into the hot broth. It dissolved, vanishing from view as if it was not there.

Magdala shivered inwardly.

"His demise must appear to be natural," Heloise confided easily. "He must look to have fallen asleep but never awaken." She fixed a look upon Magdala. "You will take his broth to him and you will ensure he consumes it."

"And if I do not."

"Then your husband's demise will be more painful than is truly necessary."

"You mean to kill Lothair."

She shrugged. "No obstacle can remain to my claiming of Tulley." Her smile broadened again. "And no one can survive who might realize that I am not you. Do as I say, and he will be assailed from behind. It will be swift and painless for him."

"And for me?"

Heloise selected another container from the collection and held it for Magdala to view. "Of course, you cannot read the label."

Magdala recognized it, though. It was the aconite.

"Again, the choice is yours. Obey me, and you will be permitted to leave Tulley to seek your fortune wherever you desire. Defy me, and this will be your reward. We might say that you were overcome with remorse for your deception." She shook her head. "No one will care, Magdala, if a little serving maid, an orphan with a taste for lying, vanishes." She reached out a hand then, her manner imperious. "I will have my ring now."

Magdala removed the circle of gold and surrendered it. She knew that Heloise would never let her live, much less walk away unscathed. She had a plan, though, one that might save both the Lord de Tulley and Lothair, the two men she held in greatest affection. "If I do as you say, you must let Lothair leave with me," she said boldly.

She watched Heloise eye Mallory. Something passed between them, an agreement no doubt to let her believe they would comply, then Heloise nodded.

She lifted the pot and offered it to Magdala. "You have a task to complete, Magdala," she said, reaching for the door as Mallory released his grip. "Do not be so fool as to defy me."

Magdala took the pot and left the chamber, climbing the stairs as if she would comply. She was thinking of doses, though, of the difference between languor and endless sleep, and hoping that her guess would come aright.

~

LOTHAIR CHARGED BACK to the keep, Gerald close on his heels. All seemed to be well when they entered the gates to the bailey. The sentries walked the walls. The guards stood at attention. The grooms swept the stalls of the stable and he could hear the bustle of activity from the kitchens. "Tell no one as yet of what we have learned," he advised Gerald in an undertone. "We must first discern her scheme."

"Your demise must be part of it, sir."

Lothair nodded at the truth of that.

Calum looked up at his appearance then and came to him, bowing low. "The Lord de Tulley has retired to the solar, and all are to gather in the hall at midday," the youth said, bowing again. "My felicitations to you, sir, on your appointment."

"You heard of it?" In truth, Lothair was not surprised. Such tidings traveled quickly.

Where was Magdala.

"All the keep is talking of it." Calum's tone turned wistful. "I suppose this means we shall not ride for Scotland soon."

His squire might be surprised. Lothair surveyed the high wall of the keep, unable to deny his sense that the sooner they left Tulley, the better.

"Where is my lady wife?"

Calum turned and pointed to the tower. "You have spoken aright about the enigma of a lady's will, sir," that youth said with a smile.

"How so?"

"Your lady wife. She wished to have me bring her garments to the chamber over the stables during the service, though I cannot fathom why she did not simply leave them in her own chamber. That is where she went once she was garbed." He shrugged, indicating his confusion.

But Lothair understood. Heloise had spoken to him, ensuring that she had a disguise, and worse, Calum had not realized she was not Magdala.

The resemblance between them must be strong.

Fortunately, the Lord de Tulley would not be deceived.

"Which kirtle did she desire?"

"The red one, from your wedding day."

Magdala had worn a blue one earlier that day. Lothair wondered what awaited him in his lady's chamber. He bade Gerald stand sentry at the entry to the tower and strode for the stairs. With every step and every sign of normalcy, his trepidation rose that all was not aright.

Where was Magdala?

LOTHAIR'S WIFE was not in their chamber, though his apothecary chest had been left open. He crossed the chamber to examine it, noting immediately that the lock was damaged and that two containers were missing. Then he heard a step behind him, one he had anticipated, and spun with fearsome speed, drawing his blade in the same moment.

A dark-haired man dove toward him but Lothair parried his blow. He flung the other man backward with the weight of his sword and pursued him, swinging his blade with power. "You must be Mallory," he said through his teeth. "We finally meet."

"But not for long," that man muttered and the battle was on.

Where was Magdala? Lothair fought with a fury he had not known he possessed. Only the defeat of his man would grant him the chance to find his lady wife. Their blades clashed with a vigor that should have alerted the household, but to his dismay, he heard a light laugh from the corridor.

"A jest," a lady said, her voice muffled. He saw the flick of her red skirts as she retreated into the chamber. "Knights always seem obliged to hone their skills." Then she closed the portal and leaned her back against it, her cool gaze landing upon Lothair.

He understood. He would have to kill them both to come to Magdala's aid.

He scarce heard her cry of dismay from the solar above, but there was no mistaking the roar of anguish of the Lord de Tulley.

"Magdala!" that man roared.

Mallory faltered. Lothair struck a fierce blow, taking advantage of that man's surprise. Mallory fell to his knees, his blood flowing over his hands, and whispered Heloise's name. Lothair finished what had been begun in time to see the flick of the lady's hems as she fled.

He raced from the room and up the stairs, kicking open the portal to the solar. His heart stopped at the sight of Magdala on the ground, the Lord de Tulley kneeling over her. The older man gathered her into his arms, moaning incoherently. To Lothair's surprise, another man strove to console the old lord, seeking to look at Magdala.

Felix?

Lothair strode to his lady wife, disinterested in any such details. All he needed to know was that Felix was yet alive, which meant that he had been deceived.

"She is dead!" the Lord de Tulley wailed. "After all my efforts. After all my plans."

"Calm yourself, my lord," Felix said. "She drank very little of the broth."

The Lord de Tulley did not listen but continued to lament.

Nor did Lothair, for time was of import. He bent over his lady, listening. He raised a hand for the older man to fall silent, listening with all his might.

And to Lothair's relief, he discerned the faintest sound of the lady's breath. He could barely feel the beat of her pulse beneath his fingertips, but she lived.

She slept. He pointed to a brass platter and Felix fetched it.

Lothair buffed it, then held it by her face. He had not erred. The fog of her breath marred the surface and he nigh wept with relief.

Magdala was not dead, and if the matter was Lothair's to resolve, she would not be. He ushered the older man out of the way, rolled Magdala to her side and encouraged her to void her stomach. He did not have to ask for Felix to pour a cup of ale and bring it to him. He cradled Magdala in his lap and coaxed the fluid over her lips, wishing she would open her eyes and soon.

The Lord de Tulley was holding his head in his hands, and raised a tormented glance to Lothair. "She chose to die!"

Lothair's glance flicked to Felix, who nodded with some measure of guilt, then to the stricken older man. "How so?"

"She drank the broth by choice. She said I had no poison-taster in the absence of Felix. She said she would do me the service. I never thought… I never imagined…but she must have known!" His voice broke as he reached for her cheek. "*My Magdala!*"

And a cold fury awakened within Lothair. She would not kill herself, not his loyal lady. She would allow herself to be injured to save another she loved, like the Lord de Tulley. He did not wish any ill to Felix, but he could not be glad that the ruse created by these two, for whatever cause, had resulted in Magdala willingly sipping of poisoned broth.

She had done as much to defend the Lord de Tulley.

It was outrageous.

It was wrong beyond belief.

And the possibility that she could have died, because of her kindness and loyalty to this meddling old man, infuriated Lothair as little else could have done.

"MALLORY!" Heloise had slipped up the stairs to find her lover, certain he would have triumphed over Lothair.

Instead, she found him dead on the floor of Magdala's chamber.

His eyes were open, staring as if he was as astonished as she by his state.

Heloise fell to her knees beside him, desperately trying to awaken him. He drew breath no longer, but she hoped her mother's lessons would allow her to aid him. There was blood, so much blood, but she strove to close his wounds with her hands. She could repair this, if only he lived. She touched her lips to his, forcing her breath into him, but his mouth was slack.

His skin grew cold already.

She rose to her feet, hating that she had been cheated of the one man who had loved her beyond all others, the man who had aided her in her schemes to ensure their future together, the man who obeyed her every whim and loved her so sweetly at night. Mallory had never judged her and found her lacking. Mallory's love for her had been pure.

And he was gone forever.

She had killed Herbert. She had lost Mallory. She knew her sister did not trust either of them and doubted that Hildegarde would even admit her to Idelstein again. She had striven to gain all but instead, Heloise had naught at all.

She spun at the sound of a footfall on the stairs. Lothair's squire was there, the red-headed youth, and his expression was grim. "My lord will wish to speak with you," he said, his body blocking the portal.

Heloise seized Mallory's blade and lunged at the squire, who neatly divested her of the weapon. He advanced into the chamber, his gaze as steady as that of his lord knight, the tip of his knife pointed toward her. "You might sit down and await him," he said, but Heloise would accept no judgement from the man who had stolen her beloved from her.

She turned toward a stool, but only to disarm the squire. As soon as he lowered the blade, she lunged to the apothecary chest, seizing a small bottle and hoping it offered salvation.

"Nay!" the squire cried but it was too late.

Heloise retreated to the window with the vial, sparing it the merest glance. Aconite. Even if she survived the fall, she would not live to tell of it. She swallowed the entire contents of the vial, cast it at the squire, then leapt from the high window of Château Tulley's tower.

As she plummeted toward the bailey, the convulsion began, a ferocious pain that made her writhe in the air.

She dared to hope she would soon be with Mallory again.

CHAPTER 16

A hue and a cry from the bailey carried to the solar, but Lothair did not care. There was no task before him beyond saving Magdala. The Lord de Tulley watched with obvious concern, but Lothair had no more patience for the older man's schemes. When he was convinced that he had done all he could for Magdala, he reached into his purse and removed the coin that Marcus had surrendered to him years before, on their departure from Jerusalem. He held it up between his finger and thumb, knowing his gaze was cold.

The Lord de Tulley watched him warily and rightly so.

"I was given this coin by a friend in Outremer, a wise man who said I might use it to buy back my soul. We laughed at the time, but I have surrendered much here in Tulley and I would be free of this place for once and for all."

"But I have made you my heir!"

"And I decline the honor. This event would never have happened, if you had allowed there to be honesty in the hall," Lothair said, his manner grim. "Magdala's life would never have been at risk if all had known her name once she confided it in me."

"I meant the best!"

"You have schemed, sir, and you have deceived. You have manipulated and you have withheld details, all in pursuit of your own objectives. You would determine the lives and situations of others as if we were no more than pawns upon your chess board. You meddle, sir, and you have no regard for the desires of those beneath your hand."

The Lord de Tulley rose to his feet with the aid of Felix, bracing his weight upon his cane. "Nay, that is not true. I care mightily for all those in Tulley. I did this for Magdala!"

"And you nigh cost me the person of greatest merit in my life." Lothair cast the coin at the Lord de Tulley and that man caught it. "I surrender this to you to end my obligation to you and pay any debt you perceive to be outstanding." He stood, lifting the unconscious Magdala in his arms. "My lady wife and I will depart from this holding as soon as she is sufficiently well to ride."

"But you cannot do this!" the Lord de Tulley shouted. "You are my vassal and my heir. She is my heiress."

"There is no longer any bond between us, sir, for you have betrayed that which is most precious."

The Lord de Tulley cried out when Lothair reached the portal. "You desire truth, sir? I believe she is my daughter."

Lothair looked back. "My blood daughter. My sole offspring. Do you know how long I sought her? Do you know how far I have searched for proof of the truth?" The Lord de Tulley shook a fist at Lothair. "You cannot take her from me. You cannot deny me the solace of my own blood in my final days."

There was silence between them for long moments.

"I could," Lothair said. "But I will leave the choice to the lady. You have best prepare a persuasive argument in your own defense."

And with that, he carried Magdala down the stairs, past the chamber with Mallory's corpse on the floor, across the great hall crowded with curious servants. He carried her through the bailey to his chamber over the stables and laid her gently on the bed. He sent Calum to collect their belongings, charged Gerald with his former duties, and sat beside his lady, willing her to open her eyes and soon.

Without Magdala, there could be no future for Lothair of Sutherland.

MAGDALA AWAKENED to the steady sound of rain.

Her eyelids were heavy and she felt drowsy as seldom she did in the morning. She stretched a little, noting the distant rumble of thunder, and smiled at the scent of Lothair on the linens. There was a ring on her left hand, but no longer one on her right, though she could not explain the change. She stretched and opened her eyes, surprised to find herself in the chamber over the stables. The light was so soft and pearly that she guessed it was morning, and she heard the patter of the rain upon the stones in the bailey.

She remembered the broth and the acrid taste of it upon her tongue. She remembered the animosity of Heloise and the avarice of Herbert. She saw again the frailty of the Lord de Tulley, and remembered the kindness of the abbess. None of them held her heart so securely as the man so close by her side. Lothair sat in a chair drawn close to the narrow bed, his head in his hands.

He slept, keeping vigil over her, and the realization both warmed her heart and made her smile.

Of course, this knight would never forget his vows.

"Defending the weak," she said, surprised to hear that her voice was so husky, and Lothair was immediately startled to wakefulness.

"Magdala!" he whispered and captured her hand in his. His gaze searched hers, his eyes so very blue that she knew of his concern. She reached out and touched his chin, seeing that he had not shaved in some days, and noted the shadows beneath his eyes.

"How long?" she asked.

"Two days and two nights," he replied.

"Have you eaten or slept?"

He shook his head, dismissive of such details and held fast to her hand. "I feared to lose you," he confessed and she shook her head, smiling.

"I had too good a teacher for that."

"Magdala! You took such a risk."

"I could see no other escape." She sat up then, surprised to find herself so weak, and found his arm behind her. "She meant to kill you and then me, after the Lord de Tulley's demise, to claim possession of the holding."

"No one would mistake her for you for long."

"She would reveal me, she said, then I would be found dead of poison, apparently by my own hand. I could not let her triumph so readily, Lothair."

He nodded and lowered his gaze.

She clutched his sleeve. "What happened to her?"

He told her of Mallory's assault upon him and death. He told her of Herbert's demise, undoubtedly by Heloise's hand and with a concoction of aconite she remembered how to make. He told her of Heloise's death.

"It seemed she did not wish to live without Mallory."

"And the baron?"

"He was her lover, deemed unworthy by Herbert, according to his manservant. He knew the baron's name and word has been sent to his holding. I believe they will find that he met his demise when his lady wife tired of his charms."

Magdala shivered and he pulled her into his embrace. "And the Lord de Tulley?"

Lothair made a sound in his throat that did not sound approving, and pulled back to look at her. "He lied, Magdala. Felix is not dead." She gasped at that. "It was a ruse. They two pretended that the figs were poisoned to discredit Herbert, so that he could not appeal to the emperor to overturn the granting of Tulley to you and me. As the sole male of the same lineage, he might have found or bought a willing ear."

"But why?"

"Because he wished for you to inherit Tulley, but with a husband to aid in defending your legacy." Lothair's voice rose. "The entire situation, from the summoning of me from Provins, was his scheme."

Magdala nodded understanding. She was not surprised that the old lord would plan so diligently to secure the future of one he loved, and she was honored to have won his support. She knew, though, that Lothair did not appreciate that he had been manipulated, and truly, she wished that the old lord might have followed her husband's own dictate of honesty and truth being tantamount.

"And now?"

"I told him we would leave." Lothair shook his head. "But he would appeal to you, likely because he knows you will indulge him."

She smiled at him. "You do not look so troubled as I might have expected."

Lothair sighed in concession. "He has a secret, and it is one would go far to justifying his choices if it is proven aright."

"Will you tell me of it?"

He shook his head. "We must ride in search of the truth, when you are able and willing." He touched his fingertip to her lips. "The secret is not mine to share, Magdala, but trust me—if the Lord de Tulley's suspicions are true, you might be well content indeed."

"I am already well content," she confessed, lifting his hand from her lips and kissing his palm as so often he had kissed her own. "I could be naught else with you by my side."

He whispered her name and confessed his love again. Then he bent to sweetly capture her lips beneath his own, as fine a promise for the future as any woman could desire.

IT WAS late July when Magdala and Lothair reached the abbey of Ste. Sophia outside Brennenburg and still Magdala did not know their errand. Her husband was indeed adept at keeping a secret and even the Lord de Tulley had not surrendered a detail.

The abbey was located on the south slope of the valley, accessed by a narrow and winding route bordered by pine forest. Their horses climbed steadily and Magdala was glad she had insisted upon riding. She could see so much further than in the cart, and still she craned her neck in an effort to peer beyond the next curve.

"You improve daily," Lothair said when she had let the mare find her own route across a shallow bed of pebbles that crossed the path. A stream flowed down to the valley there, crossing the path, though the water was shallow this time of year.

She cast him a smile. "I learn to trust the horse, as you taught me."

He nodded, a glint of satisfaction in his gaze. How curious that she had once thought him inscrutable when now she could read all the subtleties of his mood with a glance. "Is it close?"

"Around the next curve, I believe," she said, her heart rising to her throat in anticipation. What secret could await her at the convent where she had been raised? Perhaps the Lord de Tulley sent only a donation and the truth they sought was at Idelstein, yet a few days further. "And still you will not tell me the contents of the missive?"

Lothair smiled then, as mysterious as it was possible for a man to be. "I made a promise."

"You and your vows," Magdala complained good-naturedly. "What of me and my curiosity?"

"You will know the truth soon enough, and it will be better for the waiting."

Magdala sighed with mock forbearance. "I suppose I have learned to trust you, as well."

He cast her a glance so filled with satisfaction that she laughed at him. It was true that she had a secret of her own, so did not feel so neglected.

She could not wait to see his response to her own tidings.

Calum rode in the cart on this day, guiding the palfreys onward. As neither of the steeds were particularly accustomed to the cart, the task required enough of his attention that he was fairly quiet. Magdala liked that she could hear the birds in the forest around her.

The sound and the smell evoked powerful memories of her childhood. She had been happy in this place and hoped that many of the nuns were yet there.

They rounded the turn and she caught her breath to see the walls of the foundation ahead of her. It looked to be so much smaller than she recalled, more humble and less affluent. There was moss on the stone walls and only the faintest sound of the occupants at their prayers.

Lothair dismounted and strode to the closed portal, pulling hard on the rope to ring the bell. It rang, a sound so familiar that it made Magdala catch her breath, then was followed by a silence she found expectant. She could close her eyes and recall how the porter would stir and push to his feet, how he would make his way to the door at his own steady pace. Once behind the portal, he would then peer through the narrow opening.

"Who rings?" he demanded, as irritable as ever. Magdala did not imagine he had changed much—his voice was the same, as was his manner, though she could not see his face behind the small opening.

"My name is Lothair of Sutherland," her husband said. "My lady wife was raised in these walls and seeks to visit the abbess."

"The abbess accepts no callers on this day."

"I also have a missive to deliver to her own hand, from Everard, Lord de Tulley."

A larger panel was opened in the door so that the porter could view the entire company. He peered at them, made a sound of skepticism, then slammed both panels. There was a long interval of silence and Lothair turned to Magdala as if seeking her counsel of how to proceed. She simply smiled and held up a finger.

Magdala imagined the porter's path through the foundation and saw the route in her memories. She could count the steps he would have to take. He would knock upon the door securing the abbess's own chamber, they would murmur to each other and a decision would be made. He would then shuffle back to the door, while speculation ran rampant from cell to cell.

Magdala nodded in relief as she heard a bolt slide home.

A moment later, the entire portal yawned open, revealing the short and stout porter framed within the opening. He had not changed a whit.

He also did not recognize Magdala. His gaze flitted over the party before landing upon Lothair. "She will see the lady, and you alone may accompany her. No horses."

Calum left the cart and took the reins of Lothair's destrier from the knight. Lothair then lifted Magdala from the saddle, surrendering those reins to Calum, who stood tall amidst the steeds, important in his responsibility and markedly quiet. Lothair led Magdala to the portal and she felt the porter's scrutiny. She let her hood slide back as she approached and smiled at the curious man. "Good day, Anthony. I trust that you are hale."

His mouth opened then closed again, his astonishment complete. "Our little Magdala," he whispered, then grinned. "Bless my soul!" He bowed low before her then, his gaze flying to Lothair with a measure of awe as they passed him.

Magdala could only see the woman who stood in the corridor ahead of them. That lady was dressed in undyed linen, her kirtle and chemise unornamented, her wimple and veil just as unembellished. She wore a dark crucifix on a chain and Magdala remembered that it was carved of ivory, darkened by reverent touch. The abbess's hands were lined but her face was smooth, her expression serene.

She smiled and held out her hands in greeting. "Magdala!"

Magdala dropped to her knees before the older woman, clutching her hands, blinking back joyous tears. The abbess kissed her cheeks and raised her to her feet, making Magdala aware that she now towered over the woman who had been her teacher for so long.

"I feared for you when I heard that Lady Verena had passed," the abbess said finally, but the weight of her words indicated that this was only part of what had concerned her. She gripped Magdala's hands tightly, as if she could not believe Magdala stood before her.

"I remained with Lady Heloise," Magdala explained. "Until she journeyed to the abode of her uncle, the Lord de Tulley."

"And was attacked in Grimwald Forest," the abbess said, her words strained. "They said her maid had been killed."

"Lady Verena favored a disguise in travel, one also followed by her daughter. It was Lady Heloise who was attacked, dressed as a maid."

The abbess searched Magdala's gaze. "That must have been a horrible ordeal."

"It was."

They stared at each other for long moments and Magdala wondered how much more of the truth the older woman knew. Then the abbess turned abruptly, fixing an inquisitive glance upon Lothair. "And who is this?"

"This is Lothair of Sutherland, the Captain of the Guard at Château Tulley." Magdala could not help but watch him as he bowed deeply to the abbess. He looked larger in this place, more powerful and more vehemently male. "A knight and crusader, and my lord husband."

"At your service, my lady," he murmured.

The abbess's finger found the gold ring on Magdala's left hand and she rubbed it once, as if for good fortune, then her gaze fell to Magdala's belly. "Praise be," she said almost beneath her breath and Magdala blushed, for she had no secrets from this woman.

Lothair, curse him, did not look surprised either.

"A knight and a crusader. You have wed well, Magdala."

"And a healer, as well. Lothair is most knowledgeable of the useful plants."

The abbess smiled. "A common interest, then. Magdala was always of great help in the garden."

"So, she has told me."

"Perhaps you would like to see our garden, small as it is."

Lothair bowed again. "I should be honored, my lady. My lady has often spoken of it."

The abbess turned, still holding Magdala's hand as if she would never surrender her grip, and leading her along the familiar route. Naught had changed and Magdala knew it, but all seemed so much smaller than she recalled, including the abbess herself.

The silence. How had she forgotten the silence? It was like a protective shroud, sheltering all within from the storm of the world beyond the walls. Magdala realized that the only place within Château Tulley that came close to having the tranquility of this foundation was the garden.

Perhaps that was why she loved it so.

The abbess gestured that they should enter her chamber ahead of her. It was simply furnished, with only a pair of stools, a small table and a bed. The walls were white and sunlight flowed into the space. Beside the bed was a smaller table with a single unlit candle.

Lothair declined to sit, indicating that the women should do as much. The abbess sat with Magdala's encouragement, surrendering a small sigh once she did as much. "I tire in these times, Magdala," she confessed quietly. "It is the way of things." She studied Magdala again, taking her hand and smiling. "You look so well." She raised a hand to her cheek and stroked it, the gesture prompting Magdala to blink back joyous tears.

As ever, her heart swelled with gratitude that she had been raised and tutored by this woman, as well as the others here who had shown her kindness. She smiled back, wondering how she would ever leave this place this day.

Lothair cleared his throat slightly and produced the missive from the Lord de Tulley, which Magdala had almost forgotten. Before he could hand it to the abbess, she shook her head.

"My sight is not what it was, sir. Will you read it for me?"

"Of course," Lothair agreed and unfurled the parchment. Magdala knew that he was fully aware of the contents. Perhaps he had stood by the Lord de Tulley's elbow while it was written.

He began to read clearly but in a low voice, so all the foundation would not overhear.

"I send greetings to the foundation of Ste. Sophia and all those who live and pray within its walls. I particularly send this missive to the abbess, with regard to a girl raised there known as Magdala. She accompanies the bearer of this communication and is, in fact, his wife."

The abbess and Magdala smiled at each other again, the abbess' grip tightening a little more on Magdala's hand.

"Magdala confided in me that she was taken from the foundation several years ago by my sister, Lady Verena von Idelstein, to serve as a maid for my niece, Heloise. She also has told me that she was left at the foundation's door while an infant, and that she was taken in and raised there, with no one knowing the names of her parents."

Magdala wondered why the Lord de Tulley had troubled to write a missive filled with such obvious and known detail, but she kept her silence.

"I believe, madame, that this is untrue."

Magdala gasped but the abbess did not. Her lips tightened slightly but she gave no other sign of disagreement.

"I believe that you know full well who Magdala's parents were and that she was not found outside the door one night. I believe she was born within those walls, and that you yourself retired to Ste. Sophia because you ripened with child and were unwed."

Magdala felt her lips part in surprise.

The abbess did not meet her gaze but stared fixedly at Lothair.

"I believe that you are my own beloved Marguerite, whose father forbade my courtship, the lady who declined all other suitors in my stead, by all reports, and vanished some months after we last saw each other. For years I feared that you were dead, but after my brothers passed and I gained a legacy beyond expectation, I would not accept such a rumor as a solution. I had to know. I sought you, Marguerite, but without success. I could find no evidence of your demise and so I concluded that you must have taken your vows. I thought you to be lost to me forever."

The abbess blinked rapidly but did not speak.

"When Magdala arrived at my gates almost three years ago,

disguised as my niece, I knew immediately that she was not Heloise. In fact, I suspected that she might be your daughter. I had never seen another maiden with such a perfect echo of your beauty. When I learned her age, I dared to hope that she might be not just your daughter but mine as well."

Magdala stared at Lothair in astonishment.

"You should know that every day that I spent in Magdala's company brought me more memories of you, Marguerite. She has a kindness of manner, a gentle sweetness and eagerness to be of aid, that is precisely like your own. I believe she will be a gifted healer, as I hear the abbess of Ste. Sophia is reputed to be. When I realized that she spoke like you, not just in the timbre of her voice but the choice of her words, I wondered whether you not only survived but that you knew each other."

Lothair paused for a moment as the abbess bowed her head.

"Aye, you raised her, our own daughter, keeping her safe and holding your secret close. And I suspect that you recognized the name of my sister, using your considerable charm to influence her choice of a maid for her daughter, hoping to put Magdala into my path. Never have I known a woman so persuasive as you can be when your decision is made."

The abbess smiled and bowed her head.

"I do not intend to reveal you, my Marguerite, but to thank you for so defending our child. I wish you might have appealed for my aid. I wish I might have inherited a holding sooner. I wish I could have made matters simpler for both you and our daughter in those times."

The abbess caught her breath. "I wrote to him," she admitted softly. "Three times, each by a different courier, in the hope that my father would not intercept them all."

"He must have done," Magdala whispered and the abbess, her mother, nodded.

"He was so concerned with the reputation of our house," she said.

"He worried more about shame than about the glory of love." She nodded for Lothair to continue.

"I would have done anything, Marguerite, if you had but asked."

The abbess nodded sadly.

"Know this, though the confession comes late. There could never be another woman to claim my heart as you so surely did. In honor of both that love and you, I have made Magdala my heiress. She will be the Lady de Tulley as surely as her husband, whom I have chosen for her, will be its lord. And so I dispatch them both, one to learn the truth of your place in her life, and one to make your acquaintance and, I hope, earn your approval. I remember how you always liked to know the conclusion of the story."

The abbess chuckled at that, then blinked away the remaining tears. "Oh, Everard," she whispered.

"I would be honored to see you again, but I fear I have not the strength to journey to Ste. Sophia myself. I heartily regret that I am unlikely to see you ever again as a result of my own weakness. If you desire to come to Château Tulley, you have only to ask my Captain of the Guard to make it so. You do not need to ask my desire in this, for you must know it. I scarce dare to hope that you might be persuaded to leave your foundation for even a short interval, but it cannot hurt to ask. Whatever you choose, my heart, Marguerite, will always be with yours alone."

The missive was signed by Everard, the Lord de Tulley.

Lothair fell silent then and the abbess accepted the missive, her fingertips sliding over the Lord de Tulley's signature and seal. "I should have known," she whispered "that if any soul saw through my deception, it would be Everard. That man could discern the heart of any riddle."

"Then it is true?" Magdala whispered, needing to hear the confession from the abbess.

That lady raised her gaze to Magdala's and smiled, her eyes glowing as she studied the younger woman. "You are my child. You are Everard's child, created in love and joy." Her tone turned fierce. "Never doubt it, Magdala."

"I will not," Magdala vowed, her own tears slipping over her cheeks. All the years that she had desired a family and a home, she had been in possession of both, here at Ste. Sophia under her mother's loving care. She felt blessed as never she had before.

"I am so glad you came. I have feared for you since the rumors came of the attack upon Lady Heloise in Grimwald Forest and the death of her maid." The abbess took a great breath. "I confess that I prayed for you with fervor. I feared I had erred in sending you to Idelstein."

Magdala stood and drew her mother to her feet, catching her close in a sweet embrace. She met Lothair's gaze over her mother's shoulder and saw the satisfaction in his gaze. "*You knew,*" she mouthed and he smiled before he nodded once in admission. Their gazes clung and Magdala's heart glowed that she should have so much happiness all at once.

The abbess pulled away , then kissed Magdala's cheeks. "Your lord husband must see the garden, as promised," she said, taking a reluctant step back. She still held fast to Magdala's hand. "And I must make arrangements for my absence."

"Then you will come to Tulley?"

"Only if your lord husband vows to escort me back again."

"Of course," Lothair said and bowed to her again. "It would be my honor."

The abbess nodded and seemed to stand taller. "Then I will make the journey, perhaps my last great journey. I have yearned to see Everard again for a very long time." She smiled, her manner brisk now that her choice was made. "Come. The garden already is past its greatest glory, but it is a joy yet."

She led the way down the corridor, new purpose in her step, and Magdala followed behind her. "I had thought to find a maid," she confessed and the abbess glanced over her shoulder with eyes alight. "A girl who might aid me with the apothecary and the babe to come."

The abbess smiled and invited them into the cloister.

It was as perfect as Magdala recalled. At this hour of the afternoon, the square space was filled with sunlight and the hum of bees. An open corridor bordered the garden on all sides, the roof over the middle open to the sky, and a well was in its very center. The paths were made of stone, each garden bed a wedge with smaller plants near the well and taller ones at the perimeter. Each bed was bordered with calendula, the plants already becoming lanky and heavy with seeds.

The proportions were perfect, the sunlight was bright and the plants were healthy. Lothair stood and looked about himself, his approval clear.

Two little girls crouched in the path, sufficiently close to each other to touch, plucking the seeds from the plants and gathering them in a pottery bowl. They looked to be of an age until they stood up at the abbess's arrival, then Magdala realized that one was taller than the other. They were sisters, she guessed for their features were similar. One had hair of ebony and one had hair of gold. They were dressed simply in plain garments and their feet were bare, the hair of each pulled back into a single long plait. They regarded Magdala and Lothair with a measure of suspicion and the smaller one, the blond girl, eased closer to the older one, slipping her hand into that of her sister.

The very sight made Magdala's heart clench.

The abbess spoke crisply. "This is Ursula—" the dark-haired one curtseyed neatly "—and this is Andrea." The smaller girl endeavored to curtsey with less success. She could not have been four summers of age, to Magdala's thinking while the other was perhaps six.

"They are sisters?" Magdala asked.

"They are, indeed, come to us three years ago upon the passing of their mother. Their father could not ensure the welfare of two so young for he labors long each day." The abbess stepped forward, taking the older girl's hand and drawing her forward. "Ursula is adept with a needle and is very eager to please."

The younger girl's eyes welled with tears and she gripped her sister's hand more tightly.

The older one bit her lip. The expressions of the two of them rent Magdala's heart, but she and Lothair had agreed upon one addition to their household.

Before she make an appeal, Lothair cleared his throat. "Would it not be unfair to divide sisters?"

"I would be happiest to see them together," the abbess admitted, much to the evident relief of both girls. She smiled a little herself and Magdala guessed that she had been guided to this choice.

The Lord de Tulley was not her sole parent with firm views of what should be.

Magdala turned to Lothair and he nodded once, the decision made. "The choice is yours, my lady."

"Then I would have them both come with us," she said. They were uncertain and Magdala recognized as much, just as she knew that only time with herself and Lothair would give them confidence in their new situation. The abbess' presence on their homeward journey would doubtless reassure them.

As Lothair had said, there could be no question of dividing them. These two girls already had claimed Magdala's heart and she would have fought any foe in their defense. She was beyond glad to have been able to give them a home and vowed that it would be a good one.

The Lord de Tulley, she was certain, would be charmed by them.

For her own part, she was filled with joy to have the secrets of her own past revealed, and to be riding for Château Tulley with her own mother by her side. She would be witness to her parents' reunion and that gave her almost as much joy as riding alongside Lothair.

Magdala was pleased, and that was sufficient for Lothair.

The journey to Tulley was uneventful and the two young girls gained confidence each day. By the time the mount that was crowned by Château Tulley came into view, they were chattering ceaselessly. They made the abbess laugh, and seemingly had hundreds of questions, but the stars in Magdala's eyes satisfied Lothair.

They dismounted in the bailey, and Lothair shook hands with the knights who had defended the keep in his absence. Gerald had tales aplenty to share, but first they had to see Magdala's parents reunited. The abbess wore her wimple and plain gown, her appearance in the bailey prompting some curious glances. She was curious as well, openly surveying the keep and its defenses. She asked Lothair questions, making it clear that she had grown up in a similarly well-defended fortress. He led both women into the hall, fully intending to escort them to the solar to meet the Lord de Tulley.

Instead, he halted in the great hall when he spied the Lord de Tulley in his chair by the fire. Felix stood on his one side and Thomas on the other, their anticipation making it evident that the arriving party had been spotted on the road below.

Magdala crossed the hall with quick steps, bending to kiss the older man's cheeks. "You knew I was your daughter all along," she chided, her smile taking any sting from her words.

"Aye, a man with eyes in his head could not miss the truth," he said, his manner as gruff as ever. His gaze, though, clung to the lady in white who stood beside Lothair.

The abbess and the Lord de Tulley stared at each other across the great hall for so long that Lothair began to fear they would never speak. Then the Lord de Tulley rose to his feet, bracing himself upon his walking stick, and stretched out a hand.

"Marguerite," he said, his voice husky. "You have not changed a whit."

"You silver-tongued scoundrel," she said with a laugh, startling all of those gathered. "Are you blind in these times or would you charm me all over again?"

The Lord de Tulley grinned, looking like the handsome rogue she accused him of being.

She laughed again, then she hastened across the floor to him.

Against every expectation, the Lord de Tulley dropped to one knee to kiss her hand. "Marguerite," he whispered, his heart in his voice.

"Everard," she replied, then raised her hand to his jaw and bent to kiss him full on the lips.

If any were astounded that an abbess kissed the Lord de Tulley with such fervor, they had the wits to remain silent on the matter.

"Naught has changed," the Lord de Tulley said when she finally broke their kiss. He leaned a little harder on his cane, remaining on one knee, gazing upon her with such wonder that he might never avert his gaze. Then he lifted one silver brow. "Save that I do not rise to my feet so readily as was once the case." He smiled at her as if untroubled by this, though Lothair guessed it was only that he was so glad to see her.

The abbess laughed lightly and made a comment about change coming to all of them. In the meantime, Lothair stepped forward and helped the Lord de Tulley to rise, then to take his seat again. The pair scarce noticed him.

"Sit with me, Marguerite," the Lord de Tulley invited. "Tell me all that you have done since last we met."

She took a seat at his side, her manner more merry than it had yet been. Lothair could see that she had been enchanting in her time, perhaps even as beguiling as his own lady wife. "I hope the fare is good in this abode," she teased her host. "I have not eaten meat in years."

"You always liked fish."

"I like it less well than I had once imagined," she agreed. "But I will need sustenance to recount the events of some twenty years."

"And you shall have it! Thomas."

"Of course, my lord." The châtelain bowed. "There is a cask of new wine from Annossy that might be opened to celebrate our guest."

"Then open it with all haste, and bid Antoine to make this evening's meal most fine." The Lord de Tulley beamed at the abbess, as if he could not tear his gaze from her. "My lady and queen of my heart has finally stepped into my hall and I would not have her regret the choice."

"Never," she said with fervor, and they smiled at each other before their voices dropped low.

Lothair found himself smiling at their satisfaction, his own heart leaping as Magdala came to his side. She was smiling herself and he marveled that she had ever believed he might overlook the signs of her pregnancy. She was radiant as well as both softer and sweeter, and he liked how she stepped right into his embrace with complete confidence.

"Thank you," she said. "All I have desired in my life is a home and a family. I have both, thanks to you, and I have a husband to adore, as well." She lifted her face for his kiss. "Thank you, Lothair."

"Nay, Magdala, thank you, for awakening me from a life of solitude. I never believed I could have a home and family, but you have shown me otherwise." He kissed her slowly, loving how she welcomed his touch.

"And now you are fulsome, too," she teased. "As well as openly affectionate."

Lothair smiled. "I could not leave any in doubt of my regard for my beguiling wife."

"Nor could I let any believe I lack satisfaction in my match," she countered, her eyes dancing. She smiled up at him. "We shall remain at Tulley then?"

"If you so choose it."

"And you?"

Lothair took a breath. "I find it a most admirable abode, especially as your father makes progress in his need to manage all."

She laughed. "You are not discontent with the scheme he devised for you."

"Solely because he had the wits to choose you for me."

"And you for me," she agreed happily. "And you are content about the babe?"

"Of course." He would be with her to ensure that all went well.

"And we shall be a family," she concluded, her gaze trailing to her parents.

"We *are* a family, Magdala," Lothair said to her. "And whether we are two or twenty, so shall we always be." He waited for her to smile, then bent to kiss her soundly once again.

For this lady would always be his heart and his home, and he would never cease to court her smile. She had been the destination he had long sought and he, too, was content to have found the home he had not even realized he desired.

EPILOGUE

The March wind was chilly but the Lord de Tulley had not succumbed to illness as yet. He sat in the solar, fires blazing all around him, and beamed at the infant boy swaddled in his arms.

"I thought Godwyn," Magdala said to him. "What do you think, Uncle?"

The couple had brought the child to the old lord as soon as the babe had been cleaned and wrapped. Magdala, Lothair had confirmed quietly, was hale for all had gone well.

To the Lord de Tulley's thinking, the new mother was radiant in her happiness and the sight warmed his heart

"Perfect?" he asked, indicating the boy.

"Perfect," Lothair agreed.

"If uncommonly tall," Magdala added and the pair shared a glance of such affection that the Lord de Tulley had to avert his gaze.

He snorted, knowing full well where the child had earned that trait.

The babe had a dusting of fair hair and when he opened his eyes to consider the older man, they were fiercely blue. Of course. The Lord de Tulley wagered they would not change hue. The infant surveyed him then grimaced, a precursor to a cry that any man might recognize, and the Lord de Tulley hastily returned the babe to his father.

"Godwyn," he agreed, watching the knight rock his son and reassure him with an ease he did not himself share.

The Lord de Tulley wished in that moment that he might live long enough to see this boy train with his father, to watch him grow tall and strong. He wished he might see how the family resemblance developed and take note of which parent the boy favored more. The Lord de Tulley guessed though that this boy would become a knight of valor, one whose judgement was tempered by kindness and compassion. He would become a man worthy of honor and respect, to be sure, and a fitting heir to Tulley.

He wished he might see how many more children Magdala would bear. There had to be at least one daughter, as sweet and kind as Magdala herself. He was proud of how she had blossomed in marriage, learning more of the healing plants beneath Lothair's instruction and concocting balms. The vassals of Tulley came to her for their minor ailments, and the Lord de Tulley knew that often-times, it was her attention and understanding that set matters to rights. She would be a glorious Lady de Tulley, one fit to rival the memory of his mother and grandmother.

The Lord de Tulley, though, knew that his time would not be so long in this realm. He dreamed of his brothers at night and imagined them around him during the day. It was as if their ghosts drew near to summon him onward. The news from Ste. Sophia that his beloved Marguerite had passed only encouraged him to relinquish his grip upon this life. All those he knew and loved were gone, save for Magdala, her husband and child. She was content, more than content, and his final challenge had been fulfilled with triumph. Ursula and Andrea flourished in their new home, and they called him 'Uncle' at his request. Calum would be knighted at Easter, and had already vowed to pledge himself to Tulley.

There was only Hildegarde who might have been his concern, though by all reports, she governed Idelstein well. A dispassionate and clever child, her missives to him were composed with all the rigor of a military commander. He wondered whether he would see her at Easter or if his days would end before then.

He was not certain.

The truth was that the Lord de Tulley felt the shadow of death more clearly than the heat of the braziers. He would see one last deed completed, just in case.

He fumbled with his signet ring and beckoned to Felix.

"Lothair," he said and that knight looked up, no doubt surprised that he addressed him by his name. "I would place this upon your hand myself," the Lord de Tulley said gruffly, offering the ring. "When a man desires a deed to be done, he should do it himself."

"Uncle!" Magdala protested but the Lord de Tulley shook his head.

"It is time, Magdala. The responsibility for Tulley must pass to a stronger lord, and Godwyn's legacy must be secured."

Understanding dawned in Lothair's eyes. He touched Magdala's shoulder when she might have protested and shouted for Thomas from the portal. Calum arrived with Thomas, Gerald appearing shortly thereafter, a suitable gathering of witnesses as Lothair dropped to one knee before the Lord de Tulley.

The Lord de Tulley surrendered his ring, the keys to the treasury and the keep, and felt the weight of a long-held responsibility lift from his shoulders as Lothair accepted the lordship of Tulley. He leaned back in his chair, content to watch as Thomas summoned the entire household, all of them filing through the solar to pledge themselves to Lothair's service. Magdala stood beside her lord husband, their child in her arms, as regal a pair as Everard might have hoped to see.

As Thomas planned the evening meal to celebrate all, and Felix fussed with the fur pelts over the former lord's lap, as the cries of admiration over the new babe filled the solar, Everard saw his brothers step out of the shadows to approach him. He lifted his hands, one to Godwyn and one to Ulric, vaguely aware of Felix's confusion, then they gestured to the lady who appeared behind them.

Marguerite. As lovely as ever she had been, smiling with a welcome he would not deny. Everard, formerly the Lord de Tulley, closed his eyes one last time in the bustling solar, content to claim his eternal reward. The last sound he heard was Magdala's joyous laughter, and that made him smile with contentment at a task well completed.

Everard would not have been the man he was if he had not hoped, in that last moment, to be remembered forevermore in this realm as well.

Part of the inspiration for Everard and Marguerite's story was that of Abelard and Heloise, two 12th century lovers. Héloise d'Argenteuil was the ward of her uncle, Canon Fulbert, and renowned for her intellectual accomplishments even as a maiden, while Peter Abelard was a scholar hired to be her tutor. The two became intimate and had a secret affair, which was revealed when she became pregnant. The couple married secretly to appease Héloise's uncle, but she continued to live at her uncle's house while Abelard moved on. Her uncle, however, did not keep the marriage secret, despite his promise to do as much. Heloise denied that she and Abelard were married —she feared that being married would adversely influence Abelard's career as canons were expected to be celibate—and the relationship between uncle and ward took a turn for the worse.

Abelard retrieved Héloise from her uncle's house, fearful of her uncle's wrath, and took her to a convent. She lived amongst nuns "unveiled", which means without taking her vows. Her furious uncle concluded the worst and had Abelard attacked and castrated one night. As a result, Abelard joined a monastery and Héloise had no choice but to take her own vows after he took his. Their son, Astrolabe, was raised by Abelard's sister, Denise.

Abelard ultimately became abbot at St. Gildas in Brittany, while Héloise became prioress and abbess of the Paraclete, gaining a status of *prelate nullus*. The pair are remembered for their copious correspondence: they wrote letters to each other throughout their lives. I have the Penguin Classic compilation and translation, **The Letters of Peter Abelard and Heloise**, edited by Betty Radice, on my shelf.

There is no evidence that Héloise and Abelard ever saw each other again after taking their vows. I always thought that was a bit sad. Would Marguerite have left the abbey to see Everard one last time? Probably not, but I wanted this fictional couple to have one final farewell, even if the odds were against it in real life.

ABOUT THE AUTHOR

Deborah Cooke sold her first book in 1992, a medieval romance called **Romance of the Rose** published under her pseudonym Claire Delacroix. Since then, she has published over fifty novels in a wide variety of sub-genres, including historical romance, contemporary romance, paranormal romance, fantasy romance, time-travel romance, women's fiction, paranormal young adult and fantasy with romantic elements. She has published under the names Claire Delacroix, Claire Cross and Deborah Cooke. **The Beauty**, part of her successful Bride Quest series of historical romances, was her first title to land on the *New York Times* List of Bestselling Books. Her books routinely appear on other bestseller lists and have won numerous awards. In 2009, she was the writer-in-residence at the Toronto Public Library, the first time the library has hosted a residency focused on the romance genre. In 2012, she was honored to receive the Romance Writers of America's Mentor of the Year Award.

Currently, she writes contemporary romances and paranormal romances under the name Deborah Cooke. She also writes medieval romances as Claire Delacroix. Deborah lives in Canada with her husband and family, as well as far too many unfinished knitting projects.

Visit her websites to learn more about her books:

Delacroix.net

DeborahCooke.com

THE ROSE RED BRIDE

THE SNOW WHITE BRIDE

The Ballad of Rosamunde

The True Love Brides

THE RENEGADE'S HEART

THE HIGHLANDER'S CURSE

THE FROST MAIDEN'S KISS

THE WARRIOR'S PRIZE

The Brides of Inverfyre

THE MERCENARY'S BRIDE

THE RUNAWAY BRIDE

The Bride Quest

THE PRINCESS

THE DAMSEL

THE HEIRESS

THE COUNTESS

THE BEAUTY

THE TEMPTRESS

Christmas at Tullymullagh

Easter at Airdfinnan

Harlequin Historicals

UNICORN BRIDE

PEARL BEYOND PRICE

Regency Romance

The Ladies' Essential Guide to the Art of Seduction

THE CHRISTMAS CONQUEST

THE MASQUERADE OF THE MARCHIONESS

THE WIDOW'S WAGER

The Brides of North Barrows

Something Wicked This Way Comes

A Duke By Any Other Name

A Baron for All Seasons

A Most Inconvenient Earl

Time Travel Romance

ONCE UPON A KISS

THE LAST HIGHLANDER

THE MOONSTONE

LOVE POTION #9

Short Stories and Novellas

BEGUILED

An Elegy for Melusine

To learn more about Deborah's contemporary and paranormal romances,

please visit

DeborahCooke.com